The Potential *for* Love

CATHERINE KULLMANN

This historical novel is a work of fiction. Names, characters, places and incidents are the products of the author's imagination or are used fictitiously. Except where actual historical events, locales, businesses and characters are described for the storyline of this novel, all situations in this publication are fictitious and any resemblance to actual persons living or dead, businesses, events or locales is purely coincidental.

Cover image *Premières Escarmouches* by Lucius Rossi, from an antique print in the author's collection.
Cover design by BookGoSocial

ISBN: 978-1-913545-20-8

First published 2020 by
Willow Books
D04 H397, Ireland

Regency Novels by Catherine Kullmann

The Duchess of Gracechurch Trilogy **The Malvins**

The Murmur of Masks

↓

Perception & Illusion → → The Potential for Love

↓

The Duke's Regret

Stand Alone

A Suggestion of Scandal

Novella

The Zombi of Caisteal Dun

In loving memory of my dear husband, Kurt, who slipped out of this life on 17 September 2019. For almost fifty years we explored together the potential of love and, even now, have not reached its boundaries.

Chapter One

Arabella squinted into the midday sun, desperate to make out the features shaded by the peak of the tall, black shako that sat foursquare on the head of the officer approaching her. His uniform was concealed by the boat cloak hanging from his shoulders—Arthur had purchased just such a one before he left for the continent. General Kempt's letter had left no room for doubt but—one heard of such mistakes. Yet he strode so confidently through the Abbey gates, as if he were indeed coming home.

"Arth—?" Heart in her mouth, she stretched out trembling hands just as the newcomer turned his head. Dark eyes stared into hers from beneath black brows that drew together above a beak of a nose. Black, curling side-whiskers, longer than usual, angled towards a grim, disapproving mouth that showed no sign of softness. She swallowed hard as a wave of desolation swept through her. There was no comfort to be found in this forbidding face.

She jumped when the lodge-keeper's wife spoke behind her. "Good day, Miss Malvin. Is something wrong? Good day, sir," she added to the visitor, with a rising inflection as if to say, 'what may I do for you?'

Arabella forced herself to smile. "Good morning, Mrs Smith. It was foolish of me, I know. I could not see this gentleman clearly, just his silhouette against the sun, and for a moment I thought—" Her voice broke.

"Oh, Miss Arabella!" Mrs Smith's voice was full of shocked sympathy.

"Miss Arabella Malvin!"

The stranger came to life. He swept off his shako and bowed. "Forgive me. Major Thomas Ferraunt of the Twenty-third Foot, at your service."

"Thomas Ferraunt," Arabella repeated faintly. "Dr Ferraunt's son?" The rector's son had been wounded at Waterloo and was now with the army of occupation in France. Drawing on all her reserves, she conjured up a smile. "Welcome home, Major."

"Thank you, Miss Malvin."

"You brought the sun with you. It has been a long, dreary winter."

"'Fill February, fill dyke'," he quoted. "English weather has not changed, apparently."

"I suppose not. You will find it very different to France or Spain."

His mouth twitched. "There were many times in Spain where I longed for our cooler climate, I assure you."

"My brother said the same."

He hesitated and then said, "I had thought to call on Lord and Lady Malvin, but now wonder if my presence would distress them."

"Oh, no; they will be most happy to receive you. I was just about to turn back towards the house, if you would like to accompany me."

He smoothed down the hair on the right side of his face. "I should be delighted to, Miss Malvin."

When he turned she had to suppress a gasp at the sight of the raised scar that ran from above his right ear to the corner of his mouth, tweaking and puckering the mottled skin and turning his lips down in that disapproving sneer. Poor man! Did he grow the whiskers to conceal the disfigurement or because the area was too tender to shave?

His arm was firm under her fingers as they started back up the avenue, and he had no difficulty in adjusting his longer stride to her shorter one so that they quickly fell into a comfortable rhythm. The air was definitely warmer today. Not precisely balmy, of course, but no longer so cold that her breath puffed in front of her as she walked. The blanket of snow and ice on the lawns had thinned and the banks of piled up snow along the sides of the avenue dripped incessantly, creating little rivulets that trickled merrily downhill.

They stopped to watch a pair of blue-tits chase one another through the branches of a tall lime tree. "Oh look! The buds are beginning to swell at last," she said. "Spring is on the way."

"Indubitably. Look there." He pointed to two hares zig-zagging across the snow. As they watched, the animals reared up on their hind legs to bat at one another with their front paws as if they were boxing. "March hares."

"They are even a day early."

"Perhaps in celebration of leap year," he offered, surprising a little spurt of laughter from her.

A pair of brindle hounds darted from a small copse and arrowed across towards the combatants who immediately bounded away, their pursuers on their heels. Arabella watched, aghast, as the hounds closed on their prey despite the hares' rapid jinks and turns. The day was too beautiful to be marred by bloodshed. To her relief, the dogs' onward rush was halted by a piercing whistle. They looked back with all the appearance of children whose fun had been unfairly curtailed, but returned obediently to their master who had changed direction to intercept Arabella and her companion.

When he neared, she said, "Do you remember my eldest brother, Major? Julian, this is—"

"Thomas Ferraunt, by all that's holy," Julian interrupted her, extending his hand. "How many years has it been?"

"A little more than five, I think, just before we were sent to the Peninsula. I was home again in '14, but I don't think we met then."

"I hope you are coming up to the house. My parents will wish to see you."

"That was my intention."

Julian snapped his fingers at the dogs sniffing interestedly at the newcomer.

"A handsome pair." The major bent down to pat the inquisitive heads.

"They are young—suffer from an excess of energy," Julian said as they continued towards the house, the hounds padding at their heels. "When did you arrive home, Ferraunt?"

"Five days ago."

"You are stationed in Paris, I believe."

"Not any longer. We have recently moved to Cambrai, nearer the border to Belgium."

"We, that is my parents, my brothers and I spent several months in Brussels after the first peace," Arabella put in.

"Did you like Brussels, Miss Malvin?"

"Yes, although with so many English there, in many ways we might as well have remained at home. Before we knew it, we were riding in the Park and going to the same round of entertainments, as if we had brought our world with us, like snails with their shells. You did not feel you were really abroad." She sighed. "I would love to travel properly one day, up the Rhine perhaps, or even across the Alps. You must have seen a lot of the world, Major."

"I have, although not by choice. A solider must go where he is sent. In the eleven years since I joined, I have served in Nova Scotia, the West Indies, the Peninsula, the Netherlands and now France. But I could not honestly say I have lived in those countries. The army, too, brings its customs and traditions with it; to a great extent we live in our own world, especially when on campaign."

"Perhaps now the war is over you will be able to travel privately," she suggested.

"First, I should like to get to know my own country," he said seriously. "Apart from the few months I was stationed here, I know England only as a schoolboy and a student." He stood back to let her precede him into the vaulted hall of Malvin Abbey.

"Julian, you two go ahead," she instructed her brother. "It will be best if you take the Major directly to the library. Papa will be there and I'll run up and tell Mamma. I'm sure they would like to talk to him undisturbed."

Julian looked blank for a moment and then smiled slowly. "Good God, yes. We have a maiden aunt squatting in the morning room," he explained to their visitor. "She is one of those tabbies who must be a part of every conversation."

"James will take your cloak," she told the major. "I'll join you as soon as possible with Mamma."

Major Ferraunt repressed the urge to knuckle his forehead and mutter, 'yes ma'am'. *A young lady who knows what she wants,* he thought as he obediently unfastened his cloak and handed it to the footman. Amused, he watched her hurry upstairs, her skirts raised to reveal a sturdy pair of boots, more like a man's. Much more sensible for such weather, he supposed, but he could not but regret the foregone glimpse of slim ankles and a lady's delicate footwear.

"This way," Julian Malvin said.

Recalled to himself, Thomas followed him through an arched oak door to the library. Lord Malvin looked up at their entry.

"You remember Thomas Ferraunt, don't you, sir?" Julian said. "Major Ferraunt, now."

His lordship rounded his big desk to take Thomas's hand in a warm clasp. "Welcome home, Major; it is good of you to call."

He looked at his son as if wondering why he had brought the visitor here and not to the morning-room, but nodded when Julian explained his desire to avoid his aunt.

"Arabella has gone to fetch my mother and I'll go in search of Millie and Matthew."

"Of course, of course. Ring for James to come and move these chairs nearer the fire, before you go. I hope you'll take a glass of Madeira, Major, while we wait. First, let me say how pleased I am to see you safe and well, if not unharmed."

"Thank you, my lord. Poor Arthur was not so fortunate. He was a sad loss; a brave officer and the best of companions. You would have smiled to see us in the Peninsula whenever our paths crossed, sharing news from home or laughing at the tricks we used to play when we were my father's pupils."

"I had forgotten you and he shared a schoolroom for some years. It is good of you to call," Lord Malvin said again. "We have read the despatches, of course, and several of Arthur's fellow-officers wrote to express their condolences, but it is not the same as talking to one who was there."

The major swallowed and eased a large finger between his neck and the stock that was suddenly too tight. He had not expected this. Apart from boys eager to hear about the cut and thrust of battle, civilians generally did not wish to be confronted with the realities of war. Clearly the Malvins were different.

Lady Malvin looked up wanly from her seat beside her bedroom fire. Arthur's letters lay in her lap on her dove-grey morning gown. Arabella eyed the plain cap pulled over simply dressed hair, wishing that Mamma would make a little more effort with her toilette. She had always been so well turned out. It could not be good for her to cling to her mourning or to spend her days huddled in her room. Arthur would scold her if he knew. She tugged the bell pull.

"Why are you ringing, Arabella and—good heavens, what have you on your feet?"

"Roderick's old boots, Mamma." She lifted her skirts to her knees with an impish grin. "And his pantaloons. I am going to have some made before next winter. They are so comfortable. I walked down to the village gate and back. My feet are dry and I am as warm as toast. But that's not what I came to tell you. Major Thomas Ferraunt is below. He is home from France and has come to call on us."

Her mother's face lit up. "Thomas home? I hope you didn't tell him I was indisposed; I have so longed to talk to someone who was there."

"No, no. he is in the library with Papa and Julian. I thought it best to keep him away from my aunt."

"I'll go down immediately."

"Wait. Take five minutes to let Bates tidy you, make you look more the thing. A prettier cap and that lavender shawl would make all the difference. And the lavender half-boots. I'll just go and take off my bonnet."

"And those boots and pantaloons," Lady Malvin said firmly. "Whatever about wearing them in the park, you cannot wear them indoors."

"Yes, Mamma."

Was it the boots or the pantaloons that had stirred her mother from the apathy she too easily fell into since Arthur's death? Or was it Thomas's visit? Arabella did not care. "I'll be back in a trice," she promised as she sped away.

Sipping his host's excellent Madeira, Thomas looked around the library, admiring the gothic, mullioned windows and vaulted ceilings high enough to permit the installation of a gallery on three of the four sides. This must be one of the oldest parts of the original abbey. The walls were lined floor to ceiling with book-filled oak shelves. Argand lamps placed at intervals on tables around the large room cast a mellow glow on gilded leather spines while comfortable chairs invited the visitor to sit and peruse a volume at his ease.

Lady Malvin came in, hands outstretched. She had aged since he last saw her. She stood as erect as ever, but her face was haggard and the hair that framed it beneath her cap was now silver. Her fingers clung to his when he took her hands.

"Welcome home, Thomas. It seems like only yesterday when you and Arthur were up to all sorts of mischief together and now he's gone forever. But I am so happy to see you safe; you must never think otherwise."

"Thank you, my lady."

As she continued to gaze up at him, he stooped and gently touched his lips to the cheek she had, perhaps unconsciously, tilted towards him.

"Will you accept this from me on his behalf? He would have asked me to give it to you, I know."

She smiled through the tears that veiled her blue eyes. "Gladly. Now, here are the others."

Thomas bowed to Julian's wife and turned to Matthew, the third of the Malvin brothers. There was no trace of the lanky schoolboy he remembered in this elegant gentleman whose carefully disordered curls, elaborately tied neckcloth, beautifully tailored coat and gleaming hessians all proclaimed his interest in the latest fashions. Was this what they called 'a pink of the ton'?

Matthew's smile was genuine and he wrung Thomas's hand painfully. "Good to see you safely returned, Thomas. Welcome home."

Soon they were settled in a semi-circle around the blazing fire. Thomas found himself next to Lady Malvin, seated across from her daughter. Miss Malvin now wore a high-necked gown of very pale lilac trimmed with darker ribbons.

They matched a little velvet jacket that just covered her bosom, showing off her high, rounded breasts. Apples, not pears. My God, what was he thinking? This was Arthur's little sister. He remembered her as a golden-curled moppet, and later as a gawky girl just out of the schoolroom and too shy to talk to him. When had she grown so beautiful? Her hair was now the colour of dark honey that gleamed and glinted in the fire light. Her mouth was not the fashionable prim rosebud but generous and inviting, with a tempting dip in the middle of her upper lip. Her eyes had always been that clear, silvery blue, but why had he never noticed how they were framed by winged dark gold brows and fringed with impossibly long eyelashes?

She turned to speak to her father, revealing an exquisite profile and the lovely long line of her leg from hip to knee. Bright-eyed Athena, Thomas thought as he accepted a cup of tea from Mrs Malvin. Far above us mortals.

A hush fell on the little group. Lord Malvin looked over to Thomas. "Your regiment was sent to Belgium in May, I believe, Major. Did you happen to meet Arthur before the battle?"

All eyes were fixed on him. The interrogation had begun. He must speak truthfully but try to spare them the worst of the slaughter. He drained his cup and Miss Malvin came quietly to take it from him. He waited until she had resumed her seat before answering.

"I did, my lord, at the beginning of June. We ran into each other at the Namur Gate in Brussels and he invited me to join a party he was getting up that evening at the Couronne d'Espagne. We made a good night of it."

"I'm sure you did," Matthew murmured.

"Then we met again on the thirteenth at a big race meeting at Grammont. We, I mean the 23rd, were stationed there, but thousands came from all around Brussels, all in the best of spirits and determined to enjoy themselves. Both Arthur and I backed a few winners and he dined with me before leaving for Brussels."

"The thirteenth?" Lady Malvin said wonderingly. "But that was just five days before—and he was well then?"

"Very cheerful, ma'am. A little fidgety like most of us, to be frank, wondering what way things would go. We had no idea then that Bonaparte was so near. He could as easily have remained in France and forced us to hunt him down."

"And that was the last time you saw Arthur?"

Thomas nodded. "I waved him off about seven o'clock. He had another engagement, he said. The fighting started just three days later at Quatre Bras. His battalion was involved in that, but we weren't."

"So he survived that battle," Lord Malvin said slowly.

"So I understand, sir."

"And then Waterloo. What can you tell us about it?"

"You must understand that the 23rd's position was not near that of the 95th and at the time I had very little idea of how they fared. The corn—mostly rye—was about five foot high and visibility was poor, especially once the artillery started up. What general information I have was gathered piecemeal afterwards. But I will try and explain the action to you. Have you seen a plan of the battlefield?"

"No."

"Then allow me to draw you one. Might I have a pencil and paper?"

Miss Malvin jumped up. “I’ll get them. Or, Major, would you prefer to sketch your plan over here at the table?”

Thomas rose, grateful to escape the hopeful eyes fixed on him.

“Do you need a ruler?” she asked when he joined her.

“If you please.”

She bent to open a drawer. Her head close to his, she whispered, “General Kempt wrote that Arthur was killed instantly by a musket ball to the temple.” As she straightened up, her eyes met his.

“I understand,” he said under his breath, then, louder, “thank you, Miss Malvin.”

“Sit here, Major. I’ll just sharpen another pencil for you and leave you in peace.”

It was the first time he had deliberately tried to recall the events of that day. He had read the despatches, of course, and discussed various happenings with one or other of his fellow-officers but he had never tried to put it all together. *Start by making a plan of the field*, he told himself. *Wellington’s ridge was here. Then the roads, then* Houguomont, La Haye Sainte *and Bonaparte’s Headquarters at* La Belle Alliance. *That looks about right. Now, we were here*.

As he worked, he was vaguely aware of the murmur of voices and the chink of china as more tea was poured. Someone left the room and returned sometime later, but he did not look up. In his head clamoured the ear-battering cacophony of battle—the deep roar of the artillery, the crack of muskets, the rubdidub of drums punctuating the piercing bugle and trumpet calls, and the voices of officers exhorting their men to ‘hold steady, lads’. His lungs filled with the smoke that billowed all day, becoming progressively darker and thicker until he could not rid his mouth of its foul taste; he felt the ground tremble at the pounding of oncoming cavalry, heard the volleys as the English squares repelled the charge. His sword grew heavy in his hand.

The Malvins need not know any of this. Such knowledge was not for them but was reserved to the men who had stood shoulder to shoulder in that hell for hours on end.

He was finished. He went over to the group at the fire. "If I might ask you to come to the table where I have spread out the plan?"

They listened attentively as he described how they had arrived the day before and spent the night huddled in their cloaks, bedded on straw in a muddy field before going to their assigned stations the next morning.

"As if Wellington and Bonaparte were setting out a giant chessboard," Julian's wife remarked.

"Yes, but unlike in chess, they have the freedom to place the pieces where they choose."

"That is part of the commander's skill, I suppose," Julian commented.

"Yes. The Duke knew exactly what he wanted."

"Who was the first to fire?"

"The French. They attacked mid-morning."

"Why so late?"

"Heaven knows. Bonaparte took time to review his troops. We could hear them singing and the cries of 'vive l'Empereur'. But that may have been to keep the men in good heart while they waited. It had rained very heavily the night before and the ground was sodden, which would make it difficult to manoeuvre, especially for the artillery."

Thomas shook his head to dispel the memory of the muddy, blood-soaked soil and began to explain as dryly as he could the allied and French dispositions of their troops. Arthur's family clustered around him as he outlined the course of the battle over the long day. When he showed them where the 1st/95th had been deployed, near La Haye Sainte, Lady Malvin laid a tender finger on the plan as if in a last caress.

"I was wounded late in the afternoon," he told them. "They took me back to a dressing station and, after the French were routed, I was brought to a cottage where I remained some days before being removed to Brussels."

"I know we must first think of the living," Lady Malvin said, "but it is very hard to think of poor Arthur lying there. One reads such terrible accounts of mass graves and, and funeral pyres."

Lord Malvin put his arm around her. "Come and sit down, my love. He would not wish you to dwell on such things."

"Then he should not have got himself killed," she sobbed. "Oh, listen to me! You will think I am a foolish old woman, Thomas."

"Never that," he said. He went and squatted in front of her. "But—did no one tell you? Arthur was carried from the field and his remains are buried in a little churchyard not far away."

She clutched at his hands. "Truly?"

"Truly. I stood at his grave myself before I left for France in mid-July. He is not alone. Other British officers are buried there too." He looked from her to Lord Malvin. "I'm so sorry. It never occurred to me that you might not know."

Her ladyship's tears fell freely now. "Buried. In a churchyard. Oh, Tony!"

"I know, my dear, I know," her husband said gruffly.

Thomas gently withdrew his hands from her ladyship's clasp and rose to his feet, uncertain what to do next. A soft hand slipped into his arm and tugged him away.

"We'll leave them for a moment," Miss Malvin murmured and walked with him to the window where they were joined by her brothers and sister-in-law.

Matthew Malvin looked over at his weeping mother and shook his head. "You're a hero, Ferraunt! I'd rather face a charging bull than do what you have just done."

"I am sorry to be the cause of such distress."

"It is more relief than distress," Miss Malvin said. "We must thank you for calling today, Major. I think Mamma will be very much the better for your visit."

"I agree," Mrs Malvin said. "Julian, pour us all a glass of Madeira, if you please. Matthew, you may take two to your parents. While you are doing so, perhaps the major will inform us about the latest Paris fashions."

Thomas welcomed the change of subject even if he could not contribute much to it. "The ladies are all very neat and elegant, but pray do not ask me to describe their gowns. I should only make a hash of it."

"Are waists still worn so high?"

"If you mean under the arms, yes."

"I've never known anything else," Miss Malvin remarked.

"I suppose you haven't." Mrs Malvin was clearly startled. "I well remember the change from hoops to straighter gowns and how elaborate my mother's costumes were when I was a girl, especially when she wore full dress. Such beautiful fabrics, too—rich brocades and laces, so unlike the simple muslins that were all the rage when I made my come-out."

"But much less comfortable, I imagine," Miss Malvin said.

Her sister-in-law flicked a glance towards Thomas as if concerned that the conversation might drift into uncharted waters. "Oh, one gets used to anything, even these ridiculous flat slippers they have us wear nowadays instead of a proper shoe with a heel."

"Thomas?" Despite Lady Malvin's obvious exhaustion, she seemed less strained.

"Yes, my lady?"

"I cannot sufficiently express my gratitude to you."

"There is nothing to thank me for, ma'am."

"You have given me peace of mind," she answered. "I am so happy to know that my boy is at rest in hallowed ground; that one day we may visit his grave. You are here for the next few days, at least?"

"I am, ma'am."

"You must come and dine, with your parents. I'll send a note to Mrs Ferraunt."

He bowed. "We shall be honoured."

"Until then, Thomas."

Once the elder Malvins had left the room, he picked up his shako. "I'll say goodbye for now."

"Wait, I'll walk down to the village with you, Thomas," Matthew said abruptly. "I haven't been outside all day."

"That cannot have been easy for you," Matthew said as they strolled down the avenue.

"No, but it was worth it if it eased Lady Malvin's mind. Just—Matthew, she mentioned visiting Waterloo. Don't let her go."

"It's not for me to allow my mother anything," Matthew said with a grin. "She is not generally such a watering-pot. In fact, she is a very resolute lady."

"I remember. Have a word with your father—he should try to dissuade her, for the next couple of years at least. The area has become a magnet for tourists and I understand that there is a thriving trade in mementoes—buttons, belts, epaulettes, that sort of thing. She would find it distressing. And, even worse, a macabre demand has developed for the teeth of the dead."

"The teeth?"

"Yes, the battle-field has proved surprisingly lucrative for dentists and those seeking replacement teeth."

"Good God!" Mathew sounded sickened. "I agree that is no place for my parents. Thank you again, Ferraunt. Come and have a pint at the inn. I need one to take the taste of that last out of my mouth. "

Chapter Two

"I wish Mamma had not invited the Halworths," Arabella muttered to Matthew as they waited for the guests to arrive. Admiral Sir Jeremiah Halworth had purchased Longcroft Manor three years previously, and moved there with his family when forced by rheumatism to retire from the sea. The connection between the Manor and the Abbey had deepened when Lallie Grey, the step-daughter of Sir Jeremiah's niece, married Lady Malvin's brother Hugo Tamrisk, but Arabella and Matthew had not become close friends with the younger Halworths, Ruth and John, although they were more or less the same age.

"I agree. They have no sense of humour. You cannot crack a joke or make a pun, for they stare at you as if you are stupid, but they are the stupid ones."

"That's it. When you cannot laugh with somebody, they make for very dull company. Besides—I don't know what it is about Ruth, but I feel she is always watching me, assessing me somehow."

"Perhaps she envies you. She is a drab sparrow beside your—"

Arabella narrowed her eyes. "Beside my what?"

"Your golden oriole," her brother concluded triumphantly.

She stared at him, stunned by this unwonted and extravagant tribute. "And when, pray, have you ever seen a golden oriole?"

"When I was staying at Barsham last year, one of the chaps shot one. A pity, really, for it was a beautiful thing and they are quite rare, I believe." He grinned at her. "That was a very pretty compliment. You should thank me, Sis."

Her lips twitched. "I should indeed. I shall certainly note it in my journal; I may never hear another such from you. Oh, here's Mamma. Doesn't she look so much better?"

There was a sparkle in her mother's eyes that Arabella had not seen for almost a year. She had lightened her mourning, wearing a cream shell-lace tippet over a long-sleeved gown of deep purple velvet trimmed with amethyst ribbons. A cunningly twisted turban of amethyst and cream striped silk sat elegantly on her beautifully waved hair.

Her father smiled fondly and kissed his wife's cheek. "You look very handsome tonight, my dear—positively regal."

"Thank you, Tony. Arabella and I walked around the old cloisters today after your sister left us and I feel much the better for it."

"Better for the walk or for Agatha's departure?" he asked with a little twinkle in his eye.

She tried to look reproving but could not suppress a smile. "I found her particularly trying this year, I confess."

"When is she not?" Matthew drawled. "She says he was drowned, but I would not be surprised to learn that her dearest John simply decided to remain in India rather than face life with her."

"No, no. That would have been too cruel to his parents," his mother cried. "I remember them well—his father was a cousin of Lord Nugent's."

"Did you know John?" Arabella asked. "Was he really such a paragon as my aunt makes him out to be?"

"I never met him—he died before we were married, but your father knew him."

Lord Malvin laughed. "To be frank, he was something of a scapegrace. That is why he was sent to India. His parents hoped he would make something of himself."

"I have heard that while he was very charming, he was not very steady," Lady Malvin added.

Arabella frowned. "Do you mean he led Aunt Agatha on?"

"Oh, his offer was genuine enough," her father said, "but it would have been a very advantageous match for him and my father was reluctant to agree to a formal betrothal as things stood. However, they were permitted to write. Ironically, John was in funds when he died and, as he had made a will leaving everything to your aunt, it all came to her."

"I am sure she would rather have had her lover safely returned to her," Millie said.

"She never talks about what sort of a person he was, just about her loss, as if his death was more important to her than his life. I suppose in a way it was." Arabella looked at the others. "We must remember Arthur and talk about him just as we always did."

"You are right, my dear," her father said, "but we must also resume our normal lives and will have done nothing wrong if at times he slips to the backs of our minds. It is fortunate that time dulls the edge of grief. We could not survive, otherwise."

He had lost Julian's and Mattie's mother after only five years of marriage, Arabella remembered. And her still-born baby too. And yet she was not forgotten. Her portrait still hung beside his, with Mamma on his other side. How wise Mamma had been, not to insist that all traces of her predecessor be removed. Sometimes she even spoke of her in the same tone as she spoke of her sisters. And Arabella had never known her to treat Julian and Mattie any differently than her own children. To them she was Mamma, and to their children, Grandmamma.

"Black looks so well on you—it positively drains me of colour." Ruth Halworth inspected the black net gown that Arabella wore over a white satin slip trimmed with narrow silver ribbon. "I suppose that is another of Madame Hortense's creations."

"Yes," was all Arabella could reply. It wasn't her fault that her gowns came from one of London's foremost *modistes* or that Lady Halworth was not overly interested in fashion. Then, too, the other girl's short stature and full bosom did not lend themselves to the current styles, although a clever dress-maker could do much to minimise such shortcomings. "Your pink is most becoming," she added.

"Thank you." Ruth complacently smoothed her skirts. Her hazel eyes shone and she smiled engagingly at Matthew. "I was so delighted when Lady Malvin's invitation came. We have not seen one another for an age."

Arabella nodded. "We were cooped up for so long that it felt like winter would never end, but today I found coltsfoot along the lane. I always find it so cheerful, like little suns."

Ruth sniffed. "I much prefer daffodils."

"Who does not? But the coltsfoot also deserves our appreciation, for it blossoms now, even through the lacy frills of the melting snow."

"How poetic!" Ruth sniffed again then gripped Arabella's arm and hissed, "Who's that with the rector and his wife? Doesn't he look truly ferocious?"

"It's their son, Major Ferraunt," Arabella whispered back, thinking he looked magnificent in his scarlet dress uniform. He had the calves for knee-breeches, too.

He was making the rounds of the company now, and was inevitably delayed by the Admiral who was always pleased to find a companion in arms, but at last was able to move on to Arabella's former governess.

"Miss Lambton! I am happy to find you still here," he said. "I trust I see you well, ma'am."

The little governess smiled up at him. "Indeed you do, Major. The Abbey schoolroom still has two pupils, although I shall lose Charles to your father this year."

"I am sure he looks forward to receiving him. He often says he wishes all his pupils were as well grounded as yours."

Miss Lambton pinked. "The rector is too kind."

"Miss Malvin." The major was now bowing before her.

"Good evening, Major Ferraunt."

There was a subtle warmth in his dark eyes. The left one crinkled at the corner and the left side of his mouth lifted. He was smiling, she realised and her own smile deepened in response.

"Malvin." He nodded to Matthew and looked enquiringly at Arabella who immediately turned to Ruth.

"Miss Halworth, may I present Major Ferraunt? Major Ferraunt, Miss Halworth and Mr Halworth."

The major bowed. "Your servant, Miss Halworth, your servant, sir. You are new to Longcroft?"

"Not so new; it's almost three years since my father purchased the manor," John Halworth replied.

"Where had you lived before?"

"Near Rye."

"I have often wondered why the Admiral chose to settle so far from the sea," Matthew remarked.

"So have I," the Admiral's son replied, "but he just says going to sea and living beside it are two different things. Where are you stationed at present, Major?"

"Until recently I was in Paris but when I return it will be to Cambrai."

John raised an eyebrow. "You will find it deuced slow here, after Paris."

"It is more restful, certainly, although I found it hard to become accustomed to the deep silence. An army camp is always noisy and a big city is no better. You get used to a certain hubbub. Even in winter, Paris never sleeps. London is the same, I imagine, although I have never spent much time there."

"I suppose it is," Arabella said. "During the season, certainly. Most *ton* entertainments are in the afternoon and evening and frequently continue into the early hours of the morning so the whole daily round is pushed back. I found it very strange the first time I was invited to a breakfast at three o'clock in the afternoon. What the *ton* call a breakfast is more what in Brussels they called a '*déjeuner à la fourchette*'."

"You did not starve until then, I hope."

She shook her head. "I like to ride early in the morning, when the Park is less crowded, and return for a real breakfast."

"How early is early?" Major Ferraunt wanted to know.

"Oh, about nine o'clock. It's also a good time to visit the shops, especially if you seriously want to buy something and not just while away the time."

Dinner was announced and, to Arabella's disgust, John Halworth immediately offered her his arm. Ruth looked expectantly at Matthew and the major politely approached Mrs Malvin.

Once the soup was served, Arabella turned to her neighbour. He was a keen rider to hounds and prided himself on his accuracy with a gun. Another time it might have amused her to see how long she could prevent him from monopolising the conversation with an account of his exploits, but today she had no patience for it.

"Did you have good sport this winter?" She knew from experience that this enquiry would wind him up as tightly as a clock and, once ticking, all he would require of her was an attentive expression and some admiring interjections to punctuate his narrative. This left her free to look around the table.

Major Ferraunt ate sparingly and slowly. Was it because of his wound that he cut his food into small pieces and chewed so deliberately? His choice of dishes confirmed this supposition. He ignored the *Maintenon* cutlets wrapped in paper that were always a favourite with the gentlemen, preferring a fricassee of chicken and, having tested it with his fork, left the thick crust of a game pie although he ate the flavoursome filling with relish.

Arabella glanced down the table towards her mother who was eating at an even more leisurely pace than usual. She placed one of the little parcels of mutton and herbs on her own plate and pushed the platter towards Mr Halworth, who took another without pausing in his description of how he had taken a flying leap over a five-bar gate. She was encouraged to see the major help himself to some cabbage pudding when Miss Lambton recommended it to him.

By the end of the course, John had progressed from hunting to shooting. It was beyond tedious.

"A rose-pink pheasant," Arabella murmured in a suitably impressed tone.

John did not react, but across the table the major looked up. Emboldened, she continued, "And a purple swan. Was it a difficult shot?"

"Not difficult, no, but not everyone could have taken it, I fancy," John said with a self-satisfied smile.

The major's dark eyes gleamed and his left eyelid drooped in what only could be a wink. She dimpled back at him. He had sharp ears and was clearly no clod. Still, it was perhaps time to change the subject. Resisting the lure of a brace of silver snipe, she waited for a suitable pause and said, "I read that *Guy Mannering* has been adapted as a musical play and will open next week at the Covent Garden Theatre."

"How exciting," Ruth said. "I should love to see it. Have you read it, Major Ferraunt? It is by the author of *Waverley*."

"I fear I have not, Miss Halworth. What is it about?"

The ensuing babble as several people corrected one another in an attempt to explain the convoluted plot carried them through the clearing of the first course and the laying of the second. Major Ferraunt accepted a helping of hashed calf's head and some cauliflower frittered in the French style. He followed this with a slice of potato pudding which cook had sent up with an orange sauce.

"How long do you remain at home, Major Ferraunt?" Miss Lambton asked.

"Do you mean here at Longcroft or in England?"

"Both, I suppose."

"If all remains quiet in France I hope to be in England until July. I must go to London to see the regimental agent, of course, and I have some commissions to fulfil for fellow-officers, but have not yet decided what else to do. I shall be here for the next couple of weeks at least."

"Your mother will be loath to see you go, I am sure," she remarked with a sympathetic glance at Mrs Ferraunt.

"Let us not speak of parting when he has only just come home," that lady countered briskly. "The rector hopes to arrange for a good friend to act as locum and then perhaps we may all have a little holiday together."

"Just tell me where you wish to go, ma'am, and I shall make the arrangements," her son replied promptly.

"I have been waiting until we are alone to tell you our news," Lady Halworth said to Lady Malvin once the ladies had left the gentlemen to their port and were comfortably ensconced in the drawing room. "Dear Lady Tamm has been so kind as to invite us to join them in town after Easter for some weeks." She spoke with a sort of proprietary pride, for it was while staying with the Halworths that Miss Lallie Grey had caught the eye of the then Hugo Tamrisk.

Arabella's heart sank. Although Parliament had been sitting for over a month, Mamma had not yet said anything about going to town this Season. It would be Arabella's fourth Season, but, when she thought about it, only her first in 1813 had been in any way normal. In 1814 they had gone to Brussels at the end of May to be near Arthur who had rejoined his regiment in Belgium, then last year Mamma's father had died in February. They had remained at Tamm to await the birth of Hugo's and Lallie's child so it was mid-May before they came to town—and just a month later had come Waterloo. That was the end of everything.

Perhaps it was selfish of her, but surely Mamma did not mean to continue with such excessive mourning? This had been the dreariest winter ever. It was different for the men—their hunting and their shooting took them out of the house, and Millie, as the heir's wife, had long since taken over many of Mamma's duties at the Abbey. She had her children, too, but Arabella had been left to drift aimlessly through the chill, stone corridors. By December, all the still room tasks had been completed and the herb garden had sunk into its winter sleep; she didn't want to set another stitch and her writing-desk reminded her too much of one who could no longer receive her letters. Music had always been one of her great joys but now it brought pain rather than solace.

She had thought to ask Lallie and Hugo if she might come to them if Mamma decided to stay in the country. Her young aunt by marriage was not quite six years older and they understood each other very well, but Arabella could hardly suggest she come and stay when Lallie had already invited the Halworths. She looked hopefully at her mother. Perhaps she would say something about the Halworths calling on them when they were in town, but Mamma merely replied, "I am sure you will enjoy yourselves greatly."

"A splendid opportunity for Ruth," Mrs Ferraunt pronounced.

"Indeed, and it will do John no harm to acquire a little 'town bronze', as they say," Lady Halworth replied. She had seemed somewhat crestfallen at her hostess's subdued response but now perked up again.

"I can just imagine him cutting a dash in the Park," Arabella whispered to Millie.

"Wretch!" Her sister-in-law choked back a laugh. "I cannot see the Admiral footing the bill for him to play the dandy."

"I suppose not, but Ruth must have a new wardrobe," Arabella said decidedly.

"What did you say, Miss Malvin?" Lady Halworth asked.

"Ruth and you will want new wardrobes, ma'am. You may wish to consider going to town for a few days in advance. If you order your gowns now, they will be ready for you after Easter."

"What a wonderful idea, Arabella," Ruth exclaimed. "You must give me the direction of your favourite shops."

"Have gowns made in London?" Lady Halworth said. "Surely that is not necessary?"

Arabella's mother stirred. "It is if you wish to move in the first circles," she said flatly. "You will not wish to be stigmatised as provincials. I do not wish to frighten you, but you have no idea how unforgiving, even cruel, the *beau monde* can be. Arabella, bring over the most recent issues of *La Belle Assemblée* and we can consider the latest fashions."

Chapter Three

"I don't believe it," Thomas heard Miss Malvin exclaim. "Who could possibly wear half-boots of drake's neck coloured silk, laced and fringed with dark blue and yellow kid and spotted and ornamented with purple?"

"One of Astley's *equestriennes,* perhaps," Julian Malvin said dryly. "Or are you making that up, Bella?"

"No. See for yourself." She thrust a magazine into her brother's hands and went to join her sister-in-law at the tea board.

Thomas fetched a cup of tea for Miss Lambton and returned to the table to request a cup of coffee. Miss Malvin poured him one and then filled the remaining cup.

"To whom should I bring the other?"

"Oh, that is mine."

He glanced around and, spying an empty sofa, placed the cups on the table in front of it. "Will you bear me company, Miss Malvin, as an Irish friend says?"

She smiled as she took her seat. "What a charming turn of phrase—so much more expressive than, 'may I join you'."

He angled himself comfortably into the corner of the sofa and stretched out his long legs. His companion sat more upright, but turned slightly towards him so that she could meet his eyes. Tonight she wore black and white; it was too severe for her—he preferred her in colours. The vivid blue-green of a drake's neck-feathers would suit her, especially against that lusciously creamy skin.

He shifted restlessly, abruptly conscious that he had not been with a woman since Waterloo. A son of the rectory, he had never seduced an unmarried girl or intruded on a marriage and had nothing but pity for tawdry prostitutes, but the Bible accepted concubines, or mistresses as they would be described today, and when they were stationed somewhere for a length of time he liked to find a companion—a willing widow, for example—who could provide a refuge from military life. He had had a pretty little *Madame* in Grammont, but had been reluctant to set up a mistress in occupied Paris.

"What did you do with your horses, Major," Miss Malvin asked. "Are they still in France?"

"No, I brought them with me. I don't like to leave them with strangers for so long."

"How many do you have?"

"At present, two saddle horses plus a baggage mule. I cannot break the habit of being able to pack up all my traps and move instanter."

"What about hounds? Arthur spoke of a fellow-officer in the 95th who hunted regularly in the Peninsula."

"That was Harry Smith, I expect. A capital fellow! He was recently appointed Town-Major of Cambrai and arrived with eighteen couple of hounds. He and Wellington have divided up the country between their two packs. I have none myself."

"But you do hunt?"

He didn't trust the expression of bright interest on her lovely face, especially given her obvious tedium while listening to Mr Halworth at dinner. Yet here she was taking the same tack with him. Did she think gentlemen could only talk about horses and sport? Or was it a test? A test or a trap? Her way of weeding out the dullards?

"If the opportunity presents itself, but I am not hunting-mad," he replied carefully. "I shall not bore you with tales of runs and kills."

A small smile touched her lips. "I never thought you would."

"Rose-coloured pheasants?" he asked softly.

She coloured slightly, then laughed outright. "It was unfair of me to make fun of him, perhaps, but he was not listening to me either."

"True. What would you have said if he had challenged you on it?"

"Oh, that I was thinking about a new gown." She fluttered her eyelashes as she spoke. "Every man knows that females are featherheads and their thoughts likely to stray towards their wardrobes."

She looked so consciously silly that he wanted to laugh, but the usual twinge stopped him. He pressed his hand against his cheek and asked, "What was your opinion of *Guy Mannering*?"

"I thought it very far-fetched. I prefer more prosaic tales but I imagine it will make a splendid musical play."

"What do you call a prosaic tale?"

"One that deals with normal everyday life as we might experience it, but in a way that both diverts and helps us better understand ourselves. There is a new authoress who has published such works in recent years but you may not have come across them abroad."

"What is her name?"

"That I cannot tell you, Major, for she remains anonymous. Her first book was called *Sense and Sensibility* and her second, *Pride and Prejudice*."

He raised an eyebrow. "Interesting titles."

"What do you read?"

He shrugged. "In the army one learns not to be over-particular but to be grateful for every new book."

"Arthur said the same, but what did you take with you?"

"When I sailed for Portugal, I took the *Iliad* and the *Odyssey,* Mr Hooper's *Rational Recreations*, *Paradise Lost* and Smollett's translation of *Don Quixote*."

"*Don Quixote*?" She repeated his Spanish pronunciation carefully. "Is that how you say it? He's the madman who tilts at windmills, is he not? I found the book most absurd."

"Perhaps, but it is a particular sort of high absurdity. It was especially interesting to read it in Spain. Then, at the last moment, my mother presented me with her copy of *Thaddeus of Warsaw*."

"What? All four volumes? Did you have room for them?"

"Just about. But when she said that besides entertaining me, she hoped it would remind me to write to her, I could not refuse."

"I suppose not. Did you read it?"

"Yes. Is that what you would you call a prosaic tale?"

She began to laugh. "Not in the slightest. I cannot speak for the accuracy of the Polish events, but the English part is ridiculous. I have never known anyone to speak or behave as her characters do. Remember how the count finally makes his proposals, 'his lady's passive hand pressed warmly to his heart'? I thought it the epitome of romance when I was thirteen. But now—it is too long-winded and all he can do is talk about himself and his parents. The only compliment he makes is to speak of his lady's 'noble heart'. And his language is so swollen, but then none of the characters seems able to speak without falling into transports of one sort or another."

"How does your prosaic authoress make her proposals?

"Do you know, it is very strange but the ones I recall were unsuccessful? The others are briefly described—it is almost as if they happen offstage. And yet, you are in no doubt that her couples love one another."

"And that is what a proposal should be about?"

"I think so. Don't you? Real love, I mean, not the exaggerated, superficial devotion you read about in too many novels. But it is difficult to describe."

"So how do you recognise it in her characters?"

"By their behaviour," she answered slowly, "and also by the behaviour of others whose professed love is but a poor imitation of the real thing."

"That is skillful indeed. I shall make a point of looking out for the lady's work."

"I should be interested to hear what you think of it. But now we must be silent. Miss Halworth is going to sing."

"None of your lovelorn lasses, Miss Halworth," Lord Malvin said jovially as Miss Halworth passed his chair on the way to the pianoforte.

Miss Malvin raised her eyes to heaven. "Papa cannot abide what he calls lachrymose laments," she whispered to Thomas. "Miss Halworth knows this, of course, but it can prove difficult for young ladies who visit us for the first time."

"Why?"

"It is a sad fact that very many songs are about abandoned or lovesick maidens and if they may not sing them, they don't know what to choose."

"What could they sing?" he asked curiously.

"Shakespeare is always useful, or something patriotic like "Rule Britannia"."

Miss Halworth had opted for Shakespeare and sang a sprightly version of "Where the Bee Sucks, There Suck I". She had a light, high soprano that was well suited to Ariel's gaiety and he listened with pleasure. She followed this with "It was a Lover and his Lass", prefixing it with the remark that his lordship had not forbidden her to sing of cheerful lovers.

So she has a little backbone, Thomas thought approvingly. When had he last sat in a drawing-room and listened to a young lady sing? Had he ever done so? What a rough life he had led, compared with this sheltered gentility. And how many such homes had been plundered as the warring armies marched and counter-marched across Europe? England was a blessed isle, indeed, to have been spared such despoiling.

"Now what have you chosen for us, Arabella?" Lord Malvin enquired after Miss Halworth had smilingly acknowledged her applause and compliments and resumed her seat.

"I must beg to be excused, sir. I am not in good voice today, I fear."

"Then you'll play something for us. It's been too long since we had music in the evenings."

Thomas thought he heard her sigh but she removed her gloves obediently and went to leaf through the sheets of music in the slatted Canterbury beside the pianoforte. Once seated at the instrument, she squared her shoulders as if steeling herself for an ordeal and began to play. He didn't recognise the piece, Mozart, he thought, but it did not seem too difficult, yet she bit her lip as if she had to concentrate. Once she blinked rapidly and brushed at her eye as if something irritated it. She paused for a moment and then broke into a strident, aggressive melody *alla Turca*, the sharp rhythm and slashing staccato a reminder that this style of music was inspired by the Sultan's Janissary bands that had once played before the gates of Vienna. When she got to the end, she closed the lid of the instrument firmly, bowed briefly and returned to her seat beside him. She was trembling and her eyes brimmed with unshed tears. He watched, horrified, as she struggled to contain them.

No-one else seemed to have noticed. She took a deep breath, pressed her lips firmly together and swallowed, her hands clenched on her gloves. A teardrop stole down her cheek and she hastily knuckled it away. There was a second door at the end of the room. If he could get her down there, she could leave the room discreetly.

He indicated the portrait that hung on the far wall. "I should like a closer look at the background of that painting, Miss Malvin. Will you show it to me?"

She nodded and accepted his hand to help her rise. Her hand shook and he tucked it into the crook of his arm with a comforting clasp.

Another tear threatened to overflow. He ignored it and, as they slowly paced down the long room, began to describe how the French had protested against the removal of looted paintings from the Louvre. "But Wellington held firm. He even had the four bronze horses of St Mark taken down from the Arc de Triomphe and returned to Venice. Although the Venetians did not acquire them honestly either—they were part of their plunder from Constantinople during the crusades. Ah, here we are. It's very fine, indeed. I shall take a step behind you, so as to better judge the perspective." He stood back and to the right, screening her from the others.

She cast him a grateful look through wet eyelashes before dabbing at her eyes with a little lace-trimmed handkerchief, then discreetly blew her nose. "That's better." She smiled weakly. "Thank you for rescuing me. It is very foolish, but since Arthur was killed, music tends to make me weep. The tears just come—I cannot stop them."

"It is because music can unlock what is hidden away in our heart," he said sympathetically. "As time passes, you will find it easier. Would you prefer to slip away until you have recovered your composure?"

"No. I'll do now." She squared her shoulders and pointed to the painting. "Here you see my grandfather posed rather pompously against the ruins of Rome, his elbow propped casually on a convenient antique altar. I have seen similar works in other families; I suspect the artists kept a supply of half-finished canvases, ready for the next young Englishman who wanted to bring back proof of his grand tour. He has a look of Arthur, don't you think?"

"Provided one removes the wig," he agreed tactfully He couldn't see the resemblance himself, but if it pleased her to think so—

"My mother insisted on having his likeness taken when he was at home after Vittoria. He grumbled, of course, but now we are so glad to have it. It hangs in her sitting-room." She looked up at him. "It helps to talk normally about him. We couldn't before—Mamma became so distressed."

"Arabella, Ferraunt, should we play Pope Joan or speculation?" Matthew called down the room.

"Pope Joan," Miss Malvin said. "I hate speculation. Who else is playing?"

"Everyone except Admiral and Lady Halworth who have challenged the rector and Papa to a game of whist."

"That makes us ten. Shall we draw for partners?" Mrs Malvin asked as she placed an ornate, round, staking board in the middle of the table. "A hand of four cards is really too small to play properly. Matrimony and intrigue will get out of hand."

Without waiting for a reply, she rapidly created five pairs of cards, shuffled them and spread them into a fan for each player to take one.

I've never before played a game that involved 'matrimony' and 'intrigue'," Thomas remarked.

"They are both winning combinations," Miss Malvin replied, her eyes dancing. "The first is when you play the queen and king of trumps in succession; the second is if you play the knave and queen."

"And supposing your neighbour has the king to your queen?"

"Then we share the matrimony pool."

"All four? I thought we were playing Pope Joan, not the Grand Turk!" He flipped over his card. "Five of hearts. And you?"

She displayed the five of diamonds.

"Excellent. I shall rely on you to advise me," He pulled out a chair for her and took the one beside it. "How is this played?" he asked as he accepted a pile of ivory fish from Mrs Malvin. "What are the stakes?"

"And Pope clears all." Mrs Ferraunt triumphantly put down the nine of diamonds and helped herself to the counters for 'pope' and 'game'.

"I think the rectory has an unfair advantage," Julian Malvin protested as he shuffled the cards before the new deal. "That is your second pope, ma'am and I don't know how many matrimonies you and my brother have celebrated this evening."

"Pure luck," she said complacently.

Thomas rarely played cards. Even now, his income was not so great that he could comfortably afford to lose a large sum and in his early days in the regiment, where an ensign's pay had barely covered his living expenses, he had not been prepared to risk the allowance his father made him on top of it. It had been simpler to say he did not gamble. Some of his more well-to-do fellows had sneered at him as the 'parson's son,' but he had simply replied, 'And proud to be so, sir'.

This was different. While the game was important, it was the company that mattered; the jokes and quips tossed across the table, the teasing when a pair took matrimony or Lady Malvin's smug look when she emptied her hand by laying down one after another five clubs so that she and Miss

Lambton took the game. And he could lean over the shoulder of a pretty girl and whisper confidentially in her ear as he advised her which suit to lead next. She obligingly followed his instructions although she knew the game far better than he did. She smelt of roses and sunshine, somehow, of lazy summer days—English summer, of course, with its dappled shade and countless blossoms, not the baking, parched heat of Spain.

"Hearts, then spades," he murmured and she obediently placed the four of hearts in front of her, followed by the five and six. Spades were trumps and they held knave and queen. She could have played them first—there was nothing more provoking than to be prevented from playing such a combination—but the seven of hearts had already been played. This way she could dispose of five cards even if someone held the King.

"That's a stop," he announced when she put down the six. Now she could play her spades.

"Intrigue," she said, laying down the Knave and Queen and Matthew pushed the staking board towards her. It was the first intrigue of the night and she smiled over her shoulder at Thomas as she scooped the counters from the compartment.

"What a pity we're not playing for guineas."

"I think you'll find you've at most recouped your losses, Sis," Matthew said dryly.

She sighed. "I suppose you're right."

"What sort of intrigue are you and Ferraunt plotting, Bella?" Mr Halworth asked with a grin.

Thomas stiffened but Miss Malvin only laughed.

"You surely don't expect us to reveal all," she retorted gaily. "We are better conspirators than that, are we not, Major."

"As Lord Lansdowne has it, ''Tis the talk, and not the intrigue, that's the crime', " Miss Lambton put in.

"Aye, it's better to hold your peace," Julian Malvin agreed.

"But I shall speak now," his wife declared, laying down the king of spades. "Matrimony and that's the game."

"That was a very pleasant evening indeed," Dr Ferraunt declared as they arrived back at the rectory, "but it is time for bed. There is poor Johnson's funeral in the morning."

"I'll come up with you," his wife said. "Goodnight, Thomas."

"Good night, Mother." He kissed her cheek. "Good night, sir," he added to his father who waited at the foot of the stairs. "I'll catch a breath of air before turning in."

The wooden floor creaked as he walked to the side door where he paused to light a small lantern. He carried it across the terrace and placed it on the square pillar that separated the balustrade from the shallow steps leading down to the garden. It was a clear night; the brilliant first-quarter moon hung so low that it seemed as if it would soon be pierced by the church steeple looming shadow-like, against the starry sky. His nose tingled from the crisp night air. He took a deep breath, identifying the various scents that made up the smell of home. Aromatic wood-smoke—the maid would have stirred the fire in his mother's room when she heard the carriage approach. The earthy smell of rich, damp soil. The familiar whiff of the stables and the midden—almost pleasant, especially when compared with the ripe stench of horses and unwashed men that surrounded an army on the march. Something stirred below him—some creature, a cat perhaps, had brushed against his mother's rosemary bush, releasing its spicy fragrance. It spoke not only of home, but of meals of spatchcocked fowl or coarse country sausage, hastily snatched around a campfire in Spain.

He took out a cheroot and lit it at the candle in the lantern. Now the smell was definitely that of Spain. What was wrong with him? Why could he not settle? Must he always long to be elsewhere?

But where? Or what? He was increasingly disenchanted with military life. Now that Bonaparte had been so thoroughly defeated, no immediate enemy remained. Did he want to be a peace-time soldier, chiefly occupied in ceremonious display, forever ready for action but rarely called upon? Or did he want to serve abroad, the strong arm of an occupying or colonial power?

He had not asked himself these questions when he first joined the army. Then he had been mad for action and adventure, horrified by the suggestion that he might follow in his father's scholarly footsteps. 'If none of his lordship's sons want the living, I am sure you could have it when I retire,' the rector had said, 'and if that is not possible, the college has other livings in its gift should you not wish to continue as a fellow.'

In the end, they had compromised. Thomas would take his degree and if afterwards he was still averse to academic life, he might appeal to his mother's uncle, a half-pay colonel, for a recommendation as an officer. Great-uncle Bowen had been happy to oblige and both an ensignship and a lieutenancy had been Thomas's free of purchase. In addition, he had made his great-nephew his heir, so enabling him to buy a captaincy some years later. With the promotion to major after Toulouse, Thomas's feet were firmly on the ladder of success. Now was a fine time to discover he didn't want it. But what did he want? Neither the Church nor Oxford's cloistered common-rooms appealed, but what alternatives were there for a gentleman who had to make his way in the world?

He had liked Nova Scotia, he remembered. There were splendid opportunities there for a man of reasonable fortune and enterprising spirit. But could he leave his parents? His father had not been well this past winter. His mother had written, urging him to seek a leave of absence as he longed to see his son, 'before it was too late'. There was nothing specifically wrong, she had admitted; just the general fragility of old age combined with a lowness of spirits. And she was also over seventy and Thomas an only child. Did he not have a responsibility there?

He sighed and tapped the ash off the cheroot. His mother was right. It had been a very pleasant evening, one of friendly, neighbourly entertainment that was a far cry from the masculine atmosphere of an officers' mess or the larger routs and parties to which unattached officers were invited. He wanted a home, he realised, and for that he needed a wife. He was not impecunious—far from it. His uncle's legacy brought him five hundred pounds a year in addition to his pay. Supposing he were to retire on half-pay—would his means be sufficient to provide a wife and family with the comforts of life? And, more importantly, what sort of wife did he want?

Chapter Four

"I have been talking to Julian, Clarissa," Millie said at breakfast a few days later. "If you do not wish to go to town this year, we shall go. I should be happy to chaperon Bella, if she likes to come with us."

Arabella gasped, "Millie! What a wonderful idea. But what about the children?"

"We could leave them here but I would prefer to take them and Miss Lambton with us. It should be easy to manage now that Anne has left the nursery."

Lady Malvin looked down the table to her husband. "What do you think, Anthony?"

"It is up to you, my dear. We shall remain here if you wish. But I think it is time we resumed our normal lives. The longer we leave it, the harder it will be."

"Why don't we all go to town?" Arabella suggested. "You would be lonely here by yourselves, Mamma. And if Millie comes, you will not be obliged to go to all the parties with me, but may select the ones you wish to attend."

"If we all go, then it cannot be until after Lady Day," Lord Malvin said. "Either Julian or I must be here on quarter-day."

"We shall travel on the twenty-sixth," Lady Malvin decreed. "However, Millie, I think you and Julian should go up for a night or two as soon as possible. Arabella and I have gowns from last year that we have hardly worn, but you will need a complete new wardrobe. It will also give you an opportunity to view the schoolroom and night nursery and arrange to have them refurbished."

After breakfast, Arabella threw her arms around her sister-in-law. "Thank you, Millie. I was so downhearted after Ruth said they were to go to Lallie. Are you sure you will not mind?"

"No. In fact it will be good for Julian and me. We have got very staid here in the country. Are you doing anything in particular this morning, Bella?"

"No. I thought to go for a walk while the sun is shining, but that is all. Is there something I can do for you?"

"Would you go to see Mrs Bates? Her baby was born three days ago and it's time we called. I had planned to do it this morning but I must write immediately to the Belshaws if we are to go to town on Monday. Hampton will put up a basket for her."

"Miss Malvin." Young Mrs Bates struggled to sit up. "It's good of you to call, Miss."

Her mother-in-law set a chair for Arabella. "Will you sit down, Miss?"

"Thank you, Mrs Bates, but first I must see the baby." She went over to look at the little figure tucked into the cradle beside the bed. "Oh, he's beautiful—and so tiny." She gently laid a finger on the little palm and smiled when he closed his fist around it. "I remember my niece doing that."

"Would you like to hold him, Miss?"

"May I?"

"He'll be waking soon anyway. Will you take him up, Mother?"

The proud grandmother carefully lifted the swaddled infant and placed him in Arabella's arms. For all that he was so tiny, he felt warm and solid.

"You forget how small they are," she said, cradling him to her breast. He turned his head and nuzzled at it but did not open his eyes.

"He knows what's good for him," his grandmother said. "I hope it won't be long until you hold one of your own, Miss."

"Don't be putting the young lady to the blush," her daughter-in-law scolded. "But it is a great joy," she added softly. "His daddy's that proud. He loves his girls, but a man wants his son."

Arabella looked down at the baby. He was making little snuffling noises and his eyelids fluttered. "His eyes are open. What a beautiful dark blue." He seemed to look directly at her and she smiled and gently stroked his cheek. "What have you called him?"

"Jem, after his granddaddy."

The baby started to cry and his mother held out her arms. "He's hungry. Give him to me, if you please, Miss."

Arabella found she was surprisingly reluctant to relinquish him. Once he was settled, she said, "I'll leave you now, Mrs Bates. There is a basket on the table with some things you might find useful and Lady Malvin sends you this." She tucked the little purse under the woman's pillow. Her mother insisted that her guineas be given directly to the new mothers. 'Generally the fathers are sensible, but there are some who will spend it directly in the ale-house.'

"Thank you, Miss Malvin and please give her ladyship my respectful thanks."

Arabella smiled to herself as she continued down the lane. Little Jem was so sweet. He had felt so right in her arms. What would it be like to hold her own baby? She had never found herself wishing for one, but today she had felt a strange tug on her heartstrings and an unexpected yearning in her breasts and belly as if her body reminded her that she, too, was made for this. But a baby needed a father who would be her husband. There's the rub, she thought gloomily. Oh, she had been charmed before now by a beguiling smile and dazzled by a handsome face but it had never lasted, nor had she been tempted by any of her suitors. They had been more interested in the viscount's daughter than Arabella Malvin.

She had heard the Season described as the marriage mart of the *beau monde* and indeed young ladies were required to show their paces as much as any filly at Tattersall's. Last year she had overheard some gentlemen, all over thirty, discussing what they looked for in a bride.

'Sound in wind and limb, a pretty mover, from a good stable and with a handsome fortune.'

'A young wife is easier to break in; she hasn't had time to develop her own ideas.'

'She must not interfere with my way of life.'

'Trust me, I'll see to that,' the first had retorted and they had all laughed.

And yet they were all three regarded as excellent *partis.* How could you be sure you could safely entrust your heart and yourself to a man? She wanted the deep bond she could sense between her parents and between Julian and Millie. Like any plant it must be cared for, given water and protected against threats. But first it must be rooted in good soil, better soil than the Season offered. Mamma and Papa had met when they both accompanied their mothers to Bath. Mamma was used to say that she had first been attracted to Papa when she saw him help Julian and Mattie fly a kite on the lower lawn in front of the Crescent. And Millie had met Julian when he visited her brother who had been his closest friend at Oxford. Such a house party was ideal. Nobody could be on their best behaviour for a whole week at a time. And it provided countless opportunities for a couple to talk more or less privately without arousing any suspicion. Just look at the way she had been able to talk to Major Ferraunt yesterday evening.

She had felt comfortable with him and he had been both quick-witted and kind when faced with her distress. Would it be worth suggesting to Millie that they host a house-party in September like the one Mamma had held when Arthur was convalescing after Vittoria? Lallie and Hugo had met then.

She had reached the bridge over the little stream that usually purled quietly between the village and the park. Today it was swollen to the brim with the last of the melting snow, flowing strongly in dizzying swirls and eddies that rippled over the top of the banks. When they were children, they used to drop sticks in at one side of the bridge and dash across to see them emerge on the other. Lighter of heart than she had been since they heard of Arthur's death, she picked one up now and let it fall, then crossed to the other side just as a small child squeezed through a gap in the garden fence that gave onto the river bank below her. Nobody followed or called to it to stop as it toddled down to the water.

"Stop, go back!" she called, but either it couldn't hear her above the rushing water or paid no heed. Picking up her skirts, she ran down the slippery little path that led to the stream.

The child now squatted at the water's edge, inspecting something closely. It was the little Perkins boy—Sammy. Arabella was afraid to call again in case she startled him into losing his balance. She went as fast as she could. Ahead of her, Sammy leaned further forward to reach for a floating leaf. Splash! He had overbalanced and, skirts billowing, was carried into the centre of the flood.

Arabella screamed at the top of her voice. She looked around desperately but there was no-one in sight. She dare not run back to the inn for help; he would be carried away by the time anyone could return. She tore off her bonnet and pelisse, dropping them behind her as she scrambled down the sodden riverbank. Bracing herself, she stepped into the icy flow. It was deeper and faster than she had expected, coming up to her shoulders and sweeping her off her feet. Ignoring the stabbing cold she kicked out, struggling to keep her head above the water, and let the current take her towards the bobbing child. She was getting nearer! She kicked harder and reached out, cursing the tight sleeve of her gown. She stretched further and felt it give. There! She caught a fistful of the child's soaking skirts, then another, and tugged him to her. The little legs jerked against her grasp. Thank God! He was alive—or was it a false movement caused by the stream? She lifted him so that he was half out of the water, clamping him to her with her right arm. For an interminable moment he was still, then he began to cough in spluttered sobs.

Now she had to get them out before the inexorable flow swept them away. At the top of her voice, she shouted, "Help! In the stream! Help!"

A clump of alders on the opposite bank offered some protection. Supporting the clinging boy with one arm, she fought her way over to it, struggling to find her feet again. At last she could seize an overhanging branch and leaned against it, gulping great lungfuls of air.

Sammy was crying weakly. They must be looking for him by now.

"Help! The stream! Help!" Arabella called again, as loudly as she could, then turned her attention to the sobbing child. "It's almost over. You're safe now and we'll soon get out of this nasty stream and take you home to your mother."

"Mam?"

"That's right. We'll go home to your mam," she promised. "Hold on tight."

She hitched him up and his arms came around her neck in a stranglehold. Clinging to the branch with her free hand, she inched gingerly forward, slipping on the slick mud and wet leaves. Sammy grew heavier with each passing minute. As she neared the edge, the water got deeper again and she saw that the flow had undercut the riverbank, creating a barrel-shaped hollow beneath the grassy ledge. Try as she could, she was unable to climb out. She would have to pull herself up, but she would need both hands for that.

If she lifted Sammy as high as she could, would he be able to clamber onto the bank? She must tell him to crawl away as fast as he could. Would he obey and scramble to safety or would he roll back in? Her ankle turned on a stone and she stumbled but was able to right herself. She was getting tired. She would try one last call for help and then she must at least get Sammy to safety. Then she would try and swim downstream, find an easier place to get out. What was that? A man's voice. She strained to hear.

"Hallooo! Help is coming. Where are you?"

She closed her eyes in relief. "By the alders."

"Hold on."

Someone crashed through the trees and shrubs that lined the bank. Major Ferraunt stood above her. They were saved.

"Miss Malvin! Good God!"

"Be careful," she said as he came nearer. "The bank is overhanging here and might break away. I can't get out," she added with a shaky laugh. "I keep slipping back."

He knelt and held out his arms. "Give me the child and then we'll have you out of there in no time."

But Sammy clung even more tightly.

"You must let go, sweetheart," she whispered. "I'll hand you up to the gentleman and he'll take you back to your mam."

"You come too."

"I'll follow you," she promised.

His hands slipped from around her neck and with an effort she held him up to the major.

"I have him," he said and she let go.

"I'll take him, sir," another voice said.

Free of Sammy's weight and clinging to the branch with both hands, she slowly edged nearer the bank.

"Just a little closer, Miss Malvin," the major's deep voice encouraged her. "Take my hands, I won't let you go."

The relief of his strong clasp!

He steadied her as she moved forward. "Small steps; get your balance before you take the next one. That's it. Put your arms around my neck. First one, then the other."

When she obeyed, his strong arms locked her to him and he lifted her out of the water, swinging her around as he backed away from the treacherous edge.

"You are a marvel, Miss Malvin," he said in her ear. "That child would have drowned if not for you."

"Aye, Miss," a gruff voice said. The speaker had removed his frieze waistcoat and swathed the child in it.

Arabella said through chattering teeth, "You must get him home and warm so that he doesn't catch a chill."

"The same applies to you," Major Ferraunt said, stripping off his scarlet coat and draping it around her shoulders. "Come. My horse is over there. Can you walk so far?"

At her whispered 'Yes', he put his arm around her waist, supporting her as they crossed the wet grass. "I'll take you to the rectory. It's nearest. My mother will look after you."

She nodded, shivering, and clutched his coat to her.

"How long were you in the water?"

"I saw him fall in when I was on the bridge."

"You went in from there?"

"The bank below it on the village side. It seemed calmer by the alders and they gave me something to cling to so I headed for them."

They had reached a big bay standing stolidly beneath an oak. Her rescuer looked down at her, frowning, then threaded her arms through the sleeves of the coat and buttoned it down the front as if she were a child. What came just to his waist reached to her thighs, something she was grateful for when he lifted her into the unaccustomed man's saddle. There was no pommel to hook her leg around and in her wet gown she might have slipped and been deposited in an ignominious heap at his feet.

He fished in his pocket and produced a flask. "Drink this."

"What is it?"

"Cognac." She sipped cautiously and he urged, "Come. A little more—it will stave off the chill."

When she had taken another mouthful, he opened the gate and led the horse onto the road.

"Thank heavens you heard me."

"How often did you call?"

"I don't know. Three or four times."

"I was passing when I heard a cry and then, 'the stream'."

"I had him by then, but I couldn't get any purchase underfoot. I didn't know how long I could hold fast. I was going to try and throw him up onto the bank, but he wouldn't let go. And he seemed to get heavier by the minute."

"You are a heroine, Miss Malvin." There was true admiration in the brown eyes that looked up at her.

She shook her head. "Anyone would have done the same. It was just that I was there."

At last they arrived at the rectory. Thomas lifted Miss Malvin down. She clung to him, stiff and shaking, and without further ado he picked her up and carried her into the house, shouting for his mother as he went.

"Thomas! What has happened that you must set the whole house in uproar?" His mother bustled down the stairs, her housekeeper at her heels. "Miss Malvin! Good heavens!"

"She went into the stream after some brat," he explained.

"Sammy Perkins," a weak voice murmured against his chest.

"She needs a fire, a hot bath and a change of clothes," he ordered, "and something hot to drink."

"You had better bring her up to my bedchamber. Gribbins will see to everything else."

"I can walk," Miss Malvin protested faintly, her eyes half-closed.

"I'm sure you can," he said, heading for the stairs, "but this will be quicker."

Her head fell against his shoulder. She was deathly pale, her body racked by long shudders.

He took the stairs two at a time, Mrs Gribbins hurrying ahead to open the bedroom door and stir the fire into new life.

"Bring her over here," his mother commanded.

He put her down carefully so that she was supported by the high back of the chair and gently put back the soaked hair from her face. Heavy lids lifted over dull eyes.

"Thomas?" The hoarse whisper was barely audible.

"Yes?"

"Thank you for saving us."

Tears stung his eyes. She was so brave and so modest. "You did the saving, Miss Malvin. Without you, Sammy would be dead. I only came at the end."

"Just in time." Her eyes closed.

"Out, Thomas," his mother snapped. "When you have changed your clothes, go directly to the Abbey and assure the Malvins that she is safe here with me. I don't want them to hear heaven knows what elsewhere."

"I shall enquire if my lord and my lady are at home, Major," the Abbey butler said stiffly, superbly ignoring the agitated voices behind him.

"Silence!" Lord Malvin roared. "Now, Bart, what is this story of Miss Malvin falling into the stream? Where is she?" His voice broke.

Thomas brushed past the butler and strode down to the library where two grooms faced their employers. When Thomas arrived, the younger was saying, "All I know is they said the major pulled her out."

"Thomas!" Lady Malvin held out appealing hands while her husband snapped, "Is this true, Ferraunt?"

"Up to a point, my lord. Miss Malvin is safe and with my mother at the rectory. But she didn't fall into the stream; she went in deliberately to save a child—Sammy Perkins, I believe he's called."

"Good God!"

"But the stream's in full spate," Matthew said blankly.

"Yes. She had a little difficulty getting out, burdened as she was by the boy, but fortunately I came along in time to help them."

"You had better sit down and tell us the full story." Malvin's voice shook and he visibly fought for control before saying, "That will be all, Jones. Except—Bart, you say you accompanied Miss Malvin in the gig. Why the devil didn't you wait for her?"

The younger man swallowed nervously. "The cob cast a shoe, my lord, and Miss said I should take him to the blacksmith and she would start to walk home if she was ready before I came back."

"I see. That will be all."

"He could hardly have foreseen such an event, I suppose," Julian remarked as the door closed behind the two men. "How is the boy?"

"He was snivelling when I saw him last but otherwise seems to have taken no harm."

Lady Malvin shivered. "How could Arabella put herself into such danger?"

"She would not have been able to live with herself if she had walked away," Matthew answered.

"That's it," Thomas agreed. "I didn't see what happened myself, you understand, but this is what she told me."

"I left her with my mother," Thomas finished. He had tried to make light of Miss Malvin's predicament but the others knew the spot and were well aware that things might have gone differently if he had not come along just then.

"I am in your debt, Thomas," Lord Malvin said gruffly. "If we had lost our girl—it doesn't bear thinking about."

"There is no debt, sir. I thank Providence that I was there at the right time."

Lady Malvin rose. "I must go to her. She'll need fresh clothes and her warmest cloak."

He would find out how the boy was doing before he returned to the rectory. Miss Malvin would want to know. She had called him Thomas. He smiled inwardly at a sudden memory of a curly-headed moppet, not much older than the errant Sammy, holding her hands up to him and Arthur. 'Swing me, Art'ur and T'omas,' she had demanded. 'One, two, t'ree, whoooosh!' Her brother had had to explain to him what she wanted and she had kept them at it until her nursery-maid came looking for her.

"Perkins? The second cottage on Church Lane, sir. And, Major, if I might shake your hand? 'Tis grateful we all are to you for saving Miss Arabella and the little one."

He suffered having his hand wrung but felt obliged to protest. "Miss Malvin had done most of it by the time I got there. I just helped them from the water."

Really, he thought, as he continued towards the small cottage, did they seriously think he would stand by and let her jump into the water while he remained safely on the bank? He rapped on the wooden door and lifted the latch.

"Yes, sir?" A tired-looking woman looked up from where she was stirring a black iron pot hanging from a crane over the fire. A cradle stood near her and two children were tucked into blankets on a long settle, one at each end. Sammy was asleep while an older girl played with a rag doll. Her hand was bandaged.

"Major Ferraunt!" The wooden spoon splashed back into the pot and she pushed the crane aside to move it from the heat.

"I came to see how the boy was doing."

"He's asleep now. Worn out and no wonder. I'm making a bit of broth for when he wakes up. I don't know how to thank you, sir."

"There is no need to thank me," he said brusquely. "It is Miss Malvin you should thank. Without her, he would not have survived."

"You lifted them out," she said simply.

"What happened to your little girl?"

"She got hold of my husband's knife and cut herself. I asked him to mind Sammy while I tended to her and he took him into the garden. I've been at him and at him to mend the fence but he didn't and that's how Sammy got away."

"Where is he now?"

"At the inn, most likely," she said wearily.

"Not at work?"

"He doesn't have regular work, sir. He has his pension of ninepence a day; he got some prize money too but that's all spent."

"An old soldier, is he? How long is he home?"

"Since Boney was beat the first time. Only the baby's his, sir. I was a widow when I married him."

"I see." Thomas fished in his pocket for some coins. He gave sixpence to the little girl and put two more on the dresser saying, "For the other little ones. And this is for you, ma'am."

"There is no need for that, Major," she said proudly, putting her hands behind her back.

"In case you need anything from the physician or the apothecary for either of them." He nodded towards the children on the settle. "I don't want to frighten you, but after such a drenching, he might run a fever."

"Well, thank you, sir." She put the guinea into her apron pocket. The baby began to cry and she said, "Excuse me, sir. I'll try and feed him while Sammy is asleep."

He nodded. "Good-day, ma'am."

Chapter Five

Arabella woke in a strange bed. Her entire body ached and her throat felt scratchy. Where was she? It was twilight—but morning or evening? She turned her head and saw her mother sitting in a chair beside the bed.

"Mamma?"

Mamma jumped up immediately. "Oh, my dear child, you are awake." She laid a cool hand on Arabella's forehead. "No fever, thank goodness."

"Fever? Have I been ill?"

Why did Mamma look at her so oddly? "Ill, no. But—don't you remember?"

"Remember what? Where am I?"

Her mother looked even more worried. "The rectory. Thomas Ferraunt brought you here."

Why would Thomas bring her here? Suddenly she had an image of him lifting her out of the stream. He was so strong. First he had taken Sammy from her arms. She had gone in after him.

"How is Sammy?"

"Thomas sent up a note an hour ago to say that he seems to have taken no harm. And you? I'm very proud of you, but how could you frighten me so?"

"I didn't mean to, but there was no-one else there. He was carried away so fast it would have been too late if I ran for help. I did call, but nobody came."

"Until Thomas did, God bless him. Are you warm enough? Will you take another glass of negus? I've been keeping it hot beside the fire."

"No, thank you. Whose room is this?"

"Mrs Ferraunt's. It was the warmest, she said."

She pushed away the bed clothes. "I don't want to stay here. Can we go home? Have I something to wear?"

Mamma didn't ring for a maid but herself helped her daughter to dress, as if she could not relinquish her even for that short space of time.

Arabella felt quite unsteady on her feet when she rose. Mamma wrapped her in a fur-lined cloak and pulled up the hood. "Go slowly, now."

As they left the room, Major Ferraunt came along the landing towards them.

"Thomas, give Arabella your arm," Mamma ordered before he could say anything.

He was beside her in an instant, his elbow bent at just the right angle. "I'm glad to see you recovered, Miss Malvin."

"Arabella," she corrected him without thinking. "After today, I think you should call me Arabella, Thomas."

His eyes gleamed and he bowed his head briefly. "Arabella."

His arm was firm and steady under her hand as she carefully made her way down the stairs and into the parlour where her father sat with the rector and Mrs Ferraunt.

Papa crushed her to him so that she felt her ribs might break. "I had to see for myself that you were unharmed. My brave, foolhardy girl! I don't know whether to praise you or berate you."

His voice cracked and that was bad enough, but then Dr Ferraunt came forward and solemnly kissed her brow.

"'Greater love hath no man than this, that a man lay down his life for his friends'," he quoted. "My dear Miss Malvin, you are an inspiration to us all."

She managed to splutter an acknowledgement, sure that her cheeks were scarlet.

"I must apologise for causing such a disturbance, ma'am," she said to Mrs Ferraunt who stood calmly to one side. Arabella had a hazy memory of being undressed and towelled vigorously before being wrapped in a warm, flannel nightgown and tucked between warmed sheets. "Thank you for your kindness in making your own room available to me and for looking after me so well."

"There is no need to apologise, my dear Miss Malvin. I am pleased Thomas had the wit to bring you to me. Now, we must not keep you standing any longer. You must still be exhausted from your ordeal."

Thomas took this as his cue to recover her hand. "Come, I'll take you to the carriage."

She clung to him gratefully as he led her out, the others following like lambs. Just before she ducked into the carriage, she turned and looked down into his concerned eyes.

"Thank you," she murmured.

He pressed her hand and released it. Her mother followed her and promptly swathed her in blankets so that perspiration trickled between her breasts by the time they reached the Abbey. Here she had to endure her brothers' and sister-in-law's hugs and relieved exclamations before receiving the 'respectful congratulations' of the staff. At last she could escape to her bedchamber where Horton waited.

The maid burst into tears when she saw her. "Thank heavens you're safe, Miss Arabella. My heart stopped when Bart told us. I don't know how you had the nerve to go into the stream."

"Neither do I," Arabella said tiredly. "But I couldn't watch Sammy drown."

It was only now that she realised the risk she had taken. She might have died today. It would all have been for nothing, if Thomas had not come. She shivered suddenly.

"Will you take a bath, Miss?" Horton asked. "There's hot water ready."

"Yes, and you must wash my hair."

Every bone in her body ached and her head felt enlarged and clogged with mud. Her hair was full of tangles and Horton had to comb it twice; once before she washed it and again afterwards. She did it as gently as she could but by the time she was finished, Arabella was near tears. At last Horton put a dry towel around her shoulders and carefully arranged the long tresses over it.

"Half an hour by the fire should do it. Should I bring you up a tray, Miss?"

"Just some chicken broth and a cream or a syllabub if there is one. And make me some willow bark tea. I don't feel at all the thing."

"And no wonder, Miss. I won't be long."

Arabella's reward for her drenching was a violent chill and wearying cough that so alarmed her mother that she insisted her daughter keep her room for over a week. At least this had spared her the well-meaning—or inquisitive—calls of neighbours who learned of her adventure. Next week they would go to town for several months. By the time they returned all would be forgotten.

Was Thomas still at the rectory, she wondered as they strolled across the park to church on Sunday. His mother had called to enquire how she did, but he had not been with her and nobody had mentioned seeing him. She would have liked to talk to him about that day. She could remember very little of it and her sleep was haunted by unquiet dreams of watery battles against surging currents that dragged her ever further away from safety.

As usual, they arrived at three minutes to the hour. The little church was full and there was a stir as the Abbey party entered.

"Three cheers for Miss Malvin," somebody called from the gallery and to Arabella's utter mortification, the congregation erupted into cheers and applause. She didn't know where to look and was forced to pace solemnly at Matthew's side until they reached the shelter of their pew.

Her father turned at the door of the pew. "Enough!" he barked and the noise subsided, the rector entered and the service began.

Although Admiral Halworth occupied the first pew as holder of Longcroft Manor, he was very particular in giving precedence to the Malvins when the service was over. Today Julian indicated that Matthew and Arabella should go ahead of him and Millie. Arabella fixed her eyes firmly on the back of her mother's bonnet, looking neither to the right nor the left as they proceeded down the aisle. But outside there was no escape.

"I don't know how you dared," Ruth Halworth said breathlessly. "I should have been terrified."

"No other lady would have done it," her brother said, his tone leaving Arabella unsure whether he commended or condemned her actions.

The Admiral pushed him aside and took both her hands in his. "Well done, Miss Malvin," he said simply. "I am proud to know you."

"Thank you, sir."

"Are you quite recovered from your indisposition, Miss Malvin?" Lady Halworth asked kindly.

"I am, thank you, ma'am. It was no more than a cold. I believe you were in town last week?"

"Yes. Dear Lallie kindly put us up for a few nights—little Geoffrey has grown so big, you would hardly credit it—and everything is in train for when we come up after Easter."

"Yes. I could not believe the number of gowns I shall need," Ruth put in complacently.

"I shall look forward to seeing them." Arabella began to move away before Ruth could launch into a description of her new finery. "We must not delay my mother any longer."

"Wait, Sis." Matthew held her back, tilting his chin towards the churchyard gate where Mrs Perkins stood hand in hand with Sammy and his elder sister. The other villagers fell back to let them pass. Arabella swallowed. How was she to face this? She felt uncomfortable with so much praise. Did they not realise that without Thomas it would all have gone awry?

There were tears in Mrs Perkins's eyes. She bobbed a curtsey and reached to take Arabella's hand in both of hers. "We'll pray for you 'til the day we die, Miss. Won't we, Becky and Sammy?"

The children nodded.

"Every night," Becky whispered. "God bless Miss Malvin and keep her from harm." She handed Arabella a little basket of primroses, snow-drops and violets set like jewels in damp moss. "This is to say thank you."

"Oh, how pretty. You made me a flower garden. What a lovely idea."

"Mam did it, but I helped."

"I'm sure you did."

Sammy, who had been hiding his face in his mother's skirts, now released her to look up at Arabella.

"We was in the stream," he announced with an engaging smile.

"We were, and very cold and wet it was too," she replied seriously. "You won't go near it again, will you?"

"No." He rubbed his behind reflectively. "Da said he'd baste me."

"That will remind you not to," she agreed.

"And what do you say to the lady?" his mother urged.

"Thank you."

"You are most welcome." Arabella ruffled his hair. "I'm sure you'll be a good boy in future, Sammy."

He nodded and put his thumb in his mouth, resting his head against his mother's side.

To Arabella's relief, Mrs Perkins took this as a sign that it was time to leave.

Before anyone else could approach, she seized Matthew's arm. "Mamma and Papa are over there with the Ferraunts."

"Did you notice Thomas's togs? I suppose they're from Paris."

He looked different out of uniform, less severe though still very neat. She liked his coat of pale olive superfine with a black velvet collar but wasn't sure about the yellow striped waistcoat. Still, when he was used to wearing gold-trimmed scarlet, everything else probably seemed dull.

"I hope I see you well, Arabella?"

"You do, thank you, Thomas. You are very elegant today."

"Is that style of waistcoat all the crack in Paris?" Matthew demanded.

Thomas shrugged. "It was made there at any rate. When you have spent most of your life in regimentals, it is hard to know what to choose. I left it to Staub."

"Is he the tailor?"

"Yes, in the Rue Richelieu."

Matthew grinned. "I must make a note of that. I know men whose chief passion is to visit their tailors and their bootmakers. They spend hours getting dressed."

"And then strut along Bond Street like a crow in the gutter, displaying their magnificence," Arabella agreed. "But smart as Thomas is, I imagine he can still put on his coat without the assistance of two others and stoop to pick up a dropped handkerchief, so he need not fear being counted among the dandies."

"You relieve me greatly," Thomas retorted with the narrowing of his left eye and that little lift to the left corner of his mouth that she had come to recognise as a smile. "You leave for London soon, I understand?"

"Yes. We shall probably be there until mid-June." She swallowed. It would be too brazen to ask him to call before they left. But a general invitation for later? She could issue that. She smiled warmly at him. "If you should be in town, do call at Malvin House."

"Yes, please do, Thomas," her mother put in. "We should be delighted to see you."

But would he call? Thomas wasn't so sure. The ladies' invitation was well-meant, but their world was not his. Oh, he could claim to belong there by birth, perhaps—his father's father had been the younger son of the then Earl of Hawebury so the present earl was a cousin of sorts—but not by fortune.

He shook his head. It would be better not to seek her out. It was too easy to be in her company. He liked her… 'practicality', he supposed you'd call it. She was neither missish nor flirtatious. Take me as I am, she seemed to say. She was brave and resourceful. And—not beautiful, precisely—she was too vivid for that—but striking. She had felt 'right' in his arms when he carried her up to his mother's room. But he would not ask her to accept a husband who could not afford to keep her in the station of life to which she was accustomed.

He could take his capital and seek his fortune overseas—in India, perhaps. He shook his head impatiently. He could not hope that she would remain unattached, especially as it would be impossible to declare himself before he left. Only the shabbiest of fellows would seek to secure a lady's affections and then ask her to waste her youth hoping that he would return wealthy enough to marry her.

Chapter Six

A *ton* ball! Was there anything more uplifting to the spirits?

Scarlet uniforms and sober dark coats bent attentively over pale muslins and richer silks; gloved hands were raised as dancers swirled and twirled to an exhilarating melody. From the top of the stairs leading to Lady Benton's ballroom, Arabella looked down on a whirl of colours and textures made up of gowns, hair, head-dresses, nodding feathers, and elegantly draped wisps of gauze and net that claimed to be shawls. Jewels sparkled in the candle-light and the murmur of voices was punctuated by the beat of feet taking up the rhythm of the violins. She inhaled deeply, savouring that unique smell created by a myriad of lotions and waters blended with the hot wax of hundreds of candles.

The music stopped and, after a wave of bows and curtsies, ladies claimed their partners' arms to stroll a little before propriety obliged them to separate. Arabella and Millie were immediately spotted by Lallie who was talking to Mrs Rembleton. No—she was Mrs Fitzmaurice now. She looked different, younger, and had lost that air of icy reserve. She smiled at Arabella and professed herself delighted to meet Millie again after so many years.

"Is Clarissa not with you?" Lallie asked quietly when the two older ladies had become engrossed in a discussion of their children.

"No. We have decided that in general Millie will chaperon me at the balls. Is Hugo here?"

"He will come later."

"Cousin!" An elegant young man bowed to Lallie and then to Arabella. "Miss Malvin."

Arabella curtsied to Lord Marfield, Lord Benton's heir. She had forgotten his mother was Lallie's great-aunt. "Good evening, my lord."

Lord Henry Danlow, youngest brother of the Marquess of Rickersby, sauntered up to them, immaculate in severely tailored black and crisp white, the only touch of colour provided by sleek blond hair that gleamed in the candlelight and dark blue eyes that were too beautiful to be wasted on a man. He nodded to Marfield and bowed to Arabella.

"How delightful to see you again, Miss Malvin."

"Thank you, Lord Henry. When did you return from your travels?"

"Rather foolishly, at the beginning of winter. I would have been better advised to remain in the south but I had used up my supplies of tea and found it impossible to replenish them."

She smiled. "Perhaps you should have journeyed to China. Were you not tempted to seek a place on Lord Amherst's mission?"

He shook his head dismissively. "It would be too tedious. And such a long voyage, too. I am not the best of sailors, I fear. It is the carriage for me. Give me a comfortable *dormeuse* and I shall go to the ends of the earth."

The last was said so dramatically that she had to laugh. "A boat has the advantage that one is not cooped up for hours."

"Only as long as the weather is fine," he pointed out. He bowed with an elegant flourish of his slim hand. "I believe we are to have a waltz next. May I have the pleasure of dancing it with you?"

As they walked onto the dance floor Arabella was aware of sidelong, envious glances. Lord Henry, a notable dancer, was known to be extremely selective in choosing his partners, favouring only ladies whose grace and skill complemented his. It was over a year since she had waltzed. Perhaps it would have been better to start with a less demanding gentleman. How would his lordship react if she missed a step?

The musicians raised their instruments and the waiting couples moved into the opening position. Arabella's apprehension vanished with the first steps. She responded instinctively as Lord Henry's subtle touch guided her into the succeeding figures, giving herself up to the music and the joy of movement. He made no attempt to break the silence, but selected just the right steps for the space available to them so that they could move easily without interruption or hesitation. The tempo quickened. He clasped her waist; she put her hands on his shoulders and sprang with him into the *valse sauteuse*. As he lifted and turned, he skilfully slowed the movement so that for a fraction of an instant their eyes met before he lightly set her down.

The music slowed again. He turned so that, hands joined, they danced side by side and back to back, heads turned to look into one another's eyes. At the final bar, he gracefully twirled her under his arm to face him again. She curtsied, he bowed and they smiled in recognition of their mutual pleasure.

"Thank you, Miss Malvin. I think we have earned a glass of champagne, don't you?"

"Indeed we have." She placed her hand on his arm. All eyes were on them as they strolled towards the refreshments room. "Tell me about your travels," she suggested. "Where did you go from Brussels?"

"To Cologne and from there up the Rhine, then through Switzerland and down into Italy—Florence, Rome and Naples." He took two glasses from a tray and handed her one. "Your good health, Miss Malvin."

"And yours, Lord Henry." She sipped appreciatively. This was the first time a gentleman had suggested champagne and not lemonade or orgeat. "Did you have your portrait painted while you were away?"

He drew himself up and presented her with a view of his left profile, displaying an aquiline nose and a sculpted cheekbone just brushed by narrowly trimmed side-whiskers. "Yes, in Florence by Monsieur Fabre, with a panorama of the city behind. It turned out very well."

"I am sure it did. How does one manage on such tours? Do you have everything shipped home at the end or as you leave each city?"

"Generally the latter. One tends to travel with friends, so a fair amount accumulates. The local *cicerones* deal with it. As they are dependent on recommendations for future business, they cannot afford to be careless or neglectful."

"I suppose not. So you were home in time for the hunting?"

He looked at her, an odd smile on his lips. "Shall I tell you a secret, Miss Malvin?"

"Nothing too dreadful, I trust?"

"There are many who would consider it so." He bent his head to whisper, "I find hunting, and those who talk of it, deadly boring."

His warm breath brushed her ear and she jerked her head away.

"There—I have shocked you!"

"Surprised, rather, sir," she countered. "I did not think such a gentleman existed."

He bowed slightly. "Thank you. One likes to consider oneself unique."

"Does not everyone?"

"I don't think so. Only consider those who always slavishly follow the latest fashion for," he looked deliberately around the room, "circassian turbans, shall we say? They should only be worn by tall, willowy ladies, but just look about you."

"I think they are hideous, no matter who wears them," Arabella said frankly, "but I agree they suit some better than others."

She should return to Millie. She drained her glass. Lord Henry took it from her and handed it to a footman. He extended his arm. "Shall we resume our stroll, Miss Malvin?"

"I always enjoy these early balls at the start of the Season when town is still quite thin of company."

"I agree. Before Easter, society is more select."

She had meant she preferred not to have to force her way through a crush but before she could say so, he asked, “May I call on you, Miss Malvin?”

Her eyes flew to his. He looked very serious. They had enjoyed a pleasant acquaintanceship in Brussels, but he had never given any indication that he wished to court her. She felt a little prickle of excitement as she inclined her head slightly.

“You may, Lord Henry.”

“I shall look forward to it.”

Arabella was delighted to find her Uncle Hugo talking to Millie. She hadn’t seen her mother’s brother since he had come to Malvin Abbey for Arthur’s memorial service. The youngest of her mother’s siblings, he was nearer her children in age and Arabella thought of him more as another brother, especially since he had married Lallie.

“My lord,” she said solemnly and curtsied.

He nodded curtly. “I am glad to see you finally treat me with the proper respect, Miss Malvin.”

She stared at him, shocked, and was relieved to see his grin.

“If you could only see your face, Bella! And that will be enough of that. I felt like my father there for a moment, and most unpleasant it was, too.”

“We certainly don’t want to encourage you in that line,” she retorted. “I never know whether to be glad or sorry that he died before Geoffrey was born.”

“Why?”

“He would have been appallingly pleased to have an heir presumptive in the direct line to follow you but I think also deeply chagrined that your first-born was a son, given that it took him so long to father one."

"Very probably, but I don't know why we are talking about him. Do you know Gervase Naughton? He is my closest friend. We met at Oxford and he has taken the Tamm seat in the House of Commons." He raised his hand as he spoke and a pleasant looking, dark-haired gentleman obligingly veered towards them.

Hugo had never before made a point of presenting his friends to her, she reflected as the introductions were made. This was going to be a very different Season.

"You have taken the Tamm seat, I believe, Mr Naughton," she said. "Are you also from that part of the country?"

"Yes and no, Miss Malvin. My family is originally from Suffolk, but my father held the living of Barnstaple for many years and that is where I grew up. Now he is a canon of Exeter cathedral and lives there."

"So you lost your home," she said sympathetically. Thomas would also lose his when his father died or retired.

Mr Naughton shrugged. "What is home? Home is where I live. But if you mean a connection to childhood and family, my parents and sisters still provide that. The bricks and mortar we occupied in the past would be empty without them."

"It is not always an advantage to be tied to bricks and mortar," Hugo said wryly. "Old buildings can be deuced uncomfortable. Sometimes I dream of building a new house with all the modern conveniences."

"Wouldn't that be wonderful?" Millie said.

Arabella was surprised by her sister-in-law's fervour but then remembered that Millie would be responsible for Malvin Abbey when Julian succeeded Papa. "Perhaps Mr Naughton will be fortunate enough to do so one day. Where would you choose to live, sir?"

"At present I am very content with my rooms in Albany. Later? I have always liked Richmond. It is a most agreeable place and still convenient to London."

"You could have your own shallop and go to the House by water."

"Propelled by liveried oarsmen while I sit sternly under an awning perusing important documents?"

"Or lolling on silken cushions while listening to some water music or—what is it the gondoliers sing in Venice? A *Barcarola*?"

His smile deepened. "Then I should certainly not be reading papers. May I have this dance, Miss Malvin?"

This was going to be an interesting Season, Arabella reflected as she snuggled under the bedclothes. There was no doubt that she was attracting a different type of gentleman; those who had reached a marrying age. She was able to hold her own with them too. She liked Mr Naughton. Could she see herself as a politician's wife, even a political hostess? She must pay more attention to the newssheets so that she could participate in more serious conversations.

Lord Marfield was a very personable man, but she did not think he was ready to marry. And his father was not yet fifty. She did not want to spend years as the heir's wife, playing second fiddle to his mother. Lord Henry was a younger son whose brother had already succeeded to the title. He was also the best dancer but that was hardly a reason to select a husband. What were the right reasons? She yawned. She must think about that tomorrow.

"What shall you do today, my love? Tomorrow you must call on Lady Benton but we also have other calls to make. What other young ladies were there last night?"

"Caro Nugent, both Misses Frome, Lady Maud Whitbourne, Lady Elizabeth Hope, Lady Juliet Martyn—but, Mamma, I am not sure whether I should go out today."

"Why? Are you indisposed?"

Arabella shook her head. "It's not that. Last night Lord Henry Danlow asked if he might call on me."

Lady Malvin put down the stack of invitation cards she was sorting and considered her daughter thoughtfully. "How did you reply?"

"I said he may. I did not feel I could say anything else. He might not call today, but I felt I should be here in case."

Her mother nodded. "Just today. Now that he has expressed his interest, it is only fair to give him a chance—unless he is completely repugnant to you, that is."

"No, no. I enjoy dancing with him and he is pleasant company, but he has a very high opinion of himself."

"I suppose he feels he must assert himself. Younger sons must carve their own paths, after all. A good wife might be the making of him."

"That doesn't sound very romantic—as if a wife were a sort of governess."

Mamma laughed. "No, but if he seeks to please her, he will take himself less seriously. Don't be disheartened, my love. If he decides to pay court to you, it will give you the opportunity to get to know him better, but will not commit you to anything. And you must admit it would be a great triumph—I have never heard of him paying particular attention to another lady and where he leads, others will follow. Now I think you should wear the cream gown with the sea-green spencer and with matching ribbons through your hair—have Horton dress it quite *dégagé*."

The cream gown had only arrived yesterday from Madame Hortense and Arabella would not normally have wasted it on an afternoon spent at home. Deceptively simple, it was caught under the high waist with a broad, sea-green ribbon below a bodice of finest muslin embroidered with sea-green flowers and pleated so as to hint at rather than reveal the curves below. The gathered skirts were made of heavier muslin, lined with satin and trimmed near the hem with two borders of narrow ribbon, with flowers embroidered in between. As she was not going out, she left the matching spencer unbuttoned, so that her bosom was displayed becomingly while the high collar framed her neck. Green slippers peeped from beneath her skirts. Horton had brushed her hair back from her forehead before piling it loosely on top of her head so that it looked as if it was restrained only by ribbons, instead of the dozen and more hair-pins that anchored it firmly.

"You're a picture, Miss," Horton said as she handed her a lace handkerchief.

It was Arabella's turn to read. They had decided they would read aloud in turns when expecting callers. There was nothing drearier than sitting waiting for the sound of the knocker, Arabella had declared, and to be ushered into a drawing-room where the ladies of a family waited listlessly to be relieved from the necessity of staring at one another was too depressing. Mamma had concurred and they had selected Lord Byron's latest epic, *The Siege of Corinth*.

"One must have read him, but I must admit I find his long poems and tortured heroes a little boring," Arabella had said.

"Too much sends me to sleep," Millie agreed. "It is the monotony of the rhythm, I suppose."

"Lady Nugent, Miss Nugent and Mr Nugent," Belshaw announced and Arabella closed the book on "Alp, the Adrian renegade" with a sigh of relief.

The Nugents were the Malvin's nearest noble neighbours and the Ladies Nugent and Malvin had been firm friends since they came to Berkshire in the same year as brides. Their children knew each other since their nursery days and Francis cocked an irreverent eyebrow once the preliminaries had been disposed of.

"Are you starting a new literary saloon, Bella? I had not thought to find you among the blue-stockings."

"How am I to take that? Do you mean I am not clever?"

"Now, Bella, you know I didn't mean it that way. You will admit it is strange to call on a lady and find her reading poetry."

"Would you have preferred to find us reading a sermon, Francis?"

"No, I dashed well would not, and you know it."

"What do you like to read?" she asked curiously.

"He pretends to read *The Gentlemen's Magazine*, but really prefers *The Sportsman in Town*," his sister said.

"*The Sporting Magazine*, you mean," Francis corrected her. "The other is just a collection of *on-dits*."

"Which you never glance at, I suppose."

"Of course not. Where is Matthew? We spoke of going to Tattersall's."

Arabella raised her eyebrows. "You don't think he would risk being trapped in the drawing-room, do you? And, unless you wish to hazard your luck, you had better go down again and have Malton tell him you are here."

Chapter Seven

Lord Henry Danlow's valet wiped the perspiration from his master's face and neck. "Shall I increase the speed, my lord?"

"Yes. Ten miles an hour."

Henry repositioned his feet on the treadles of the gymnasticon and tightened his grip on the upper cranks. The treadles also turned the cranks so that in addition to trampling vigorously he was forced to rotate his arms in rapid circles. He continued at the higher speed until he was panting in short, sharp breaths and the muscles of his calves and shoulders burned.

"Reduce gradually," he gasped.

Jones readjusted the gears and Henry slowed down one stage at a time until he reached an easy walk.

"Enough." He extricated himself from Dr Lowndes's machine, then revolved slowly in front of the cheval glass. There could be no doubt that his calves were more defined and his shoulders broader. His tailor had commented accordingly only last week.

On his previous visit, the man had had the impertinence to suggest that his pantaloons would benefit from a judicious padding of his calves. "You would be surprised how many gentlemen do so, my lord."

"Be damned to that," Henry had replied, "and if you wish to keep my custom, you will never mention such a thing again."

"No, my lord."

It had been Jones who suggested the gymnasticon. "You may exercise at home in all privacy and in all weathers, my lord," he had said persuasively.

"I could try it, I suppose," he had answered and within a week the thing was installed in his dressing-room.

Now, two months later, the benefits were noticeable—and not only in his muscular development. Only yesterday Angelo had commended the extension of his lunge and remarked on his increased stamina. Whistling under his breath, he stripped off his loose shirt and breeches and stepped into the bath.

"I'll wear the new hessians and the dark blue coat with the yellow poplin waistcoat."

"Very good, my lord. Should I put out the pink under-waistcoat too?"

"Yes." Only a thin strip of it would appear but it added a certain something to the ensemble.

He washed meticulously, using the vanilla soap he had bought in Florence, at the end working the rich lather into his hair. Jones stood ready with fresh warm water to rinse him and had towels heating beside the fire.

Freshly shaven and dressed in a loose-fitting brocade banyan over a fresh shirt and clinging pantaloons, Henry strolled back into his bed-chamber. All was prepared for breakfast. He poured a glass of burgundy and drank, his ear cocked for the sound of rapid footsteps. A footman hurried in bearing two chafing dishes, which he placed on waiting silver braziers and lifted the lids for his master to inspect the contents. As the man withdrew, Jones came in with a plate of hot-buttered toast he had made at the dressing-room fire. He set it down wordlessly, moved the *Morning Chronicle* nearer Henry's hand and disappeared again.

Simple pleasures, Henry thought, helping himself to breaded lamb cutlets and devilled kidneys. His staff knew what he expected of them. He was a generous master, or so he thought, but he made it clear that he would not tolerate careless work. A cook might send up a poor dish once, but the second time would see him turned off the same day. Fortunately, the premium Henry gave for good service—a fifth quarter's wages paid at Whitsun to all who had completed the previous twelve months in his employment—encouraged his servants to respect his wishes.

The kettle of freshly-drawn water on the hob was simmering by now and he rose to warm two teapots. A fine souchong this morning, he thought, as he emptied the water in the first into the slop-bowl. He inhaled, enjoying the first release of the tangy aroma as the leaves hit the warm porcelain and hurried to pour the boiling water over them. Why did so many hostesses make such foul tea? Was it so difficult to have freshly boiling water and good quality leaves? His eyes on his watch, he waited for the tea to draw, then drained the second teapot and strained the fragrant brew into the warmed vessel. Finally, he dropped a small piece of sugar in his cup and, already anticipating the first refreshing sip, filled it with the hot liquid.

"Aaaah."

It was just right, very hot but not scalding. The smoky fragrance lifted his spirits. He had never had tea prepared by

Miss Malvin. Although he had been invited to the house her parents had taken in Brussels, it had been to a rout rather than a dinner where afterwards the daughter of the house would have displayed her skill at the tea-table. Still, she could be taught to do it exactly as he liked it. She had taken his breath away last night. Her girlish plumpness had been replaced by a more refined beauty. Her gown had been quite out of the common way—fine silver net over a slip of palest amethyst satin, so pale that it was barely not white. The net was scattered with matching spangles and at times she seemed to be wrapped in dawn mists. Her beautiful hair was held by combs set with amethysts and pearls.

As soon as he saw her, he had had to speak to her. She had greeted him calmly, as if they had last met only recently and not over eighteen months ago, but he fancied she had been pleased to see him and, when they danced, she had come into his arms as if made for them. Their waltz had exalted him. He had not wanted to release her. He could have called on her without first seeking her permission, of course, but somehow it had been important to indicate his interest. Perhaps he should make it more apparent.

He rang for his valet. "Has it stopped raining?"

"Yes, my lord."

"Provided it remains dry, I shall require the phaeton and greys at four o'clock. If the rain resumes, have the carriage brought round."

The gods were with him. The clouds had cleared and the sun shone. Should he have brought a posy of flowers? It seemed too particular for a first call.

Naughton, the new Member of Parliament, came down the Malvin stairs as Henry went up. They nodded civilly to each other, but that was all. Two older ladies were in the drawing-room with the Malvin ladies. Henry made his bow to Lady Malvin and claimed a seat beside her daughter.

"I trust I see you recovered from your exertions, Miss Malvin."

"I assure you I am not such a poor honey as to be laid low by one ball, Lord Henry," she replied, a delicious twinkle in her eyes. "On the contrary, I found it invigorating."

"I am delighted to hear it. Could I persuade you to take a turn with me in the Park? My phaeton is below."

"I should love to. Pray excuse me while I put on a bonnet."

He rose with her. When he resumed his seat, he turned to Mrs Malvin. "I hope you are enjoying your stay in town, ma'am. It is some years since you have been here, is it not?"

"Yes. Generally I prefer the country but after this last winter I longed for a change."

"It seemed to me to be particularly dreary. I spent the previous one in Naples and there it was quite different. The days are not so short and the temperatures more clement."

"Perhaps we should all travel south for the winter," she suggested.

"And return here for our more pleasant summer, thus avoiding the extremes of heat and cold? What an excellent idea!"

Miss Malvin took Henry's hand and climbed lightly into his 'high-flyer'. He took his place beside her, nodding to his tiger who let go the greys' heads and scrambled up behind as they drew away from the kerb. She had replaced her spencer with a green pelisse that was buttoned to the throat, and paired it with a spring bonnet in shades of yellow with green ribbons. After a few minutes she opened a matching parasol, tilting it at just the right angle to shade her face without blocking her sight of him. He liked the way it created an intimate little space just for them.

"You dare block the sun on one of his rare appearances?"

"You told me one of your secrets yesterday, Lord Henry. Now I shall reveal one of mine."

He could hear the smile in her voice. "I am all ears, Miss Malvin."

"If I do not take immediate precautions against the sun, I quickly have a red nose, and worse!"

"Worse?"

"Freckles," she said dolefully. "They are the curse of my hair colour, or so I am told."

"Your hair is glorious." She reminded him of Botticelli's Venus, but better not say that! "It is like spun sunlight."

A faint colour tinted her cheek. "What an original compliment. Thank you, sir."

"A sprinkling of freckles can be quite—enticing," he remarked as he eased into the line of carriages entering Hyde Park. "Did not our grandmothers apply patches?"

She laughed. "Unfortunately, one cannot arrange for a freckle to appear in the most becoming spot. Better to prevent them altogether."

How charmingly direct she was. Here was no artifice. Take me as I am, she seemed to say. She ignored the stir their appearance caused, looking around her with interest but in no way preening herself or trying to attract attention. The only other lady he had driven in the Park was his sister, Lady Allenby, but very likely Miss Malvin didn't know that. That stout matron did, judging by the way she nudged her fubsy-faced companion.

"My nieces and nephew are with us for the first time this year," Miss Malvin said.

"Oh? How old are they?"

"Hermione is eleven, Anthony is ten and Anne is five. They spend most of their time in the school-room, of course, but we must arrange some outings for them—to the Tower of London, perhaps. I am ashamed to admit I have never visited it."

He raised his whip to acknowledge Mr Theo Frome who approached them in his curricle. "I have, and I do not recommend it, especially for children."

She shifted on the seat to look at him. "Why not? I thought the wild animals—"

"That is precisely why," he interrupted her. "They belong in the wild. Have you ever seen a magnificent stag with his crown of antlers? Imagine taking such an animal and penning him between stone walls and iron bars in a cage where all he can do is pace and turn, pace and turn; trapped where he can scent other animals, some his rivals and some his mates but is unable to respond naturally to them? Other beasts may also detect the presence of their prey or their enemies. The misery in the Lion House at the Tower is indescribable. And these are some of God's most magnificent creatures. Then there is the stench and the noise—there is always some fool who demands to hear the lion roar and torments it until it does."

He took a breath. "Believe me, Miss Malvin, neither the Tower menagerie nor the one at the Exeter 'Change is the right place for children. Take them to Bullock's museum in Piccadilly. There you will find admirable examples of the taxidermist's art, including elephants, and the children may approach as near as they like without fear of injury. Mishaps are not unknown at the Tower."

"It is not my decision, of course, but I shall tell my sister-in-law what you said."

They had reached the end of the Row and she was silent while he turned his equipage. He accomplished the manoeuvre neatly and they joined the slow procession back.

"Now I understand why you don't like hunting," she remarked.

"I disapprove of hunting or otherwise tormenting animals for sport. What sort of savages are we that we pursue animals with dogs and indulge in bull and bear-baiting and cock-fighting for entertainment? If a man wants food for his table, let him take out a gun or a rod. If a fox persists in taking a farmer's chickens, let it be shot humanely. But if a man wants to ride cross-country, he should participate in a steeplechase." His breath quickened but he continued to hold his team to a smooth, steady pace.

"I cannot disagree with you," Miss Malvin said. "In fairness, I should point out that these are all masculine pursuits."

"I have known some ladies ride to hounds, but in general you are correct."

The sky had clouded over and Arabella closed her parasol. She had never sat in a high-flyer before. At first it had felt strange to sway so high above the road but Lord Henry was no Jehu and capably guided his team through the crowded streets. From her perch she could look down into the open barouches and landaus, conscious of many a curious glance. She smiled at Caro and Lady Nugent, raising her hand in greeting. They must have come to the Park after completing their calls. If it remained fine, she would coax Mamma to come out with her tomorrow.

"My late brother, Captain Malvin, could not understand this custom of driving in the Park at a snail's pace, staring at one's coachman's back, as he put it. Its only purpose, as far as he could see, was for a group of people who meet several times a day to display themselves again."

"It is one of the more absurd aspects of the Season," his lordship agreed. "However, it offers one supreme advantage to a gentleman who drives his own carriage, and that is the opportunity to have an uninterrupted, private conversation with the young lady of his choice."

She glanced sideways. What did he mean by 'the young lady of his choice'? He was going very fast. Best to ignore his comment and continue to talk about Arthur.

"My brother would have been the first to admit that he was an indifferent whip, for lack of practice, he said. He enjoyed tooling the gig around the countryside until he was able to ride again, but had no wish to drive in town."

"It is a wise man who knows his limitations. Miss Malvin, while we are private, let me express my sympathy on your loss. I did not know your brother well, but enough to know him to be an admirable officer and a congenial companion."

"Thank you. It seems strange to be grateful that he was wounded, but we became much better acquainted in the months he was at home. Before we had never met as adults; I was the little sister who wrote to him every week—my governess said it was a good exercise—and once a month my father sent the letters to him." She smiled wistfully. "He didn't write to me as often—generally, he added a few lines in his letter to my parents, but he kept all my letters. We found them in his room at Malvin Abbey, afterwards."

"They must provide an interesting record of your juvenile years."

"I suppose so." She inclined her head in acknowledgment of Lord Marfield's bow. "Do you enjoy the theatre, Lord Henry?"

He looked down his nose. "I should enjoy it more if it were not for the audience. I don't know which is worse, the pit or the boxes. At times it is impossible to hear what is being said on the stage. And I detest the habit of pairing a serious work—one of Shakespeare's tragedies, for example—with an inferior musical piece or even a farce."

"Then you shall have to arrange private performances," she said with a little laugh. "I enjoy the whole experience, including seeing who visits whom in the interval. Besides, sometimes we need something lighter to bring us down to earth again."

"Ah, you are only of that opinion because you know nothing better. Believe me, my dear Miss Malvin, if you were once to experience and appreciate the perfect *Othello*, for example, you would wish to leave in silence, hoping to re-live the performance and the language with 'that inward eye which is the bliss of solitude', as Mr Wordsworth puts it."

Arabella was torn between indignation at his patronising tone, in particular in connection with a play that she found in no way elevating, for what was there to admire in an easily-tricked, jealous husband strangling his wife, and appreciation of his admiration of one of her favourite poets.

"There is something so cheerful about daffodils," she remarked. "Somehow it seems as if they are about to blow their own trumpets."

"Proclaiming the arrival of spring?"

"Precisely."

"They must have inspired your charming bonnet, in particular the fluting of the brim."

"Do you think so? Perhaps that is why I fell in love with it instantly."

"It suits you perfectly."

"Thank you, Lord Henry."

He sent her a little smile and asked, "Do you drive, Miss Malvin?" as he turned into Curzon Street.

"I drive the gig at home, but have not yet driven in town."

In fact, she must ask Matthew or Julian to teach her to drive a pair. She looked sideways at her companion. Or would he be willing to teach her? Perhaps, but she was not yet willing to ask.

"I trust you never will," he said as he drew up in front of Malvin House. "It is too dangerous for a lady."

He jumped down without waiting for a reply and handed the reins to his tiger, then came to assist Arabella to alight. It had been easier to get in, she found, as she felt for the first small step with her foot. This achieved, she released one hand from the side to take his proffered one, then steadied herself with her other hand on his shoulder before hopping down, praying that her skirts would not catch on the big wheels.

He immediately offered his arm to escort her to the door of Malvin House.

"Thank you for my outing, Lord Henry."

"It was my pleasure, Miss Malvin."

As she went into the house, all she could think of was how easily Thomas had lifted her from the stream. If he invited a lady to drive, he would not leave her to climb down by herself, she thought and seemed again to feel the comforting clasp of his large hands. Would he call when he came to London? She hoped so.

"Did you have an enjoyable drive," Mamma asked when Arabella peeped into her dressing-room where she was resting before changing into her dinner gown.

"Yes." Arabella came in and sat down. "It was very pleasant in the Park and he has a magnificent equipage—bang-up prime, as Matthew would say."

"You know I don't like you repeating Matthew's cant. You will get into the habit of it and use it in the wrong place one day!"

"And be drummed out of Almack's?" Arabella asked saucily. "Are you afraid the patronesses will instruct Mr Willis to tear up my voucher and snap my feathers in two—not that I wear any—then pluck the flowers from my hair and trample them underfoot?"

"You dreadful child," Mamma said, laughing. "No, but some people might consider you a romping girl or a hoyden."

"Mamma! Believe me; I know the difference between using the odd cant expression at home and tying my garter in public. And frankly, I think I would be well rid of any censorious person who took undue offence at such a phrase."

"You are very likely right. I suppose it comes from having so many brothers."

"They will never let me turn missish," Arabella agreed, "and I am grateful to them for it. I have noticed that girls without brothers tend to be skittish around gentlemen and don't know how to talk to them. Lallie was a little in that way when we met her first, but Arthur and Hugo soon put her at ease—and Matthew too."

Chapter Eight

Sixteen young ladies sat elegantly dispersed around Lady Neary's drawing room, near enough one another to converse but separate enough to permit a gentleman to find a seat beside the lady of his choice when he joined them after dinner. They would not have a long wait. Lady Neary's guests were for the most part aged twenty-five and younger, and her husband would not be inclined to waste his port on such young men. Miss Constance Neary was making her come-out this Season and her mother wanted to give her the opportunity to make new friends before her ball, which would be held after Easter.

"I think it ridiculous to pitchfork girls into the *ton* by keeping them in seclusion just so they can make a grand entrance at their own ball," she had explained privately to Lady Malvin. "Constance is inclined to be shy until she gets to know people. I thought sixteen couples—enough that there is some variety but not a crush. Dinner and some music—perhaps dancing—Miss Peters, our governess, could play some quadrilles."

It sounded like a pleasant change from the usual round of balls, Arabella had thought when her mother informed her and Matthew of the invitation. But to her dismay, not only was Lord Henry among the guests—apart from Miss Peters and Lord Neary's secretary Mr Holmes, who must both be more than thirty, he was the eldest, she fancied—he had also been assigned to take her in to dinner.

She could not escape him. He seemed to lie in wait for her each evening to the extent that other gentlemen apparently regarded the first waltz as his private preserve. Their drive in the park had not gone unnoticed but fortunately it had not been repeated. He had called twice since then but she had not been at home. He had been driving his phaeton both times, Millie told her, and had not come up to the drawing-room but merely left his card. His attentions had begun to make her feel uneasy and the fact that Lady Neary appeared to consider them a match in the making made her realise that it was time she hinted him away. But how? He had done nothing to give overt offence or earn a set-down.

"Francis is so proud of his new turn-out," Caro Nugent said. "He's been cursing the east wind that kept so many ladies at home this last week. I think he intends to invite one after the other to drive in the Park."

"So that's why he sent me a note this morning," Arabella said, highly entertained. "'Dear Bella, I'll call at half-past three this afternoon, and take you up in my new curricle. Be ready on time, mind. I don't want to keep my horses waiting in this wind. Yours, Francis.'"

Caro raised her eyes to heaven. "Eloquently put! I hope you told him that that was not the way to a lady's heart."

"You may be sure I did. He only laughed and said that if he was trying to fix his interest with someone, of course he would phrase it differently but that he regarded me as a sister and didn't have to do the pretty with me anymore than with you."

"That's Francis for you. He's a rogue, but you couldn't ask for a more loyal brother."

"I know. Matthew is the same. He might provoke and tease but he would do anything for me."

"I wonder what sort of a brother Lord Henry is. Does he have a sister?"

"I don't know. He has never mentioned his family."

Caro stared at her. "Never? And you have not asked or at least looked in the Peerage?"

Arabella shrugged. Some girls, Ruth Halworth, for example, studied the Peerage and Baronetage assiduously but she had never seen the need, nor had she been inclined to familiarise herself in this way with a gentleman's family. She could rely on Mamma to tell her anything important, and for the rest, she preferred to get to know people directly rather than look them up in a book. She was about to say this when the gentlemen arrived and they had to drop the subject.

The tea-tray was brought in and Miss Neary took up her position behind it. She completed her task gracefully and unhurriedly, passing the cups to the gentlemen who clustered around the table. Lord Henry was among them, scrutinising the girl's every move.

"Tea, Miss Malvin?"

Arabella sighed inwardly. Lord Henry stood before her, holding two cups. He handed her one and, with a murmured, "May I", took the vacant place on the sofa beside her. He frowned slightly, looking from her to Caro on the adjacent sofa and back again.

"The Nugents are from your part of the country, are they not?"

"Yes." Had he heard Francis had taken her driving? What of it? She owed him no explanations. "Where is your family seat?"

"Northumberland. It is a dreadful old pile. I don't care if I never see it again." He smiled at her surprised look. "I like to be comfortable, Miss Malvin." He sipped his tea and with a faint shudder, set the cup down.

How pretentious, Arabella thought. What sort of a finicky fop was he that he would not drink a perfectly good cup of tea? She looked around. Matthew sat beside Miss Neary, listening intently to what she was saying. Almost as if he had felt his sister's gaze, he looked up and caught Arabella's eye. She touched her ear as if fiddling with an ear-bob. He nodded and after a moment came over to her.

"Miss Neary has something to ask of you."

She rose with a polite, "Pray excuse me."

"Please." His lordship gestured graciously as if to sanction her departure and she was sorely tempted to inform him that she had not been seeking his permission.

"That was very convenient," she whispered to her brother as they crossed the room.

He grinned. "It's nothing but the truth. I was describing Papa's abhorrence of sentimental pap and she asked did we know "Dermot and Sheelah"? She was used to sing it with her elder sister, but she has not come to town this year, so when I said you knew it, she wondered would you like to sing it with her later. She would rather not perform on her own. I think she is shy," he added with a fatuous smile.

Arabella forbore to comment on this unwonted solicitude. "Of course I'll sing with her."

"Here she is." Matthew was as proud as a cat laying a mouse at its mistress's feet.

Arabella smiled at Miss Neary, a pretty girl with soft, fair curls and a rosebud mouth. "I should be very happy to sing with you, but I have never played the accompaniment."

"Oh, thank you, Miss Malvin. My sister's governess will play for us. If you like, we can slip into the music room and run through it quickly while people finish their tea." She gave Matthew a dazzling smile. "Pray excuse us, Mr Malvin—and thank you."

When they returned to the drawing-room, Lord Henry had moved to the corner of the sofa where he sat sideways, his legs crossed and one arm thrown nonchalantly along its back, presenting his chiselled profile to the company. His supercilious expression did not alter as Arabella launched into the sprightly melody which strangely belied the woebegone tale of poor Dermot lamenting his lost love 'all under the willow, the willow so green'.

Miss Neary's lighter soprano took up the story as she, in the role of Sheelah, a forsaken maiden, volunteered to share the young man's anguish as ''tis dismal, you know, to be dying alone'. The final verse they sang together, recounting to laughter and warm applause how,

He was so comely, and she was so fair,
They somehow forgot all their sorrow and care,
And thinking it better a while to delay,
They put off their dying to toy and to play
All under the willow, the willow so green.

His lordship did not appear particularly moved by their performance, his expression remaining unaltered even as he briefly touched his hands together. Arabella would have preferred not to return to her place beside him but she felt it would look too particular to sit elsewhere, especially as there was no other obvious seat available.

He rose briefly when she approached. "Very diverting, Miss Malvin."

There wasn't even a trace of a smile on his face. Was he being sarcastic? If so, she would ignore it.

"Thank you, my lord. It is one of Herr van Beethoven's Irish Songs," she replied brightly, sitting as far into the opposite corner of the sofa as she could. "It is a pleasure to sing with Miss Neary."

"Would you not find the same enjoyment with another singer?"

"With some, but not all. It's like dancing, I suppose; one is more attuned to some partners than to others. Do you play or sing yourself, sir?"

"Not in public," he returned briefly, looking down his nose in a way that made her feel she had just appeared on the stage of Covent Garden.

A flurry of notes drew their attention to the pianoforte where seventeen-year-old Miss Gatton stood, her hands clasped tightly in front of her generous bosom. After a long introduction, she inhaled deeply and with tragic fervour proclaimed, "'She never told her love; She never told her love, But let concealment, like a worm i' the bud, Feed on her damask cheek'."

Arabella had to bite the inside of her cheek to stop herself smiling at the overly dramatic interpretation of Viola's lines. She would have sung them more reflectively, conveying both the girl's inner pain and her strange joy at being able to speak of her love, even anonymously, to Orsino. She must find out who the composer was, even if she could never sing it in her father's presence.

"That was a more seemly choice than your romping hoyden," Lord Henry observed when Miss Gatton was finished. Arabella stared at him and he added with a faint smile, "You will not mind my giving you a hint, I know."

She did mind. She regarded it as an arrant impertinence but he stood before she could give him a piece of her mind.

"I see Miss Haydon moving forward. You will forgive me if I leave you before she begins. My sensitive ears, you know."

"But of course," Arabella said sweetly.

His eyes narrowed. "Then, farewell for now."

She sighed with relief and smiled encouragingly at Mr Neary when he came to compliment her on her singing.

"It is easy to sing well with your sister," she replied. "This is a splendid idea of Lady Neary's. It is like a family party but without the obligatory elderly relatives. The ones who sit in a corner and complain, I mean."

"I know. We have some of them too. And then there are the ones who insist on repeating the same anecdotes time after time."

They laughed comfortably together and settled to listen to Miss Haydon.

To Millie's surprise, Matthew insisted on accompanying his sister and sister-in-law to Almack's the next evening. Only the previous week, after his first foray, he had sworn never to darken its doors again, condemning it as the worst of marriage marts, full of harpies.

Now he just said, "When I heard Julian was dining with Gracechurch, I didn't want to leave you two unescorted."

"How gallant," Arabella murmured.

All was revealed when the Nearys arrived. Matthew's eyes lit up and he immediately urged his ladies forward to greet them. It was Miss Neary's first appearance, and she looked entrancing in a white gown of figured gauze worn over a white satin slip and decorated with a wreath of pink rosebuds to match the ones in her hair. Mr Neary insisted on partnering his sister in the first quadrille, but Matthew successfully claimed her for the second when Arabella and Lord Marfield were their opposite couple.

Miss Neary and Matthew looked somehow right together, Arabella thought as the four of them began "Le Pantalon". She seemed to have thrown off her shyness and was very graceful and light on her feet. All four couples in the set had danced together the previous evening and were well matched; no-one stumbled or had to be pulled back into place. Arabella was sorry when the music stopped. There were to be three waltzes, the first one after this. At least Lord Henry rarely graced Almack's with his presence; she had the impression that his occasional visits were more to show that he had the *entrée* than for enjoyment's sake.

As she took Marfield's arm there was a little stir at the door. Her heart sank. Immaculately clad, if a trifle spindle-shanked in the prescribed knee-breeches—perhaps that was another reason why he came so rarely—Lord Henry made his bows to the Ladies Jersey and Castlereagh. Perhaps Marfield would suggest a glass of Almack's insipid lemonade, Arabella thought hopefully, but no. To her disgust, he returned her so promptly to Millie that she arrived at her sister-in-law's side at the same time as Lord Henry, who nodded to Marfield as if to thank him for safely delivering her to him.

"May I have the pleasure, Miss Malvin?" he drawled.

She had no choice. But tomorrow would be different.

All eyes were on them as they walked onto the dance floor. She racked her brains for something innocuous to say, finally remarking, "It is still very cold, is it not? If it were not for the longer days it would feel more like Christmas than Easter."

"Do you know, Miss Malvin, in other countries one does not constantly discuss the weather?"

"One probably has no need to," she said with a sigh. "Just imagine being able to assume that it will not rain if one is planning a picnic, for example."

"True," he said, "but we need not talk about such boring topics."

This was too much, especially after his 'hoyden' remark the previous evening. But she couldn't cause a scene at Almack's. Thank heavens the musicians struck up and they could take up their positions. They danced as usual in silence but the harmony of Lady Benton's ball had long fled. A polite smile pasted on her lips, Arabella concentrated on her steps in what had become more an exercise than a dance. She made no attempt to meet her partner's eyes, not even in the attitudes that almost demanded a flirtatious glance.

"I don't think we'll risk Almack's lemonade," Lord Henry decided when the dance was over. "And as for their tea!"

"I believe they also serve orgeat," Arabella offered, curious to see how he would respond to her implied wish.

He shuddered. "No, Miss Malvin. Allow me to advise you on this. Champagne is the only drink at a ball."

It was enough. Arabella lifted her hand from his sleeve a moment before they had reached Millie. "Thank you, Lord Henry."

He bowed briefly. "Miss Malvin."

Mr Neary immediately begged her hand for the next quadrille and after a few moments Lord Henry moved on.

"Can you and Francis ride in the Row with Matthew and me tomorrow morning?" Arabella muttered to Caro an hour later.

"I would love to. Shall we say half-past nine? If Francis is unable to come, Matthew may escort us both."

Arabella bit her lip. "I particularly want to talk privately to Francis and I don't want to drive with him two days in a row. You know how people talk. But if the four of us go riding together, that would be quite unexceptional."

"I'll see what I can do. I'll send a note first thing if he can't come."

Francis brought his bay gelding up beside Arabella's grey mare. "And how may I serve you, fair lady?"

"By engaging to dance the first waltz with me at Lady Needham's tonight."

He whistled softly. "Is Danlow making a nuisance of himself?"

"Not precisely, at least not in the way you mean. His behaviour is always very proper, except—he has asked me to dance the first waltz with him at every ball I've attended since we came to town two weeks ago. He is not the only gentleman with whom I have danced at each ball, but he has made a little ritual out of it. It is always the first waltz; after we dance, we drink a glass of champagne together and then he escorts me back to Millie in quite a proprietary manner. I don't know whether he leaves then or goes into the card-room, but he does not dance again. It has gone so far that no other gentleman requests the first waltz. Then, last evening at Almack's—"

"He turned up at Almack's?" Francis interrupted. "I'm surprised he got a voucher, considering his habit of dancing only with the select few."

"One of whom is Lady Jersey," Arabella said dryly. "He did dance a quadrille with her last night, but waltzed only with me—the first waltz again. People are assuming there is something more between us, Francis. Look how Lady Neary seated us together the other evening. And you thought of him immediately when I mentioned the first waltz. Yet I can't refuse him without sitting out at least that set. And if I do that, who is to stop him remaining by my side? No, it is best to make clear that he does not have any sort of claim on me."

"Why not ask your father to have a word with him?"

"On what pretext? Because Lord Henry makes me feel uncomfortable? That's as good as saying I am a silly chit who imagines things."

"He might declare that his intentions are honourable and ask permission to court you."

"That would be even worse. I think it is best to hint him away."

"True. Some would regard it as a good match though, Bella."

"Perhaps, but not for me."

"Why not? You seemed happy enough with his attentions at first. Don't misunderstand me—it's a woman's prerogative and all that. You are entitled to change your mind."

"He is too self-contained, self-centred even," Arabella said slowly. "He seems unwilling or unable to put himself in another person's place. It would never occur to him that I might object to his behaviour or that it might make me the subject of unwelcome conjecture. He just does what pleases him. There may be a dozen ladies without partners at a ball, but he will not dance with any if they do not meet his ridiculously high standards. If his tea is not made to his satisfaction, he will let it stand. And as for the way he left Lady Neary's! If it were not for Mr Holmes, we would have been short one gentleman for the quadrilles. If he is like that as a guest, what would he be like in his own home?"

"He would be a domestic tyrant, you think?"

"I am sure of it. I don't think he can brook any opinion contrary to his own. No matter how trivial the topic, he lays down the law so dogmatically that I am infuriated even when I agree with him."

"And when you disagree with him? You were always one to speak your mind."

"Yes, but he just smiles condescendingly and says, 'You will allow me to know better in this' or something of that nature and repeats his argument."

Francis laughed. "I can imagine how that impressed you. It is time you put an end to it and I agree it is best to avoid a direct confrontation."

She nodded. "He can hardly complain if another gentleman has asked me to dance before he arrived."

"Well, I'm your man tonight."

"Thank you, Francis. I think we'll tell Caro and Matthew that I want to nudge Lord Henry away without making a huge commotion."

"I'm glad you've come to your senses, Sis," Matthew said when she explained. "I couldn't understand what you saw in him."

"He's an excellent dancer," she replied with a rueful smile.

"Any lady must be pleased to have him as a partner," Caro agreed. "But other than that—you must tell your mother as well, Bella, so that she is up to snuff if he calls again. I don't mean she should refuse to receive him, but she should know why you decline another invitation to drive with him, for example."

"Are you nervous?" Caro whispered as the guests gathered in Lady Needham's ballroom.

Arabella shook her head. "Mamma insisted on coming. She said it was too delicate a matter for Millie to deal with on her own."

"'She saith among the trumpets, Ha ha'," Caro murmured, "'and she smelleth the battle afar off'."

"Sssh." Arabella stifled a giggle and turned to greet the Nearys.

Miss Neary rather shyly asked if Arabella would be willing to practise some more duets with her. She agreed and Matthew immediately offered to escort her to the Nearys any time she wished. He followed this by inviting Miss Neary to stand up with him for the first waltz.

"May I have the pleasure of dancing the first waltz with you, Miss Malvin?" Mr Neary said.

Nothing could be better, Arabella thought. "I should have been delighted, sir, but I am afraid Mr Nugent is before you."

"Ah. Then perhaps the second one?"

"It will be my pleasure."

"Thank you." He turned to Caro. "Miss Nugent, dare I hope you are free for the first waltz?"

"Here he comes," Caro murmured to Arabella. "His appearance is always too pat. You never see him until just before the first waltz. How does he manage it?"

Arabella shrugged. "Very likely he waits in the card room and tips a footman to tell him when the time comes. It's rather ridiculous, isn't it? As if he feels he must make an entrance."

Lord Henry did not seem disconcerted to find her at the centre of a larger group than usual but deftly made his way through it until he reached her side.

"Good evening, Miss Malvin."

"Good evening, Lord Henry."

Her heart began to beat faster. Should she mention casually that Francis had been before him? No, when he asked her to dance would be time enough. To forestall him would suggest that she felt the need to justify a perfectly normal occurrence. The mere fact that she considered it showed how uneasy he had made her.

"You were not in the Park this afternoon," he remarked.

"No." She would not mention her preference for early morning rides in case he took it as an invitation to join her. "Were there many there?"

"Very few worthy of notice."

"Do you stay in town over Easter, Lord Henry?"

"I have not yet decided. Will your family return to Berkshire?"

"Yes."

He continued to chat lightly but did not ask her to dance. She shrugged mentally. Perhaps he had noticed her reserve at Almack's and this was his way of putting her in her place. When the waltz was announced, he would stroll away and leave her without a partner, making it clear that she no longer met his strict standards in what would be an equivalent of the cut direct.

When the musicians touched their bows to the strings, she looked over to Francis. Before he could say anything, Lord Henry smiled coolly at her, took her hand and placed it on his sleeve.

"Our dance, I believe, Miss Malvin."

This was the outside of enough! Arabella pulled her hand free, saying coldly, "I fear you are mistaken, my lord. I am engaged to Mr Nugent for this waltz."

Her words created a pool of silence that spread outwards, quenching the usual chatter.

Dull red stained Lord Henry's cheeks and his eyes flashed. He drew himself up to his full height. "Indeed, I see I was mistaken," he said icily. "Your servant, Miss Malvin."

He barely inclined his head and turned on his heel. There was a collective exhalation as he stalked away, the fascinated onlookers parting to let him pass. Matthew looked furious and Mamma was frowning.

Francis made an elaborate, old-fashioned leg, straightening to offer his hand to Arabella. "Our dance, I believe, Miss Malvin?"

She placed her hand on his wrist to a ripple of laughter.

"That did not go so well," she murmured when they had left the group.

"On the contrary, I think it went extremely well. He has shown himself in his true colours, and before your mother as well. But it was high time you put a stop to it, Bella. He didn't even bother asking you tonight, but assumed you had waited for him."

Mocking laughter rang in Henry's ears as he passed through the crowds that thronged the Needhams' ballroom and staircase without looking to the right or the left. He was shaking with rage.

"My carriage, instantly." He pressed some coins into a footman's hand and waited impatiently as the man hurried away.

"He's on the opposite side of the street, my lord," the man gasped twenty minutes later. "There's no chance of him pulling up to the steps."

Henry brushed past him, hurrying down the carpet and out onto the road in front of a conveyance disgorging a sour-faced matriarch and her gaggle of giggling chits. A young boy ran up, brandishing his broom.

"I'll sweep for you, sir."

Henry followed him, flipping the boy a penny when he reached his carriage. He had, after all, prevented him from soiling his pumps or splashing his pantaloons with the ordure of a hundred horses.

"Home," he instructed his coachman.

How dare she reject him so publicly? She would pay for it, he resolved and that ass Nugent, too.

"That is a very arrogant young man who clearly cannot bear being crossed," Lady Malvin declared four hours later as they drove home. "How foolish of him to display his chagrin so openly. I felt I must explain the situation to Ladies Neary and Nugent, for he quite gave the impression that you had previously committed to standing up with him, Arabella. Lady Neary was horrified and said at once that she would not send him a card for Constance's ball and I should not be surprised if other mothers follow suit. We shall not be at home if he tries to call, my love, and if he dares to ask you to dance again, Julian or your father will have a word with him."

"I hope people will not say I led him on. I wanted to make clear that there was no understanding of any sort between us, but that was all. I should hate to be considered a flirt or even a jilt."

"No one will think that. You were put in an awkward situation and did your best to deal with it tactfully. It is not your fault that he could not behave in a gentlemanly fashion. All he had to do was apologise for his mistake and request a later dance."

"As Mr Neary did."

"Precisely. It is fortunate that most of the *ton* go out of town for Easter, and by the time they return everything should have blown over. However, although we had planned to leave tomorrow, I think we should remain here until Saturday. If the curious call tomorrow, as I imagine they will, we must be here to explain what really happened."

"What should we say?"

"That his lordship presumed an engagement that did not exist and took umbrage when he learned that another gentleman was before him."

"Mamma, supposing he does call, should we not receive him? He might wish to apologise."

"Do you think it likely?"

"No, but I would prefer to continue on civil terms with him if possible."

"It would serve to dampen any gossip," her mother acknowledged, "but you must not be seen to favour him in any way. If he invites you for a drive, you must decline and I prefer that you do not waltz with him again."

"Yes, Mamma."

Lord Henry did not call on Friday although over twenty others did. Most came to show their support but one or two were overly inquisitive or even censorious.

"That's what comes of all this waltzing," one dowager sniffed. "Girls today are allowed too much freedom."

"Nonsense," Lady Neary snorted. "If you ask me, too many young men are puffed up with their own consequence. We have had enough of these self-proclaimed arbiters of good taste who consider themselves unconstrained by the customs and etiquette of polite society. Lord Henry Danlow apparently fancies himself a second Brummel. Miss Malvin found herself in a disagreeable situation and she dealt with it with grace and poise. It is a pity that he could not match her."

"Hear, hear," Mr Naughton said.

Arabella, who had been flattered and encouraged by the appearance of several of her usual dancing partners, had to suppress a smile when Lady Neary added severely, "It is also a pity that the other gentlemen spinelessly accepted Lord Henry's claim to the first waltz. If one of them had challenged it earlier, it might never have come to this. And I must admit that I also consider myself to blame, for I invited him to my little dinner, thinking I might be doing both of you a service. I am sorry, my dear."

Arabella smiled gratefully at her. "There is no need to apologise, my lady."

Chapter Nine

They left for Malvin Abbey on a cold, blustery Easter Saturday. It snowed on Easter Day but despite this, the Malvins attended church. Thomas was no longer at the rectory. He had travelled with a fellow-officer to Ireland to purchase remounts, his mother told Lady Malvin.

Arabella was bored at home. She was no longer a green girl but an adult woman and there was no role for her here. If only she were a boy! Roderick had left Eton and would go up to Oxford at the commencement of the Easter term. Julian and Matthew were to accompany him and see him established. It was so unfair. He was only seventeen but already allowed to make his own way in the world. Matthew came and went as he pleased; he had spent most of last winter at home but that was only because of Arthur's death—generally he was away hunting or shooting or whatever it was gentlemen did outside the Season.

Why was it that the only way a young lady could escape from under her parents' roof was through marriage? Not that she wanted to 'escape' her parents precisely; she loved her family very much and the three generations lived together most harmoniously. But at present she felt as if she were waiting for her real life to begin. She was ready to take charge of her own household but, unless she wanted to end up like Aunt Agatha, she must marry before she could establish it. And marriage was not without its dangers. A wife was a '*feme covert*', a woman whose very being or legal existence was suspended, and incorporated and consolidated into that of her husband. All she owned would become his—she would become his in the eyes of the law. Mamma had explained it very carefully before her first season.

"*I tell you this, my love, so that you will be wary of any gentleman who tries to lure you into an engagement without Papa's approval. You may be sure that your father will be most particular in his choice of your suitors, because once you are married, he will have no say in your life and he will want to be sure that he entrusts you to an honourable, considerate and affectionate husband. You will not be undowered and you must be aware of fortune-hunters.*"

Would he have refused Lord Henry's offer, Arabella wondered. She must talk to him about it and also about her fortune. Arthur had made a will a month before he died, leaving everything to her, prompted, he wrote, by Lord Tamm's decision to bequeath two thousand pounds to each grandson but nothing to his granddaughters. Arthur had left three and a half thousand pounds. To this would be added the dowry her father gave her. What would her total fortune amount to? Would it provide her with an independence if she didn't marry? Why did nobody talk to girls about these matters? They got so many lectures about propriety but nobody spoke about the important things.

Arabella's father looked up when she opened the library door. "Come in, my pet. Is there something I can do for you?"

"No, yes." She picked up the latest *Gentleman's Magazine*, looked at it blankly and put it down again. "Papa, what did you think of Lord Henry?"

He put down his pen. "Why do you ask, Bella?"

"I remember Mamma saying you would be particular in your choice of a husband for me and wondered whether you would have agreed to his suit."

"I knew nothing to his detriment and if you have been inclined to accept him, I would not have objected provided I was assured he could support you in the proper style," he said slowly. "But I would have been wrong. He is not the right man for you."

"Who is? How does one know?"

"Would you not prefer to discuss this with your mother?" he asked uneasily.

She lifted a hand and let it fall. "We have frequently talked about a suitable match, but I want to hear what a man has to say. You proposed twice. What made you choose Mamma and Julian's mother over other eligible ladies?"

The silence stretched until she wondered would he answer at all.

"Come and sit over here," he said, getting up from his desk. "If we're going to talk about such weighty matters, let us be comfortable." He waved her to a deep armchair and threw another log on the fire before sitting opposite her.

"Why do we decide for one person and not another? Let us assume we have free choice—that we are not forced to marry for any reason other than the natural desire to be one with the person we choose as our life's companion, the other parent of our children."

"Yes."

"I think that person will be similar to us in many ways—birth and upbringing, for example, general outlook on life, their sense of the ridiculous—but they must also be different so that they complement us, so that we can learn from them and they from us. That is very important. But apart from that, there is an essential something that calls us to them, something that we recognise or that resounds within us on the most intimate level."

"Love, you mean?"

"Rather the possibility or potential for love." He shook his head. "It's impossible to describe, Arabella, and it may take us some time to recognise it, but we do know when it is not there. You realised quickly enough that Lord Henry was not for you. If a different suitor had made a habit of claiming the first waltz, you might not have objected, might even have been flattered by his attentions."

She nodded thoughtfully. "It was not just that; it was his general behaviour. If that had been different—but he was not interested in me—the real me, I mean. In the end I found it hard to talk to him because he only sought my views to ensure that they agreed with his."

"So now you know that the right man must respect you as Arabella, a person in your own right, and be willing to discuss things with you as an equal."

"That's it," she recognised. "I don't wish to be my husband's satellite, subservient in all things."

"Nor should you. The gospel tells us '*a man shall be joined unto his wife, and they two shall be one flesh*'. To me, that means that together they will create something new, not that she is subsumed by him."

"He leaves his parents and is joined unto her, not she unto him," Arabella said reflectively. "Who is the stronger?"

"Harrumph!" Papa cleared his throat loudly. "I never thought of that and we are straying into deep waters, too deep, perhaps. You asked why I proposed to your mother and before her to Hermione. Quite simply, because they had taken up residence in my heart and my mind. I could not imagine a future without them. I could picture them here at the Abbey, opposite me at dinner, with my children in the nursery. I am a very fortunate man, Bella, to have found that twice."

"But you had a chance to get to know them first."

"I knew Hermione all her life—she was Nugent's sister, you remember—and with your mother—well, in Bath one stood less on ceremony, I suppose. Have I helped you at all, pet?"

"I must think about the potential for love," she said with a sigh.

"I think the seed is there with many people—that is the initial attraction, if you like—but will it take root? In some cases it may happen slowly, in others very quickly. Sometimes it shoots up in an intense infatuation and dies as quickly. You will have seen that, I imagine?"

She nodded. "Our first season, Caro was crazy about Mr Fitzmaurice, and the fact that he danced only with married ladies made it worse. She was determined he would ask her to stand up with him. But when he did, she decided he was too dull for words."

Her father smiled. "I always knew him for a clever man."

"Do you think he was dull on purpose?"

"I imagine so, but don't say anything to Caro."

"No, it would be too mortifying."

"To come back to love, Bella, the important thing is 'to thine own self be true'. Be honest with yourself and, when the time comes, be honest with him. There is no place for dissimulation within love and if you feel you must pretend to be someone other than you are, then he is not the right man for you."

"How can I be sure he is being honest with me?"

"You must be willing to listen to what your instincts tell you, but also take into account how others speak of him. And watch how he behaves with others. Do not let yourself be distracted by notions of a great match or the fact that it is your fourth season and you still have not met the man with whom you want to share your life." He cocked an eyebrow as he said this and she felt her cheeks grow warm.

"No, Papa." She came over and kissed him. "Thank you."

Papa had helped, she found, as she pondered his comments. Someone to share her life with—and who would share his with her. That was just as important. She knew of many *ton* couples where husband and wife more or less went their separate ways. The Gracechurches for one.

The potential for love—there would have to be a little prickle of excitement, the initial attraction, Papa had said. But you would also have to be at ease with him, albeit not in a sisterly way. And both of you must be willing to provide the 'mutual society, help, and comfort, that the one ought to have of the other, both in prosperity and adversity,' as the marriage ceremony had it. Thomas would provide it, she thought suddenly. But Thomas was in Ireland purchasing remounts in preparation for his return to his regiment.

Chapter Ten

Easter was over and the *ton* had come to town in force. A rare sunny afternoon had everyone flocking to the Park and the ladies' attention was divided between inspecting the passing throng and deciding which party to attend. With the Season in full swing, one had to be selective in one's choice of entertainment or run the risk of being overcome by exhaustion before the end of June. In the Nugent's barouche-landau, Arabella, Caro and their mothers reviewed the latest invitations.

"Do you go to Lady Lutterworth's tonight?" Caro asked.

The marriage of Lord Franklin, a second son urgently recalled from the army after his elder brother broke his neck attempting a five-bar gate with an unschooled hunter, to Miss Sally Gregg, companion to Mrs Frome, had astounded the polite world the previous summer. As it had taken place at the tail-end of the Season and during the aftermath of Waterloo, society had not yet had the opportunity to express its opinion of the match but Lady Lutterworth had now sent out cards for a ball to celebrate her son's marriage.

"Yes," Arabella said. "I met Miss Gregg at Mrs Frome's musicale last year. Some idiot stood on my gown and tore the flounce. She noticed it and took me to a little parlour and pinned it for me. I liked her. Lord Franklin was there too, escorting his mother and sister and Mrs Frome was so puffed up about it. She seated him next to her daughter and he looked quite bored, grim, almost. I don't think she was aware of his interest in Miss Gregg."

"I heard someone say that she trapped him. He took her to the continent intending to make her his mistress and she contrived to get him to marry her."

"I am surprised at you repeating such gossip, Caroline," Lady Nugent said languidly. "You may be sure it is merely sour grapes on the part of those who are envious of Lady Franklin's making such an eligible match."

"I am sure you are right, ma'am," Arabella said. "It is true he escorted her to Belgium but it was because her brother was very seriously wounded at Waterloo. Mrs Rembleton, as she was then, accompanied them. Captain Gregg and Lord Franklin were in the same regiment, as was Mr Fitzmaurice, who wrote to his lordship. His lordship had procured a special licence in advance and once Captain Gregg was out of danger they were married by the chaplain to the Embassy. Lallie told us the full story last evening."

"The Greggs are connected to the Fromes, I believe. That is why Mrs Frome offered Miss Gregg a home when her father died," Lady Malvin remarked.

The two elder ladies settled to tracing Lady Franklin's antecedents while Caro and Arabella returned to their review of the *ton*.

"Who else was at the Tamms'?" Caro asked.

"Oh, it was just a small dinner to welcome the Halworths. Apart from us, Lallie's father and stepmother, who is the Admiral's niece, were there and my Aunt Forbes and her husband."

"Were Miss Halworth's new gowns ready?"

Arabella nodded. "She sent a note asking me to come early so I could see them. They're beautiful and suit her very well. Madame Lemartin used fabrics with a suggestion of vertical lines and just a little narrow trimming at the hem so that the effect is to make Ruth taller. She also recommended a *corsetière.* The new stays flatter her figure."

"Flatter or flatten?"

"Neither, I would say. It is more that they fit properly so that she is not so billowy."

"And Lady Halworth?"

"She also looks much more the thing. She will never be supremely stylish—she does not have the interest in her appearance—but she no longer looks such a provincial dowd."

Caro grasped Arabella's arm. "Lord Henry's phaeton is coming up behind us," she hissed. "He is about to over-take us. I can't believe that someone is still wearing an Oldenburg bonnet," she added in a louder voice.

"They must be the ugliest hats ever created," Arabella agreed. She glanced up when the phaeton pulled out to pass them, prepared to acknowledge its driver civilly, but he deliberately turned his head away as he came abreast of their carriage.

"Cut, by Heavens!" Caro said when he was safely past. "That will teach you to show him a proper respect, Bella."

Arabella burst out laughing. "Indeed it will. He is an even bigger fool than I thought him."

Trapped while two dowagers exchanged lengthy greetings from barouche to barouche, Lord Henry Danlow fought to retain his impassive expression as the girls' laughter rang in his ears. Impertinent chits! And to think he had considered making Miss Malvin his wife, had thought she would be worth schooling. He was well out of that *galère*. His hands tightened on the reins, making his horses shift restlessly.

At last the beldam in front of him gave the signal to move on. Once out of the Park, he took his team at a spanking trot through the crowded streets, ignoring the angry looks of those who had to make way for him. Back at Jermyn Street, he pulled up in front of his house and jumped down, swore at his tiger for not being quick enough to take the horses from him, then stalked indoors where he threw his hat and gloves at his butler who backed away as his master headed for his little book room.

Instead of making his usual cup of tea, Henry headed for the decanters and swallowed half a sizeable measure of brandy before going to his desk. The pile of cards was smaller than usual, especially now that everyone was in town. The Lutterworths' was the main ball tonight. He would look in for a few minutes, he decided, flicking through the unopened correspondence until he found a note sealed with Lady Jersey's crest.

He broke the wax and scanned the sheet, swore and threw it in the fire. She regretted she was unable to oblige him with further vouchers for Almack's. The impertinence! Be damned to her and to all women. Doxies every one of them!

The *beau monde* had arrived in droves to inspect the new Lady Franklin, who appeared to stand up well to the ordeal of being made known to her mother-in-law's guests. Arabella took a small pencil from her reticule and scribbled her partners' names discreetly on the spokes of her fan so that she would not forget the order of battle, as Arthur had irreverently called it. No sign of Lord Henry, thank heavens. This promised to be a wonderful evening. She had been inundated with requests for the first waltz. She was to dance it with Mr Neary but had already engaged herself for all other dances.

She turned to smile at the Tamms and the Halworths. Ruth looked very pretty in a slip of pale primrose satin under a white striped gauze gown trimmed with a narrow flounce and a wreath of small yellow primroses with dark green leaves. John, who was equally well turned out, seemed overawed by his surroundings and was less bumptious than usual while the Admiral and his lady were as comfortable here as they would have been in their drawing-room at home or on his quarter-deck.

"Is Matthew still in Oxford?" Ruth demanded. "I was relying on him to stand up with me. When will he be back?"

"I'm afraid I don't know," Arabella said briefly. Matthew would not thank her if she encouraged Ruth to think she had a claim on him. Still, this was Ruth's first outing in the *ton.* Arabella introduced her to the others in the group and had the satisfaction of seeing her engaged for a respectable number of dances before the music started.

"Here. Write their names on your fan," she murmured, handing Ruth the little pencil when there was a slight lull. "Otherwise you won't remember."

"Thank you, Bella. I was wondering how to manage without muttering their names in turn as if I were reciting my multiplication tables. You know; number one, Hugo, number two, Mr Nugent, number three, Mr Neary." She giggled. "I don't think it would make the best of impressions, do you? I wish the dancing would start. I'm so excited." She looked over to the staircase that led down into the ballroom. "Surely all the guests are here now. I have never seen such a crush."

"This is nothing out of the ordinary," Arabella assured her but Ruth wasn't listening.

"There they come. Isn't she beautiful? It's so romantic."

Lord Franklin led his wife into the middle of the dance floor where they were joined by three other couples to dance an elegant quadrille.

"What a charming figure," Arabella exclaimed, as the dance ended with the bride enclosed within an arch formed over her head by the arms of the gentlemen dancing on either side of her.

"It is called "Les Graces"," Lady Alys Franklin, who had come up to them with Lord Marfield, explained later. "Generally, all couples would dance it in turn, but today we felt it fitting that only my brother and his wife should dance it. He chose Mr Fitzmaurice as the other gentleman because he was a witness at their wedding.

"You could call this version "La Mariée"," Arabella suggested. "It is perfect for a bridal."

"But first they should dance "Le Captif", where the bride and bridesmaid bag the bridegroom," Francis suggested.

"I have made a note of that for your wedding," his sister informed him sweetly. "It shall be danced at your special request."

"Who is that leading out Lady Alys?" a girl whispered behind Arabella. "Over there—the tall, black-haired officer. I haven't seen him before. He looks positively grim."

"I don't know. Doesn't he look deliciously dangerous?" her friend murmured. "I saw him dancing earlier. He moves beautifully but never smiles."

"Our dance, I believe, Miss Malvin." Lord Marfield bowed before her.

Arabella put her hand on his arm and let him lead her onto the dancefloor. She liked him and he was easy to talk to, but her heart did not beat any faster when he approached and she did not find herself thinking of him at odd moments. They were the fourth couple and, as the first two couples led off, she turned her head discreetly, trying to spy Lady Alys and her partner. There they were, nimbly chasséing to the right and the left so that they separated and returned to face one another. Lady Alys's partner had his back to her, but there was something about the set of his head on his shoulders that was familiar.

The figure ended and he returned to Lady Alys's side. Now she could see his face. It wasn't! It couldn't be! Arabella stumbled as Marfield drew her forward to begin the figure. She stole a last quick glance at the other couple. It was indeed Thomas. He was in town and had not called. And he could not plead as an excuse that he did not intend to move among the *ton*.

They were not in the same set, thank goodness. She had time to compose herself before they met—if indeed they met this evening. She had no intention of going in search of him. She forced herself to concentrate on her own partner and the other couples in her set, to resist the temptation to watch Lady Alys smiling up at him. The music stopped and she curtsied to Marfield, then accepted his arm for the obligatory stroll.

After the fourth set Thomas found his way to where the Malvins stood with the Nugents and the Halworths.

"This is indeed a pleasure," he said, bowing to the group.

Arabella had herself well in hand and murmured a polite greeting. Her mother's response was cooler. Was she also miffed that he had not called?

Ruth, of course, beamed at him, saying, "There is something particularly delightful in meeting someone from home in town, Major."

"Indeed there is, Miss Halworth," he replied.

Mamma had to present him to the Nugents but once the formalities were concluded, he turned to Arabella.

"May I have the pleasure of dancing with you, Miss Malvin?"

She smiled calmly. "I'm afraid, Major, that I am engaged for the rest of the evening."

He did not appear downcast by the news.

"I should have expected it," he said simply and turned to Ruth. "Miss Halworth, will you favour me with your next free dance?"

To crown Arabella's misery, he danced the supper dance with Caro, afterwards leading her to join a merry group of officers and their ladies. Arabella resolutely shifted her chair so that she had her back to them and smiled at Mr Naughton.

"Do you think it was right to abolish income tax?"

"Major Ferraunt is wonderful," Caro murmured to Arabella as they returned from the ladies' retiring room. "So masculine, and those sinister looks; have you noticed how he prowls, like a black tiger? And, like all of Wellington's officers, a superb dancer. How is it you have never mentioned him before?"

Arabella laughed. "I've known him all my life but hadn't seen him for years until he came home last month. His father is our rector."

"Oh." Caro's interest cooled rapidly. "I thought he was one of the Gloucestershire Ferraunts."

"There is a connection, I believe, but it is quite distant."

Thomas did not dance again after supper. Some of the other officers had also disappeared, Arabella noticed, but there was a steady trickle of guests arriving, coming on from other entertainments.

"Are you feeling quite the thing, Bella?" Francis asked quietly as he set his hands at her waist. "Not in the dumps, are you?"

She clasped his shoulders and shook her head as they revolved to the music. "Not at all. A little tired, perhaps, just for a moment. I don't have to hide it from you."

"As long as that's all—I was afraid Danlow was pestering you again."

"I don't think he's here. I haven't seen him at any rate."

"Nor I."

They moved to an open hold and she turned gracefully under his arm before sinking in the final curtsey. "Thank you, Francis."

He raised an eyebrow. "Shall we have some champagne?"

She chuckled at his imitation of Lord Henry's drawl. "I'd love some. Let's take it to that window and get some air."

"Speak of the devil," he muttered a few minutes later.

"Why?"

"Look there." He nodded towards Lord Henry who gracefully descended the stairs, his head in the air and a faint smile on his thin lips.

Arabella took a step back into the window embrasure.

"You're not afraid of him, are you, Bella?"

"No. But I don't want him to make a scene. He cut us in the Park today, you know."

"Idiot! Him, I mean, not you. But look, Bella."

They watched his lordship slowly make the circuit of the big room. Was it Arabella's imagination or was his progress accompanied by little eddies in the groups about the eligible girls? No, there was a subtle closing of ranks, a turning away instead of the usual nods and becks when chaperons acknowledged a suitable gentleman or the smiling flutterings of fans and flounces where young ladies sought to attract him. No-one wanted to catch his eye. He paused to bow to his hostess and then spoke to Lady Alys who was seen to smile and shake her head. He bowed again, completed his tour of the ballroom without acknowledging another person and within fifteen minutes had mounted the stairs and disappeared to a rising hum of conversation.

"Well!" Francis expelled his breath. "The matrons have turned against him. I've never seen anything like it."

Arabella pinned a bright smile to her lips for the remainder of the ball. She could not have borne solicitous questions as to her state of mind. At last it was over. Her slippers threatened to fray and her feet ached, but that was nothing compared with the sting in her heart. She could not believe that Thomas would slight them so. Or were they merely dull country neighbours and she a romp of a girl who had to be fished out of a stream?

He had not gone unnoticed; speculative eyes had followed him and more than one young lady had admitted to experiencing a peculiar frisson when his eyes rested on her. Caro's description of him as a black tiger had made the rounds and Miss Gatton had remarked that she was sure he had suffered a secret sorrow. "He is so haggard and never smiles. It is so romantic."

No, you are so hen-witted, Arabella had thought. She refused to be drawn into a discussion of Major Thomas Ferraunt.

Chapter Eleven

Thomas turned into the narrow entrance of Craig's Court. The offices of Greenwood, Cox & Co., the 23rd's regimental agents, were in one of the first houses. He had been here twice before—once to open his account and once to arrange the purchase of his captaincy.

A clerk rose from his high stool. "Major Ferraunt, I presume? Good morning, sir. If you will be good enough to wait a moment, I shall let Mr Greenwood know you are here."

The clerks here are probably the most expert of all in recognising uniforms and insignia, Thomas reflected, impressed. He had written advising that he would call but had not expected to meet Mr Greenwood himself.

An elderly, affable-looking gentleman emerged from a mahogany doorway, his hand outstretched. "Major Ferraunt! I am happy to meet you, sir. Please come this way."

He ushered Thomas into a richly furnished office full of gleaming wood and turkey carpets. He did not retreat behind his desk but waved his visitor to a comfortable armchair at a round table and took the seat opposite him.

"A glass of Madeira before we begin, or do you prefer port?"

"Madeira, by all means." Thomas waited patiently for the glasses to be poured, his health toasted and the first savouring sip taken.

"We are always pleased to welcome one of our officers home," his host said, picking up a sheaf of papers. "Now, I presume you wish to know how you stand."

"I do, sir."

Mr Greenwood detached the top sheet and slid it across the polished table. "You are doing very well, if I may say so. Many of our officers would wish to be in a similar position."

Thomas glanced at the page and looked again, puzzled by the balance of more than six thousand pounds. He expected to be in funds, but not to that extent.

"Forgive me, sir, but are you sure this is accurate?"

"Unless you have taken to writing extravagant drafts that have not yet been presented, yes."

"Not I," Thomas murmured. On Malcolm's advice, he had taken cash with him to Ireland so there was nothing outstanding from there. "May I see the rest?"

He flicked through the other papers. The quarterly payments from his uncle's estate had more than doubled compared with six years ago, and an additional sum of several hundred pounds had been deposited the previous February.

"What was this, sir?"

Mr Greenwood peered at the page. "Prize money for the Peninsula and Waterloo. As a major, you received the equivalent of eighteen months pay for the latter. The captain's share for the Peninsula was not so generous, but all in all, it came to a pretty sum."

"Indeed."

"What are your plans, Major, if I may ask? If you have no immediate need for the full amount that has accumulated, you must put it to work."

Thomas sipped his Madeira. "To be frank, Mr Greenwood, I don't know what my plans are. I left my great-uncle's estate in the hands of Mr Benson, his man of business—there was no time to do anything else—and judging by this, he has managed it well."

"It would appear so." Mr Greenwood looked over his spectacles. "You are now in a position not only to support a wife and family but to command the elegancies of life for them."

Thomas's head was in a whirl. He entered the first coffee house he passed and found a quiet corner where he stared unseeing at that morning's *Times*. *Support a wife and family*; *Command the elegancies of life*. He had thought it would be years before he could hope to be in such a position. He must write to Benson at once—ascertain whether the increase in income was well-founded and would continue. If so, what then?

Greenwood had enquired whether he wished to remain in the army, pointing out that a major's half-pay would amount to more than half of what he currently received because it would not be liable to the usual stoppages. "Now, while they are reducing the army to a peace-time level, is the time to consider it," he had said. "Afterwards, there may not be as many opportunities to do so."

They had agreed that he would make tentative enquiries without mentioning his client's name.

While Thomas had often wondered about leaving the army, it had been more along the lines of 'one day, perhaps' than 'should I do it now?' Something in him yearned for the possibility to put down roots, for permanence. But where and in what style did he wish to live? He beckoned a passing waiter and ordered more coffee.

He couldn't see himself as a gentleman-farmer, managing his own acres. But he would need some interest, something to occupy his time. He could keep a small stud like Sir John Malcolm; hobbyhorses, he thought, smiling to himself, although he would not turn up his nose at a little profit. If you are going to do something, do it properly. He was sure that Martin, who had been very taken by Colduff, would stay as his head groom. So, a house with good stables and land with good grazing for horses. An exercise ring too.

Happier now that he had the outlines of a plan, he took out a cheroot and lit it pensively. How would he take to civilian life? He would have to learn all its shibboleths. Cards, for example—he couldn't pay calls without them. He must collect the new ones from the stationers if he wanted to present himself at Malvin House later.

It had been a stroke of luck stumbling upon The Crossed Swords the other day. He had gone in for a pint of beer and recognised the former Captain Franklin who, after a brief exchange, had taken him upstairs to the long room where ex-military men and off-duty fencing masters tested one another's skill. Thomas had immediately been matched with a former cavalry sergeant who also topped six feet and afterwards introduced to Luke Fitzmaurice, a man of about his own age who had served as an ensign at Waterloo and was now a member of parliament. He had felt comfortable there, would go back.

And so had come the invitation to the Lutterworth ball, including dinner before it as someone had cried off at the last moment. Dark-haired, dark-eyed Lady Alys had taken him under her wing. And a very pretty wing it was too. But she was not Arabella, who had looked ravishing in white with touches of sea-green that brought out the colour of her eyes. She put all the other girls in the shade. It was not surprising that she was so much in demand. And that could well be the only ball invitation he received, he thought gloomily. He would have liked to have danced with her, even once.

"Major Ferraunt, my lady."

He had come! Arabella's heart leaped and then she remembered he must have called on the Lutterworths days ago. They were only second best. Still, she could not but watch as he walked confidently down the long room to bow to her mother.

"How good of you to call, Major Ferraunt."

Mamma was at her most majestic. Had she taken snuff too? They had not discussed it, but it was very likely. But Thomas was not daunted.

"It is my pleasure, my lady," he murmured and then turned to Arabella.

That tell-tale warmth came into his eyes and the left corner of his mouth lifted. She felt her own lips quiver in response and curve into a smile.

"I trust I see you well, Miss Malvin."

"You do, Major, thank you."

"May I?" He indicated the place on the sofa beside her and she gestured with her open hand as if to say, 'please'.

He sat, casually balancing his shako on his knee. Not for the first time, she was irritated by the conventions of morning calls. Six other persons sat in the room, so it was impossible to have a private conversation, and etiquette required that he remain thirty minutes at most. Lady Halworth and Ruth were about to leave. That left Mrs Milward, Lady Haydon and their silly daughters, both of whom preened themselves on the other side of the circle. She would ignore them.

"I believe you have been in Ireland, purchasing remounts."

He stared at her and his mouth twitched again. "I take it you have been at home in Berkshire recently."

"For Easter. Your father revealed all," she added dramatically.

"I have no secrets left, have I?"

He sounded amused. It was amazing how well he was able to convey such subtleties despite his lack of expression on one side.

"I wouldn't go that far," she said, laughing. "Did you have a successful journey?"

"Too successful, almost. I have three new horses eating their heads off at livery. I should probably sell one—I find I am loath to part with Lochinvar; he has been a faithful servant these many years."

"Lochinvar?

"Yes. He came out of the west, you see."

"Was he with you in the Peninsula? Did he "stay not for brake and stop not for stone"?"

"And swam more rivers than I care to remember." He glanced over to where the Milwards and Haydons had begun to make their farewells. Beneath the little hubbub he murmured, "But talking of rivers, I hope you suffered no further ill-effects after your soaking?"

"No, and Sammy is as adventurous as ever, his mother tells me."

"I have no doubt of it."

"Did you take your other horses with you to Ireland?"

"No, in fact I took Perkins on to look after them while I was away because Martin—my man—came with me. I must see about selling the other one."

"What about the mule?"

"That depends," he said vaguely. "Do you still like to ride in Rotten Row at nine o'clock each morning?"

"When I can. Both Matthew and Julian are out of town at present. They went with Roderick to see him settled at Oxford."

"But you will when they return? With three horses to exercise, I am there almost every morning. You must tell me what you think of my purchases."

"We'll see. How long do you remain in town?"

"Until the end of May, at least. I have been putting up at Gordon's Hotel, but our regimental agent told me of a pleasant set of rooms in Poland Street that is passed from one officer on furlough to another. The present occupant leaves at the end of the month and I shall replace him."

"How do you find life in London after so many years on campaign?"

"The disconcerting thing is that while London, and indeed England, should be familiar, it is not. I went from the rectory to Oxford and from there to the regiment. When you are abroad, you are always conscious of the fact that you are somewhere 'other', but you are supposed to be, well, 'at home' in your own country."

"And you are not?" she asked gently.

His gaze softened. "Not always. With you, I am."

A warm glow suffused her. "I think that is the nicest thing anyone has ever said to me, Thomas. But don't worry. I am sure you will become accustomed to our odd customs and habits."

"I hope I may rely on you to put me right if necessary. I am not used to the ways of the *ton*."

She laughed. "You probably find them just as arcane as I would military ones. Is there a special etiquette that applies to ladies within military society? Do wives take their husband's rank, for example? I don't mean in terms of formal precedence—there are clear rules for that—but does Mrs Captain Brown condescend to Mrs Lieutenant Smith? And where do daughters and sisters fit in?"

"I don't know, to be frank. I have no real experience of a station where there are many ladies. Most do not accompany their husbands on campaign and the few who do are not generally sticklers for needless etiquette. Of course, a wise junior officer will not offend a senior officer's lady, let alone his daughter."

"I can well imagine. So the army in peacetime will be very different to the army at war?"

"Very different."

"Have you been to the theatre yet?" she asked impulsively. "Edmund Kean is appearing as *Richard the*

Third on Tuesday evening at Drury Lane. Would you like to join us in our box?"

His eyes lit up. "I should like it above all things, Arabella. Thank you. I have never had the opportunity to see him. In fact, I have never been inside a London theatre."

"Never?" She could not imagine it.

He rose to his feet as her mother approached. "I fear I have stayed too long."

"Nonsense, Thomas," Lady Malvin said. "You will take a cup of tea with us, I hope. I vow I am parched after so many callers. Ring for it, please, Arabella. And tell Belshaw we are not at home to further visitors."

Chapter Twelve

The vestibule of the Theatre Royal, Drury Lane, was crammed with elegantly dressed persons. Lady Malvin's party forged its way through the clusters of people exchanging greetings as if had been several months and not some hours since they had last set eyes on one another. Preceded by a sturdy, liveried footman, they advanced in a quincunx, his lordship with his lady taking the front rank, Mrs Malvin the middle and Thomas and Arabella following close on her heels. At last they reached the left of the pair of grand staircases that led to the three circles surrounding the pit.

"It will be quicker now. Our box is in the dress circle, so we must only take the first flight and then we'll be out of this crush." Arabella's eyes sparkled. "I am so looking forward to the play. I saw Kean as Shylock—you could not but feel for him, even though he remained stubborn to the end, and his Richard is said to be even better."

But when they entered the wide, elegantly furnished corridor that curved behind the boxes, Thomas felt her falter and her hand tightened on his arm. He looked down. The light had gone from her face.

He slowed and murmured, "Is something wrong?"

"I hope not," she whispered.

She moved a little closer to him, as if seeking shelter, and he put his hand over hers. He could see nothing that might have distressed her. Her parents and sister-in-law had stopped to speak to a stiff-rumped couple and a younger, fair-haired man of average to middling size who stood very erect, his head tilted either to display his profile or to enable him to look down his nose. Arabella took a deep breath as they reached the group, slipping her hand from his arm but remaining close to his side.

She curtsied. "My lords, my lady."

The two men bowed.

"Good evening, Miss Malvin, I am pleased to see you well." The unknown ladyship's graciousness was overpowering.

"Thank you."

"May I present Major Ferraunt, who is at present home on furlough?" Lady Malvin asked. "Major Ferraunt, the Marquess and Marchioness of Rickersby and Lord Henry Danlow."

Thomas bowed. "My lords, my lady."

"What regiment are you with, Major?" the marquess enquired.

"The 23rd, my lord, the Royal Welch Fusiliers."

"And you are at present in France?" Lord Henry drawled.

"Yes, at Cambrai."

"How dreary. My commiserations."

"I think we should go in," Lord Malvin intervened. "Your servant, Lady Rickersby." He nodded to the other two and gestured to his ladies to go on.

"Thank heavens they don't have the box beside ours," Arabella hissed when they were safely in their own domain. "Did Lord Henry say anything before we came up?"

"Just 'good evening'," Millie said. "Does he usually accompany his brother and sister-in-law to the theatre?"

"I don't recall seeing him with them before, but that is not their usual box."

What was all that about, Thomas wondered as the three ladies took the front seats. He and Lord Malvin sat behind and between them, with an excellent view of the boxes opposite. The Malvin party was apparently equally visible. A battery of lorgnettes and quizzing glasses swivelled towards them as soon as they appeared. Thomas noticed heads turning, looking past them, presumably to the Rickersby's box and then back again. Arabella's hand tightened on her fan but she sat as still as a soldier on parade. In a way she was, he supposed.

She glanced over her shoulder. "There is nothing as inquisitive as a London audience. They are probably wondering who you are, Thomas."

He smoothed his side whiskers. "How long will it take them to discover I am nobody?"

Her brows drew together but her eyes still smiled. "You must not fish for compliments!"

"Is that what I was doing?"

"You know very well you were," she answered severely. "If you were sitting beside me, you would feel my fan on your knuckles, sir."

He leaned forward and stretched out his hand, palm down. "You only have to turn around a little more."

She laughed. "You are incorrigible. My poor fan would be broken by the end of the evening. Ssh. They are drawing up the curtain."

By turning his chair to the side and craning forward to look past Arabella, he could see about half the stage. In some of the other boxes, the gentlemen remained standing, presumably to have a better view. Perhaps he would do that later, but for now Thomas was happy to divide his attention between the play and the lady just in front of him.

What a delicate neck she had, what a sweet curve where it joined her shoulder. Her hair was dressed quite simply, parted on her forehead and swept back and curled into a roll that caressed the rounded base of her skull. He itched to touch just one ungloved finger to the little tendrils that curled at her nape, or pluck one of the little bunches of lily of the valley that matched the delicate headpiece that dipped onto her forehead and secured her tresses.

The steady hum of conversation from the pit scarcely abated during the first scene at the Tower of London. King Henry received the news of his son's death and withdrew. Silence fell. It seemed to Thomas as if the great house held its breath. A short, dark-haired, strong-featured man walked on the stage and the play-goers broke into rapturous applause. He acknowledged the ovation and then stepped back and gathered himself. As they watched, he changed. His fierce brooding look was tempered by a faint, sardonic smile; a shift in stance caused one shoulder to hunch slightly. As his torso twisted, the fingers of one hand contracted, claw-like.

"Now is the winter of our discontent
Made glorious summer by this sun of York"

As Kean spoke, he became Richard, Duke of Gloster, revealing both the anguish and the viciousness of one twisted in body and mind. He did not declaim—it was as if one could eavesdrop on the man's most intimate thoughts and feelings. The audience was rapt, sighing in unison when he turned to the back of the stage where King Henry was revealed in his tower room, about to face his son's murderer, and his own.

"It is strangely compelling, isn't it?" Arabella said after the curtain had dropped again.

Thomas nodded. "As if Richard himself stands before us and lures us into sympathy for him."

"Do you think his villainy is part of his deformity—that his appearance reflects his base character?" Mrs Malvin asked.

"He seems to think so," Arabella said, "but I don't agree. If that were the case, the opposite must also apply, and we have all known handsome people who appear to have every advantage the world offers and yet are mean-spirited."

"That is very true. Think of the beauties who cannot bear to hear another lady praised."

"I know a man who walks very haltingly but is the merriest, kindest person one could meet," Thomas said. "He is a shoemaker, respected in his village and loved by his wife and children. Richard seems to have always been 'crooked Richard,' despised and scorned for his appearance from the beginning. Might that not have twisted his soul?"

"I think it very likely," Lady Malvin said.

"Does anyone want to stroll?" Arabella asked. "Hugo and Lallie are opposite with the Halworths. I thought we might call on them."

Her face fell when both her mother and sister-in-law declined to face the crush.

"May I escort you?" Thomas offered.

She beamed and tucked her hand into his arm. "Thank you, Thomas. Visiting other boxes is half the pleasure of the theatre."

Others also sauntered along the corridor. When they reached the Rickersby's box, Lord Henry stood in the open door as if about to leave. He stepped out, but Arabella did not slacken her pace or give any indication that she had noticed him. Lord Henry hesitated, a strange smile on his lips. He bowed, ostentatiously yielding the floor to them.

Thomas nodded briefly. "My lord."

Arabella had as good as snubbed the other man. Had there been something between them in the past that caused her to ignore him now? He must have been very importunate or offensive for her to behave so.

"We must cross the rotunda and go up to the first circle on the other side," she said.

"It seems as if half of those here are calling on the other half," Thomas remarked as they made their way through the crowds. "How do people know whose turn it is to visit whom?"

"It's not as bad as that—it is only the people in the boxes who make calls, though there are saloons where those in the pit and the gallery can refresh themselves. There is one in there," she nodded to a door in the rotunda, "but ladies generally do not go in there."

Thomas was amused by the way she ignored the alluring females entering the saloon on the arms of aging rakes and young bucks, some of whom on another evening might be among her dancing partners, but now strolled by without a flicker of recognition on either side. Young ladies seemed obliged to spend a lot of their time with their eyes closed to the world around them. Did they feel the restriction?

They stopped to exchange greetings with the Franklins and Mr and Mrs Fitzmaurice and continued up the stairs to the Tamms' box where they were met by a vivacious Miss Halworth.

"Isn't it exciting? I have never seen so many people together in all my life. There must be about two thousand here. Just think—that's four times the population of Longcroft. You're looking very fine, Bella. What shade of blue is your slip? I have never seen it before."

"The modiste called it 'Marie-Louise.'"

Ruth sniffed. "After the Empress? How strange!"

Thomas looked to see how Arabella took this comment, but she appeared to find nothing untoward in her friend's remark, ignoring it as she continued past her to greet her uncle and aunt and their other guests. He followed and accepted a glass of champagne.

"This is a real treat for us," Lady Halworth said. "It is so kind of dear Lady Tamm to arrange it. Do you know, Major, this is the first time I have spent several weeks in town. Generally, we just pass through, stopping for a night or two, and we rarely manage to get tickets for the theatre. Next week, our niece Mrs Grey—she is Lady Tamm's stepmother, you know—and her daughters are to join us and her ladyship has promised us all manner of delights suitable for her younger sisters, including Astley's Amphitheatre and the Academy's summer exhibition, which I find an odd choice but apparently the elder girl is a talented artist."

"You clearly enjoy London, ma'am."

"Who could not?"

"Dr Johnson had the right of it," the Admiral said. "When a man is tired of London, he is tired of life."

"I don't agree," Lady Tamm said. "I enjoy London, but I shall be glad to go home."

"I shall hate to go home," Ruth cried. "Longcroft will be so dull, won't it, Bella?"

"It will be different, less frenzied, certainly," Arabella answered.

"Who is that in your parents' box?" Ruth asked suddenly.

Arabella turned to look. "Lord and Lady Rickersby."

She had turned quite pale and Thomas noticed the Tamms exchanging speaking glances.

"Lord Rickersby—he's Lord Henry's brother, isn't he?" Ruth asked.

"Yes."

"I am looking forward to seeing Miss Boyce as Lady Anne," Lady Tamm declared before the discussion could go any further. "I believe she is Lord Byron's latest inamorata. She was seen with him in his box here."

Miss Halworth immediately demanded to have Byron's box pointed out to her. To her disappointment, it was empty, and she then wanted to know were there any other 'notorieties' among the spectators.

When the Rickersbys had returned to their own box, Arabella said, "I think we should go back. I'll call during the week to see Geoffrey, Lallie. How many teeth has he now?"

"Eight," Lady Tamm said proudly, "and he can stand by himself. It won't be long until he is walking."

"How old is Tamm's child?" Thomas asked as they descended the stairs to the dress circle.

"Thirteen months. I was there when he was born last year—we had all gone to Tamm for my grandfather's funeral and then Geoffrey came."

"I don't think I ever saw your grandfather."

"He rarely came to Malvin, even when he was well enough to travel. He was a horrible old man," she said dispassionately. "He despised all females, especially his wife and daughters. It served him right that it took him so long to have his heir—a male heir, that is, because, failing one, the barony can descend in the female line—but that wasn't good enough for him. Mamma only discovered it after he died, from something the solicitor said."

He opened the door to the rotunda. She smiled her thanks as she went through and tucked her hand into his arm. Again, her fingers tightened when she spied Lord Henry who now lounged against the circular railing, his eyes glistening as he drank champagne with a dazzling bird of paradise. Under these circumstances, there could be no acknowledgement of his lordship, and Thomas took care to lead Arabella around to the opposite side so that she would not have to pass too closely. The woman laughed—a high, artificial titter. Her reddish-blonde hair was not as beautiful as Arabella's but there was a faint resemblance, he thought and immediately reproved himself for thinking of them together.

"Are your brothers still in Oxford?" he asked.

"Yes. They want to wait for May morning but will return by Saturday at latest."

"So I may hope to see you soon in Rotten Row?"

She looked up at him with an enchanting smile. "I hope so."

"I saw the Rickersbys here," Arabella said as soon as they were back in the box.

"Yes," Lady Malvin said. "They were perfectly affable; enquired after Julian—was he in town—they would send cards for a little dinner when he returned—it was too long since he and Rickersby had been at Oxford together—he would not like the friendship between our families to wane."

"Oh," Arabella said.

"It might be for the best," her mother said. "It would smooth everything over. Now, we must take our seats again."

Gloster leaned casually against the side of the stage, looking on as Lady Anne, widow of the dead monarch's son, entered with the King's funeral procession. It did not take long for his taunts to turn into a perverted wooing. Thomas could not believe that any woman might yield in such dire circumstances but, again, Kean carried all before him—the lady and the spectators.

Something flashed and cracked in the pit. A pistol shot! Thomas kicked his chair away as he grabbed those of Arabella and her mother, dragging them backwards so fast that they skidded across the floor. "Get down and stay out of sight," he snapped, crouching forward to pull Mrs Malvin back.

Screams and shouts were mixed with the bark of another shot.

"Take that, damn you!" A man's voice rose to a shriek.

"Get back! Stay down!" Thomas shouted as pellets hit the front of the box.

"I have his weapon," someone called from below. "You others hold him pinned while we fetch a constable."

Still kneeling, Thomas looked down into the tumultuous pit where several men grappled with a tall figure amid overturned benches while shocked spectators huddled together at either side beneath the boxes. On stage, Lady Anne had sunk onto a stool, holding a blood-stained cloth to her ear.

"What happened?" Lady Malvin demanded. "Thomas?"

"Some lunatic fired a pistol at the stage."

"Good heavens! Was anyone hurt?"

"Lady Anne, it seems, but it does not appear too serious."

"Someone fired at Miss Boyce?" Arabella exclaimed. "Let me see."

Her father put a restraining hand on her arm. "Wait. Is the danger over, Thomas?"

"Yes. A constable has the assailant in handcuffs."

As Thomas got to his feet, an officer wearing the dark green of the Rifles rose in the box opposite. He, too, had sent his party to the rear and now grinned ruefully as he surveyed the ladies hanging out of the other boxes, determined not to miss anything. He nodded to Thomas and, like him, turned to restore order among his own company.

"What's that?" Mrs Malvin had picked something up from the floor of the box.

Thomas took it from her. "It's a pellet. He must have loaded the pistol with shot."

"How did he manage to fire twice?" Lord Malvin asked.

Thomas shrugged. "Either he had two pistols, or a pepperbox pistol with several barrels. They are rare, but one sees them occasionally. I imagine people were struggling with him as he fired the second shot, which is why it went wide."

"You were so fast, Thomas," Arabella said admiringly. "I had barely registered the shot when you pulled us back." She rubbed her elbow as she spoke.

"Are you hurt?" he asked sharply.

"It's nothing. I knocked my funny-bone. You know how painful it is, but it's almost gone."

"Let me see." Without thinking, he felt for the little groove in her elbow and began to rub it gently to ease the sting. His big hand circled her arm—he could feel its warmth beneath the soft kid of her long glove. She smelled of flowers and a subtle spice. How fine her skin was. She stood quietly, letting him help her. Did he imagine it or had her breathing quickened? Or was it his breath that came faster? He tried to slow it, to ignore the tightening in his groin and his growing need to take her in his arms.

"It looks as if they will resume shortly," said Mrs Malvin, who had been watching the efforts to restore order in the pit and on the stage.

Thomas looked up. Arabella was a little flushed and there was a sweet smile on her lips.

"Is that better?"

"Very much. Thank you, Thomas. You are always coming to my aid."

"It's nothing."

He wished he could return her smile. The best he could offer was an anguished rictus. But she was neither repulsed nor morbidly fascinated by his destroyed features. To her, he was simply Thomas, he realised gratefully.

"You take my place, Thomas," Lady Malvin said. "Such an upset! I shall be more comfortable here with Malvin. Is my turban straight?" she added to her husband.

He smiled at her and adjusted her headdress a little. "You'll do, my love."

The actors of the interrupted scene returned to the stage. Miss Boyce received a thunderous ovation when she reappeared in a new headdress.

A stentorian voice called. "Three cheers for a lady with pluck! Hip, Hip!"

The roared response threatened to bring down the roof and the actress came forward and curtsied deeply. "Thank you, my friends, thank you."

She assumed the attitude she had taken when the shot was fired and Kean, who had waited quietly to one side, approached her.

I swear, bright saint, I am not what I was.
Those eyes have turned my stubborn heart to woman:
Thy goodness makes me soft in penitence.
And my harsh thoughts are turned to peace and love.

Once again, he held the excited house in the palm of his hand. At last, Lady Anne and the cortege departed, leaving Gloster to gloat over the progress of his courtship. But it was not long until, the lady won and wed, "she had outlived his liking" and his thoughts turned to another woman. Soon he allowed himself to be persuaded to take the crown. Death followed upon death; among them the young princes and his hapless queen until, finally, an army gathered to oppose him.

When the first ghost appeared on the stage, Arabella caught Thomas's hand and did not let go until Kean/Richard lay dead on Bosworth Field.

She took a long, shuddering breath. "He holds one fast, as in a nightmare. It is impossible to look away and even while you abhor his every action, you must applaud the skill with which it is portrayed."

"Would he impress as much in a less villainous part, do you think?"

"I don't know. I cannot imagine him as Romeo or Orlando, can you?"

"No, but I would certainly try and see him if he were to appear in such a role."

Her ladyship had decided not to remain for *The Two Misers*.

"Too tedious," Arabella had agreed and, although he would happily have sat through the dullest of plays if she were by his side, Thomas had regretfully to be content with escorting her to the carriage. How soon could he call on the Malvins again, he wondered, raising a hand in farewell as their carriage drew away.

Chapter Thirteen

Caro handed her friend a sweetmeat glass. "You must try this, Bella. It is Cook's latest idea; coffee and chocolate creams swirled together and sprinkled with crushed macaroons."

The two girls sat on the cushioned window-seat in Caro's sitting-room. There had been no opportunity for a private coze since Lady Lutterworth's ball and they were anxious to pass the intervening week under review.

"Mmm—delicious!" Arabella took another spoonful, letting the flavours of the smooth, rich creams and crisp, nutty macaroons linger on her tongue.

"You were at Drury Lane the other night when shots were fired at Miss Boyce, weren't you? Was it very frightening?" Caro asked.

Arabella shook her head. "It all happened so quickly and Thomas was so fast. We women were in the front row and he—Major Ferraunt I mean—sat behind with Papa. There was a flash below and a loud explosion. Thomas just grabbed Mamma's and my chairs and whisked us backwards while our ears were still ringing. Then he pulled Millie back and sort of surged forward and crouched to look over the parapet. He called to us to stay back and down and there was another explosion—the madman managed to fire again while people were struggling with him. He had loaded the pistol with shot—we found a pellet on the floor of our box. Thomas wouldn't allow us to come forward until the villain was in handcuffs. Even then, he resisted those holding him but they finally succeeded in dragging him out. The pit was in an uproar, with benches overturned and all the men crowding around."

"Was Miss Boyce really wounded?"

"In the ear, it looked like. She was fortunate it was no worse."

"I heard someone say it was because the assassin disapproved of her affair with Byron."

"I doubt that, somehow. If it's true, all Byron's lights-o'-love must be in a pother. And why now? He has left the country—for good, they say."

"What?"

"Hadn't you heard? Millie had it from her sister who knows his wife's family. They say he treated her abominably. He was forced to sign a deed of separation on the twenty-first and left a few days later."

"Good heavens! He had to fall from favour sooner or later, I suppose. But tell me, how long have you been on such familiar terms with Major Ferraunt?"

Arabella felt her face grow warm but did her best to reply with a matter-of-fact, "Since I was a child. Even my mother calls him Thomas in private."

"Arabella Malvin, I vow you are blushing. Methinks he is more than a childhood friend." Caro wiggled herself more comfortably into the corner of the seat. "Admit it now."

"I cannot deny that I like him and feel very—comfortable with him."

Caroline raised a mocking eyebrow. "Comfortable? Like with Francis?"

Arabella bit her lip as she remembered Thomas's caressing touch as he gently eased the little sting on her elbow, how she had looked down at his head and wanted more than anything to stroke his dark hair. She had never felt such a compulsion for Francis—or any other man if it came to that.

"I'm right," Caro said triumphantly. "But, Bella, will your parents accept the rector's son?"

"Caro! There is no talk of that—but, since you ask, I do not see why they should object. Papa knows Dr Ferraunt since his Oxford days and Thomas is an officer and a gentleman."

"But money, my pet, money! Has he anything more than his pay?"

"How should I know? I am very sure he is not a fortune-hunter. If it comes to that, how can we know how any gentleman is fixed, financially, I mean? Many a nobleman or nobleman's son lives on the banks of the River Tick."

"And some even marry a future queen," Caro said wickedly. "Did you hear that Princess Charlotte giggled when Leopold vowed to endow her with all his worldly goods? All he has is the fifty thousand pounds per annum voted to him by our Parliament."

"Unfortunately, we cannot expect Parliament to do the same for our husbands. We must rely on our fathers to make the proper enquiries and settlements for us."

"And on our brothers, who might know if a gentleman is given to excessive gambling or other vices."

"When I came out, Mamma made me promise that I would never elope or marry against her and Papa's wishes. They would never make a match for me, or force me into a marriage, no matter how advantageous it might appear, she said, nor would they oppose one unreasonably. I should know that their only aim would be to ensure my future happiness. 'The rest of your life is a very long time to be miserable,' she said, and that she had seen in her own parents how unhappy wedlock could be, especially for a woman."

"That sounds quite promising. They do not object to your being in the major's company?"

"No. But it is too soon for anything more, Caro. I would like to know him better, I admit. The thing is, he is not acquainted with so many people here in town and as a result does not receive very many invitations. And it would look too pointed if we were to introduce him into society."

"I suppose it would. Hmm. If you can arrange for me to meet him, I'll suggest he call on Mamma. Then she can invite him to her archery fête."

Arabella smiled at her friend. "Thank you, I knew I might rely on you. But, Caro, you won't say anything, will you?"

Caro licked her spoon. "Of course not, other than we should be kind to returning officers—and one can never have too many single gentlemen at a party, both of which are quite true. Perhaps Lady Tamm would send him a card for her ball. Lord Tamm was much attached to Arthur, after all, and he and the major were good friends."

"Perhaps. He escorted me to their box the other evening. I'll suggest it to Lallie. In the meantime, there are always the mornings on Rotten Row."

"Why? Does he ride there?"

"He bought three new horses in Ireland and they must be exercised."

"Who bought new horses?" Francis enquired as he came into the room. He sauntered over to inspect the array of sweetmeats and selected a trifle. "Cook should use more brandy," he remarked after the first mouthful, then dropped into a chair, swinging his legs over the arm. "What horses?"

"Major Ferraunt's. He went to Ireland to purchase remounts."

"Where?"

"To Ireland," Arabella repeated patiently.

He sighed gustily. "I hadn't thought you so dense, Bella. Where in Ireland?"

"Oh. County Wicklow, I think. He mentioned a Sir John Malcolm."

"Of Colduff? His horses are very sound."

"If you want to see them, you may ride with me early on Monday morning," Caro said sweetly. "Is Matthew back, Bella, or should we call for you?"

"He should be home this evening. If not, or it doesn't suit him, I'll send you a note tomorrow."

She would wear her new riding-habit, Arabella decided on Monday morning. "You don't think the double ruff is too much?" she asked her maid later, as she considered the effect in the long mirror.

"No, Miss, not at all. The cream lace lightens the mulberry of the habit, especially with the paler pink handkerchief inside it. "Here, try the hat."

Horton picked up the small-brimmed, high-crowned hat of pleated mulberry silk and set it on her mistress's head. "It still needs something," she muttered and went to a drawer, returning with a small plume of curling, pale pink feathers which she deftly fixed to the side of the hat with a little pearl brooch.

"That's perfect, Horton."

A little bubble of anticipation rose within her as she drew on her gloves, took the long riding switch and hurried down the stairs. A strange groom waited in front of the house with Grey Lady.

"Where is Bart?" Arabella asked.

"He broke his leg, Miss," Matthew's groom volunteered. "This is Jeb Marsden, who'll be working for us until Bart's leg is mended."

She nodded to the stocky young man. "Good morning, Jeb. What happened to Bart, Dick?"

"He fell at the farrier's on Friday, Miss. Jeb was helping there. He brought our horses back and told us about Bart's mishap."

"Was the bonesetter fetched?"

"Yes, Miss."

"Good. I'll come and see how Bart does later this morning."

"There's no need, Miss. He went back to the Abbey with the cart that brought up the vegetables and such on Saturday. Mrs Belshaw thought he would do better there."

"I suppose he will," Arabella said, although she was doubtful about the effects of the jolting journey on a broken leg.

"Come, Sis. We don't want to keep the horses standing any longer." Matthew stooped and cupped his hands. She placed her foot in them and he threw her into the saddle, then helped her find the stirrup. She settled herself and took the reins from Jeb.

"Ready?" Matthew asked and at her nod headed for the Park.

London was different in the early morning. Everyone was more purposeful. Later, in the fashionable lounges of Mayfair and the Park, it would be all about seeing and being seen. A little dog darted towards them and Arabella flicked at it with her switch to keep it away from the sharp hooves.

The sun shone but a brisk breeze lent an invigorating crispness to the air. The Row was almost empty at this hour. Grooms exercising their charges had left and the *ton* had not yet made an appearance. Arabella sighed with happiness and guided Grey Lady into a smooth canter. A tall man turned at the far end of the Row and rode swiftly towards them. He sat as easily in the saddle as Arthur had; his left hand held the reins, leaving his sword arm free. He raised his hand to shade his eyes from the morning sun behind her and immediately slowed down. As he drew near, he removed his hat.

"Good morning, Arabella. Good morning, Matthew. How did you find Oxford?"

"Unchanged—but Julian and I felt we had got older."

"Or the students had got younger?"

"That, too." He eyed the chestnut gelding. "Is this one of your Irish purchases?"

"'Morning." Francis Nugent and Caro trotted up.

To Arabella's amused frustration, the gentlemen immediately became immersed in horse-talk. She caught Caro's eye and nodded ahead. "Shall we?"

Caro grinned and skirted the cluster of men to move forward beside Arabella. She touched her heel to her horse's side and raced down the broad ride and back up the other side. Arabella followed more slowly.

"We should have expected that, I suppose," Caro said when they pulled up again at the start of the row. She patted her mare's neck. "Good girl. That shook the fidgets out!"

"Yours or hers?"

"Both. Let's go again."

"A little slower, perhaps." Arabella suggested. "Grey Lady is no longer so keen to gallop."

When they came abreast of the gentlemen, Thomas wheeled his horse to fall in beside her.

"Good morning, Thomas. He is a handsome fellow. What have you called him?"

"Samson."

"Why?"

He shrugged helplessly. "I don't know. He looks like a Samson, I suppose. Why do you smile?"

"I was wondering would you name your children the same way. I could see you cradling a new-born infant, muttering names to yourself—Gideon, no; Gerard, no; Jeremiah—not Jeremiah."

"I have never thought of it," he said with his lop-sided smile. "But I imagine the child's mother would have something to say too, don't you?"

"I'm sure she would," she answered hastily, dazzled by a new image of herself propped up against her pillows, laughing and shaking her head at his suggestions. That was what she wanted in marriage, she realised suddenly, love and laughter and a bond that was much more than two signatures on the marriage register.

"Arabella?"

His deep voice brought her back to herself. He was looking at her intently, a new ardour in his eyes. Had he divined her thoughts? Her hands tightened on the reins and Grey Lady shifted restlessly.

She smiled at him and moved into a walk and then an easy canter. "What do you look for in a horse?"

"Stamina—endurance. It must be—biddable is not quite the right world—amenable to army life, not too temperamental but able to cope with—"

"Alarums and excursions?"

"And languor and tedium as well as long route marches with only a makeshift stable at the end, and drill and parades."

"In other words, you need the same qualities that you need in a good soldier."

"That's it. How do you find the first Season of the peace?"

"It is a little quiet. It is not yet a year since Waterloo and some families have not come to town—the Harburys, for example, who lost both a son and a son-in-law—while others are abroad. Everyone must make their own decision, of course, but I think it was right for us to come. We had become too engrossed in our mourning, I think."

"Are you able to enjoy your music again?"

"Yes. You helped me that evening—I hadn't spoken about it to anyone else, you see—and afterwards I found that I was able to play and even sing again."

"I'm glad," he said simply.

"Shall I see you at Lady Falconer's ball?" Thomas asked as they completed their turn around the bridle path and started up again. "She is the sister of Captain Malcolm and was kind enough to invite me."

"How came you to know the Lutterworths?" Arabella asked before she could stop herself. It still rankled that he had called there before coming to Malvin House.

He did not seem to find her question impertinent but answered willingly. "Through Lord Franklin, who was Captain Franklin when I knew him. I met him by chance, and he insisted I call to meet his wife. I know her brother too, but not as well."

"He wasn't at the ball, was he?"

"No, he is in France with his regiment. But you haven't answered me about Lady Falconer."

"Yes, we hope to attend. Why?"

"Because I would very much like to waltz with you, Arabella, and I do not want to risk another rebuff by being too tardy."

His deepened voice sent shivers down her spine.

"Oh." A little smile danced on her lips.

"Well?" His eyes challenged her.

"Well what, sir?"

He bowed from the saddle. "May I have the pleasure of waltzing with you at Lady Falconer's ball, Miss Malvin?"

She inclined her head graciously. "You may have the first waltz, Major."

"Thank you. And a quadrille later?" he added hopefully. "Or, better still, the supper dance?"

She looked at him. Did he know that to ask a lady to stand up with him twice at the same ball would be construed as a clear declaration of interest? She could hardly ask him. If he did it only once, it might be ascribed to his not knowing so many ladies. And otherwise—"You have to make hay while the sun shines," she had once overheard a maid say to another when they were discussing their sweethearts. She would do the same.

"The supper dance," she decided.

He shifted the reins to his right hand for a moment and reached over to touch hers. "Thank you."

"We'll take Bella home, Ferraunt, and I'll ride on with you to see your other purchases," Matthew announced.

For the first time Arabella wished Malvin House was further away from the Park. They reached it all too soon. Thomas immediately dismounted, tossed his reins to Matthew and came to stand beside Grey Lady. She brought her leg over the pommel and slipped her foot from the stirrup, then she felt his strong hands at her waist. She remembered the ease with which he had drawn her from the stream and afterwards carried her up the stairs. Now he lifted her as if she were a feather and set her on her feet as if she were the most precious of objects. He released her reluctantly—or was she reluctant to lose his touch?

"Thank you, Thomas," she said softly.

"Thank you for the pleasure of your company," he replied with that little lift at the corner of his mouth that had become so intimate and so treasured.

The new groom—Jeb?—came up from the area to take Grey Lady's reins and Thomas swung himself back into the saddle. Arabella paused at the open front door and looked back. He touched his hand to his hat in salute and she went into the house. If only the rest of the day would be as happy, but tonight was Lady Rickersby's 'little dinner'.

Chapter Fourteen

To Arabella's dismay, Lady Rickersby had realised that there was no important party planned for Monday and swiftly sent out her cards.

"Must I go," she had asked her mother.

"I think you must; in fact, I have accepted for all of us."

"Will Lord Henry be there?"

"Yes. Lady Rickersby called earlier and assured me that he would do nothing to make you feel uncomfortable. He will not be your dinner partner. There will be dancing, but no waltzes, and if you will but dance one quadrille with him, all may be forgotten."

Arabella stared at her. "And he has agreed to this?"

"So her ladyship gave me to understand."

"But why? They do not secretly think we might still make a match of it?"

"No, no. There is nothing like that. It will show the world that there is no dissension between our families and give that foolish young man the opportunity to redeem himself. It would be an unforgivable slight to refuse, Arabella. You must go."

The Malvin carriages had to wait their turn to pull up at the portico of Rickersby House. Not so small a dinner, then.

"We shan't be the first, at least," Arabella said.

"Are you nervous, Puss?" her father asked.

"Yes. I feel everyone will be watching Lord Henry and me."

"There may be a little interest at first, but if you treat him the same way as you do the other gentlemen, it will soon pass off," her mother said firmly. "Here we are."

Matthew jumped down and assisted first his mother, then his sister to alight.

"Pluck up, Sis," he hissed as they followed their parents to the shallow steps. "You don't want him to think you're afraid to face him, do you? Have a little pride!"

Her back stiffened and her head went up.

"That's better—don't glare at me; a gracious smile is what you want. Pretend you're Mamma squashing a beetle—an upstart, I mean."

This made her smile and he nodded approvingly. "That's the barber. Here we go."

They made their way up the grand staircase to the large drawing-room where Lord and Lady Rickersby awaited their guests. They did not offer Arabella anything more than the conventional greeting, but Rickersby welcomed Julian warmly, commenting on their Oxford days together and saying they must meet at Brooks's while they were all in town.

"There are the Nearys," Matthew muttered and headed towards them.

Arabella glanced up at him. There was an expectant, joyful look on his face that she had never seen before. Was he seriously interested in Miss Neary? She was so busy pondering this question that she failed to notice Lord Henry until he stood before them.

"Good evening, Miss Malvin, Mr Malvin," he said with a slight bow. His stance was even more rigid than usual and there was a faint flush along his cheekbones.

She felt a rush of sympathy. He too must feel all eyes upon him. She offered a polite smile.

"Good evening, Lord Henry. Did you enjoy the play the other evening?"

"I did. You were not too shocked by the drama in the pit, I hope?"

"The drama in the pit? Oh, you mean the attack on Miss Boyce? It was all over so fast, that there was no time to be shocked. I thought the way she and Mr Kean resumed their performance as if nothing had happened most impressive."

"Why, what happened?" Matthew asked. "You never said anything about an attack."

Others turned to listen and by the time Arabella and Lord Henry had described the events, any awkwardness had passed. The little group separated; she and Matthew to continue on to the Nearys, while Lord Henry went to talk to Lord Marfield.

"Well done," Matthew said under his breath.

This was the dullest of parties, Arabella thought as she caught snatches of the stilted conversations along the huge dinner table. Mr Neary, who had taken her in, was carving the pair of roast fowl that sat on a platter in front of him and Lord Marfield on her other side was very properly talking to his own lady.

"A wing, Miss Malvin?" Mr Neary enquired, laying the knife so that her portion would include a generous slice of the breast.

"Thank you, Mr Neary," she murmured, grateful that someone had taught him properly. A wing was the only part of the bird that a young lady might request with propriety, but there was very little meat on it. She helped herself to bread sauce and buttered carrots. That would do. She had already taken soup and a filet of sole with delicate green peas.

"Pray excuse me, Miss Malvin."

She sat back as Lord Marfield passed a plate with the request for a wing.

"Is there anything I might send down to you, Miss Malvin?" he enquired courteously. "Some asparagus, perhaps?"

She took a couple of spears out of politeness. "Thank you, Lord Marfield. After the long winter, it is a treat to have spring vegetables again."

His task completed, Mr Neary filled his own plate.

"You do that very neatly," Arabella complimented him.

"Oh, chickens and ducks are easy enough. A haunch of mutton is worse and, worst of all, a cod's head. Usually some old lady requests some and she is most particular about what she wants. 'A little of the sound and some of the palate, if you please, Mr Neary'," he quoted in mincing tones. "Ugh!"

She shuddered. "I promise faithfully I shall never make such a request of you or of any gentleman. I think it is the most revolting thing imaginable."

"Precisely. And you are left staring at the skull and gaping jaws until the end of the course. I have never understood why we do not have servants carve and serve the joints from a sideboard, but it remains a gentleman's duty."

"Perhaps it is to show that he is able to provide for his family."

"Do you know, Miss Malvin, you could well be right? How else are we to prove ourselves? We 'toil not, neither do we spin'. But when we pick up the carving knife, we are men! We feed others and they are dependent upon our largesse." His eyes danced as he made this outrageous pronouncement.

She laughed. "I see this discovery is a great comfort to you, sir. I need have no qualms about asking you to crack walnuts for me later."

"Excellent. And will you take wine with me now?"

"With pleasure."

"Will you play for us, Miss Malvin?"

Arabella was surprised to be singled out. There were other young ladies present, Lady Juliet Martyn, for example, whom she would have expected to be invited to perform first. But she could not refuse. As she went to the pianoforte, she remembered the evening at the Abbey when Thomas had been so kind. Smiling to herself, she began the same Mozart sonata she had played then. She had never played it so well—it seemed to her that she was inside the music. It transported her to Thomas—she could see his dear, crooked little smile, feel the clasp of his hand, glimpse his intense gaze. If it didn't rain, she would see him again tomorrow morning.

When she finished there was a moment's silence and then genuine applause. Someone called, "Encore!" but she shook her head and rose to join Millie on the sofa where she sat and listened dreamily to the rest of the performers.

When the dancing started, Mr Neary came at once to claim her hand. To her relief, Lord Henry was not in the same set, but she found herself dancing opposite him in the next one. In one figure, the opposite lady and gentleman danced more with each other than with their own partners, but she might as well have been dancing with an automaton. His steps were as perfect as ever, but that sense of accord with the music that was the mark of the true dancer was missing. As the evening wore on, she saw that he invited the single young ladies, all peers' daughters, to stand up with him in strict order of rank. Would he go so far as to take the two viscounts' daughters according to their fathers' precedence? As Papa was the more junior, this would place her last but one, ahead of Miss Neary, daughter of a baron. Her suspicion proved correct. His lordship approached her before the fifth quadrille.

"May I have the pleasure, Miss Malvin?"

"You may, Lord Henry." She placed her fingertips on his arm and let him lead her to the nearest set.

"You played charmingly earlier."

"Thank you."

"What was the piece?"

"A sonata by Mozart. It is one of my favourites."

"I recall my grandmother telling me how she heard him play at court—a young prodigy of seven or eight, a most charming child. He had already started composing, she said."

"How wonderful!"

The opening bars of the dance brought their conversation to a close, but everyone could see that Lord Henry Danlow and Miss Malvin were again in perfect charity with one another. Their dance passed off without incident and Lady Rickersby announced that they would finish, according to tradition, with Sir Roger de Coverley. His features as impassive as they had been all evening, Lord Henry led Miss Neary to the top of the set while Arabella and Lord Marfield found places lower down. After two hours of more demanding quadrilles, the old-fashioned dance proved a welcome respite. A glass of negus to fortify them against the night air and they could make their farewells.

"That wasn't so bad," Arabella said as soon as they were in the privacy of their carriage.

"You behaved just as you ought," her mother said approvingly.

"What should I do if he asks me to stand up with him elsewhere?"

"I doubt if he will. Lady Rickersby promised me he would not embarrass you in any way."

Henry was the last to leave his brother's house.

"I hope that has done the trick," his sister-in-law said after he mumbled a few polite words about 'a delightful evening'. "Mrs Drummond-Burrell has promised to send you vouchers for Almack's. She says she is sure she can convince Lady Jersey that the whole affair was blown up out of all proportion. Now mind you do not let us down, Henry. We may not be able to retrieve another such situation and you need to marry well. Rickersby cannot continue to make you such a generous allowance."

He bit back a stinging retort. He must see about obtaining some sort of office, a sinecure that would make him less dependent on his brother, but until then he could not afford to alienate him—or his shrew of a wife.

A brief bow, a muttered 'good night' and he was free, but still burned with angry humiliation. Should he go to Watier's, see if his luck still held? Later, perhaps. He called a hackney and gave the Jehu an address in Covent Garden. The abbess there could provide just what he wanted.

Chapter Fifteen

"You look ravishing, Miss Malvin."

"Thank you, Mr Neary."

Arabella could not stop smiling. Thomas was already here. His eyes had immediately sought hers across Lady Falconer's ballroom. 'Later,' they promised.

It was delicious to wait for the first waltz, to hug her secret anticipation to her. She had never danced as lightly. Her happiness was infectious, causing a smiling exhilaration to ripple through the ballroom. 'Tonight,' it seemed to whisper as couples exchanged laughing glances and mute signals. It reached the musicians, lending a sensuous tone to their playing, adding subtle, coaxing rallentandos where time was suspended, where everything was possible.

"Miss Malvin."

Her breath caught and all she could say was, "Major Ferraunt." But it seemed to be enough.

There was a tender gleam in his eyes. "Shall we?"

She linked her arm with his, rested her hand on his scarlet sleeve, and let him lead her onto the floor. For the next twenty minutes they would be alone—or alone as one could be in a crowded ballroom. He angled his body towards hers, creating a little intimate space among the hubbub.

"Every time I see you, you are more beautiful."

She felt herself blush. "Thank you, Thomas."

"How did you spend your day? You did not ride this morning."

"No. Matthew was not free. I went shopping with my sister-in-law before breakfast, then practised my music. Afterwards I visited Lady Tamm and played with her baby. My mother collected me and we drove in the Park. We dined at home and then came here. And you?"

"After exercising the horses, I had breakfast and read *The Times*. You have no idea what a pleasure it is to have today's newspaper today and not several weeks later. Afterwards I looked in at Tattersall's."

"Tattersalls? Have you decided to sell one of the Irish horses?"

"No. I require a new saddle and don't know who the best saddlers are. I thought I was bound to get a recommendation or two there."

She laughed at his dry tone. "I take it you received more than one or two?"

His mouth twitched. "It was the topic of the day, but they were so occupied discussing it with each other that in the end I gave up and left them to it. I'll have a word with Franklin—he will have a better idea of my requirements."

The dance floor was now full of couples and the musicians began the introduction to the waltz. She shivered inwardly when his arm came around her shoulders and it seemed almost unbearably intimate and yet so right when she mirrored his gesture. Although he was several inches taller, she did not feel awkward or unbalanced in his arms. His embrace was not impersonal; she knew who held her, whose light clasp guided her through the different attitudes. He smelt fresh, with an underlying spice and hint of distant forests, perhaps from the lotion he used to tame the dark curls which fell onto his forehead and temples, blending into his side-whiskers.

He gripped her waist and, smiling, she clasped her hands behind her back, yielding full control to him. She generally did not adopt this pose because of the way it thrust her breasts forward, but his admiring look did not make her feel uncomfortable.

“You dance excellently, but I knew that.”

“So do you.”

He turned so they were back to back and side to side. Despite their difference in height, she did not have had to stretch uncomfortably—he seemed to accommodate himself to her in the most unobtrusive way. Her heart beat faster when he brought her back to face him and looked into her eyes. She felt a new, deeper smile tremble on her lips. His gaze became even more intent and he held her there for an additional beat before turning her quickly under his arm. She spun away from him but he twirled her back and caught her neatly.

“Is that a French step?”

“I call it the Arabella Step. One of the advantages of the waltz is that one can be a little creative without upsetting a whole set.”

“You are full of surprises, Thomas.”

A sound that was almost a laugh escaped him. “Follow my lead,” he ordered, raising their joined hands as high as possible and holding them together between them. “First I turn under, then you. Don’t let go!”

She gasped and instinctively rose on tiptoe to make it easier for him to complete a full turn, then he swiftly urged her to do the same, repeating the manoeuvre another three times. She was laughing when she faced him at the end.

"What an interesting variation."

He placed his hands on her waist again and this time she clasped his shoulders. "It comes from south Germany or Austria, I believe," he told her as they continued to revolve in time to the music. "Both dancers must be confident or they'll botch it sadly."

"I can imagine."

As the musicians played the closing bars, he lifted her hands from his shoulders, retaining only the right one which he raised briefly to his lips before spinning her into a final pirouette. As the last note faded, she sank into a curtsey while he bowed.

"Now that is the French way of doing it," he said blandly.

"How strange that I never heard of it before."

"It is the very latest in Paris," he assured her. "Would you like a glass of champagne?"

The house Lady Falconer had taken for the Season was one of Arabella's favourites among those regularly leased by *ton* families. Its suite of rooms was admirably designed and included various alcoves and corners where a couple might have a private conversation yet remain in view of the company. Best of all was the extensive terrace where lamps created pools of light and corners of mysterious shade. Lady Falconer had had the doors to it set wide and a few couples had already strolled out to enjoy the mild air.

"Let's go out," Arabella said impulsively. "It is such a beautiful evening."

Thomas obligingly veered towards the nearest door and led her into the welcoming shadows. They wandered over to the balustrade and stood with their backs to the ballroom, looking down into the moonlit garden.

"I was beginning to despair of ever having you to myself," he said huskily.

"Did—do you want to?" Her voice shook.

"More than anything in the world."

He removed the glove from his right hand, then gently cupped her cheek before tracing the curve of her eyebrow with one finger. She quivered at his touch.

"Ah, Arabella, I've wanted to do that for so long, and this." He mapped the shape of her lips, exploring the soft, yielding textures. Did he imagine it, or had she brushed a kiss onto his finger, like the caress of a butterfly's wing?

He had to kiss her. Everything in him yearned for the touch of his lips on hers. He tilted her chin up. She did not resist but stood stock-still, her wide eyes fixed on his. Then, at a sudden cascade of laughter from within, she reached up to clasp his wrist.

"You mustn't. Someone will see."

The spell was broken. He lifted his hand and they stood for a moment, his wrist still in her grasp. She nervously moistened her lips. He swallowed, then released her.

They continued to face each other silently.

Inside, the musicians began to tune their instruments. She picked his glove up from the balustrade. "You must not forget this."

"What? Oh, yes. Thank you."

"We must go in. I am engaged for the next dance. And you?"

He shook his head. "I only want to dance with you tonight."

"No!" She gripped his arm. "You must not single me out, Thomas. Please invite other ladies to stand up with you. Promise me!"

"As you wish," he said stiffly, wondering at her vehemence.

"There you are." Young Nugent spoke lightly but his face was serious. "I thought you had forgotten our dance."

Arabella released Thomas's arm. "How could I?" she answered as blithely.

Thomas bowed. "Thank you, Miss Malvin."

"Until later, Major."

Thomas didn't dance the next set, but later stood up with Ruth Halworth for a quadrille. To Arabella's astonishment, he led Lady Jersey out for the second waltz, but then she remembered that her ladyship was known to enjoy dancing and must always know the latest steps. They looked well together, she had to admit, both tall and graceful, and were well-matched for his four-hand turn.

The supper dance was a quadrille and, whether by accident or design—she was inclined to suspect that there was very little 'accident' in Thomas's doings—their set was made up of officers and their ladies who all went into supper together. One, who wore the dark green of the 95th, said on being presented to her, "Miss Malvin? Aren't you Arthur's sister? I had the pleasure of making your acquaintance in Brussels two years ago."

"Yes." To her surprise, it was not overly painful to think of her brother; on the contrary, she could imagine him in just such a light-hearted round.

"He was the best of good fellows, always up for a lark," Captain Hawthorne echoed her thoughts.

"He was." That was how she would remember him.

Thomas returned from the supper table bearing two plates and set one in front of her.

"I hope it is what you like," he murmured in her ear. "I seem to remember hearing something about lobster patties, but I'll go back for some if you wish."

"No, thank you," she replied hastily. A youthful encounter with a platter of lobster patties that Arthur had pilfered and insisted on sharing with her and Matthew had left her with a life-long aversion to them. "I can't believe Arthur told you that."

"He had to explain why he preferred to stand during his lessons the next day."

She laughed. "Poor Arthur. I was so ill that Mamma said I had brought my punishment upon myself as I had to spend the next day in bed with only gruel to eat. This galantine of veal is much more to my taste, I assure you and the dressed cucumbers are excellent."

"All your regiments are presently in France," Captain Hawthorne's partner said. "You must find London very dull after Paris."

The four officers exchanged glances.

"It is different," Captain Malcolm said tactfully. "There we are among strangers but here we are with our families and friends."

And must behave ourselves, Arabella translated mentally, recalling some of Arthur's stories of Madrid. "It must be a relief to speak English," she said aloud, although she had no doubt that English was not necessarily required for some masculine pursuits.

"Oh, one can always make oneself understood," Captain Hawthorne replied, "but what we miss most is the company of charming young English ladies like you."

The other three men murmured agreement and Captain Malcolm raised his glass. "To your bright eyes, ladies."

Arabella would have been as happy to leave the ball after supper, but was forced to remain as she was engaged for all the dances. She did her best to concentrate on her partners and not let her eyes stray to Thomas who was greatly in demand, judging by the number of introductions Lady Falconer made, including one to Lady Westland, a married lady of dubious reputation. Arabella's belly clenched when, as the waltz came to a close, she heard her ladyship's sultry voice purr, "And now, your final flourish, Major."

She didn't want to look but couldn't stop herself. If he kissed that woman's hand, she would claw first her eyes out—and then his! But Thomas brought his partner to a sedate halt.

"I vow, Major, I am dying of thirst," Lady Westland remarked.

"That will never do." He signalled to a passing footman, took a glass from his tray and handed it to her. "Pray excuse me." He bowed briefly and made his escape.

Arabella sighed inwardly with relief and returned her attention to Mr Naughton.

"A glass of champagne, Miss Malvin?"

"No, thank you, sir. I wish to speak to Lady Tamm before she leaves."

"Then permit me to take you to her."

She and Thomas met as opposite couples in the final set, and she had the satisfaction of dancing again with him, even if only for a short time. After he had returned his partner to her mother, he joined the Malvin ladies in the upper hall at the top of the grand staircase.

"Your new steps were all the rage, Major," Arabella said teasingly. "Everyone wanted to dance "Major Ferraunt's Fancy". You were quite the beau of the ball; put all the others in the shade."

His lips twitched. "Minx! I will have you know that I do not consider myself either a beau or a caper-merchant."

"No?" she asked with a laughing glance over her shoulder as they descended the stairs.

"No." he said firmly.

In the hall, a harried-looking maid was distributing ladies' wraps.

"I think this is yours, Miss," she said, offering Arabella a cashmere shawl.

With a quiet, "Allow me," Thomas took it from the girl and laid it gently around Arabella's shoulders. "Will you be warm enough?" he asked frowning.

Men were all the same, she thought, as she said, "Yes."

"Mrs Malvin's carriage," a footman bawled.

She took Thomas's arm as they crossed the pavement.

He looked down and covered her hand with his. "Thank you again for my dances. Shall I see you in the morning?"

"If I can persuade Matthew to get up so early." They had reached the carriage. "Good night, Thomas."

His fingers gripped hers as he handed her in. "Good night, Arabella."

He closed the door and waited on the pavement until they had driven off, then she saw him turn and stride down the street. Was he going home, or to one of those masculine haunts ladies were supposed to know nothing of?

Chapter Sixteen

Mrs Platts believed in giving 'her officers' a good breakfast. This morning, in addition to potted salmon and fresh toast, she had provided a dish she called 'bacon fraise' which proved to be a thick pancake studded with cubes of crisp bacon. It was very tasty, Thomas found, especially when accompanied by pickled cucumbers.

He had been doubly fortunate in finding these rooms. From his seat at the square table that stood between two windows he looked with satisfaction at the low, deep armchairs at the hearth and the capacious bureau bookcase against one wall. Everything was tidy, down to the squared stack of correspondence that awaited his attention and the two swords, a shako and a dress bicorne neatly arranged on a side-table. The bedroom was just as neat and well-furnished and Sergeant Platts and his wife were assiduous in attending to his comfort.

He finished *The Times* and folded it, pushed his coffee cup aside and started to go through the little pile of letters, notes and cards. Mrs Forbes requested the pleasure of his company at an evening of music—he frowned, then remembered she was Lady Malvin's sister, Henrietta Tamrisk who had lived at the Abbey for some years before her marriage. Lady Nugent's archery fête, Lady Tamm's ball.

Lady Westland—he had no recollection of her—invited him to a little supper—now he remembered—an opulent matron with dark curls and a come-hither eye—a note from Captain Malcolm about a prize-fight—another from Captain Hawthorne about a cockfight—a letter from his father. He broke the seal and scanned it quickly.

His parents were well, his father wrote. *To my astonishment I have received a letter from my cousin Hawebury who requests that I pay him a visit at my earliest convenience. His health does not permit him to travel, he writes, and he would like to see me before the End comes. I am sure he would not be averse to receiving you too and I own I should welcome your company on the journey. My old friend Morton has agreed to lend me his curate so we could leave next week if it suited you. It is true that my cousin and I have not had much contact in recent years*—decades, Thomas thought—*but I do not like to ignore such a wish. Pray advise me by return when I may expect you.*

What the devil? And now, of all times, when he had so many other things on his mind. Most important of all was his courtship of Arabella. What would she think if he suddenly disappeared? But he did not like to disoblige his father. He had been a poor sort of son, after all, even if his prolonged absence from England had been in the service of his country. He put the letter to one side, to be answered in time for this evening's mail. Perhaps he might be able to combine the visit to Ferraunt Court with one to Cheltenham. He really should see his great-uncle's man of business—letters were not enough. And he had promised his mother to accompany them on a little holiday.

What was left? A note from Hoby begging to inform him that his new boots were ready for collection, a letter from Mr Greenwood requesting him to call on Friday morning if this suited him. The last one was addressed in a flowing, feminine hand. He had just broken the elaborate seal when there was a tap on his door.

"Enter."

His landlady handed him a card. "A gentleman to see you, Major."

Francis Nugent. "Send him up, Mrs Platts, if you please."

"Yes, Major. Will you want more ale or coffee?"

"Bring up both, please."

"Very good, Major." She quickly piled the breakfast dishes onto a tray and whisked them out of the room.

"Come in, Nugent."

"Good day, Ferraunt." Mr Nugent surveyed the airy room. "Comfortable place you have here; you're well cared for, by the looks of it."

"I am, indeed. Thank you, Mrs Platts," Thomas said when his landlady returned with a laden tray. "We'll look after ourselves. Coffee or ale, Nugent, or would you prefer a glass of Madeira?"

"Ale, please." Mr Nugent removed his gloves and laid them on the side-table with his hat and cane.

"Sit down and tell me what I may do for you."

"Do for me? Why nothing," his guest protested, collapsing elegantly into an armchair. "I was passing and thought I'd pop in."

"Deuced civil of you." Thomas handed him a foaming tankard and poured himself more coffee, then took the seat opposite.

"How do you find it being back in England? It must be very different to what you are used to."

"London is different to Paris, I own," Thomas replied without betraying even a glimmer of his amusement at this original question, "but not so very much after all. And I am accustomed to finding my feet in a new society."

"I daresay. You've certainly got your foot in the door here quickly enough."

Thomas raised an eyebrow. "What precisely do you mean by that?"

"Nothing, nothing at all. Dashed good ale, this; of course you're next door to The King's Arms, you lucky devil! If I could find some rooms as snug as these, I swear I'd take them. I'll be mouldering in Nugent House long enough."

"As the only son, your path is set from the cradle, is it not? Do you find it onerous?"

"Not precisely onerous, but—it constricts one, I suppose. And you know, too, that there is only one way you can succeed to the title. On the one hand you want your father to live for ever while on the other—" he broke off.

"You do not wish to stand eternally in the wings," Thomas suggested.

"Oh, it's not quite as bad as that. There is a lot to learn and we have agreed that I shall take over the running of the estate when I am thirty."

"So you still have some years to enjoy your freedom. Do you smoke, Nugent?"

"I blow a cloud from time to time, but have never tried one of those."

Thomas held out his cheroot case invitingly. "I got to like them in Spain. They are more convenient than a pipe."

"Thank you."

Thomas handed a burning spill to his guest and put a small plate at his elbow. "Mrs Platts does not object to the smell, but she will not tolerate ash on her carpet."

"Fair enough, I suppose," Mr Nugent said, with the look of a man who had never given any thought to the wishes of an inferior, let alone a servant. He followed Thomas's example in lighting the cheroot, turning it so that the tobacco caught evenly, and inhaled cautiously. "Not bad, not bad at all."

"How long do you generally stay in town?" Thomas asked.

The other shrugged. "We shan't take the knocker off the door until Parliament rises, which can be as late as the end of July, but that don't mean I'm here all the time. There's Ascot, for instance, and if I get word of a mill somewhere, I'll be off at once. Are you one of the Fancy, Ferraunt?"

"The what?"

Mr Nugent smiled pityingly. "That you need ask, answers the question. I mean an amateur of pugilism."

"No," Thomas said shortly.

"Tell me, what do you fellows do in the army now that the war is over?"

"Apart from lolling around, paring our fingernails, you mean?"

Mr Nugent reddened. "There are no more battles to be fought."

"Very true, but you and your men must be ready at all times. It is too late to start drilling when war breaks out."

"Of course. When are you expected back at your regiment?"

"Sometime next month."

Nugent drew on the little cigar and exhaled slowly. "Damn it, this is deuced awkward. It's none of my business, but I can't bear to see her hurt."

"See who hurt?"

"Miss Malvin."

Thomas sprang to his feet. "Arabella! What happened? Who has hurt her?"

"I'm afraid you will."

"How dare you, sir!"

Mr Nugent held up a pacifying hand. "I'm sure it is unintentional."

"And that would make it all right and tight?" Thomas asked sarcastically. "Are you accusing me of trifling with her affections? You impertinent pup!"

Nugent jumped up to face him. "Calm down, Ferraunt. I'm only thinking of her, dash it! She is getting too fond of you; any fool can see that. Malvin won't agree to her following the drum and what sort of life would she have here, while you are soldiering abroad? You military men never think of that but let me tell you it's a damn, lonely existence for a woman left to fend for herself, especially when she's neither maiden, wife nor widow. I saw it with my own cousin. It's no wonder some of them kick over the traces—not that Arabella would, of course."

He looked so earnest that Thomas's rage abated. He refrained from retorting that if he married Arabella, he and not her father would decide whether or not she accompanied him and demanded, "What the devil has it to do with you? You are neither her father nor her brother."

"I might as well be her brother. I've known her all my life. She turned to me when that cur Danlow started singling her out."

Thomas raised his eyebrows. He had suspected from the beginning there had been something between Arabella and Danlow that made her nervous of him. "Singling her out? In what way?"

"He made a damn nuisance of himself, dancing only with her. People were beginning to talk."

Thomas poured himself some ale. He replenished Nugent's tankard and waved him back to his chair. "Tell me the whole story."

Nugent shrugged. "He'd come to a ball and dance only with her and always the first waltz, even turned up at Almack's to do so. What's the harm in that, you might ask, but it was remarked upon. You have no idea how the *ton* talk, Ferraunt. People started coupling their names and other men did not challenge the arrangement. I know I assumed she had agreed to it, but she hadn't. It got deuced awkward for her. So she asked me to dance the first waltz with her one evening—to show his lordship he did not have a claim on it or on her. He took snuff when she told him she was already engaged—by that time he behaved as if it was his by right. He looked her up and down saying that he saw he was mistaken and turned on his heel and stalked out. It caused quite a bit of talk."

Thomas smiled involuntarily. So that was why she had insisted he dance with other ladies. She had not been trying to hint him away or suggest his attentions were not welcome.

"Fortunately, the matrons supported Bella," Mr Nugent continued, "but it could as easily have gone the other way. Danlow is generally reckoned to be a good catch and they might have said she was overly particular or had led him on. But, you see, if she is now associated with you, and you return to France before the Season is over, people might start calling her a flirt or even say she got a taste of her own medicine when you left her high and dry."

"Miss Malvin has nothing to fear from me," Thomas said firmly. That was as far as he was prepared to go to alleviate Nugent's concern.

"I apologise if I seemed to imply that she did." Mr Nugent's stiff tone echoed his own. "It's just that I'm fond of her, you know."

More than fond, Thomas thought, observing the miserable face opposite him. Would his guest be happy to know that rather than warning Thomas off, this visit had served to fix his resolve to propose as soon as possible? Hardly, but there was no need to rub salt in the wound.

"Yes, of course," he said hastily. "You mentioned boxing—do you frequent Gentleman Jackson's Saloon?"

Having sung the praises of the Gentleman, Mr Nugent moved to a blow by blow account of the best mills he had witnessed, letting his cheroot burn out on the little plate while he demonstrated how, "Haydon then planted a desperate right-handed hit upon Smith's upper works that made a dice-box of his swallow. Smith's claret flowed freely but he was full of game and put in a most severe blow on Haydon's jaw, flooring him."

Thomas listened, mildly entertained but waiting for the moment when he could send his uninvited guest on his way. A sharp rat-tat of the door-knocker jerked him upright. He sprang up when it was followed by agitated voices and erratic steps on the stairs and had the door open by the time Matthew Malvin appeared, escorted by Thomas's landlady who retained a steadying hand under his elbow. He was paste-white and swayed on his feet.

"Thank you, Mrs Platts. I'll take him," Thomas said, steering him to a chair.

"Matt! You can't cast up your accounts here," Nugent exclaimed when Matthew swallowed vigorously.

"He's not jug-bitten," Thomas said, frowning. He had got a whiff of vomit but there was no smell of alcohol. "I think he's had a shock. The brandy decanter is over there, Nugent."

Mr Nugent was across the room in a flash, returning to squat and hold a glass to his friend's lips. "Here, Matt. Take it slowly."

Matthew managed to swallow and then took the glass himself. "Thank you. It was the shock. Has me all to pieces. Thank the Lord I remembered your rooms were here, Thomas. I couldn't go home yet."

He sipped again and closed his eyes but shuddered and opened them at once. "I can still see her."

"See her? Who?"

"I was strolling down Poland Street, thinking that it was a damn shame that such a fine building as the Pantheon has been let go to rack and ruin and in Oxford Street, too, when I noticed that the wicket gate in the side entrance was ajar. I thought I'd look in and see what was left after they gutted the place—they even sold the floor-boards of the pit, I'm told. I thought maybe someone was going to renovate it —open it up again."

Matthew's voice grew steadier as he continued his story. "There wasn't much to be seen—nothing, in fact, but some poor unfortunate huddled in a blanket in a corner. I don't know what made me go over." He took a long drink and corrected himself. "Well, I do. Her hair reminded me of Bella's and I thought she is some man's daughter or sister. What are we coming to that she has to sleep in a place like this?" He looked slightly mortified and added defiantly, "What's a yellow boy or two to me, eh?"

"Nothing," Mr Nugent confirmed.

"So I went over and said, 'Excuse me, ma'am. I see you are in sad straits.' But she didn't answer. I was trying to think of some way to say I just wanted to help her and was not looking for a quick screw or any sort of *quid pro quo*, when it occurred to me that she was too still. And then a cursed rat scurried away. I jumped, I may tell you, but she didn't move, although it must have run over her feet." He shuddered again. "So I," he swallowed audibly, "I just put back the covering from her face. Well, I couldn't leave her there, could I?"

"No. No decent man could," Thomas said quietly. "She was dead, I take it?"

Matthew nodded convulsively and drained his glass. "Worse. She had been strangled, Thomas," he whispered. "Her face. I think I'll never forget her face."

"Good God!" Mr Nugent exclaimed and fetched the decanter.

"Wait." Thomas took the coffee pot from the trivet by the fire. He poured some into a cup and added cream and sugar. "Put a little into this. We don't want him foxed."

"Wouldn't it be better for him?"

"Not at this stage, no. What did you do then, Matthew?"

"I sent a ragamuffin to the watch house. What else could I do? And I waited with her until they came with a cart." He stared into the cup. "When they carried her out into daylight, I recognised her," he said painfully.

"What?"

"I said, 'Good God' or something like that." He looked at Mr Nugent. "You'd have known her too, Francis. She was that blonde bit of muslin Chesson had in keeping last year."

"What? Not that pretty little tit? Annie or Fanny or something like that?"

Matthew nodded. "She's not pretty now. Well, when the man heard I recognised her, he wanted to arrest me there and then. But I said, 'Nonsense, man. Would I be so foolish as to send for you if I had killed her? And you can see she's been dead for several hours, what's more.'"

"Good God! You didn't peach on Chesson, did you?" Nugent asked uneasily.

"No. I just said I recognised her as Haymarket ware but that I had never had any dealings with her, which is true. If he enquires among her sisters, he's bound to find someone who knew her. But he didn't seem to care. Said she wasn't the first whore to be throttled and wouldn't be the last. Damned hard-hearted bastard, if you ask me."

"Yes," Thomas agreed, "but you did the right thing and that is what matters."

Matthew smiled faintly. "Thank you. I'm sorry for intruding like this, but I couldn't think where else to go. You don't mind, do you, Thomas?"

"No. You were right to come here," Thomas said at once. He would not have turned anyone away in such circumstances, but as Arabella's brother, Matthew was entitled to call on him for assistance.

"We'll keep this to ourselves, shall we?" his prospective brother-in-law said. "No need to mention it to my father, let alone the ladies."

"Best to not to dwell upon it," Nugent agreed.

Chapter Seventeen

Arabella dozed on the chaise longue in the small parlour. She had begged off paying calls with her mother and Millie—if she had been up early to ride, she needed to rest in the afternoon, especially when she had danced into the early hours of the morning. But it was the best way to see Thomas. Her Aunt Henrietta had promised she would send him a card for her musical evening tomorrow—she hoped he would come.

Belshaw cleared his throat loudly and she sat up, rubbing the sleep from her eyes. "Major Ferraunt has called, Miss Malvin."

"Major Ferraunt! Show him in here, Belshaw, but I am not at home to anyone else."

"Very good, Miss. Should I request Miss Horton to join you?"

Horton? Why on earth? She laughed. "No, that will not be necessary. The major is the son of our rector at home—I shall be quite safe with him."

"Very good, Miss."

She quickly shook out her skirts and folded the shawl she had spread over her legs before running to the overmantel mirror where she stood on tiptoe to tidy her hair. Thomas's firm steps grew louder.

"Major Ferraunt," Belshaw announced and withdrew, leaving the door ajar.

"Thomas!" She came forward smiling, both hands outstretched.

His crooked smile deepened as he gripped them. "I had not dared hope to find you alone. There is so much I want to say to you."

Arabella's heart beat faster and she drew him to a sofa that was out of sight from the open door. "Come and sit down."

He put his hat on the floor, then released her to strip off his gloves. He dropped them into his hat and took her bare hand in his. An electric shock went through her at the intimate touch. He raised her hand and kissed it—a real kiss, not the token kiss that hovered over a lady's glove, but firm, cool lips pressing against her skin.

She gasped, her fingers clinging to his.

He raised his head and looked into her eyes. "Arabella, I have come to love you very dearly. Will you entrust yourself to me, be my wife and, God willing, the mother of my children?"

He looked so serious. How could he have become so dear to her so quickly? She had received other proposals but never before had part of her screamed, *say yes, say yes*. Another, more prudent voice urged, *If you are to entrust yourself to him, what sort of a husband will he be*?

"Arabella?" There was a caress in his voice when he spoke her name. He never shortened it, although almost everyone else did.

She cleared her throat. "Would you want me to follow the drum?"

"That is one of the things I want to discuss with you."

"I see." She withdrew her hand from his and turned to face him. "I cannot answer you yet, Thomas, and should I consent, it must be dependent on my parents' approval—"

"I know." He captured her hand again.

Generally, it was left to a young lady's father to interrogate her suitors, but why should she not put her questions herself? But how to do it?

"Arabella?" he repeated. Was there a slight edge to his voice?

"I want to know what my life would be like if I married you," she blurted out. "You want me to entrust myself to you. Are you offering me your protection in exchange for my services as a wife and mother?"

His eyebrows snapped together. "My protection? Your services? I am not looking for a mistress!"

"To many men, a wife is nothing but a legal mistress, with the advantage that the law gives him complete control of her."

He dropped her hand. "And you think I am such a man?"

"I don't know. I have no idea of your thoughts on marriage or on the rights of women; how you would see our life together."

"Arabella, all I know is that I cannot imagine a future without you. To my surprise, I have discovered that there are different futures possible for me. I have decisions to make and I do not want to make them by myself. I've put the cart before the horse, I fear, and asked the most important question first."

"Oh," she said, mollified. "You want my opinion, my advice?"

"Yes."

"About what?"

"I'll explain, but before that, can you at least tell me if the idea of marrying me is not repugnant to you?"

He looked so anxious that she found herself saying, "No, of course not." Hastily she added, "If it were, we would not be having this conversation. You should know that I would put these questions to any gentleman whom I seriously considered as a possible husband before I made up my mind about him."

"Have there been so many?"

She shook her head. "Mamma always says one should try and hint away a man if one does not intend to accept him. Some reveal their true colours early on so that you rule them out at once and others—well, the potential for love, married love, I mean, is missing."

"The potential for love?"

"Papa described it as an essential something that calls us to another person on the deepest, most intimate level." And now she had as good as admitted that she found it in him, she thought resignedly, noting the triumphant gleam in his eyes.

When he turned her hand to kiss the palm, she had to resist the urge to raise her face for a more intimate kiss. Mamma would return soon. "We must not waste time, Thomas. I don't know how long we shall be undisturbed."

"That is true." His shoulders fell as he huffed out a breath. "What are my thoughts on marriage? To be frank, I have never consciously considered it—in the abstract, I mean. But when I think of being married to you—I want to provide for you and our children, protect you as far as humanly possible from harm and do my best to ensure that you are happy. That is what I meant when I asked you to entrust yourself to me. I have no wish to control you, as you put it, or to play thc domcstic tyrant. I will never fail to treat you with respect, I promise you."

His clasp tightened. "As to how I see our life together—and I say our life, Arabella, for when I think of a wife, I think only of you—I see us as companions, friends and lovers; sharing the joys and sorrows of life, making our own family. I don't want to exchange the officers' mess for a gentlemen's club. In time, God willing, we'll have children to love too."

"Yes," she whispered.

"You asked about following the drum, but I am thinking of leaving the army if we marry. I should like to put down some roots. The rectory is not a true family home, remember; it is ours only as long as my father holds the living."

"I never thought of that. What would you do if you left the army?"

It had never occurred to her that he might wish to do so. She did not want to ask directly if he could afford to, but she had never had the impression that the rector was a wealthy man.

He sat back. "Just before I went to the Peninsula, my mother's uncle died and left me everything. There was no time to do anything with the estate, so I instructed his man of business to continue as he thought best and forward the income to my account at Greenwood and Cox. When I called there last week, I discovered that I am wealthier than I had thought."

She beamed at him. "You must have been very pleased."

"I was, especially when Mr Greenwood told me I now have an income that enables me not only to support a wife and family but to command the elegancies of life for them."

"But that is wonderful, Thomas." She was not hanging out for a rich husband but had no wish to live in poverty either. And Papa certainly wouldn't have approved if she had proposed to do so.

He nodded. "Then Greenwood said now would be a good time to apply to retire on half-pay, as there will be a general reduction in the size of the army. And I have to admit that the more I think about it, the more attractive I find the notion, especially now that all my visions of the future include you. I would hate to have you traipse with me from lodging to lodging in garrison towns, trying to make a home as best you can and never knowing when we might be ordered elsewhere or, worse, when I must leave you behind if war should break out again somewhere overseas."

"I shouldn't like that either," she confessed. She had never thought about the practicalities of being an army wife, although Arthur had always sworn that he would not marry so long as he remained in the military.

"Would you prefer to live in the town or in the country?" Thomas asked.

"The country," she said at once. "I like to visit London, and I am sure we could always stay here or at Tamm House if we wanted to come up for a few weeks, but I should not like to be here all the year round."

"I had thought of purchasing an estate and keeping a small stud. I must have something to keep me occupied. It would depend on what I could afford."

"We," she corrected him. "We could afford. I have some money too, Thomas. Arthur made me his heiress and my father intends to dower me. I just don't know the exact sum."

"That is your money," he said equally firmly.

She raised her eyebrows. "True companions should share everything, should they not?"

He kissed her hand again. "I see I shall be living under the cat's paw, and a very pretty one it is too."

When she replied to this impertinence with a sarcastic, "Meow," he leaned over and pressed a kiss onto her laughing mouth.

"Ohhh." She gazed up at him, lost for words.

He slid nearer and put his arm around her, holding her to him. "Arabella," he said, and kissed her again, so sweetly.

She had never felt anything like it. She melted into him, her arms closing about his neck to hold him to her.

He raised his head and looked down at her. "Will you marry me, Arabella, share my life and be my true companion in all things?"

"Yes, Thomas."

He crushed her to him, his kiss now more demanding, his tongue probing at the seam of her lips until she opened and permitted him entrance. As he deepened the kiss, sensation speared through her to curl in strange excitement deep in her stomach. She slipped her fingers into the curls at the smooth, rounded base of his skull, exploring its shape just as he ran a finger down her spine, causing her to shiver against him. Was this what they meant when they said man and wife would be one flesh? Somewhere a clock struck four and she gasped and broke the kiss.

"Thomas," she stammered and then, "Mamma will be back any minute."

"Arabella." He smiled down at her and kissed her quickly again before releasing her. "My father wrote requesting me to accompany him to Gloucestershire to visit our cousin Hawebury. They have been estranged all their lives, but apparently Hawebury is not well and wishes to see my father before the End, as he put it. I feel it my duty to go. While I am away, I thought to call on my great-uncle's man of business in Cheltenham. There is some property there, but I don't know whether it is an estate or just a large house and grounds. It is leased at present, but I don't know upon what terms. We may decide to sell it, but I would like to see it first."

"Cheltenham is not even fifty miles from home," she said excitedly.

"That had occurred to me, too. But I shall probably be away for a fortnight, Arabella, and, depending on how matters can be arranged with the regiment, I may have to return to France soon afterwards for some months at least. I shall hate to leave you but may not be able to avoid doing so. Should you find it awkward if we announced our betrothal and I immediately left England? Is it likely to cause talk?"

"There are always people who talk, but why should it matter to us? Besides, everyone knows you will have to return to your regiment. And if we are formally betrothed, we could write to each other."

"That is true. I should like to receive letters from you."

"And reply to them, I hope."

"You may depend upon it."

"When do you leave for Gloucestershire?"

"This is where I need your advice. My father is keen to leave at once, but Greenwood has written asking me to call and I had a note from Lady Jersey enclosing vouchers for Almack's."

"What?" Arabella stared at him. "She just sent them to you? You didn't apply for them?"

"It would never have occurred to me to do so."

"Did she flirt with you at Lady Falconer's?"

"Not at all, which puzzled me, I confess."

A twinkle in his eye accompanied this piece of conceit, but, before she could think of a suitable reproof, he continued, "We drank a glass of champagne after our waltz and she asked if my interest in you was serious."

"And you say she wasn't flirting?" Arabella asked incredulously.

"It wasn't like that, I promise you. If I had to describe how she was, I would say, 'concerned'. I simply said 'yes,' but that I had not yet spoken to your father. She nodded and said she would send me vouchers for Almack's and suggested I escort you there next week, by which she meant this coming Wednesday. I think I should obey her instructions, don't you?"

"It would be very foolish not to, but it is most strange. I have never heard of her doing such a thing. Do you mind if I tell Mamma?"

"Of course not. But that would mean I could not set out before Thursday."

"If you want to reach Hawebury this week, you cannot leave any later as you must first go to Longcroft and it will take you two days from there if you are travelling with your father, especially if your mother accompanies him. And don't forget the rector will refuse to travel on a Sunday."

"Why?"

She laughed. "He has preached so often about keeping the Sabbath-day holy that it would have to be a matter of life and death, but you should easily manage it in two days, at a pace that will not be too demanding for your parents. Why don't you borrow our travelling coach? It will be more comfortable than a yellow bounder, especially with three of you."

"I can't do that, Arabella."

"Nonsense, of course you can. We don't use it in town. I shall ask Papa."

Thomas's mouth twitched in a tiny grin. "I think I had better obtain his consent to marrying his daughter before I start borrowing his carriages. Have I your permission to do so?"

She reached out and smoothed his tousled hair. "You do, Thomas. Come, I'll take you down to the library."

"Where is Miss Malvin?"

Arabella closed the library door behind her and came into the hall. "I'm here, Mamma."

"Come up with me, my love. Belshaw, send up some tea."

"At once, my lady."

Mamma looked tired and climbing the stairs seemed more of an effort for her. Once free of her bonnet and pelisse, she sank with a grateful sigh into her favourite, high-backed armchair. Her maid brought a footstool and spread a Norfolk shawl across her mistress's lap.

"Thank you, Bates. That will be all."

"Would you not prefer to lie down?" Arabella asked.

"No. I'll just close my eyes for a few minutes until the tea comes. That will set me up in a trice."

"I have something to tell you, Mamma."

"What is it, Bella?"

"Thomas is with Papa, seeking my hand in marriage."

Her mother's cup and saucer rattled and she set them down carefully. "What? Thomas Ferraunt? How can he afford to marry you? I had not thought him a fortune-hunter!"

Arabella's breath caught in her throat and her eyes stung. "What an unfair thing to say! Can you not be happy for me?"

"Love on a pittance may seem romantic, but it rarely endures," Mamma said dryly. "Do you even know if he has any money other than his pay?"

"As it happens, he was his mother's uncle's heir and he can offer his wife the elegancies of life. He will explain it all to Papa, I'm sure." Her voice trailed away and she tried not to sniff. This was not how she expected Mamma to receive her news.

Mamma held out her hand. "I am sorry, my love, I did not mean to hurt you. Come and tell me all about it."

"Do you love him?" Mamma asked when Arabella had finished.

"I think I must. I cannot imagine my life without him, and he says the same about me. I like that he consulted me about his plans. He would like to put down roots. We can do that together—he has no wish to exchange the officers' mess for a gentlemen's club, he says."

"It will be a big change for him, if he leaves the military, but at least he will not have acquired the bad habits of the idle bachelors of the *ton*."

"I don't think he can be idle. That is why he plans to breed horses."

"Well, my love, if Papa agrees, I shall too and wish you both very happy."

Arabella hugged her mother. "And Thomas says we shall not live so far away that I may not visit you easily. And you must come and visit us."

Lord Malvin held out his hand. "Well, Major, if my lady agrees, I shall too and wish you and Bella very happy."

"Thank you, my lord."

"What is this about Hawebury? What precisely is the connection?"

"The present man is the sixth earl. My father is the grandson of the fourth earl, through a second marriage. His father was twenty-five years younger than his half-brother, the fifth earl, and only ten years older than his nephew. There was bad blood between the half-brothers from the outset—apparently the elder resented his father's second marriage—and the situation between uncle and nephew wasn't much better. When the old man died in 1740, my grandfather was more or less shown the door, although he was not yet of age. My father wrote to inform Hawebury of his father's death in '85 and his own subsequent marriage and my birth. He received a civil reply each time, but apart from advice of the marriage of Hawebury's heir and the births of his two grandsons, which my father acknowledged equally civilly, there has been no communication between them since."

"And now Hawebury is on his death-bed and has sent for your father?"

"As to the death-bed, I cannot say, but he must be eighty-six now."

"A fine age. Presumably, he seeks a reconciliation before he dies."

"One would hope so. In any event, my father is not the man to ignore such an appeal."

"No, of course not."

When Tony Malvin entered Clarissa's bedchamber, he found her sitting hand in hand with Arabella. Both ladies were misty-eyed but they smiled on seeing him.

"I think you are before me with my errand," he said, bending to kiss them.

"What did you say to Thomas?" Arabella demanded.

"That if your mother agreed to his suit, I would too and would wish you both well."

"Oh, Papa!" She jumped up and hugged him then wiped her eyes. "I don't know why I am such a watering-pot. I am so happy!"

He held her close. "You have chosen a good man, Bella. Now you should go down and put him out of suspense."

"Where is he?"

"In the library."

"Bring him to the small parlour," Clarissa said. "We'll meet you there."

When the door closed behind their daughter, Tony turned to his wife. "Well, my love?"

She sniffed and blotted her eyes. "I am happy for her, Tony, truly I am, but we'll miss her."

He sat beside her and slipped his arm around her. "I know, my love. But we must let her go—and Matthew and Roderick too, when the time comes. At least we have Julian and Millie and the children with us. And Thomas proposes to establish himself within a day's journey of Longcroft. She might have married someone from the other end of the country."

"That is true. You could make some enquiries about suitable properties."

He shook his head. "We must not interfere."

"But you can offer your advice," she said persuasively. "He would be very foolish not to take it, for you have much more knowledge of such matters than he has. I must own I was surprised to learn he was so comfortably off."

"Twelve hundred a year is not an immense amount of money, but Arabella's fortune will add eight hundred to that so together they will have more than enough for their needs. He is a sensible man, doesn't gamble and will agree to a good settlement for our daughter. What is more important, he will be a loving husband and neither a tyrant nor a wastrel."

Clarissa sighed. "A loving husband with sufficient means. That is all I have ever wanted for her. Of course I would like her to have made what the world would recognise as a splendid match—what mother would not? But the other is more important." She smiled up at him. "I hope she finds with him what I have found with you, Tony. I still sometimes dream about Tamm, and wake up and touch you to assure myself that that life is over."

His arm tightened around her waist. "That morning in Bath, when you picked Mattie up and comforted her while I was chasing after Julian's wretched kite—I knew then that you were what we, all three of us, needed. But I thought I was too old for you."

He felt her shake her head. "No. You were just right. You still are."

He tilted her chin up and kissed her. "Let us hope that in thirty years' time, Bella and Thomas say the same."

"Bella! Thomas! What a surprise!"

The whole family awaited them in the small parlour, eager to hug Arabella and welcome Thomas in a whirl of congratulations, felicitations and questions about their future. Reassured that he would not immediately whisk their sister away to France, Julian and Matthew enthusiastically supported his idea of breeding horses, Matthew immediately volunteering his assistance in selecting 'prime bits of blood' for the foundation stock and demanding first refusal of their progeny.

Millie had a more pressing question. "When will the wedding be, and where? If it is to be before the end of the Season in Hanover Square, you must order your bride-clothes as soon as possible."

Arabella wrinkled her nose. "I have no wish to marry in St George's. I believe eleven weddings were held there one day last month. Can you imagine having to wait for the couple ahead of you to be fired off and the one after you panting at your heels? I should think there would be very little reverence in the ceremony. I should much prefer to marry at home, with Thomas's father officiating. As to when—we haven't even begun to discuss it. There are other things we must talk about first. Almack's, for example."

"Almack's? What has Almack's to do with your marriage?"

"Nothing. It's just—Lady Jersey sent Thomas vouchers, unrequested, and said he should escort me tomorrow."

"What!"

"But not before enquiring if my intentions towards you were serious," Thomas reminded her.

"That makes it even more puzzling," Millie said. "Have you ever heard of such a thing, Clarissa?"

"Never. I wonder why she did it. She is said to be capricious, but I have always found there is method in her madness."

"That's what I think too," Arabella said, "and we both feel he must obey, even though his father has called him away on a family matter."

"It would have to be a matter of life and death before you ignored such a mark of favour. Indeed, if you are unable to attend the following week it would be wise to let her know. It would not do to be unappreciative of such consideration."

"Yes, but why has she done it?" Matthew asked.

"I wonder," Millie said slowly and then broke off.

"Yes?" Thomas said encouragingly.

Millie hesitated before continuing, "I heard that she has refused to supply Lord Henry Danlow with further vouchers for Almack's."

"And has selected Thomas to take his place?" Arabella said sceptically. "I know he is a good dancer, but is that not a little extreme? She is not a female pasha who may summon the gentlemen of the *ton* at her pleasure."

"Bella! What a picture. It is worthy of Cruikshank or Rowlandson."

Julian and Matthew guffawed at their father's remark and took turns embellishing the theme until they were satisfied with an image of her ladyship, bejewelled, beturbaned and scantily silk-clad, reposing on cushions and fanned by palm-leaf wielding guardsmen as she made her selection from the assortment of gentlemen gambolling before her.

"If you summoned me I would come from the ends of the earth."

Thomas's deep murmur provoked a delicious thrill. Arabella shivered at his warm breath on her ear and looked up at him from beneath her eyelashes.

With the ease of long practice, Millie recaptured the floor. "If that were the case, her ladyship would not have insisted Thomas escort Bella. What is more likely is that she discovered that another patroness—Mrs Drummond Burrell, perhaps—had agreed to give Lord Henry vouchers. Remember, the Drummond Burrells were at the Rickersbys the other evening."

Arabella looked sideways at her betrothed, but he did not appear puzzled by this remark, instead saying, "And Lady Jersey would not be averse to putting a spoke in his wheel? I had not thought great ladies could be so devious."

Even Mamma had to laugh at this *naïveté*.

"They are the worst of all," Papa said jovially.

"I imagine she was piqued when Mrs Drummond Burrell overruled her," Millie added.

"There has to be more to it than that," Thomas said slowly, "otherwise, why would she ask if my interest in Arabella were serious? I wonder, does she think that Lord Henry will beset Arabella in some way."

"We must not over-indulge in speculation," Mamma said, "or have it appear that Thomas's presence there is in any way unusual." The clock struck six. "Bella and I have decided to remain at home tonight. There are two big routs so anyone who misses us at one will assume we are at the other. Will you dine with us, Thomas, or have you another engagement?"

"I should be delighted to, ma'am."

"Excellent. I'll tell Belshaw to put dinner back until eight o'clock. That will give you ample time to dress and return. We can discuss the other arrangements later."

Chapter Eighteen

Arabella caught Thomas's hands, holding him at a slight distance while she raised her face for his kiss. "You must not crush my gown or untidy my hair. It would never do to go all tousled to Almack's."

"I suppose not," he said with his little smile, then bent and proved that he could fluster her completely with just a kiss, nipping gently at her lips before slowly invading her mouth so that she longed to release his hands and pull his head down firmly to hers.

"My dearest love," he said when he lifted his head. He took a small leather box from his pocket and placed it in her hands. "To remember me when I am away from you."

"I won't need a reminder but thank you." She smiled with delight at the gold ring, its centre a flower made of precious stones set around a diamond. "Thomas, it is exquisite."

"Can you decipher it?"

"Is it an acrostic? Where should I start?" She turned the ring this way and that, muttering to herself and then said triumphantly, "Diamond, emerald, amethyst, ruby, emerald, sapphire, topaz. 'Dearest'! How beautiful and so apt because you are my dearest too. Thank you, Thomas."

Heedless of her appearance, she came into his arms to kiss him again.

"It reminds me of the flowers you wear in your hair."

"I shall have some made to match." She extended her right arm in its long kid glove. "Can you undo it, please?"

He complied and then slowly eased it down to bare her hand in a long caress that made her tremble inside. He looked up at her, his eyes gleaming. "Will you wear my ring?"

"Yes."

He slipped it onto her finger and pressed his lips to her hand.

"It fits perfectly. How did you know the size?"

"It looked right—and it looks right on you."

"It is so pretty. See how it sparkles when it catches the light."

"Will it fit under your glove?

"I'm sure it will."

"How do you put it on?"

"The same way you do a stocking—you roll the long part down and slip your hand in first," she said absently, demonstrating the method as she spoke. He stopped her when she started to unroll the soft leather from her wrist to her elbow.

"Let me."

This seemed an even more intimate service. She had never thought a man's touch could be so exciting. Of course, he wasn't just any man but her Thomas.

She ran her finger over the little bump in the glove. It was a secret reminder of their love.

Mamma and Matthew waited in the hall. Millie had cried off—she wasn't feeling well—and Julian had gone to White's with Papa. It meant they need only take one carriage. Arabella settled herself beside Mamma, with Thomas and Matthew opposite.

Going to a ball with an accepted suitor was very different. Previous prickles of uncertainty and anticipation were replaced by a possessive pride and a new expectancy. She stood at a new threshold. They had spoken of a September wedding. Soon her girlhood would be behind her and her place would be among the married women. She would leave the Abbey and create her own home and family.

"I had a very kind letter from the rector. He quoted from the book of Ruth and welcomed me as their daughter," she said as they drove off. "It does seem strange that he will be my father-in-law. I imagine you feel the same about my parents, Thomas," she added with a sidelong glance at her mother.

"I suppose it is because our families have known each other for so long," Mamma said, "and we have our fixed places in one another's lives. We must all become accustomed to the new connections between us. Isn't it strange that there is no word to denote the parents-in-law of one's child?"

"There is in Spanish," Thomas told her, "a nice neat one—*'consuegros'*, but there is an English term that I hope will describe all four of our parents and that is 'grandparents'. Although you already have grandchildren, don't you, ma'am?"

"Four, and I love them dearly, but strictly speaking they are my step-grandchildren, so your children will be very special to me as I shall be their grandmother in my own right," she said proudly.

Arabella had never seen Almack's so crowded. A glittering throng pressed up the stone stairs and into the great ballroom and she had to cling to Thomas to avoid being swept off her feet. He glanced down at her and then glared forbiddingly over his shoulder.

"This will be better." He gently lifted her hand from his arm and stretched behind her to grasp the banisters, creating a bulwark that defied any further encroachment.

It was like having her personal bodyguard Arabella thought smugly, as they continued the slow climb. At the top of the stairs she took his arm again before they joined the procession through the ante-room to the ballroom, nodding to friends and acquaintances, noting who was present and who was absent. To arrive at Almack's on the arm of a gentleman suggested that an announcement might be expected shortly and Thomas's appearance at her side caused a little stir, although there were none of the envious looks she could have expected if she had captured one of the great prizes among the bachelors.

"I never thought Miss Malvin would settle for him," she overheard one girl murmur to another. "He does not even have a handsome face to recommend him."

"And to think she might have had Lord Henry."

Arabella wanted to retort that a strong arm and a true and loving heart were more important than a pretty face and a childish disposition but contented herself with a contemptuous glance as she passed the pair. Let them have the Lord Henrys if they wanted them.

Lady Nugent and Caro greeted them with fond smiles. Caro could hardly wait to draw Arabella aside.

"So it is all settled between you?"

"Yes."

"I wish you both very happy. I shall call tomorrow to hear all about it. How did you manage to arrange a voucher for him so quickly?"

"Lady Jersey was so kind."

"She has a partiality for good dancers," Caro said. "I hope you will spare him to me for one set tonight."

"As you have never yet failed to garner an invitation from any gentleman who caught your eye, I do not think I shall need to solicit one for you."

"But I would consider it wrong to flirt with him now that you have accepted him," Caro protested plaintively. "The bonds of friendship forbid it. You must practise being a wife and select safe females for him. Indeed, when we are all old and grey and I am an old maid, I shall expect you to remind him that he must dance with 'poor Caro'."

"I promise," Arabella said solemnly. "But there are plenty of unattached gentlemen here tonight. Do I imagine it, or are there more than usual?"

"It only appears so because they are forbidden fruit to you now," Caro teased but then said, "You are right. It is as if all those who make an appearance once or twice a Season have decided to come tonight. There are Hall, Lord Rastleigh, I mean—that is the first time I have seen him this Season—and his friend Mr Graham. Ssh, they are coming this way."

Arabella smiled at the young earl and offered her condolences on his grandfather's death earlier in the year.

"Thank you, Miss Malvin. He was not young, I know, but it was still a shock."

"Especially when it brought such a change in your own life."

"That's it. I am beset by peers on both sides of the House, trying to convince me that I should sit with them."

"Must you choose one side or another?"

"There is no such obligation. Frankly, I am inclined to declare myself an independent and make up my mind according to the facts of each matter."

"I imagine it would be more rewarding than playing 'follow my leader'," Arabella said thoughtfully, "even if you have to inform yourself thoroughly rather than simply adopting the party point of view."

"That is what I think too."

"And only consider the satisfaction when you inform the next person who seeks to importune you that you intend to go your own way," she added. He couldn't be much older than Matthew and she was sure that he was sick of his elders in the Lords offering unwanted advice.

He smiled slowly. "An unforeseen bonus! Thank you for your wise counsel, Miss Malvin. May I have the pleasure of dancing with you?"

By the time they had agreed on the third quadrille, Thomas had turned back to her and she said, "May I present Major Ferraunt of the 23rd? Major Ferraunt, the Earl of Rastleigh."

Thomas bowed. "Your servant, my lord."

"I believe you were recently the guest of my mother, Lady Malcolm, Major," Rastleigh said. "Did you enjoy your visit to Ireland?"

"Very much. If only it were not so difficult to get there."

"You went by packet boat, I take it," Rastleigh said sympathetically. "It is a wretched stretch of road to Holyhead, is it not? Then, as often as not one must wait for the tide in Dublin Bay. I have my own yacht and so can leave from and put in to any harbour."

"That would make it much more bearable," Thomas agreed. "We returned from Waterford to Bristol. We bought several horses and it was certainly an easier route, especially on this side of the Irish Sea."

"Good evening, Miss Malvin."

Arabella was surprised to see Sir Denis Howe make his bow. Usually by this time in the Season, little groups and cliques had formed and the more fortunate young ladies had established their courts of admirers, but tonight her hand had been sought by several gentlemen who until now had displayed little interest in her. What would it be like once her betrothal became known? Would her regular partners go elsewhere? Generally, a different cohort of gentlemen danced with the married ladies. Next Season—but perhaps there would not be a next Season for her. Thomas might consider the time and money better spent establishing themselves. She didn't think she would mind, especially if they could come to town for a couple of weeks to keep Mamma company.

The musicians had taken their place in the orchestra gallery and were tuning their instruments. All around her, gentlemen brought their conversations to a close and found their ladies for the first dance.

"What a squeeze," Thomas said when the quadrille came to an end. "There is hardly room to dance the figures properly."

"It's worse than usual tonight. I hope that people will soon disperse to the other rooms."

"Isn't that Danlow at the door?"

Arabella looked over to where Lord Henry stood with Mr Drummond Burrell. "Drat! I want to enjoy tonight without worrying about what he might be up to." She watched the two men commence a sauntering circuit of the room that would soon have brought them to her and Thomas. "Come. Let us move ahead of them."

He immediately led her away. "What makes you nervous about him?"

"I don't know. I just feel he has not forgiven me for slighting him, as he sees it. He is very intense. I thought he was at Lady Rickersby's against his will and might explode at any moment."

"Have you any dances still free?"

"Just the last one."

"If Lord Henry should request one, you will dance it with me," Thomas said calmly. "In fact, I think you should do so anyway so you may truthfully tell him you are completely engaged tonight."

"But that would be a third dance. People would think—" She broke off, laughing. "And people would be quite right. Let us go and talk to the Tamms."

"I had not expected to see you here," Arabella said to Lallie.

"Believe it or not, it was Hugo who suggested we come. I think it is because he wants a respite from our guests."

"You did not apply for vouchers for them?"

"Clarissa advised against it. She said it would be better not to risk a rebuff as they would feel it sorely. I don't think the possibility of acquiring vouchers even occurred to them, to be frank. They cannot be dissatisfied with the invitations they receive, and Ruth has a couple of admirers, although I do not know if anything will come of them."

"Perhaps it will stop her pursuit of Matthew. He feels obliged to stand up with her if they are at the same ball, but otherwise he avoids her. There were too many hints about drives in the Park. How long do the Halworths remain with you?"

"We had originally said until the end of the month, but depending on how things develop, I might suggest they stay a little longer."

"Poor Hugo!"

Hugo grinned. "Have you a dance for me, Bella, or do you still consider it too stuffy to dance with your uncle?"

"I'm sorry, they are all taken, unless," she glanced at Thomas, "you would like the last one?"

"Which you have already promised to Major Ferraunt?"

"Yes, but I'm sure he wouldn't mind…"

"Don't try to answer that," Hugo advised Thomas. "I wouldn't dream of asking you to give it up."

"Miss Malvin." Lord Henry bowed before her.

"Good evening, Lord Henry."

"May I have the honour of dancing this next with you?"

His bow was as elegant as ever and he spoke with his usual drawl, but again she had that sense of something seething beneath the polished exterior. She did her best to answer him as calmly as she would any other gentleman. "Thank you, Lord Henry, but I am already engaged."

He took a breath. "Then perhaps later in the evening?"

She shook her head. "I'm afraid not. I am fully committed."

Something flashed in his eyes but was gone before she could recognise it.

"Thank you, Miss Malvin," he said coolly. "I shall take my leave of you."

Hugo looked after him, frowning. Mr Neary came up to claim Arabella's hand and Thomas bowed to Lallie and requested the honour of leading her out.

Once this unpleasantness was out of the way, Arabella could give herself up to the enjoyment of the evening. A whispered exchange with the Tamms had informed them of her betrothal and she had accepted their delighted felicitations.

Hugo grinned at Thomas and said, "I don't think I need another overgrown nephew. I suggest you think of us as an additional brother-and sister-in-law."

"I should be delighted," Thomas had replied, shaking his hand. "As an only child, I cannot have too many brothers and sisters."

"When is the wedding?" Lallie had asked.

"We are thinking of September," Arabella answered.

Lallie nodded. "That will give you more time to prepare than we had."

"It will be at home—you will come, won't you?"

"Our waltz, I believe, Miss Malvin."

"Are you sure, Major?" she asked with mock hesitation and laughed when he tucked her hand into the crook of his arm.

"None of your tricks," he said severely. "It is fortunate I secured my dances in advance, for otherwise I wouldn't have had a hope of getting them."

She cocked an eyebrow. "See that you remember that, sir, and don't become too complacent."

"Or what?"

"Or nothing, provided you still dance with me once we are married."

"I promise," he said solemnly. "Do your parents still dance together?"

"Papa does not attend many balls, but when he does, he will always stand up with Mamma, even if it is just for the finishing dance. They prefer the old country dances to our waltzes and quadrilles."

"I wonder what will be danced when we are their age," he said, leading her onto the dance floor.

The musicians struck up and she surrendered to the pleasure of being in his arms. Words would only have broken the spell, but afterwards they strolled downstairs to the supper room.

"I saw Greenwood today."

"Greenwood? Oh, your regimental agent."

"He recommends I apply to go on half-pay immediately, but I wonder whether I should not make a clean break and simply sell out."

"Are you sure you will not miss the army?"

"I am very sure I will not. What do you think?"

"Could you be recalled from half-pay?"

"If there were a need, certainly."

They had reached the supper room and she had to laugh when she saw him inspect the curling slices of bread and butter, and dry cake that were all the lady patronesses saw fit to offer. "Sometimes I think that they save the food from week to week. I just want a glass of lemonade; dancing makes me thirsty. I'll wait over there at that small table."

She sat quietly, a little smile on her lips. She would prefer if Thomas sold out, but might he regret his decision? Could he re-join if he wished? A suave voice interrupted her musings.

"All alone, Miss Malvin? May I fetch you something?"

She looked up into Lord Henry's glittering eyes.

"No, thank you, sir. There is no need." She smiled past him at Thomas who approached with two glasses of lemonade.

He handed her one and nodded to his lordship.

"Major—Ferraunt, isn't it? Still here?"

"As you see," Thomas replied equably.

After a moment's silence, Lord Henry withdrew.

"Now, where were we?" Thomas said.

"Talking about whether you should retire or sell-out. Do you have to decide before you leave?"

"No."

"Then why not think about it while you are away? You will know more about your circumstances once you have spoken to your uncle's man of business, will you not?"

"That is true. I can also keep an eye out for a suitable property. Have you any preferences?"

"I would like to be near a pleasant town with amenities such as a circulating library, assembly rooms and even a theatre."

"Cheltenham sounds more and more promising," he said. "There is a racecourse there too, I believe. Shall I bring you back a guide if there is one?"

"That would be truly splendid, Thomas. This is exciting, isn't it? How fortunate we are that you are not going to inherit some gloomy pile and we may choose where and how we want to live."

He nodded. "We shall decide on a place and then take a house for a year while we search for our permanent home." There was a twinkle in his eye when he added, "I doubt if your mother would agree to your jaunting around the country with me before we are married, even if it is to inspect estates. But first, we must think of our wedding journey. Where would you like to go?"

Thomas twirled Arabella into the final turn of the last waltz and final dance. She sank into her curtsey and gasped, "I'm sure I've danced through my slippers tonight. We'll leave as soon as Matthew has found us. You have an early start tomorrow."

"Your mother is holding up very well," he said, glancing over to where she stood talking to Lady Nugent, Lallie and Hugo.

"Yes. It is good to see her so cheerful. What is happening now?"

A footman had handed a note to the orchestra leader who unfolded it and proclaimed, "My lords, ladies and gentlemen, by special permission of the lady patronesses, there will be an additional waltz tonight."

"No," Arabella groaned through the gabble that followed this announcement. "I can't dance anymore."

"You don't have to," Thomas said, just as Matthew came up to them.

"Come on, Bella. The carriage is waiting."

"Excellent. Let me just say goodbye to Lallie."

"Be quick then."

"Miss Malvin?"

Lord Henry! Drat the man. What was he thinking of, popping up like a jack-in-the-box? Surely he wouldn't? Her heart sank into her shredded slippers when she realised that indeed he would. And she could not claim a previous engagement.

"May I take advantage of this both fortuitous and fortunate dispensation and beg you to favour me with this last dance?"

Before Arabella could say anything, Hugo answered curtly, "My niece will not dance with you, sir."

"Indeed, we are just about to leave," she said hastily. "Good night, Lord Henry."

"Well! I have never seen Hugo behave so like his father," Arabella exclaimed once they were safely in the carriage. "There was no need for him to give Lord Henry such a set-down. I could have dealt with him more civilly."

Matthew shook his head. "There was more to it than that. Hugo must have got wind of it, because it is unlike him to stay to the very end, but he must have wanted to keep an eye on things."

"Keep an eye on what?"

"The fact is—it was the talk of the clubs—that Danlow was offering one hundred to one that he would stand up with you tonight. There were plenty of takers, too."

"Why, that little coxcomb!"

"What the devil!"

Mamma, ignoring Arabella's and Thomas's interjections, asked awfully, "Were you aware of this before we left home tonight, Matthew?"

"No, ma'am, upon my soul, I wasn't. It was Roger Neary who tipped me the wink, but by then Bella was safe as all her dances were taken."

"Was that by design?" Arabella asked. "Sir Denis Howe, for one, has never asked me to dance before."

Matthew grinned. "I think some of the fellows felt Danlow was either too cocksure or he planned some devious trick to make it impossible for you to refuse. In any case, they decided to take him down a peg by ensuring that you had no dance free. But when he managed to have another dance added to the programme—well, to my mind, Hugo was quite right to say what he did."

"I agree," Mamma said. "You will not dance again with Lord Henry, Arabella, no matter what the circumstances. Given what has happened, you would not be required to refuse all other invitations if you refuse him."

"I doubt if he will," Matthew said. "He will feel this evening's work in his pride as well as in his pocket. I imagine he'll make himself scarce for a while and once news of your betrothal spreads, he'll give up."

"If he doesn't, I'll deal with him," Thomas said grimly.

Chapter Nineteen

Ferraunt Court, Glos.
11th May 1816

My dearest Arabella,

So much has happened since we arrived today that I hardly know where to begin except at the beginning and describe everything to you as it happened. Our journey was uneventful. My parents bore it well and arrived in good spirits, due in a large part to Lord and Lady Malvin's thoughtfulness in making their travelling coach available to us. I am charged with conveying to your parents their great appreciation of this kindness and I beg you will mention this, although I shall of course do so personally when next we meet.

I imagine it will take me several days to find my way around Ferraunt Court. It is a hodgepodge of gables and oriel windows built piecemeal over the centuries and there always seems to be an unexpected stair or passage to throw one off balance. Our arrival was expected. We were received by the steward and housekeeper and told that his lordship would see us in an hour. (It was now half-past three in the afternoon.) Our rooms are comfortable but, even to my unschooled eye, very old-fashioned. My mother commented that although well-kept, everything appears to be at least sixty years old. This is most apparent in the parlours and drawing-rooms which hold stiff and uninviting accumulations of dark wood and faded hangings.

Promptly at half-past four, the steward ushered us through an imposing oak door to a spacious saloon. From there we entered a large bedchamber where a wreck of a man lay propped upon a pile of pillows in an enormous bed whose elaborately carved headboard, tester and supporting poles displayed a higgledy-piggledy mass of interwoven figures, plants and animals. Hawebury must once have been tall and well-built, but now appears gaunt and haggard against the faded crimson and gold hangings,

A valet stood beside the bed. When we were announced, he withdrew to the window, where the steward joined him.

The earl raised a weak hand an inch from the coverlet. "Cousin."

My father went forward. "Good day, Cousin. I am grieved to see you so unwell." Receiving only an inarticulate response, he continued, "May I present my wife, Mrs Ferraunt?"

My mother curtsied. "My lord."

"You are welcome, madam." Hawebury spoke slowly, pausing frequently to gasp for breath. He looked at me. "This is your son?"

I bowed. "Major Ferraunt of the 23rd at your service, my lord."

"He is your heir?"

"He is my only son," my father answered, puzzled.

"Married?"

"I hope to marry later this year," I replied.

There was a gleam of interest in his eye. "Who is your bride?"

When I told him, he grunted, "Better than I expected."

You may imagine, dear Arabella, how annoyed I was at Hawebury's lack of respect in so speaking of you but in light of his weakness I let it pass. He began to cough and the valet held a glass of some sort of cordial to his lips. After a few moments he waved the man away.

"Well, Cousins," he said, looking from my father to me, "you are all that's left of the Ferraunt line."

"What do you mean?" my father asked sharply.

"My son—and grandsons—were—drowned—last year—sailing in the Bristol Channel."

"Good God!" My father's face turned as white as his hair.

We were all three still standing and I snapped at the valet to set chairs for Dr and Mrs Ferraunt. The earl had closed his eyes and now he opened them again. "You are my heir."

My father and mother looked at each other, horrified. You know them well enough, Arabella, to appreciate what unwelcome news this was to them. A more reluctant Earl and Countess cannot be imagined. Dumbstruck, they reached for each other's hands, drawing on the mutual support that is the foundation of their life. My mother was the first of us to gather her wits.

"I am so very sorry for your loss," she said simply.

"Why did you not let us know earlier?" my father asked then. "We would have come to you. No man should be asked to bear such suffering alone."

The earl raised his hand slightly and let it drop. "I needed to lick my wounds. Besides, it emerged afterwards that my son's wife was with child. If she carried another son—"

"Poor lady. But a daughter will comfort her," my mother said.

Hawebury shook his head. "It was a boy, born six weeks ago. Neither he nor his mother survived the birth."

"How tragic," my mother whispered.

"I would have let you discover all this after my death if it were not for one thing."

"If there is any way I can be of service, Cousin, you need only say so," my father said at once.

"There is. John," he said to his valet, who immediately left the room.

We waited in silence. Arabella, I cannot describe to you the thoughts that filled my mind. They were a mixture of pity for the earl's heartrending situation and dread of the inevitable consequences, not only for my parents but also for us. Our lives too have been irrevocably changed.

After some minutes the door to the bedchamber opened to admit a peevish-looking lady of about thirty and a thin, pale child wearing a black dress.

"Good day, Grandfather," she said solemnly, making a little curtsey. "I hope you are feeling better today."

You could see what an effort it was for him to smile at her.

"A little better, my dear. Now I want you to meet your cousins, Doctor and Mrs Ferraunt and Major Ferraunt." As she curtsied, he said to us, "Your cousin and my granddaughter Venetia Ferraunt. Will you swear to me, all three of you, that you will care for her as if she were your own child?"

"I will." We spoke in unison, then my mother held out her hand. "You have had a very sad time of it, my dear, but it will get better, I promise you. Remember, you are not alone."

After a moment, Venetia took the outstretched hand. My mother drew her to her and put her arm around her.

At that, the earl's head fell back on his pillows. "My steward will look after you and my man of business will come on Monday to discuss matters." He closed his eyes, clearly exhausted and so we left him.

Dearest Arabella, I could think of no other way of breaking this to you than of describing the desolate scene. One could not but pity the old man whose life's work lay in ruins about him and our hearts ached for the orphan who was about to lose her last remaining link to a happier past. We discovered later that she will be ten this summer. Poor child! Our own distress must fade when we consider what she has endured.

We repaired to one of the uncomfortable parlours. Dinner would be served in half an hour, we were told and my mother instructed that they set for Miss Venetia and the peevish lady who, it turned out, is her governess, a Miss Dunford. We had changed from our travelling clothes on our arrival and my mother further decreed that we would not change again. You would have smiled to see her assume command. The role of countess may be new to her but she is used to being mistress of her home. Over dinner we endeavoured to speak of lighter matters so as not to oppress the child but after she and Miss Dunford left us, we simply sat and stared at one another, trying to grasp the enormity of what was happening. My parents retired early, and I sit now writing to you, still trying to make sense of it.

I shall leave this letter open and add to it before sending it to Bristol on Monday to catch the afternoon post. By then there may be more to report. I have seen men die, and I do not think that Hawebury has long to live, especially now that he has fulfilled his last remaining duty.

Thomas put down his pen and stretched. What a coil! And there was no escape. He could not expect his parents to bear this burden alone. Such an unexpected inheritance at their age might kill them. Thank God for the Malvins. His lordship would surely advise his old friend and Arabella was very familiar with the demands made on a peer's wife. How fortunate he was. His brief foray into tonnish society left him in no doubt as to the eligibility of the heir to an earldom and of the lengths to which some mothers and daughters would go to capture such an unexpected prize, but his Arabella had chosen him when she might have made much more advantageous matches.

Sunday evening

It is as I feared. The Earl of Hawebury died in the early hours of this morning. My father, who had given instructions that he was to be called if his cousin's condition worsened, sat with him until the end. And yet the Earl of Hawebury lives. I wish you could have seen my poor father's expression when he was addressed as 'my Lord' *in what he considers to be indecent haste. But such a large household will be quite regimented, I told him, and the servants drilled in the appropriate behaviour. It comforts them to know they are doing the right thing. To my surprise, they are also 'my lording' me; I am now, apparently, Baron Ferraunt or Major*

Lord Ferraunt. I am tempted to tell them to address me as major, but fear that will be too confusing if I sell out soon.

With true fellow-feeling for his brother clergyman, my father elected not to attend morning service today, too conscious of the dual commotion the death of the old earl and the presence of the new one would create. Instead, he read the service to the household assembled in the 'Grand Saloon', which is the largest room here. This also provided an opportunity for the steward to introduce all the servants to us. It was a melancholy occasion. My father expressed his condolences, especially to those who had served his cousin for many years. We all now stood before changes, he said, not least he and his wife, but he was sure he could rely on the support of the household, particularly over the coming days.

Afterwards, in a dignified procession that was as rigidly ordered by rank as any military parade, the staff went to see their master for the last time.

Otherwise we spent the day quietly. The parson and his wife called at my father's request to discuss arrangements for the funeral which will take place on Friday. No doubt the Hawebury man of business will advise us tomorrow on the further, necessary formalities, including the notification to the appropriate authorities of the earl's passing. I do not know when we shall be able to leave here.

My dearest Arabella, it is just four days since we agreed how fortunate we were to be free to make our own lives, unencumbered by inherited responsibilities and now all has changed. I sincerely regret imposing this burden on you but cannot tell you how grateful I am that you will be by my side. You are much better prepared for your new role than I and I am certain that my family can rely on the support and advice of yours as we face this challenge.

Good night, my dearest love. Among all these changes, I remain, most importantly,

Your true and devoted servant
Thomas Ferraunt

Post scriptum. Monday. In haste, before I seal this. Notices will be sent by the same post to the Court and the Lord Chancellor and tomorrow to The Times and The Morning Chronicle.

"You are my heir."

Arabella stared blindly at Thomas's letter. The rector was heir to the Earldom of Hawebury. And Thomas was his only son. She read on mechanically, tears stinging her eyes at the description of the orphaned granddaughter in her black dress. Poor, poor child—to lose her father and brothers at one fell swoop and then, in less than a year, her mother and a newborn brother. And now her grandfather. Thomas had sworn to care for her, but he would have done so even if it had not been required of him. The old earl was dead, she read dully, and Thomas was Lord Ferraunt.

They could forget their dream of a new house. She sprang up. She must see Mamma at once.

Papa sat beside Mamma in her dressing-room, their heads together over a book. They were laughing.

"It is too over-wrought for words," Mamma exclaimed. She looked up. "Only think, Bella, your father managed to secure a copy of *Glenarvon*." Her smile faded. "What has happened?"

Arabella held out Thomas's letter. "Oh, it is so dreadful. Hawebury is dead and the rector is his heir."

"The rector! What of Hawebury's son and grandsons?" her father demanded.

"All drowned last year. And a posthumous grandson died at birth, with his mother. It is too sad." Arabella began to shake.

"Put this around you." Mamma wrapped her in a warm shawl and drew her down onto the sofa. "We'll have some tea."

"Drink this while you are waiting." Papa closed her fingers around a cordial glass.

She sipped gratefully and the trembling eased.

14th May 1816

My dearest Thomas,

I cannot tell you how shocked we were by the dreadful news conveyed in your letter of the 11th and how much we feel for you and your family, confronted without warning by such tragedy. My parents have charged me to express to you and your parents their profound sympathies on the death of your cousin the Earl of Hawebury and also on the earlier deaths of his son, grandsons and daughter-in-law, of which you have only just learned.

My heart goes out in particular to little Venetia. It is impossible to think of her without weeping. Poor child, I am sure she wonders will she ever be happy again. She cannot now appreciate how fortunate she is in being entrusted to your parents and to you. It is far too soon for you to have made any decision about her future, but please be assured that I will welcome her into to our home and care for her as if she were my own child.

My mother, aware of all the demands that will be made on you and your parents at present, and the decisions with which you are faced, has suggested that you might like to bring Venetia and her governess to us for the moment. If you explain to her that I am your future wife, she should not feel that she is being 'cast out' of her home for ever but understand that this is a temporary arrangement. She will have company in the schoolroom, which can only be good for her, as Julian's and Millie's children are also here in London, as is Miss Lambton. I promise you we shall do everything in our power to comfort Venetia and make her and Miss Dunford welcome. Mamma is having rooms prepared for them so there is no need to write in advance if you wish to bring or send them to us.

In the face of such tragedy, it seems selfish to think of one's own concerns and I am sure that most people would be surprised that neither your parents nor you and I welcome such an unexpected elevation, especially when it comes at such a cost to the innocent. But 'man proposes and God disposes' *and we have no choice but to accept it and the responsibilities that come with it. Although we must face a different challenge, we can still shape our own life, Thomas, and we shall still dream together.*

You say I am better prepared for our new role than you are. To some extent, perhaps, but remember that you are used to sizing up situations and commanding men and I am sure you will quickly take charge of the Hawebury estate. In many ways, you have an advantage over other heirs as you will not be hidebound by tradition but able to cast a fresh eye on how things are done. It occurs to me too that Lord Franklin must have found himself in a very similar position when he became heir after his brother died and I am sure you can turn to him for advice and support.

There is very little news here. Matthew says that any discussion in the clubs of Lord H.'s unfortunate wager has been obliterated by the publication the following day of Glenarvon, *a novel written by Lady Caroline Lamb which Lady Holland describes as,* 'a strange farrago and scandalous libel against her family and friends'. *The fashionable world is torn between fury at being portrayed and dismay at being ignored while many a score has been paid by loud musings as to whether the fictional Lady X might be a depiction of the actual Lady Y. Lady Jersey is furious and intends to ban Lady Caroline from Almack's.*

Lady Nugent's archery fête was a great success but I missed you sorely. Your absence was noted and several people enquired after you. I explained you had been called away on a family matter. I wonder how many of them will nod sagely and say they suspected as much when they see the notice in the newspapers.

I must close here as I want this to go with tonight's post. Dearest Thomas, you are constantly in my thoughts. Pray let me know how you go on and do not hesitate to mention any way in which I or my family can support you and yours at this difficult time.

Please give my affectionate compliments to Lord and Lady Hawebury and to you I send my fondest love,

Your Arabella

(Who shall now take a deep breath and address her letter to 'Major Lord Ferraunt'. She hopes he will not be too dismayed to see it.)

Post Scriptum. If there is to be a funeral procession, my father begs that you instruct our coachman to drive our carriage as a mark of our respect for the late earl. He is to do everything as usual, my father says—he will know what is required.

Chapter Twenty

Lord Malvin scrawled his name across the corner of Arabella's letter. "There, my pet. Are you feeling more the thing?"

She laughed shakily. "I don't know. I think so. I'll just take this out to James—he's waiting with the postbag."

After handing the letter to the footman, she returned to the library. "Where is the latest edition of *Debrett's Peerage*?"

"There, under that window. Why?"

"I want to see if there is any information about Venetia's mother—perhaps there are uncles or aunts on her side even if there are none among the Ferraunts. I don't mean that Venetia should be sent to them," she added hastily, "but it would be useful to know, especially if she comes to stay here. She must be feeling so lost and it might help to meet some of her mother's family. I didn't see any notice of her death, did you? The name would have caught my eye, especially if it was only six weeks ago."

Her father straightened in his chair. "No, and I don't recall reading anything about the tragedy last year either. Of course there is no law that says such matters must be made public and, depending on when it happened, the newssheets would have been full of other things."

She carried the thick volume to the table and flicked through the pages. “Hawebury. Here we are. Hmmm. Thomas’s grandfather is here; he died in 1784, leaving issue of one son, Thomas—that must be the rector. There is no mention of his marriage or Thomas’s birth and the deaths of Venetia’s father and brothers are not yet recorded. Her parents married in 1800. Her mother was Venetia, only daughter and heiress of Charles Haynes, Esq. of Gloucestershire. If she was the heiress, she most likely had no brothers. I wonder if her father is still alive.”

“Depending on the marriage settlements, her daughter is very likely now an heiress. Generally, a reasonable portion of a lady’s fortune passes to her daughters and younger sons and as Venetia is the sole surviving child, it will all go to her.” Papa sighed. “I could have wished, Bella, that you were not saddled with this responsibility at such a young age, but it will be better for the child if she goes to you and Thomas now rather than first to Dr Ferraunt and his wife. They are too old for such a charge.”

“Perhaps. But it is not my decision.”

“I imagine that if you were to offer, they would not say no. If she were a boy it might be different—they are used to schoolboys—but of course he would have been the new earl and it is unlikely our rector would have been named guardian.”

“I suppose not.”

“Remember your mother was even younger when she married me and took on Julian and Mattie. She will be happy to advise you.”

“Or I could ask Mattie what it was like having a young stepmother.”

Her father laughed. "I would never have thought of that. I have no doubt that you'll do very well, Pet."

"The rector can hardly continue at Longcroft, can he?"

"It would be very unusual. I suppose that means I must look for a new incumbent."

Almack's hummed with speculation. Would Lady Caroline Lamb seek entrance and would she be refused?

"Frankly, I don't care a whit," Caro Nugent said to Arabella. "I have never liked her and feel she gets what she deserves. Where were you yesterday evening? And more to the point, have you heard from your major since he left? You look quite pale—are you pining for him?"

Arabella drew her into a quiet corner. "I do miss him," she admitted, "but I received dreadful news yesterday."

"What? Has he lost all his money?"

"Caro! No, it is something else entirely. I don't want it bruited abroad tonight but the notice will be in the newssheets tomorrow or, at latest, on Friday. The old Earl of Hawebury is dead and our rector is his heir."

Caro's jaw dropped. Wide-eyed, she opened and closed her mouth a couple of times before managing to stutter, "The Longcroft rector? Major Ferraunt's father?"

"Yes."

"But why is that so dreadful?"

"Because the earl's son and grandsons were drowned last year and then, six weeks ago, a third, posthumous grandson died at birth."

"Oh. That is very sad. What will happen now?"

"I don't know. Thomas wrote at once to tell me—I received his letter yesterday—but it was too soon for them to have made any decisions about the future."

Caro smiled. "And so you have made a splendid match despite yourself."

"Yes," Arabella agreed gloomily. "We shall no longer be free to do as we wish. The rector and his wife are both more than seventy and have suffered a severe shock, Thomas says. We shall have to support them."

"Oh, I am sure they'll come about. It was a pleasant shock, after all. What sort of people are they?"

"He is very much a scholar, but his sermons are not too dull. Arthur and Matthew liked going to him for lessons—he did his best to find interesting books and would discuss ancient battles as if they had occurred only yesterday. She was more of a disciplinarian but always provided an ample nuncheon, which was of greater importance to the boys. She takes her husband's position very seriously."

"Most wives do."

"I don't think she approves of me, not since I brought the kitten to church. She shouldn't have noticed it in the box pew, but it decided to climb onto Papa's shoulder. She could hardly scold him, but the service was barely over when she descended upon Matthew and told him the rector would deal with him in the morning for bringing that animal into a sacred place."

"Whereupon you declared imperiously that she should not scold Matthew because it was your kitten."

Arabella nodded. "She shook her head and said that she could see that I was sadly lacking in discipline and she wished she could hope Miss Lambton would give me a good whipping. Then Mamma looked down her nose at her and said she was very satisfied with Miss Lambton."

"I can just picture it. Were you punished?"

"Mamma read me a lecture, then I had to return the kitten to the stables and copy out some verses about being kind to animals."

"Nothing about kindness to rectors' wives?" Caro asked impishly. "And she is to be your mother-in-law."

"It didn't matter before, as we would not have seen a lot of them, but now—" Arabella broke off as Lord Marfield and Mr Neary approached, clearly bent on dancing.

It was many years since the sixth Earl of Hawebury had last visited the capital and the notice of his death might have gone unremarked were it not for the additional information that, due to the tragic deaths within the past year of his son, Lord Ferraunt, and three grandsons, he was succeeded by his cousin the Reverend Thomas Ferraunt D.D. of Berks, grandson of the fourth Earl. It was not long before some ladies remembered that Miss Malvin had mentioned that Major Ferraunt's absence from town was due to a family matter. Two and two were quickly put together, resulting in a plethora of calls on Lady Malvin whose seat, it was recalled, was also in Berkshire.

Arabella admired the composure with which Mamma agreed that yes, the new Earl of Hawebury was the incumbent of their parish in Berkshire, adding that he and her husband had been friends since they met at Oxford. Yes, she concurred, Major Ferraunt was the earl's son.

"Has Major Ferraunt any brothers?" one ambitious mother enquired. This was the burning question. Had the future heir to an earldom been let slip through their maternal fingers?

"Major Ferraunt is an only son," Mamma answered.

"Were you aware that his father was Hawebury's heir?" another matron enquired. Her spiteful glance at Arabella suggested that her hostess had unfairly concealed such a prize from the marriage mart, to her own daughter's advantage.

Arabella waited for her mother to annihilate her, but instead of issuing a well-deserved set-down, Mamma smiled slightly. "I never thought about it, but had I been asked, I should have said I was very sure he was not."

"Perhaps he did not know himself," Lady Nugent suggested. "I do not recall seeing any notice of the deaths of the previous heirs."

"The old earl was very likely too grief-stricken to think of it," Caro said. "How old was he? Eighty-five or eighty-six?"

"And to lose his son and grandsons within one year—it doesn't bear thinking about," Arabella added.

This successfully changed the tone of the conversation and, with the exception of the Nugents, the visiting ladies departed to consider and disseminate the information they had gleaned.

"What vampires," Caro said disdainfully. "I am sure Major Ferraunt will be inundated with invitations when he returns. You were very quiet, Bella."

"I did not want to let on that I knew more than was in the papers."

"No, they would have fallen on you and not released you until they had extracted the very last drop. But show me your beautiful ring. Did he give it to you?"

The old earl's will was very simple. Drawn up hastily after the deaths of his daughter-in-law and infant grandson, it left everything to his cousin and heir, Thomas Ferraunt.

"And what of his granddaughter?" Thomas's father asked sharply.

"She is amply provided for by her mother's marriage settlement," the solicitor answered. "His lordship was unwilling to further weaken the estate after the devastation wrought by the fourth earl. On top of a jointure of one thousand pounds per annum to his widow, who queened it in Bath for over forty years, he left a considerable sum to their son." He sighed and looked at his fingernails. "A dissolute young man, I fear. We never heard how he did, but it is to be assumed that he frittered it away."

Thomas raised an eyebrow at this remark and even his mild-mannered sire was provoked enough to glare over his spectacles and say coldly, "You will speak with respect of my father and grandparents, Brierley."

"What? Oh, yes. I had not thought—I beg your pardon, my lords."

While Thomas and his father sat with the family solicitor and man of business, the new countess consulted with the steward, housekeeper and butler about the necessary domestic arrangements.

"They are weary of death," his mother said that evening as they sat in the countess's parlour. "The earl's passing on top of the other tragedies has shattered them; he ruled for almost six decades and was the only master many have known. And although relieved to know that there is an heir, they wonder what changes we may bring. But we need not think about that now. Our chief aim must be to arrange his funeral."

"We must be grateful the fashion for midnight burials of the nobility has not reached here, although I should have set my face against it," her husband said.

"The servants know the local customs and have advised which funeral furnishers to use and whom to call upon for assistance. They described Lord Ferraunt's funeral last year and the steward even found details of the obsequies of the previous earl in 1760. Times have changed, of course. We can dispense with the 'featherman' who walked ahead dressed in black and carrying a coffin lid decorated with feathers on his head, I think."

"Good heavens, yes," Thomas interjected.

"But we must have a hatchment over the door. And we must find rosemary somewhere—the stock here is sadly depleted and we need sprigs for favours, and black silk ribbon to tie them. Strictly speaking, the servants should all have new mourning clothes, but Mrs Fulcher said that those they received for poor Lady Ferraunt were still very good. But one does not wish to seem neglectful or disrespectful either, and I suggested we set the sewing woman and her late ladyship's maid to sewing new aprons and caps for the women and sashes and arm and hat-bands for the men. The senior male servants and tenants must also be provided with mourning cloaks. They all need black gloves, of course. And, Dr Ferraunt, you might like to consider giving mourning rings to the senior servants who have been here many years."

She barely waited for her husband to murmur, "Whatever you think right, my dear," before continuing, "Then there must be two feasts—one for the nobility, gentry and chief tenants here and one for the lower orders at the Ferraunt Arms. I shall tell the steward to arrange a price per adult and per child for a good ordinary and a reasonable amount of ale and we shall issue tickets to everyone entitled to attend so that we do not finish up feeding the entire county." She turned to her son. "I think, Thomas, that it would be a good idea for you to look in at the inn and make the landlord's acquaintance."

He touched his hand to his brow in salute. "Yes, ma'am."

"I see you have it all in hand, my dear," the new earl said gratefully.

She gave him a satisfied smile. "How did you fare with the solicitor?"

"Poorly. He is either ignorant or resentful or both. My cousin left everything to me, with no provision for old retainers or indeed for the child who is said to be adequately provided for through her parents' marriage settlements. We shall have to look into all of that."

"And inspect the books in general," Thomas suggested. "That is essential if you are to know where you stand."

"Where we stand, Thomas. I cannot do it by myself. In fact, I think the sensible thing would be for you to take charge of things now rather than wait for my demise."

"There are some things only the earl can do," Thomas pointed out.

His father nodded. "Then they must remain with me, provided you will take on the rest—by which I mean the estate and, in particular, Venetia. Your mother and I are too old to raise a child—it would not be fair to saddle her with us as guardians."

Although Thomas could see the sense in this, he said firmly, "It is not alone my decision to make. I must first consult Arabella."

His mother frowned. "We cannot abdicate all responsibility, Dr Ferraunt, simply return to the rectory and pretend nothing has happened."

"Do not ask me to give up my calling completely, my dear. What about my pupils? I cannot abandon them and I would miss my church."

"We are called to other duties now," she said implacably.

"You are right. Forgive me, Thomas. I suppose I should have said I would like you to take command, but I will support you to the best of my ability."

"We need not make any decisions tonight," Thomas said soothingly.

"I agree," his mother said. "I think I'll retire. Good night, my dears." She tilted her cheek first to her son and then to her husband. "Do not sit up all night brooding," she admonished the latter. "If the Lord has sent us this burden, it is because we can bear it. When there is a will, there is always a way."

Thomas closed the door behind his mother and went over to the tray of decanters that had been placed on a side table. "Will you take a glass of port with me, Father?"

"I will, Thomas. Oh dear, what a day. It is indeed providential that you are at home and were able to come with us. Thank you, my boy." He took the glass and sipped cautiously. "Very palatable indeed."

"Our cousin clearly didn't stint himself," Thomas agreed. "I confess I am curious about the considerable sum that allegedly came to my grandfather."

"Yes. It has been on my mind to talk to you about that. I don't know what his inheritances were, either from his father or later from his mother—whether she spent that thousand a year or saved some of it—and of course he was a military man himself, but when he died he left a tidy fortune. Its first charge was my own mother as long as she lived, but it paid for you at Oxford and later for the allowance I made you as a young officer. At your request, that stopped when your great-uncle died. Since then, I have drawn only half of the income each year. Together with my stipend, it provides comfortably for your mother and me as well as enabling us to do good where it is needed. There remain about forty thousand pounds in the funds and a small property in Shropshire near Shrewsbury, which is let at present. The house in Queen's Square in Bath probably reverted to the Hawebury estate when my grandmother died, for it did not come to me."

Thomas's jaw dropped so much that it pulled on the scar on his cheek. He rubbed it absently as he considered what he had just heard.

His father must have noticed his astonishment, for he continued, "If I had known sooner that you considered selling out, I would have discussed this with you and indeed had resolved to do so once you informed us of your betrothal, but of course everything has changed now."

"It might be wiser not to mention we have independent capital until we have a better idea of how the estate is fixed," Thomas said thoughtfully. "While an injection of unentailed cash may benefit it, we should be wary of making any plans or promises until we know the whole picture."

"I am sure you are right."

"What sort of settlement did you make on my mother when you married?"

"She has pin money of two hundred and fifty guineas a year—although I doubt she spends that much—and will have a jointure of five hundred if I predecease her. I suppose I should reconsider that now—increase them both."

"I think so. As a countess she will have different demands on her purse."

"We must also consider Arabella's settlement."

Thomas nodded. "We shall have to take the Hawebury estate into account, which will make the drawing-up of it considerably more complicated. I have the feeling that the people here are more loyal to the estate as they know it than they are to us. It is understandable, perhaps, but they must learn who is in charge."

His father sat up. "You have put your finger on it, my boy. They remind me of Hines, the old verger who was still in office when I came to Longcroft. He considered the church his; I was an interloper. Perhaps we should pension the older ones off."

"Not until we have the whole story," Thomas said firmly.

"No doubt you are right." His father finished his port and stood up. "I shall go and keep vigil with my cousin while I say Evening Prayer. Good night, Thomas."

The need to keep vigil over the dead earl until the funeral placed an additional strain on the household. The body lay in a coffin in a north-facing room that had been completely draped with black, its floor strewn with rosemary, lavender and other aromatic herbs to counter the more unpleasant odours that developed as the week wore on. Four beeswax candles burnt constantly, adding their sweet perfume to the heavy air. Thomas had drawn up a roster which ensured that every member of the family and upper servants with the exception of Venetia and her governess shared this duty, reserving to himself the morning hours from four to six. He was used to disturbed nights, he said.

Now he sat beside the open window. It had rained during the night and he gratefully inhaled the scent of damp soil and greenery. When the light grew stronger, he drew Arabella's letter from his pocket and read it again. He had known he could rely on her—and on her family. 'Welcome, brother,' Julian had said to him when he learnt of their betrothal.

What would it be like to be a member of a larger family? His parents had always been content with one another's company and the local society at Longcroft. His father had his parish, his pupils and his books, and his mother capably managed her household and her husband. Once the initial shock was over, she had taken her change of circumstances in her stride.

He would bring Venetia to town himself on Monday. His heart lifted at the thought of seeing Arabella again. He would write to Franklin, too; asking could they meet towards the end of the week. He must also explain matters to his colonel. He had no choice but to sell out now.

But first they must bury the old man.

He nodded to the steward who had come to relieve him and left the room, running down the back stairs to the huge kitchen where a sleepy-eyed kitchen-maid handed him a mug of hot coffee. He gulped it down and held it out for a refill.

"Thank you, Meg."

He took the coffee and the thick ham sandwich she had prepared to the east terrace. After so many years on campaign, where breakfast frequently meant a bite snatched as a bivouacking army readied itself for another day's battle or march, a peaceful breakfast in the fresh country air was a real blessing. He ate slowly, savouring each mouthful. When he was finished, he lit a cheroot and took a notebook and pencil from his pocket. Some habits died harder than others, he thought as he began meticulously to review the arrangements for the day before turning to those for tomorrow's funeral.

She had known, of course, Lord Henry told himself. Her interest in him had waned from the moment the usurper had appeared in town. Women were all the same—fickle, faithless and always with an eye to the main chance. Or was she coerced by her family? Look how Tamm had intervened at Almack's. Perhaps that was it. She had tried to appease him, with her murmured excuse and little smile. Poor girl.

Chapter Twenty-One

They closed the coffin late on Thursday, nailing down the heavy oak lid with firm blows that were muffled by the black wall-hangings. An engraved and water-silvered brass plate bearing the arms and supporters of the dead man gleamed against the pale wood but was soon hidden by the heavy, black, velvet pall.

Early the next morning, the first of a procession of carriages rolled up the long avenue. As the mourners, all male, gathered and were equipped with funeral apparel and favours according to their standing, the furnisher and his underlings bustled to and fro, ensuring the participants knew their places in the cortège, while in the hall the nobility, gentry and important tenants made the acquaintance of the new earl and his heir over a glass of wine and dry cake. At last the hearse and mourning coaches, the carriages, the escort of the local Militia, whose colonel the earl had been, the mutes, pages, pall-bearers, and the cloaked mourners were all marshalled in a fitting panoply of death.

Hats were removed and heads bowed when the new countess entered, clad in a high-waisted, long-sleeved gown of dull silk that billowed and rustled imposingly as she moved. A turban made of twisted lengths of black silk and velvet crowned her white hair, the front of which had been carefully curled. She was accompanied by a young girl—the only surviving descendant of the dead man. They stood silently with Thomas and his father as the coffin was borne through the great oak doors and placed on the hearse drawn by six black horses crowned with nodding black plumes. The men followed. Women, or ladies at least, Thomas had discovered, did not attend an interment and the female servants would be needed to put everything to rights before the guests returned.

He and his father watched as the long procession got underway, led by tenants and estate workers on foot, followed by coaches and carriages all tricked out with the black adornments of mourning. Finally, Thomas and his father took their places in front of the hearse, followed by the steward carrying the earl's coronet on a dark red velvet cushion. It was as impressive as any military parade, and for much the same purpose—to remind onlookers and participants of the dead earl's "pride, pomp and circumstance".

Despite all the doleful trappings, Thomas missed the sincere grief that had surrounded the hastily dug graves in the Peninsula, where a man's comrades gathered bareheaded in a final farewell. He would prefer such a simple ceremony. Could one lay down the nature of one's funeral in one's will? Stipulate no hired carriages, mutes or pages? Something else to be considered when this was over. He would be interested to hear what his father thought of it all but now was not the time to ask him.

In the distance, a muffled bell tolled a doleful summons to the final farewell. They paced solemnly to its mournful beat, hats pulled down so that the brims protected their eyes from the dust thrown up by those who walked before them. *Dust thou art and unto dust shalt thou return.* Thomas looked at this father anxiously. It was a good two miles to the church. They would drive back, he resolved.

"That went off well enough," the new earl remarked several hours later as the last carriage rolled down the avenue. "Too bombastic for my taste, mind, and I hope you will arrange something simpler when my time comes."

"With pleasure, sir," Thomas said, adding hastily, "I do not mean that it will be a pleasure to arrange your funeral—I hope it will be many years before I am called upon to do so, but that I agree with you about such unnecessary ostentation."

His father sighed. "I had hoped to be buried with my predecessors at Longcroft, but it is not to be."

"When the time comes, if Malvin agrees, I could erect a monument in the church there, recalling your long incumbency."

A sudden smile lit his father's face. "Would you, Thomas? I confess I should much prefer a simple marble tablet there to a pompous tomb such as my cousin had prepared for himself and his wife."

"Have you thought of editing your sermons for publication now that you will have more time? That would also be a fitting memorial. We could describe you as '*the Reverend Thomas Ferraunt DD, 7th Earl of Hawebury, sometime Fellow of New College, Oxford and Rector for over thirty years of St Mary's, Longcroft in the County of Berkshire'*."

"Thomas!" His father had tears in his eyes. "That shall be my epitaph. I would much prefer to be remembered by my achievements, such as they are, than by a title acquired through tragedy and an accident of birth."

"Where is Venetia?"

At her son's question, Thomas's mother lowered the volume of sermons she held before her face so that the page was not obscured by the triple ruff of stiff white lace that encased her neck above the high collar of her gown. "Venetia? She is in the schoolroom, I presume."

"Is she not to come down this evening?"

"I thought there was little point as we do not dine together today. I told Fulcher to have cook send up something to her and Miss Dunford and to prepare a supper later for the three of us."

"I did not see Miss Dunford in the hall this morning," he remarked. "I thought she would have been with Venetia."

"She remained in the background, as was proper."

"I see."

He would just look into the schoolroom, he thought. He must take more of an interest in the child. She had looked so lost earlier in the great hall. Had she watched as the coffins of her parents and brothers were carried out? It was too much for any child to bear.

The schoolroom was empty. Thomas examined the collection of books and primers in the little bookcase, admired the framed sampler depicting Noah, his wife and their three sons that hung on the wall and peered at a blotted transcription of the first verses of the *Elegy Written in a Country*

Churchyard—could the woman not have chosen something less melancholic for her pupil? At the other end of the room, a splendid rocking horse stood riderless beside a collection of cricket bats and battledores and shuttlecocks. Had Venetia anyone to play with now?

Where were they? He tugged the bell-pull and waited impatiently until a maid came up.

"Now what is it?" she asked in exasperated tones as she came into the room, then blanched, curtsied and stammered, "I beg your pardon, my lord."

He fixed her with a look that his men had learned to dread but merely said, "Where are Miss Venetia and Miss Dunford?"

"I'm sure I don't know, my lord." She looked at the connecting doors at either end of the long room. "Should I see if they are in one of the other rooms?"

"Yes."

There was no response to her knock on the first door. She opened it quietly then went in. "Miss Dunford is not here, my lord."

Perhaps she had taken her charge for a walk now that the bustle of the funeral was over. He nodded towards the other door. "See if Miss Venetia is within."

When the maid opened the door, he could see that the curtains had been drawn against the evening light. "Miss Venetia?" the maid said. "Miss Venetia?"

He heard a murmur and then, "Lord Ferraunt wishes to speak to you, Miss. Come, get up. Put on a spencer and wrap this shawl around you—you can't go out to his lordship like that. Here, let me tie your cap."

Within minutes, a wary-looking Venetia stood in the doorway.

"You wished to speak to me, Cousin Thomas?"

"Just to see how you go on," he reassured her. "I am sorry to disturb you, especially if you are unwell."

"I feel perfectly well."

"Then why are you in bed at half-past six o'clock?"

"Miss Dunford sent me to bed early because she said I was impertinent."

"And were you?" Thomas asked mildly. It seemed harsh, today of all days.

"I don't think so. I only asked her who the gentleman was to whom she was speaking earlier. She said it was none of my business and I said this was my home and he had come to my grandfather's funeral. And then she said I may not have my dessert, even though cook had sent up little custard cups, and that I was to go to bed at once."

What the devil was the woman about? "It's too fine an evening to go to bed," he said curtly. "Would you like to come for a walk with me?"

"If you please, Cousin Thomas."

He looked at the wide-eyed maid. "Help Miss Venetia—what is your name?"

"Fanny, my lord."

"Help Miss Venetia dress, Fanny. I'll wait here."

"Let us go to the orchard. It's this way."

"Tell me about Miss Dunford," Thomas said as they walked down the narrow path. "How long is she with you?"

"Since last June. My old governess, Miss Knox, married and went to live in Devonshire. She was much nicer."

That must have been just before her father and brothers drowned, Thomas realised. Another loss.

"Miss Dunford says it is very dull here," Venetia said. "She hopes you will stay because she does not want to dine with two old people every day or have to play ombre in the evenings. What is ombre?"

"A card game for three people," Thomas said, frowning.

Venetia put her hand to her mouth. "Pray forget I said that. She would be angry if she knew. I did not mean to tell tales."

Thomas ignored this. If the governess was foolish enough to vent her feelings within earshot of her pupil, she need not complain if what she said was repeated. "Do you like her? Is she kind to you?"

"She always seems to be cross—not just with me but about things. For instance, she grumbled about not going to Bath last winter, as Mamma had promised we would when she engaged her. But that was before Papa and the boys drowned. She doesn't like getting her hem wet or dusty, so we rarely go for a walk and I may not swing on the swing in the orchard. And she can't ride. I haven't ridden my pony since Grandfather became ill."

"I'll take you riding tomorrow."

A huge smile lit her face. "Really, Cousin Thomas? Thank you!"

"Did you know that I am to be married later this year?"

"No."

"To Miss Arabella Malvin, a beautiful and kind young lady. When I wrote telling her about you, she replied inviting you to come and stay with her family for a while."

"May I not stay here?"

"You would find it very lonely for the next weeks, as my father must return to his parish and his pupils until other arrangements have been made for them and I must see about leaving the army."

"But you will all come back here?"

"Yes, but we cannot say precisely when. Remember, when we marry, Miss Malvin will be your cousin too and this way you will get to know her and her family, including her nieces and nephew, two of whom are about your age."

"Where do they live?"

"They are all in London at present, so I would take you there, but in a few weeks they will go home to Malvin Abbey which is in my father's parish of Longcroft and you will go with them."

"May Moonlight come too?

"Moonlight?"

"My pony."

"I'll ask Miss Malvin if the other children have their ponies in London. If not, I'll have him sent to Malvin Abbey to wait for you there."

It was eight o'clock by the time they returned to the house. Venetia had played on the swing in the orchard and they had returned via the stables so that she could visit Moonlight and assure him that she would ride him the next day.

"We'll go in through the kitchen," Thomas said. "Cook may have another custard for you or a strawberry tart."

While Venetia enjoyed these treats with a glass of milk, he had a quiet word with the housekeeper.

"Yes, Fanny mentioned it to me, my lord. I don't think Miss Dunford has returned yet."

"When she does, I wish to speak to her immediately. In the meantime, I would like Fanny to stay with Miss Venetia."

"Two carriages have drawn up outside, Miss Malvin. One is the travelling coach."

Arabella jumped up, surprised. She had not expected them to travel on a Sunday. "I'll come at once."

She arrived at the front door just in time to see Thomas lift a young girl down from the coach. He had come himself! The poor child looked so wan in her black pelisse and bonnet.

Thomas set the girl on her feet. "Here is Miss Malvin to welcome you."

"And you must be Venetia." Arabella held out both her hands. "I am sure we shall be great friends. Come in to the house. You must be tired after such a long journey."

"Yes, and I need," Venetia tugged at Arabella's hand and, when she bent down, whispered, "I need the necessary."

"Of course you do. Come with me."

Arabella smiled apologetically at Thomas as she led Venetia away, saying over her shoulder, "Belshaw, show Major Ferraunt to the small parlour."

"We have put you on the schoolroom floor, beside my nephew and niece. Hermione is twelve and Tony is ten. Little Anne still sleeps in the nursery. How old are you?"

"I shall be ten in August, Miss Malvin."

"So you shall fit in very nicely. I fear we were in such a hurry earlier that we forgot your governess. Perhaps she will be in the schoolroom before us."

Venetia shook her head. "She didn't come with us, just Fanny—she is my maid," she added importantly.

"I see. We have a very kind governess here who used to be my governess and knew your cousin when he was a schoolboy. Shall we go and meet her and the other children after I have shown you your room?"

"What about Cousin Thomas? He won't leave without saying goodbye, will he?"

"I am sure he won't."

Arabella came into Thomas's arms. They closed around her like iron clamps and he kissed her hungrily. He tasted of the ale Belshaw must have brought him and of himself. After some time his grip eased and he raised his head to rest his forehead against hers.

"If you knew how much I needed you," he said on a long sigh. "You cannot imagine what it was like."

"Poor Thomas." She drew him down onto the sofa and sat so close to him that it was only natural that his arm came around her. "Tell me all about it."

"I know we talked about a September wedding," he said after he had described his dismissal of Miss Dunford, "but would you consider marrying sooner—at the end of June, perhaps? Apart from the fact that I don't think I can do it without you, there are so many decisions to be made and most of them will affect you."

She hesitated. Marry within a month? Lallie and Hugo had married quickly too. It might have saved much heartache if they had known each other better, been more comfortable with each other. She could see that it might help if she were included in the discussions at Ferraunt Court, but, once she was married, while her views might be sought, would they be heeded? Married to the heir, she might be expected to dance attendance on his mother—just the role she had always avoided.

"Let me talk to Mamma and Papa and see what they say."

Thomas did not seem to have noticed her prevarication for he pulled her back into his arms. This kiss was more tender. She felt herself melt as she opened to him, her palm against his face, holding him to her. His whiskers were crisply soft, not at all bristly. His hand moved to trace the line of her neck down to where it met her shoulder. She shivered and he paused for a moment, before going on to cup her breast. Her nipple hardened against his touch and he caressed it with his thumb, sending darts of fire to the secret place between her legs. She leaned into his hand. Suddenly a June wedding seemed more appealing.

But now they were in the small parlour. She stilled his roving hand and broke the kiss. "Someone might come."

"You are right," he said reluctantly.

"I promised Venetia you would not leave without saying goodbye."

"No, of course not. Where is she?"

"Miss Lambton said something about taking the children into the garden to let Venetia shake out the fidgets after the long journey. I'll just fetch a bonnet and shawl and come with you. Can you come back and dine with us?"

"Do you not go out this evening?"

"Later, to Lady Needham's musicale. I am sure she would be thrilled if you were to accompany us. She would steal a march on all the other hostesses."

"Good God!"

She smiled at his look of horror. "In fact, I think it an excellent idea. Her parties are always very select, and it would be an easy way of making your bow as Lord Ferraunt. Shall I ask Mamma to send Lady Needham a note letting her know that you will accompany us?"

"Whatever you think best, Arabella," he said, adding with his crooked smile. "You cannot imagine how often I heard my father say that to my mother this last week."

She laughed. "I see you have learnt the first lesson of marriage, my lord."

Millie and Miss Lambton sat in the walled garden while a game of chasing raged about them. Tony was in hot pursuit of Venetia when she suddenly leaped onto a stone bench, crowing, "You can't catch me!"

"You have to get down and then I'll tag you."

She laughed and darted to and fro along the bench while he mirrored her movements on the ground. Suddenly she pulled her skirt up to her knees, hopped up onto the low back of the seat and jumped down on the other side, taking the boy completely by surprise. After a startled moment he gave a whoop and dashed after her.

"What are they playing?" Thomas asked.

"Off-ground tig, Venetia called it," Millie explained. "She used play it with her brothers—you can't be caught if your feet are off the ground."

"I must apologise for imposing her on you, Miss Lambton," Thomas said, "but I should have been very reluctant to send her former governess here—I don't think you would have found her a sympathetic companion."

"Then there is no need to apologise, my lord. If that is the case, to have had to share the schoolroom with her would have been a much worse fate. I shall be happy to help Venetia."

"She is already a different child. She has been so subdued all week—I am glad to see her so light-hearted."

"Cousin Thomas!" Venetia caught sight of him and ran over. "Are you going? When shall I see you again?"

"Before dinner," Arabella answered. "Your cousin is coming back here to dine. When we dine at home, the children always come to the drawing-room for the hour before dinner. Your maid will help you get ready."

Arabella had decided to wear her pale amethyst gown. The very lightest of mourning, it suggested sympathy for and alliance with Thomas's family while avoiding a presumptuous assumption of personal loss.

"An excellent choice," her mother said approvingly. "Lady Needham is enchanted that Thomas comes with us and so pleased that I thought of bringing him. I think, my love, we may now tell our friends of your betrothal. Do you think the earl and countess would come to town for a night if I were to give a little party? Not a ball, of course, so soon after the old earl's death, but a *soirée*."

"I fear it might be too soon, Mamma. I doubt if Thomas's mother has a suitable gown for a start. She was always dressed very appropriately for a rector's wife, but I don't think it would be fair to invite her to a *ton* party at short notice. She was there, remember, when we talked about Ruth and her mother needing new gowns if they were to come to town."

"That is true. It just seems so odd to celebrate your betrothal without Thomas's parents."

"I'll talk to Thomas, see what he thinks. I must hurry; I want to look in on Venetia before I change, make sure she has everything she needs."

Venetia sat in front of her dressing table while her maid brushed her hair. She jumped to her feet when Arabella came in and the maid curtsied.

"Do you have everything you need?"

"Yes, thank you, Miss," the maid said promptly.

Venetia didn't answer and Arabella asked, "Is there something you would like, Venetia?"

"It's just—I only have black dresses, Miss Malvin. I have nothing pretty to wear to the drawing-room like Hermione has."

"Ssh, Miss," Fanny said. "What will Miss Malvin think, with his lordship not dead two weeks and it's not even two months since your poor mother left us."

"And not a year since my father and brothers were drowned. I know. Wearing black doesn't bring them back, Fanny. It's been so long since I could wear anything else."

"I think white with touches of black is perfectly suitable as mourning for children," Arabella said. "That was what Hermione and Anne wore when their uncle was killed last year. Have you no white muslins, Venetia? You could wear one with a black sash."

"We didn't pack any, Miss," the maid said. "They would all be too small now—Miss Venetia shot up this past year."

Arabella went to the bed and inspected the black crape dress that lay ready. "Hmm. Or you could wear a white fichu and sash with this. Black and white hair ribbons, Fanny, and dress Miss Venetia's hair less severely. And we could trim the pantalettes with white lace instead of the black."

"Oh, thank you, Miss Malvin."

"I'll send my maid Horton to you with some trimmings. When did Miss Lambton say to be ready?"

"Half-past six, Miss."

"Then you have plenty of time to change the lace."

"Yes, Miss."

"Tomorrow, we'll see about having some white muslins made, Venetia," Arabella said as she turned to go. "I'll see you downstairs in a little while."

"She is a different child," Thomas murmured to Arabella, looking over to where Venetia was 'helping' five-year old Anne put together a dissected map of the counties of England.

"She misses her brothers, I imagine. It will be good for her to be together with other children again."

"Yes. I am indebted to your mother and Mrs Malvin for taking her in."

The invitation might have been issued in Mamma's name, but it was understood that Venetia was Arabella's responsibility. Did Thomas not see it? Suddenly she felt invisible. He had thanked Miss Lambton earlier, too. Don't be so petty, she scolded herself. He does not mean to overlook you.

Chapter Twenty-Two

The Countess of Needham's select company numbered about a hundred, Thomas estimated as he waited to be announced, and included the Franklins, the Tamms and the Nugents.

"Viscount and Viscountess Malvin, Mr and Mrs Malvin, Miss Arabella Malvin, Lord Ferraunt."

All heads turned at the sound of Thomas's name and the conversation faltered before reviving with new vigour. Lady Needham offered her hand.

"Welcome, Lord Ferraunt. We are delighted you could join us."

Thomas bowed. "Thank you, my lady."

"Are we to have the pleasure of seeing your parents in town this Season?"

"I'm afraid I cannot say, ma'am."

"Pray give your father my compliments," Lord Needham said. "I remember him from Oxford—he was a fellow when I was a fellow-commoner. I was Hope then. Ask him if he remembers the bear."

"I shall make a point of doing so," Thomas said, with a little smile. It was strange to hear his father and a bear mentioned in the same sentence.

The present Viscount Hope seemed to feel the same. "I must hear that story too, sir."

"Not until after your brother comes down," his father said firmly. "I cannot afford to have my paternal authority undermined."

"Come, Ferraunt," Hope said, "let me present you to my sister."

Thomas bowed to Lady Elizabeth who looked charming in a rose-trimmed gown that just skimmed her rose-coloured, silk slippers. She offered him a matter-of-fact, friendly smile.

"I have been telling Miss Malvin that tonight we have two wonderful singers from Vienna to sing Mozart for us."

"What a treat," Arabella said. "He is my favourite composer. I would love to see one of his operas in its entirety, but even to hear some extracts will be thrilling."

"I had the pleasure of seeing *Die Zauberflöte* in Paris last year," Thomas said. "It is an entrancing work."

"Then you will especially enjoy this evening," Lady Elizabeth told him. "Herr Schneider is a noted Papageno and Fräulein Gottlieb sang Pamina for Mozart himself."

"She knew him?" Arabella said, awed. "Lady Elizabeth, would you be so very kind as to introduce me after the concert?"

"If it is possible, I should be delighted to, Miss Malvin, but sometimes these performers are quite temperamental."

Lord Hope laughed. "Are you thinking of the soprano last year? She swore the pianoforte was ill-tuned, fought with her *pianiste* and demanded champagne to soothe her throat. She was quite elevated by the end of her performance but Bolton—that's our butler—was able to get her out of the room with the promise of a little supper ready for her elsewhere."

"Fräulein Gottlieb is not like that," his sister said. "She is just terrified of draughts and we had to promise to close all the windows before she starts to sing."

"Bolton will see to all that," Hope said carelessly.

He stepped aside as a thin lady used her sharp elbows to edge her way into their little circle. A muslin-clad girl hovered beside her, meekly curtseying as the older lady completed her greetings. Thomas had no idea who she was and was grateful for Hope's curt, "Lady Haydon, Miss Haydon."

Lord Hope was not her ladyship's prime target. With a toothy smile that sat oddly on her peevish face, she uttered, "Good evening, Lord Ferraunt. You remember my daughter, of course."

Thomas bowed coolly. "I fear you have the advantage of me, ma'am."

The lady tittered. "Now don't say you have forgotten us. We met at Lady Malvin's. I suppose I must forgive you, especially as you have been occupied by other matters since we last spoke."

He cast a despairing glance at Arabella who shook her head slightly and looked past them to greet Lady Alys Franklin who came up on Lord Marfield's arm.

"I don't know whether to congratulate or commiserate with you, Lord Ferraunt," Lady Alys said with a sympathetic smile. "I know how my brother felt when he found himself in somewhat similar circumstances two years ago."

"They are rather—unsettling, I admit."

"At least Lord Franklin grew up on the family estate," Lady Elizabeth remarked. "Your case is more like that of a newly-married lady who moves to a new home."

"That is very true," Thomas said, "and ladies do it all the time, so it cannot be very difficult."

Arabella opened her mouth, but before she could say anything they were surrounded by the Halworth family, all eager to discuss the startling transformation of their parson into a peer of the realm.

"How does the rector?" the Admiral asked jovially. "I'll warrant he is not too happy at the recent turn of events."

"He will be sad to leave his parish," Thomas said.

"And we shall miss him, but I fear he has no choice. His duty now calls him elsewhere."

"Isn't it exciting?" Ruth said to Arabella. "And to think that you have known Major, I beg his pardon, I mean Lord Ferraunt forever; indeed, one could say you were almost brother and sister."

This was too much. Before his betrothed could reply, Thomas tucked her hand into the crook of his arm, declaring, "No, Miss Halworth, one could not say that. It would give quite the wrong impression."

"Indeed," Arabella confirmed composedly. "Lord Ferraunt and my brother Captain Malvin were great friends, but I have never regarded him as another brother."

"I am relieved to hear it," Thomas said. "It is not a sentiment one looks for in one's bride, after all."

"What? Is it all settled between you?" Ruth exclaimed.

Thomas bowed slightly. "Miss Malvin has done me the honour of agreeing to be my wife."

“Well, you have fooled me nicely, but I am sure I wish you both very happy.”

The Admiral and Lady Halworth hastened to add their felicitations while Lady Haydon, who continued to hover nearby, turned on her heel and towed her daughter away.

“When is the wedding?” Ruth asked eagerly.

Thomas had had enough. “We have not yet decided. Pray excuse us, Miss Halworth.”

“She is very wearing, isn’t she?” Arabella said as they moved on.

“Like a puppy. I wonder does she ever think before she speaks.”

“I doubt it. On the other hand, she gave you the opportunity to confirm our betrothal. The Haydons overheard you too. If they spread the news, it may save you from similar onslaughts. Now, where shall we sit? With the Nugents or over there with Captain Malcolm?”

The performers smiled at each other and Fräulein Gottlieb’s voice soared in airy flight above her partner’s deeper tones before spiralling down to join him again.

“Man und Weib und Weib und Mann
Reichen an die Gottheit an”

Beside Thomas, Arabella sighed softly and moved so that her hand just touched his. *Man and wife and wife and man reach towards divinity.* She felt it too, he thought, intertwining his fingers with hers. Her clasp tightened when the magical phrase floated upwards again. When the music stopped, she smiled tenderly at him, tears sparkling on her eyelashes.

"That was so beautiful. Do you know the story? Are they lovers? Is there a happy end?"

"Yes, no and yes; they both long for love and will find it but not with each other."

"Sssh. They're starting again."

"My lord." Mr Nugent nodded coolly. He seemed to brace himself and added, "I understand that congratulations are in order."

"Thank you, Nugent." Thomas offered his hand and the other man took it.

"She positively glows with happiness. Be good to her, Ferraunt."

"Trust me." Thomas nodded towards the vestibule. "Step out here for a moment and tell me if there was much talk in the clubs about Danlow's bet. You would probably have heard more than Matthew."

Mr Nugent wrinkled his brow. "Some; not a lot and not in connection with her. It was more satisfaction that he had been given his own again. He dropped about five thousand, I believe. There were some mutterings that it had not been exactly fair play as some of the fellows had made a point of standing up with Bella, but none of them had taken up the wager and there was no sign that they were put up to it by those who had. And then it emerged that Danlow had convinced Drummond Burrell to prevail upon his wife to allow the extra waltz and that wasn't felt to be fair and square either. Everyone felt Tamm behaved very properly. Danlow has been playing least in sight since."

"And will continue to do so if he knows what's good for him."

"I'll tell you something else, Ferraunt."

Thomas raised an eyebrow.

"There's been another yellow-haired bird of paradise found strangled. In Covent Garden, this time. I think it's strange, but Matthew says it's only because we know of the first one; otherwise we'd make nothing of it. After all, the constable said that they regularly find murdered whores." He glanced around to make sure they could not be overheard and lowered his voice. "Apparently, some men like to throttle a woman while they're rogering her and sometimes go too far."

"Surely you don't think this has anything to do with Danlow?"

"No, no. I never heard he was that way inclined," Nugent said. "He's a cold-blooded bastard, if you ask me. There's Marfield. I want to talk to him about a horse." He nodded to Thomas and strolled away.

But Danlow has a weakness for fair-haired women, Thomas thought, remembering the one he had seen in his lordship's company at Drury Lane. Or was that just a coincidence?

A hand clapped him on the shoulder. "At last I have a companion in misfortune," Lord Franklin said with a grin. "How do you find your elevation, Major?"

"Deuced awkward. I haven't felt so inept since I was a Johnny-raw. You at least were 'to the manner born'."

"And escaped as soon as I could. When it comes to managing the estate, I was just as much at a loss as you. But your situation is worse," he said more seriously, "because your father is very likely all at sea too."

"That's it."

"Is there anything I can do to help?"

"I'm afraid not, unless you can find me an adjutant or whatever the civilian term is—someone to help me make better sense of all the paperwork and support me with the men of business and the lawyers. I have my own affairs to deal with and my father's, to boot. Eventually our funds will become part of the Hawebury estate, but first I must be sure that all is according to Cocker. I have no reason to suppose it is not, but—"

"Better be safe than sorry," Franklin agreed. "You want a secretary with some idea of the law and estate accounts but also with *nous*; ideally a gentleman—a younger son or the son of a younger son, perhaps. I'll make some enquiries. How long do you remain in town?"

"I'm not sure. Hawebury left an orphaned granddaughter who is not yet ten. I came up chiefly to bring her to stay with the Malvins, but I had better see Greenwood and make arrangements to sell out at once."

"Good God, yes! The last thing you want is to be recalled to France."

"I don't know—it might be more peaceful, at that!"

Franklin laughed. "We'll talk again before you leave. You're still in Poland Street, I take it?"

"Yes. I'll keep it on until the end of June at least."

Thomas nodded to Franklin and returned to Lady Needham's drawing-room. Arabella was still among the group clustered around the evening's singers but, almost as if she had felt his entrance, she looked up and her eyes met his. Her uncle, Mr Forbes, stood beside her and, satisfied that she was happy and in good hands, he joined a little group of uniformed officers, perhaps for the last time as one of them. But he had The Crossed Swords, he remembered, and Franklin promised to be a good friend.

Chapter Twenty-Three

Arabella quickly slipped into a morning gown. Schoolroom prayers were at half-past seven. Millie always attended them, and she should too, as long as Venetia was with them, just as Mamma had always come for her own children when she was at home.

Miss Lambton nodded approvingly and moved away from Venetia, making room for Arabella to stand beside her. Many years ago, the rector had written a simple form of the Catechism and Morning Prayer for use by children up to the age of twelve. With a murmur of thanks, Arabella accepted the booklet Miss Lambton offered her and held it so that Venetia could read it too.

It was strange to play Mamma's role, asking the questions of the catechism in turn with Millie, but it seemed she was now a guardian, or stepmother, almost. Venetia seemed pleased to have her there. She stood close, leaning into Arabella's side, and listened carefully. At Arabella's prompt she read the answers to her questions and repeated the psalm and the Lord's Prayer with the other children.

"Can you remain with us for a little while, Miss Malvin?" Miss Lambton asked when prayers were over. "I shall set the others their first tasks and then would like to have a little chat with Venetia, see what she has been doing and how far she is."

"Certainly, Miss Lambton." Arabella smiled inwardly at this echo of her mother's gracious tones. Was this how Mamma had coped when she found herself a mother as well as a bride?

Venetia read aloud fluently, they discovered, with a lively intonation and a natural feel for punctuation, but must practise her copperplate. She liked arithmetic, she revealed, and became excited at the prospect of learning the use of the Globes. Mamma had taught her the names of the most common flowers, but she had no idea of the principles of botany and was enthralled by the copy of Miss Wakefield's letters that Miss Lambton produced. She hated embroidery. She had completed a boring sampler and never wanted to sew a stitch again. She loved to sing, but Miss Dunford had said she should not while she was in mourning, which she couldn't understand because Papa had loved to hear her—he had called her his little linnet.

"You shall sing here," Arabella said gently. "A music master comes twice a week to teach the others and we shall ask him to stay an additional hour for you. He also teaches pianoforte. What about drawing and water-colours?"

"I don't think I am very good at them," the child said doubtfully, "but I would like to try again now that I am older."

"Practise makes perfect," Miss Lambton said. "Once you can control your hand you will find it easier."

Venetia muttered, "Yes, ma'am," and then asked, "Do you teach Latin, Miss Lambton? My brothers' tutor, Mr

Markham, started to teach me when I was seven, but of course he did not stay after—" She fell silent.

"I teach beginners' Latin," the governess answered, clearly surprised. "I think it is the best way to learn grammar. When my pupils are ten, the boys go to school and the girls start to learn French instead."

"Julian and Millie will have to make other arrangements for Tony now," Arabella said. "He was due to start with Dr. Ferraunt—I mean your cousin, the earl, Venetia—after the summer holidays."

"Good Heavens! I had not thought of that," Miss Lambton said. "I must remind Mrs Malvin. Well, I think that gives us enough to get you started, Venetia. There is time to settle you at your desk before breakfast."

"That reminds me, Miss Lambton," Arabella said. "Horton will want to measure Venetia for some white dresses today. She can also make some pinafores—white is not very practical in the schoolroom."

"We could cut up my blacks," Venetia suggested. "Fanny can help."

"That's a good idea. We shall keep the best ones and see how they can be re-trimmed properly with white, not just something makeshift like yesterday evening."

Venetia jumped up and threw her arms around Arabella. "Thank you, Miss Malvin. You are most kind."

"Why, it is nothing, Venetia. I am glad to be able to help you."

"When shall I see you again?"

"I'm not sure yet what my engagements are today, but I'll look in again this afternoon. Just not between two and three o'clock."

Everyone knew not to disturb the schoolroom during quiet reading time. Miss Lambton always allocated an hour for this and an hour after dinner for quiet work when her pupils might do what they liked, and the worst sanction in her armoury was the withdrawal of these privileges with the resulting imposition of a task suitable to the offence committed.

Arabella bent and kissed the girl's cheek. "Be a good girl and mind Miss Lambton. She used to be my governess. She makes the lessons interesting and I know you will find her very kind."

Venetia nodded solemnly. "That's what Cousin Thomas said. I think he was right."

It was half-past eight. If she hurried, she should reach the Park in time, provided Matthew was prepared to accompany her. Or, wait! Now that they were betrothed, surely she no longer needed a chaperone to ride with Thomas? He could come and collect her. It was too late to send a note today, but from tomorrow that was what they would do.

Matthew met her on the stairs. "Where have you been, Sis?"

"In the schoolroom with Venetia. Are we riding this morning?"

"I'm sorry, I can't—I'm meeting some of the fellows at Angelo's. But you don't need me anymore, do you?"

"No, but I forgot to tell Thomas to call for me." She shrugged. "It doesn't matter. I have plenty to do today."

"Lord Ferraunt has called, Miss Malvin."

Arabella jumped up from the desk where she had been trying to compile the list of articles she would need for her bride-clothes. It was not yet twelve, but Thomas need no longer stand on ceremony in this house. Depending on how long he planned to stay in town, this might be her only opportunity to talk privately to him.

"Show him into the small parlour, Belshaw."

Thomas stood slump-shouldered at the window looking down into the garden. He wore his Parisian clothes instead of his usual regimentals.

"Good morning, Thomas."

He barely glanced back at her. "Arabella."

"Is something wrong?"

"No, nothing, or nothing new at least."

"You seem blue devilled."

"Do I?" He turned to face her. "I've sold out. I am no longer a soldier. Eleven years wiped out with the stroke of a pen."

"Thomas!" She put her hands on his chest and looked up into his face. "That is foolish talk and you know it. Those years have made you the man you are—they are written on your body and in your heart; they set you apart from all who have not served as you have and mark you as a Peninsula man, a Waterloo man."

"'We happy few, we band of brothers?'" he asked savagely.

She flinched at his sarcastic tone, dropping her hands and taking a step back.

"You may sneer but you cannot deny that there is a special fellow-feeling among those who have fought together, a sort of loyalty, even. Do you think your former comrades will shun you now?"

"No, of course not."

"Then what is it?"

His mouth twisted in a rueful smile. "I'm sorry. I shouldn't have taken my ill-humour out on you. I just had not thought it would happen so quickly—'Sign here and here; thank you, Lord Ferraunt'." He sighed. "Strictly speaking, I am still Major Ferraunt until my resignation is gazetted, but that, apparently, is only a formality. I feel as if I am in a strange country where I do not know the laws."

"It sounds a bit like getting married. That happens just as fast. One enters the church single and emerges married. The only difference is that there is no going back. An officer who has sold his commission may purchase another if he changes his mind, but marriage is for ever."

His tense expression eased and his lips curved into his crooked smile. "I hadn't thought of that. But, speaking of marriage, are you happy to marry by the end of June?" When she did not respond immediately his smile faded. "Do you not like the notion?"

She didn't, not exactly, but how to explain her misgivings?

"You cannot deny things have changed since you made your offer," she said defensively.

"No—although the change was not of my doing."

"But you—we—still have to deal with it. I'm not sure where I fit in anymore."

"Fit in? You will still be my wife. The only difference is that you will be Lady Ferraunt instead of Mrs Ferraunt, but you will not object to that, I am sure."

She shrugged. "Were my sole ambition to be Lady Somebody, I could have achieved it in my first season."

"Indeed? Should I be flattered that you did not accept such offers?"

"If you like. I merely meant that a title is not important to me."

"I would rather be without it too. But I am still the same man, sweetheart."

"You are, but you cannot deny that the circumstances are no longer the same."

His brows twitched together. "What do you mean?"

She sat and waved him to the chair opposite. "If I understood you correctly, your father does not wish to give up his scholarly pursuits or take on the responsibility of being earl. He wishes to abdicate in your favour as far as possible."

"Yes."

"And you have agreed to his request."

"More or less." He stretched out his legs. "I said I would have to consult you, but frankly, I do not see that I have any choice. He is too old to change his way of life so radically. He must either rely too much on his steward and man of business or effectively leave everything to me. The earldom will come to me sooner or later. I think it best for all concerned if I take charge from the outset with full authority to act on behalf of my father. Anything else can only lead to confusion and chaos." He raised an eyebrow. "May I not count on your support?"

"How do you wish me to support you? From what you say, your mother has ably stepped into the countess's shoes and picked up the reins at Ferraunt Court. I doubt she will be willing to relinquish them so quickly."

"I hadn't thought about that, but you are very likely right."

"So what will Lady Ferraunt do?"

His eyes gleamed. "What wives usually do, I hope."

"Thomas! That is precisely what I cannot do. I shall not be mistress of our household."

"What do you mean?"

"You say you want my support, but it seems to me that you and your parents have decided that you will become earl in all but name to your mother's countess. Your father will retreat to his study, you to the estate office and I? Am I to be your mother's lady-in-waiting, there to run her errands and do whatever tasks she sees fit to delegate to me?"

"What's wrong with that? A subaltern cannot immediately become commander-in-chief, after all, and I am sure you and my mother will deal splendidly together. It is not as though she is a stranger to you."

It was on the tip of her tongue to point out that that was partly the problem; there was a great difference between being a rector's wife and a countess. But then she must remind him that while his mother had very little notion of the role of the mistress of a grand estate, his betrothed had been brought up to fulfil just such a position. It would sound too much as if she sought to depose his mother. She didn't, but she refused to be subservient to her. She must have her own domain, but how could she explain this? At last she said, "If we are using military terms, to go from daughter to subordinate daughter-in-law could not be considered a promotion."

She raised her chin and met his questioning gaze.

After a couple of minutes he said, "Your position would not be that of my mother's daughter-in-law but of my wife—Lady Ferraunt and, in due course, the Countess of Hawebury."

In due course. His wife, not Arabella, a person in her own right. "When you asked me to be your wife, you also asked me to be your true companion in all things. We would share everything, you said. We were going to set up our own establishment, make a new life for ourselves. I know it is not your fault that things have changed so radically, but—Thomas, I don't want to be merely the woman to whose arms you return at night; one who otherwise has no say in how we live or what we do."

A brittle silence stretched between them. At last he said, "If you find my altered circumstances so unsatisfactory, I shall not stand in your way if you wish to withdraw from our betrothal."

Arabella's spine stiffened. There could be only one answer to such a statement. He could not withdraw but she would. When she stood, he rose with her. Tears stinging her eyes, she silently removed his ring from her finger and placed it on the palm of her hand. He said nothing, did nothing when she held it out to him. After long moments her hand began to tremble. Without saying another word, she tilted it so that the ring fell to the floor. It hit the polished boards with a dull clink, bounced and rolled under a bookcase.

She inclined her head gravely. "My lord."

Head held high, she walked towards the door. She would not cry.

She had just passed him when a strong hand caught her wrist and swung her back to face him.

"Don't you dare 'my lord' me," he growled, catching her other wrist and holding both behind her back so that she was pulled hard against his body.

He kissed her fiercely, but she was not in the mood for kisses and nipped sharply at his lip. He jerked and she snapped, "Release me this instant, sir!"

"I will never release you."

"What a change of tune, my lord. It is not five minutes since you requested I break our betrothal."

"What folly is this? I never said such a thing."

"Not directly, no. A gentleman cannot withdraw, but when he says he will not object if the lady does—well, a nod is as good as a wink—"

"Arabella—you must know I didn't mean it that way!"

"Oh? So you just wanted to put a pistol to my head? Marry you on your terms or not at all?"

"No!"

His grasp had slackened. She tugged her hands free and stepped back from the circle of his arms.

He knelt on one knee to retrieve the ring. For a long moment, he looked up at her before placing it on a table with an audible click. His crooked smile made her want to weep.

"I don't know what to say to you, Arabella. I think it best that I go." He came lithely to his feet. "Your servant, Miss Malvin."

A brief bow and he was gone.

She stood paralysed, listening as the rap of his boot-heels grew faint, fainter. He had left her. Suddenly frantic, she rushed to the parlour door, only to see him at the end of the corridor, disappearing into the hall. Even if she ran after him, he would have left the house before she could reach him. Shaking, she collapsed into a chair.

What had happened? How had it come to this? She tried to reconstruct their conversation but could not. His ring reproached her from the side table. She could not leave it here—the wound was too raw to risk comment. It was cool and heavy in her hand and the colours shimmered and blurred as she stared at it. She groped blindly for her handkerchief, sniffed inelegantly and dashed her cuff across her eyes, then headed for the back stairs, praying she could reach her room unobserved.

Chapter Twenty-Four

Thomas felt as if he had taken a knock to the head—his stomach churned and fragments of speech and broken images chased each other through his shattered brain. She had tried to give him back his ring and when he wouldn't, couldn't take it, had dropped it at his feet. She had treated him as a stranger, called him, 'my lord,' as cool as bedamned and sailed past him, her nose in the air. He had stopped her. He couldn't let her leave him.

Her hand shook as she held the ring out to him. Why had he said nothing? He had stood there like a great looby, dumbstruck and paralysed. His brain still felt numb.

And then she had said it was he who wished to dissolve their betrothal, when he had only thought of her. She was clearly unhappy, and he did not wish her to feel coerced or obliged to him in any way. She had been quick enough to take him up on his offer to release her. Very likely she now regretted her earlier acceptance. God knew that he didn't want to be Ferraunt or, later, Hawebury. But he had no alternative. Could she not see that? One had to do one's duty. But how would he manage without her? He had been sorely tempted to toss her over his shoulder and carry her off. In the end, he had thought it best to leave.

His mind a whirligig of recollection and recrimination, he wandered aimlessly through the streets, ducking past carriages and ignoring passers-by until his errant footsteps brought him back to Poland Street. He was tempted to go into the inn next door but was in no mood for company.

"A bottle of brandy, Mrs Platts," he said to his landlady when she came out from her little parlour. "I am not at home to callers."

"Certainly, my lord."

Mrs Platts had at first been overawed by his elevation but had quickly become accustomed to it and, he thought, was secretly proud of her noble tenant. He tried to imagine her face if he had arrived with Arabella over his shoulder. Would she hurry up the stairs to open the door for him or, more likely, command him, 'to put that young lady down instanter,' with a rider of, 'I had thought better of you, my lord'.

He collapsed into an armchair with a large drink. But he couldn't find oblivion in a glass. How could he retrieve the situation? Would she receive him if he called again? What could he give, what might he offer that she would accept?

At four o'clock, his heart in his mouth, Thomas again rapped the knocker at Malvin House.

"Miss Malvin is not at home, my lord."

Did Belshaw look more implacable than usual? Dare he enquire if Miss Malvin was within and prepared to make an exception for him?

While he was wondering how best to phrase his request, the butler continued, "I understand she has gone to the Green Park with the children."

"Thank you, Belshaw."

Apparently, he was still persona grata with the Malvins' butler. Encouraged, Thomas looked down at the posy of cream roses bound with ivy. "I'll leave these, in case I fail to find her. Have them put in her room." He took out one of his cards and impulsively scribbled on the back, *Your humble servant, Thomas.*

The Green Park was not far from Curzon Street. Soon Thomas was strolling across its lawns, dodging kite-flyers, avoiding hoop-bowlers and shuttlecock players and giving a wide berth to a group of very young ladies playing puss-in-corner. The greensward was unbroken by flower beds and footpaths and groups of women and children ebbed and flowed across the grass, mingling and separating, amalgamating into larger groups that as suddenly flew apart again. He looked around for the Malvin House party but could not see them.

"Look out, sir!"

He was just in time to catch the ball and toss it back to its youthful owner. He proceeded with more caution after a cherubic infant ran straight into his legs and had to be steadied, comforted and restored to its apologetic nursemaid.

In the end it was Venetia who found him, running up to exclaim, "Cousin Thomas! This is famous! Come, we are over here."

"You look very fine," he said, eying the dark green pelisse edged with black that she wore over a white muslin dress. Her simple straw bonnet was trimmed with matching green and black ribbons.

"Hermione had it last year when her grandfather died. Miss Malvin said I need not wear black all the time. She is having new clothes made for me, but Hermione lent me this."

"That was kind of her," How like Arabella to continue to care for the girl even though she was at outs with the child's guardian.

"She does not generally come to the park either, Hermione says, but came today for me. Do you know, Cousin Thomas, she even came to schoolroom prayers this morning, just as if she were my mother, and looked in yesterday to say goodnight before she went out in the evening." She sighed. "Her gowns are truly beautiful."

Venetia halted beside two blankets spread on the grass to provide seating for Arabella, Mrs Malvin, Miss Lambton and two other ladies. Two stout, liveried footmen stood nearby. "Look who is here, Miss Malvin."

"Good day, ladies." Thomas bowed to the little group and held out a hand to Arabella. "May I speak to you for a moment, Miss Malvin?"

Her eyes met his warily. She was too pale, he thought with a pang. After a moment, she placed her hand in his and permitted him to help her to her feet. Her glove was smooth beneath his fingers—she was not wearing his ring.

The other ladies smiled benevolently when he placed her hand on his sleeve and invited her to stroll with him. Her consent was silent—she had not even said 'good day' to him. When they were far enough from the little group to be unobserved, he stopped.

"I am so sorry, Arabella."

"For what?"

So he was to confess his sins. But what were they? What had he done that was wrong? Damn it, why was he so tongue-tied? He had frozen when she took the ring from her finger in a way that would have earned any soldier, let alone an officer, a severe reprimand. How was it he could face the might of Napoleon's army but not the loss of one young woman?

"For giving you cause to think I wanted to break our betrothal," he said finally. "I swear I never intended to."

"You do not seem to know what you want. One minute you say you will not stand in my way if I wish to do so, the next you will not release me and in the third, you leave. I had not thought you so volatile in your humour."

"I am not, generally,"

"And all because I said, 'my lord'?"

He shook his head. "It was the dismissive way you said it—I could have been any lordling. And then you walked away from me. I couldn't let you go."

She shrugged. "I went because you did not react or speak to me."

"I was petrified," he admitted, "unable to respond. I know I said I would not stand in your way, and perhaps I should not if you can no longer bear the thought of our marriage, but I simply could not take the ring from you, Arabella. I don't want to let you go. But I don't know what to do. I will beg you to stay, if that is what you want."

"No. That is not what I want."

"What do you want?" he asked desperately. "Tell me and I'll give it to you."

"It's not as simple as that," she said sharply. "You make it sound as if I want a new bonnet or a diamond necklace. I told you what I did not want, and you told me what you must do. I will not ask you to turn your back on your family for me—it would mean the death of any happiness we might have had."

"Do you think I can be happy if I turn my back on you? There has to be a middle way. Surely we can discover one?"

She rubbed her arms as if she were cold. "I had hoped we could. But not here and not today."

"When then? Tomorrow?"

She shook her head. "It's too soon. I need a day to think."

"The day after then?"

When she hesitated, he said, "Please, Arabella. Let us make a beginning."

"Very well."

He tucked her hand into the crook of his elbow. "Come, let us walk a little." He felt as if he had clawed his way back from a precipice when she fell into step with him.

"Thank you for caring for Venetia," he said quietly. "I am glad to see her out of black."

"I know it is not three months since her mother died, but the poor child has been wearing mourning for so long."

"I must admit that the trappings of mourning seem absurd to me."

"I agree, especially when it comes to children. Otherwise—at first it cocoons you from the world and that is no bad thing, but afterwards, as the weeks and months go on, it becomes second nature so that it seems almost a betrayal when you begin to lighten it. That was the case for me with Arthur, at least. With my grandfather, we observed the minimum permissible but then it was all outward show. None of us mourned him, not even Hugo."

"Venetia seemed to have a genuine affection for her grandfather and his last thoughts were for her."

"That is good. You must remind her of it, for I am sure she took very little in that night."

"How can I show my appreciation to Miss Lambton? Would it be insensitive to give her money?"

"It would depend on the way you present it. I think if you combined it with a gift, perhaps a book, she would not be offended. Shall I ask Mamma?"

"If you would." He glanced sidelong at her. "What are your engagements for the rest of the week? May I escort you to Almack's?"

"I do not think it would be appropriate."

He stiffened. "I'm sorry; I did not mean to importune you."

"It's not that. It is not two weeks since your cousin died, and it might be thought insensitive. I shall not go either. As far as others are concerned, we are still betrothed."

He stopped and gripped the hand that lay on his sleeve. "As far as I am concerned, too, Arabella. Our betrothal stands unless a day comes when we are forced to agree that our differences are irreconcilable. I hope it never will. Can we agree on that at least?"

Her eyes searched his. At last she said, "If you wish."

"I wish," he said softly. "And will you wear your ring again? It will excite less comment," he added persuasively. "You will not want to have others asking why you no longer do so."

She frowned at him. "You are a sad scoundrel! Give you an inch and you take an ell, my lord!"

"Bella! Take it back!"

"And if I don't?"

"I'll kiss you until you do," he threatened, "here in the middle of the Green Park."

"Oh, that would never do," she said primly. "I take it back—Thomas."

"Once we are married, you may say it," he said generously, "and I shall say 'my lady'." His voice deepened. "You will be my lady, will you not?"

"Stop it, Thomas! It is most unfair of you to press me so."

The little quiver in her voice sobered him. "I'm sorry. When may I call on you?"

"How long do you remain in town?"

"As long it takes to win you back." Telling her that wasn't pressing her, it was just the truth.

"But," she began, stopped and went on, "Come on Thursday morning, about half-past eleven—we should be undisturbed then."

"Thank you."

She glanced over to where the others were on their feet, the rugs folded and Tony's kite-strings securely coiled. "What time is it now?"

He pulled out his watch. "Half-past five. I'll escort you home, if I may."

"Are you coming with us, Cousin Thomas?"

"Your cousin is determined to see us home," Arabella said.

Thomas held out his free hand to Venetia. She slipped hers into it with a shy smile and they followed the Malvin children who ran across the grass to the Queen's Walk. At the Piccadilly Gate they stopped to take the adults' hands before venturing onto the broad thoroughfare that was crowded with tonnish equipages and riders coming or going from Hyde Park.

"I have never seen so many carriages, and so elegant too," Venetia said, her awed gaze fixed on a barouche in which two stern dowagers in imposing bonnets sat bolt upright, their bewigged footmen standing equally stony-faced behind.

A crossing-boy hurried up. He seemed to know the party for he gave them a gap-toothed grin and knuckled his forehead before sweeping vigorously before them.

Arabella reached across to put a penny into Venetia's hand. "Give it to Freddie when we are at the other side," she whispered. "The other children will do the same."

They continued down Half-Moon Street, Venetia chattering happily about her lessons. Mr Graves, the singing master was extremely handsome but she thought Herr Weber, the pianoforte instructor a better musician although he was very strict about time, or tempo as he called it.

Thomas raised his brows at this precocious pronouncement and saw his amusement reflected in Arabella's eyes.

"My first new muslins will be ready tomorrow—you don't think my cousin Lady Hawebury will disapprove of my putting off my blacks, do you, Cousin Thomas?"

It was on the tip of his tongue to reply flippantly that they would cross that bridge when they came to it when he felt Arabella stiffen beside him.

"Certainly not," he said firmly. "We may rely on Miss Malvin to know the right thing to do."

Venetia gave a little skip. "That's what I think, too."

They had reached Malvin House and Thomas made his farewells without further ado. There was no suggestion that he return to dine with them and he did not press Arabella again to receive him the next day, merely saying, "Until Thursday, unless you need me before then. I am at your service."

Chapter Twenty-Five

Thomas headed for The Crossed Swords, not dissatisfied with his progress. Venetia's artless question had cast a new light on Arabella's disquiet. Did she fear that his mother might challenge her authority or even overrule her? If he and Arabella were to be Venetia's new parents, and that was what it amounted to, then they must hold the reins, she even more than he, for what did he know of young girls? You cannot give someone a command and then interfere with them at every hand's turn, he reminded himself as he turned into Maiden Lane.

"Ho! Ferraunt!" Lord Franklin waved to him from a corner table in the crowded tap room. "What has you in such a brown study?"

"Franklin! The very man I need to talk to."

"Why, what's up?"

"You had better ask what isn't," Thomas said gloomily.

"Let's go upstairs. There's nobody there yet. You can unburden yourself over a jug of ale."

Franklin took a long draught and sat back, crossing his legs at the ankles. "There is no doubt that Jones brews the best ale in town. Now, what's bothering you? Is it the estate? And that reminds me that I have an adjutant for you."

Thomas, who had tilted his chair back on its hind legs, came forward with a thump. "Who?"

"Joel Phillips. A lieutenant invalided out last year. He took a ball in the hip at Waterloo and can no longer walk or ride for hours at a stretch but is otherwise fit. He has a pension but it is not large, and he cannot bear to be idle. The younger son of a baronet in Kent, he knows the ropes of estate management and has a good head for figures. He is personable and well-mannered; you would be happy to have him at your dinner table or in your wife's drawing-room, which is also a consideration."

"You think he may be interested in coming to work for me?"

"I know he would. Gregg—Sally's brother—wrote to ask if I knew of any post that might suit him."

"What should I give him? Would a captain's pay be adequate?"

"Generous, I should think, as he'll be living all found with you, have the stabling of his horse and the use of a gig if he needs it, and no stoppages. He's about twenty-four. You don't want to start him too high or he'll finish up a colonel, if not a general. As long as he's paid more than your steward, there will be no need to worry. Offer him a trial period of six months at a lieutenant's pay. If you get on together and you think he's worth it, you can increase it then if you like."

Thomas laughed. "I see you're up to all the rigs. Where is he putting up at present?"

"He's at home in Kent—near Wrotham. There should be no problem in his coming up to meet you. Shall I write to him for you?"

"If you would, Franklin. He may call on me on Friday at twelve noon."

Franklin nodded and took out his pocket book. "A habit I cannot break myself of," he said as he scribbled.

"Nor I," said Thomas, drawing out his own. "Lieut. Joel Phillips, you say. Of the 52nd?"

"That's it." Franklin waited until Thomas had jotted down the information before asking, "What else is on your mind?"

"Would it were as easily solved. Frankly, it is how to reconcile the requirements and expectations of my parents and my future wife."

"Separate households," his lordship said promptly. "You cannot have two mistresses under one roof and a bride expects her own home."

"The problem is that my father wishes me to be the earl *de facto* so we cannot move elsewhere, even for a year or so, as I must become familiar with the estate. On the other hand, I have seen no sign that my mother wishes to relinquish her position as countess or live anywhere other than Ferraunt Court. In addition, Arabella and I are to be *in loco parentis* to the ten-year-old orphaned granddaughter of the last earl. It is an enormous undertaking for a bride, and I do not want to make matters more difficult for her by exposing her to the risk of having her authority undermined or ignored."

Franklin whistled. "Do you think that is likely?"

"My mother is a rector's wife," Thomas said dryly. "It is fourteen years since I lived at home for any length of time, but Arabella, who has been acquainted with her all her life, is adamant that we clarify how she will fit into a joint household before she agrees to set a wedding date." Thomas smiled wryly. "Before all this happened, we planned to set up on our own, fifty miles away from our parents, and breed horses."

"And live as free as the air," Franklin said enviously. "Is there a dower house at Ferraunt Court?"

"I haven't seen any mention of one. I understand that my great-grandmother, the last dowager, lived in Bath after she was widowed."

"If there isn't, build or buy one. You and your wife can live there as long as your father is alive and afterwards your mother, if she survives him, can retire there. She probably will be no easier to live with as dowager than as reigning countess."

"And so he cuts the Gordian knot," Thomas said admiringly. "You must not think my mother is an unkind woman, Franklin."

"I am sure she is not, just used to having things her own way. Are we any different? Not having been raised as heir and having been away for so long, I had to return to Lutterworth to learn estate management. The first thing I did after we were married was refurbish a woodland cottage so that Sally and I had somewhere to escape to while the dower house was being renovated. That work is now complete and we'll remove there when we go home next month. Apart from Sally's natural preference to manage her own establishment, I am too old and too independent to live with my parents like an unlicked cub."

"So am I," Thomas realised. "Thank you, Franklin."

Now he just had to make things right with Arabella. He resisted the urge to go immediately to Malvin House and put the solution to her. She had asked for time—and perhaps she had suggestions of her own. He should listen to them first.

"Why don't you bring Miss Malvin to a quiet dinner with Sally and me on Saturday," Franklin suggested, "just the four of us."

"I would like that, provided she has no other engagement, of course."

"Excellent. I'll ask Sally to send her a note."

The first of the evening's swordsmen arrived, including his usual opponent. He should go home and immerse himself in the cursed Ferraunt papers, but a hard, sweaty bout with the blades would be just the thing to take his mind off his problems. And tomorrow? Arabella didn't want to see him until Thursday, he remembered. "On second thoughts, Franklin, if you give me Phillips's direction, I'll go and see him tomorrow. I'll send him a note with tonight's mail."

Muslin skirts fluttering, the hon. Geoffrey Anthony Tamrisk tottered gleefully towards the expectant arms held open to catch him, hug him and lift him high in the air.

"Who is the cleverest boy in the world?" Arabella cooed.

A soft hand patted her cheek. "'Bel, 'Bel," he crowed and then, imperiously, "M'ma, M'ma."

She hugged him again, obediently set him back on his feet and gave him a little nudge to set him staggering back towards his mother who knelt opposite her.

"Are you happy, Lallie?" she asked abruptly.

Lallie's smile was wide enough to embrace the whole world. "Happier than I ever dreamt possible. Why do you ask?"

"I suddenly remembered this time two years ago."

"When Hugo and I were at outs? That is all behind us. Have you quarrelled with Thomas?"

"Not quarrelled precisely, but—he doesn't listen to me. He just hears the words but doesn't reflect on them."

"Then you must make him listen," Lallie said firmly. "Explain what you mean if he does not understand you. You must engage with him. Gentlemen are not very good at reading one's mind," she added with a little smile. "And don't say if he loved me, he would know what I mean. They think in a different way than we do."

"I never looked at it that way."

"What is the real problem? The thing you did not like to say straight out? I am sure you went at it in a roundabout way and then were upset because he did not guess what you were trying to say."

"How did you know? I couldn't just say, 'I don't want to live with your parents, especially your mother,' could I?"

"Do you have to? Live with them, I mean."

"It seems so. The earl wants Thomas to take over the management of the earldom at once so he will have to live at Hawebury in order to become acquainted with the estate and the tenants. But his mother will be the mistress of Ferraunt Court and where will that leave me?"

"She always struck me as being a commanding sort of woman," Lallie said, rolling a ball to her son who promptly patted it away from him.

Arabella retrieved it and gently tossed it back. “Exactly. She and Mamma are not overly friendly, although the rector calls frequently to see Papa or consult a book in the library. They dine with us occasionally, but when Mrs Ferraunt sends out her cards, she only invites Mamma, Papa, Julian and Millie. She does not have the space for us younger ones, she says, although she did include Arthur last year. I suppose that with Thomas in the military, she was glad to talk to another officer.”

“Hmmm.”

“I am sure she is in alt at the idea of taking precedence over us all.”

“Do you think she will try to browbeat you, as countess and mother-in-law?”

“I don’t know. At best she will ignore me, but I think it more likely that she will try and make me an attendant lady, have me run her errands. Thomas sees no harm in that. He said, ‘A subaltern cannot immediately become commander-in chief’.”

“What?” Lallie’s jaw dropped.

“So I said if we were talking in military terms, to go from daughter to daughter-in-law could not be considered a promotion.”

“That was clever. How did he respond?”

“He said I would not be his mother’s daughter-in-law but his wife. But what does that mean?”

“You need to spell it out for him, Bella.”

“Perhaps. But then he said if I was not happy with the alteration in his circumstances, he would not stand in my way if I wished to break our betrothal.”

"Men!" Lallie rolled her eyes. "Hugo did the same the day we discovered the extent of my fortune. He pokered up and offered to release me. It was some strange notion of honour, I think."

"So I took off the ring he gave me and held it out to him."

Lallie gasped. "Bella! You didn't! I scolded Hugo like a harpy, but he was quite pleased about it. I think he needed reassurance that I still wished to marry him."

"Oh!" Arabella had not thought of it like that. "Thomas said nothing, but didn't take the ring either and I let it fall to the floor. I wanted to leave but he seized my wrist and pulled me to him and kissed me fiercely, saying I was his."

"What did you do then?" Lallie asked curiously.

"I bit his lip and he let me go," Arabella admitted.

"Well done! When was this?"

"Yesterday morning. We sort of made up later—he came to the Green Park where I had gone with Millie and the children—and we agreed we would try to find a middle way."

"I am sure you can. You are not making too much of this, are you, Arabella? Clarissa and Millie deal very comfortably together."

"Probably because they are not very often under the same roof. Mamma spends much of her time in London while parliament is sitting, and Millie and Julian generally visit her family and their friends once Mamma and Papa come home. I don't know whether it was deliberate or just turned out that way. But Mamma and Millie are more like sisters, perhaps because there is not such an age difference between them—only thirteen years, which is less than between Millie and me."

"I suppose it suited them to divide up the responsibilities," Lallie said thoughtfully. "Perhaps you could come to a similar arrangement with Thomas's mother."

"I don't know. I want to be mistress of my own home, Lallie; I want to be able to order the dinner and move the furniture and invite my friends and family to sit at my table—and, and fight with Thomas without being afraid that his parents will overhear."

"Then you must tell him that. You don't know yet what Ferraunt Court is like. There may be special apartments set aside for the heir and his wife like the ones at Tamm or, if that is not private enough, a dower house you could use. If not, if Thomas is wealthy enough to buy his own estate, he can also afford to buy or build a house for you. It is what my grandparents Grey, or at least their forbears, did. My uncle and his family live across the park from the main house in the heir's house. Would that satisfy you? You would have your own household, with Venetia and later your own children and more freedom to develop the life that suits you and Thomas."

"It seems very expensive for what may only be a few years."

"Years that will set the tone of your marriage. A wedding is only the beginning, Bella. There is a big difference between being bride and groom and husband and wife. You need to be with one another privately to allow the bond between you to grow—the constant presence of your parents-in-law will not make that any easier. Most couples hardly know each other when they marry. It takes a while to get used to living so intimately with someone else. You need to spend time together to develop those comfortable little habits that help you be at ease with each other; to see him and for him to see you when you are not at your best, to know that a quarrel is not the end of the world and that kissing and making up has its own appeal."

"What sort of habits?"

Lallie shrugged. "It depends on what interests you. It could be something as simple as a walk after church. Sometimes I ride out with Hugo when he visits the tenants. At least once a week we make music together. Some evenings he reads to me while I sew, while on other occasions we might each read our own book, just glad to be together, looking up from time to time to read out a passage or mention something completely different. Or just share a glance and a smile. It's impossible to explain it." She made an all-encompassing circle with her hands. "It's as if something golden grows between you and shapes your special place where the rest of the world is shut out. You cannot remain there for ever, of course, but you must make time for it. There is an intimacy of the mind as well as of the body, Bella. They are the two aspects of love."

"Lallie, can I ask you something else?"

"Of course. What is it?"

"You mentioned the 'intimacy of the body'. I presume men sire children the way other animals do, but there has to be more to it than a mere coupling or there would not be so many crim cons."

"Much more," Lallie assured her. "Don't be afraid of it. It may seem strange in the beginning and the first time can sting a little, but don't make the mistake of thinking that it is something the husband enjoys and the wife endures. It is like a dance, Bella, and if you follow Thomas's lead, you will find your body responds instinctively to him. Let it happen and you will find much pleasure and happiness together."

"I hope so," she said, remembering how easy it would have been to sink into Thomas's arms when he kissed her so ardently. She yawned suddenly. "I beg your pardon, Lallie. I hardly slept last night—it was all going through my mind again. I couldn't think what to do and then I thought of coming to you. Thank you. You have helped me to a better understanding of things."

"I am so glad," Lallie said simply. "It is vital that you talk, Bella. And be honest with him. It is only fair."

"I know."

Geoffrey reached for the ball again, overbalanced and began to cry.

"He's tired and hungry," Lallie said as she comforted him. "There, there, my precious. I think you need to be changed. Nancy will make you comfortable and then you can have a little nap. Ring for Nancy, Bella, and then we'll have some tea."

They jumped as rain rattled sharply against the window pane.

"I had better not stay for tea," Arabella said. "Papa will scold if I keep the horses waiting in this weather. Thank you, Lallie. I see my way better now, I think."

"The important thing is that Thomas is willing to try and find a middle way. Many gentlemen would not. But you must be willing to meet him half-way."

"I know. It would certainly help if we have our own front door," Arabella said thoughtfully. "I had a note from Lady Franklin inviting Thomas and me to dine with her and her husband on Saturday. Just the four of us, she said. She will have been in a similar situation."

"That sounds very promising. Thomas must have spoken to him, Lord Franklin, I mean." Lallie reached over and lifted Arabella's hand. "I see you are still—or again—wearing his ring."

"He asked me to. He said our betrothal stands unless a day comes when we must agree that our differences are irreconcilable."

"In your heart of hearts, Bella, what do you want?"

"To marry Thomas." The reply shot from Arabella's lips. She did not pause to think, not even for even a second.

"Then you will find a way," Lallie promised. "Is your maid waiting below?"

Arabella shook her head. "It is such a short drive from here to Malvin House, I said she need not come but should stay and help finish Venetia's new dresses."

Chapter Twenty-Six

Huddled into the Norwich shawl that Lallie had insisted she borrow as she only had a light pelisse, Arabella hurried across the pavement beneath the big umbrella held by one of the Tamm footmen. She nodded to Jeb who, similarly equipped, held the carriage door open for her.

"Everything's in a right snarl today, Miss Malvin," he said as she set her foot on the step. "It's the rain, I suppose. I might have to go the long way round."

"Do the best you can, Jeb."

"Yes, Miss."

The door closed behind her. The interior of the carriage was dark and she leaned forward to open the blind on the opposite window. Why make the day even drearier than it was? The shadows in the far corner stirred. A firm hand grasped the back of her head and some fabric like heavy silk was pressed over her mouth and nose. She gasped for breath, kicked out and tried to tug the restraining hand away. She couldn't breathe properly. Her limbs felt strange and she felt overly warm, then she seemed to float—float—float—

The carriage rocked as if they were travelling at breakneck speed. A wave of nausea engulfed her. She opened her eyes cautiously but when she turned her head everything revolved around her. Her eyelids sank again. Her lower lip felt sore and she touched it gingerly. Was it swollen? She needed—

"Air." Her voice sounded strange to her ears.

She heard the swish of fabric as someone moved, a click and then blessed, fresh air flowed in, cooling her face and head.

"Thank you." She must have been ill but someone was looking after her. Thank heavens she was not alone.

The next time she came to herself, she felt steadier. She was still queasy, but no longer felt she might be sick at any moment. Her mouth was dry.

"Horton?"

"I see you have recovered, Miss Malvin," a male voice said. It was not unfamiliar, but she couldn't place it. A doctor? Had she been so ill? But why were they in a carriage? She took a cautious breath and lifted her heavy eyelids. She must still be dreaming. What sort of strange dream had her driving with Lord Henry Danlow? She looked again. No, he still sat opposite her, a quizzical smile on his arrogant face.

"You're not here," she told him and closed her eyes, resting her head against the squabs. Her head pounded in time with the rapid staccato of the horses' hooves. A dog's bark was followed by the crack of a whip and a yelp. Now she heard the heavy trundle of a cart. This was a very vivid dream. She could smell tobacco and pictured the carter perched on the side of his cart, smoking his pipe.

Someone touched her knee. "Miss Malvin?"

It was the same voice. Arabella bit the inside of her mouth. It hurt.

"Miss Malvin!" At the sharp hand-clap, her eyes flew open.

She stared unbelievingly at Lord Henry who, dressed in unrelieved black, lounged in the corner opposite, his hair pale against the dark squabs. Dark squabs? She sat up and inspected her surroundings. "This isn't our carriage."

"How very astute of you. It would be the worst of bad taste to use your father's carriage to elope with his daughter, would it not?"

"Elopement? Who is eloping?"

He laughed softly. "Is it not obvious? I fear, my dear, you still suffer from the after effects of the gas."

"Gas?" Why was she parroting his every word? Really, it was all too absurd. She must be caught up in one of those interminable dreams where one thought one had woken but in fact the scene had merely shifted.

"Davy's gaseous oxyd, to be precise," he said. "I apologise for the necessity, but I considered it wiser to postpone explanations until we were outside London."

Outside London? She clamped her lips on the repetition and leaned forward to look out the window. They were bowling along a well-made road bordered by green fields. A few bedraggled cows clustered together near a hedge. From the other window she could see a narrow road that ran up to a small village—just a handful of houses and a church. What were they doing here?

She sat up straight, folded her hands in her lap and said primly, "I cannot imagine what you are about, Lord Henry, but I insist that you return me to my parents immediately."

He laughed. "Surely that is not necessary? My intentions are perfectly honourable, I assure you."

She raised an eyebrow. “You call stupefying me with gas and abducting me honourable?”

“That was a stratagem, only necessary because your family has turned against me. But now that we are on our own, my dear Miss Malvin, my dearest Arabella, will you do me the honour of accepting my hand in marriage?” He spoke as collectedly and as civilly as if he were indeed an accepted suitor making a formal offer, having received her father’s blessing.

“No, I will not,” she snapped. “You know I am betrothed to another man.”

He waved dismissively. “I know your family is keen on a match with Ferraunt, but surely you do not want to marry that clod—a jumped up parson’s son.”

“Of course I do,” she cried angrily. “He is worth a thousand of you! I would not marry you if you were the last man in the world.”

He inhaled sharply, his lips thinning to a narrow line. After some moments, he said, “Very well, if that is your reply, so be it. If you would rather be my mistress, I shall not complain. However, you only get one chance at marriage, Miss Malvin. Once I have had you, I shall no longer feel impelled to do the decent thing. It will have been your choice to be ruined, after all.”

She stared at him. “What folly is this? Stop the carriage and instruct the driver to turn back immediately.”

“No folly, I assure you. Mistress or wife—it is your choice. I have a yacht waiting at Folkestone. Tomorrow we leave for France, but it will be too late for you by then. You will already have graced my bed. You will not find me ungenerous as long as you are in my keeping, and I am sure you will have no trouble in finding another protector once I have tired of you."

Did he really sit there and threaten to ravish her? For that was what it amounted to, despite all his talk of choice. And he had clearly been scheming for some time. For a dreadful moment she thought her stomach would revolt. She swallowed hard and took a deep breath. She must try to escape. Better find out as much as she could, she thought.

"Where is my father's carriage?" She was proud that her voice was steady.

He shrugged. "Somewhere in London. Jeb, however, is no longer in your family's employ. His usefulness there is finished and it would have been unkind to leave him to pay the piper, as it were. I reward loyalty—you would do well to remember that."

"But—"

"In truth, he is my servant; I—lent him to your family, one might say."

Her hand went to her mouth. It was over three weeks since Bart had broken his leg. Had Lord Henry been spying on her all that time? And worse—"Did you have my groom injured so you could place your henchman in my service?"

He spread his hands "Needs must, my dear, needs must when the devil drives. And you are my devil. We could have done this more simply, but you would not."

"It is you who are the devil! Or a spoilt child who cannot bear to be thwarted!"

"Watch your tongue, Miss Malvin. You have thwarted me several times and cost me a lot of money into the bargain. It is time you paid your debts."

"I owe you nothing, my lord. There was never anything more between us than a mild friendship that quickly withered and died."

"Soon you will feel more for me," he said calmly.

"You will not claim you love me!"

"Do you want me too?"

She repressed a shiver at his silky tone. "Certainly not!"

"Then hate it shall be."

The carriage slowed and he glanced out of the window. "We shall stop here briefly to change horses. You, my dear, will remain here quietly or it will be the worse for you later."

The carriage lurched as it turned into the inn yard, throwing Arabella against the door. As quick as a flash, she pushed down the handle, the door flew open and she jumped down, pressing herself against the wall of the narrow entrance.

"Come back this instant!"

A furious Lord Henry ducked his head to leave the carriage and she slammed the door into his face. As soon as she saw him tumble back between the seats, she caught up her skirts and ran. A waggoner had begun the delicate task of guiding his team into the entrance to the yard. It would plug the narrow passage like a cork in a bottle for several minutes. Ignoring the oaths he flung at her, she dodged around the cumbersome equipage and edged her way past the four pairs of horses, hoping that they were steady beasts. One false movement might see her crushed between the near horse and the stone wall at her back. Then, her heart in her mouth, she squeezed past the huge wheels and ran onto the street, but had to jump back at once to avoid a cart and horse. Apart from its driver, there was no one in sight.

She looked around frantically. A massive church tower stood foursquare opposite her. Perhaps there was an adjacent parsonage. She darted across the now empty street and hastily skirted the low wall surrounding the churchyard until she came to a gate. A quick glance backwards showed the waggon still blocked the entrance to the yard, but Lord Henry and Jeb stood talking on the front steps of the inn itself. They must have gone through the taproom. After a moment, they separated, Lord Henry going right and Jeb going left. They were looking for her. Drat the man! Could he not simply give up?

If she saw a respectable-looking female, she would risk asking her for help, but none appeared. She walked around the church but there was no other building. With a vague notion of finding sanctuary, she tried the huge door. It swung open over flagstones that were worn smooth and hollow and she moved gratefully into the hushed depths, padding softly down the side aisle, hurrying from pillar to massive pillar. A small oak chair was set between two imposing tombs bearing the effigies of a long-dead knight and his lady and she sat down, gratefully shrinking back into the shadows.

Where was she? What was she to do? She had a few coins with her but not many. How could she send a message to town and how long would it take to reach her parents? If her funds stretched to it and she managed to evade Lord Henry, perhaps it would be wiser to buy a seat on a public coach. Mamma would not approve, but it couldn't be helped.

Had she been missed? Were her family already searching for her? Had they sent for Thomas? What would he think of this escapade? It would cause a great scandal if it were to become known. Lord Henry must be touched in the head. There was no other explanation for it.

She carefully emptied her reticule onto her lap. She had two guineas, three shillings and six pennies, a handkerchief, a small paper of pins and her card case with cards. At least she could prove she was the Honourable Miss Malvin.

She held her breath when the door opened again. Two be-ribboned ladies—a mother and daughter, perhaps—sailed purposefully up the aisle and established themselves in a front pew. They were followed by an older, forbidding looking dame who nodded coolly to them before taking a seat opposite. She produced a pair of steel-rimmed spectacles, perched them on her hawk nose and bent her head over a prayer book.

Not long afterwards, a stout middle-aged man emerged from a door on the opposite side of the altar and trod down the aisle to assume a watchful stance opposite the door. High above them a sonorous clock struck twice—the half-hour. But half past what? A clerk appeared from the far door—it must be the vestry—to light the altar candles and retreated again, then returned, preceded by a clergyman in choir dress. It must be time for Evening Prayer. She was safe, for the moment at least.

The great door opened again and she heard quick, booted steps. The stout man, presumably a churchwarden, moved forward to greet the newcomer who, it soon became apparent, did not wish to attend the service. She strained to hear the whispered altercation over the murmurs of the small congregation reciting the general confession. There was a pause when the prayer ended and the voices at the bottom of the nave became louder.

"There's no young lady here." A country voice—probably the churchwarden.

"I'll just see for myself." That was Lord Henry. How to escape? There was a small door on her right and she sidled towards it. Perhaps she could hide.

"Not during Prayer, sir," the other man said uncompromisingly.

"Now see here, my good man!"

The three ladies in front peered around inquisitively. Arabella cautiously opened the door. It gave onto a spiral staircase. She pulled the door to, not daring to risk the click of the latch, and carefully climbed up to a narrow gallery above the arch over the rood screen. With a sudden, vivid memory of Thomas after the shots were fired at Miss Boyce, she knelt and crept forward to peer over the balustrade.

Below, the brawny churchwarden towered over his lordship.

"Is there a problem, Mr Stokes?" the clergyman asked from the altar.

"No, sir. At least, not if this gentleman leaves quietly. If he continues to cause a disturbance, I shall have to remove him."

"I'm sure it will not come to that," the other said resolutely.

"No, sir. Now, this way, sir."

Arabella sighed with relief as the man took a firm grip of Lord Henry's arm and propelled him towards the door. She would wait until the service was over and approach the ladies. She hoped they would not consider a young lady who was unescorted and pursued by a gentleman of dubious behaviour unworthy of their assistance.

Her fears were justified. The plump, well-to-do looking matron raised her lorgnette to her eyes and looked Arabella up and down. "A likely story! I imagine that the truth is that you allowed yourself to be cozened into an elopement and now regret it. Well, you have made your bed and must lie on it. Come, Malvina. Let this be a lesson to you."

"Yes, Mama. Imagine having the temerity to approach us. In the church, what is more."

The eldest lady looked down her redoubtable nose at the pair. "And you dare to call yourselves Christians? We are commanded to help our neighbour, are we not? Only think of the Good Samaritan. I do not understand why you must always assume the worst, Mrs Browne. Unless you speak from personal experience, of course." Ignoring the matron's outraged gasp, she turned to Arabella. "Now, how may I help you, my dear?"

Arabella sighed with relief. "If you would give me shelter while I send word to my parents, ma'am, I should be eternally grateful, as would they."

"What is this?" The churchwarden, who had come back up the aisle, frowned at Arabella. "Where did you come from? I did not see you come in."

Mother and daughter broke into a babble of explanation. When the clergyman, a tall, fair gentleman of about thirty who looked as if he would be as at home on the cricket pitch as on the altar, appeared, they moved smoothly to take up a position either side of him while continuing their expostulations. He looked around the little group and held up his hand.

"One moment, ladies. Mr Stokes, if you please."

The churchwarden cleared his throat. "This is the young lady that his lordship was searching for earlier."

"A lord?" Mrs Browne frowned at Arabella. "And you dare accuse him of abduction."

The churchwarden chuckled. "They are to be married this evening—he showed me a special licence—but they had a little tiff, he said—you know how young ladies get overly excited at such times."

Arabella's heart sank when the two men exchanged masculine grins. "It is not true!" She looked pleadingly at the curate. "He stupefied me with gas and abducted me. He says that if I do not marry him, he will force me to be his mistress." Her voice broke.

The older woman took Arabella's hand in a comforting clasp. "Do not worry, my dear. I am certain Mr Ellison will help you, will you not, sir?"

"There you are!" A smiling Lord Henry strode down the aisle. He nodded affably to the churchwarden. "Did I not tell you she must have slipped in here for a period of quiet reflection? I trust you are feeling more the thing, my love. We must be on our way."

"One moment. Stokes here tells me you have a special licence." The clergyman held out a commanding hand. "May I see it? Thank you." He spread out the document. "Lord Henry Danlow to the Honourable Arabella Malvin? You are Lord Malvin's daughter?"

"Yes, and neither he nor I consented to this farce! I am betrothed to Lord Ferraunt."

"Son of the new Earl of Hawebury?" The clergyman began to smile. "I know him; his father taught me. Your brother Arthur was with us for some years."

"Yes. He was killed at Waterloo."

"I am very sorry to hear it." He bowed briefly. "Allow me to introduce myself. My name is Ellison, I am the curate here."

"How do you do, Mr Ellison." Greatly relieved, Arabella offered him her hand which he pressed reassuringly.

"Now, Miss Malvin, you tell me that you do not wish to marry Lord Henry."

She retrieved her hand, tugged off her glove and put her bare hand on the big bible. "I swear it."

"Have you ever agreed to do so?"

"Never."

The curate briskly folded the licence and tucked it into his pocket. "In that case I shall retain this."

"How dare you! You have no right!"

"I have every right." He looked scathingly at Lord Henry. "I should not have to tell you, my lord, that it is both dishonourable and an offence to obtain a licence under false pretences or to attempt to coerce a woman into marriage. I shall have to report this to his Grace, the Archbishop of Canterbury."

His lordship started forward, but the churchwarden caught his raised arm in an iron grip. "No brawling in the church, my lord!" He spoke as if to a recalcitrant youth and Arabella had to bite the inside of her cheek to keep from laughing.

Mr Ellison offered her his arm. "Miss Malvin, I think it is best if you come with me to the rectory where I am sure that Mrs Filby, our rector's wife, will offer you every hospitality until we can arrange for your family to come for you. In the meantime—Stokes, you will kindly ensure that his lordship does not leave this church for some thirty minutes after the ladies and I have departed. I suggest he use this period to reflect on his transgressions."

With this parting shot, he led Arabella out of the church, followed by the two harpies, as Arabella had mentally titled them.

The curate fixed them with a stern look. "I trust I need not remind you ladies of the dangers of idle gossip."

They bridled but said, "No, Mr Ellison."

Arabella made a point at smiling at her champion who brought up the rear. "I cannot thank you enough for your support, ma'am. Might I know your name?"

"I am Miss Eames, Miss Mary Eames. Perhaps, you would do me the honour of stepping into my parlour, Miss Malvin? I live just along here."

"I should be most obliged to you, Miss Eames."

"This way, if you please."

"Thank you, Miss Eames," Mr Ellison interrupted. "I should be grateful if you would remain with Miss Malvin while I go and hire a gig. I do not keep a carriage myself, Miss Malvin, I prefer to ride."

"Mr Ellison, if Miss Eames permits, perhaps you would first accompany us to her house. Rather than go immediately to the rectory, I should first like to consider if there is any way I might return home tonight."

"That would be best," Miss Eames agreed. "Your parents must be extremely worried." She opened a small garden gate and, with a murmured, "If you permit," led her guests up the short path to the front door of a neat cottage. Her key was already in her hand and she quickly threw open the door and stood aside to allow Arabella and the curate to enter.

"If you would take a seat in the parlour, I shall have tea made in a trice—I set the kettle on the hob before going to church. I am sure you are in need of refreshment, Miss Malvin."

Arabella could not deny it—the effect of Lord Henry's gas still lingered, or perhaps it was just the shock of the afternoon's events that had her feeling queasy and lightheaded. She sank with relief into one of the padded arm-chairs that stood either side of the unlit fireplace and looked around the comfortable room. Miss Eames clearly understood how to make the most of a small space. Two more chairs stood either side of a drop leaf table under the window. Pulled out into the centre of the room and expanded to its full size, the table would permit the hosting of a small card party. A small rosewood bureau bookcase held three shelves of tightly packed books and opposite it a matching china cabinet displayed a handsome silver tea-service, some cups and saucers and a decanter and wine glasses. The soft shades of green and pink in the carpet that covered the centre of the oak floor were echoed in the wreaths of roses stencilled on the walls. Everything gleamed and sparkled as if regularly tended by a loving hand.

Miss Eames hurried in. She took a cloth from a drawer and spread it on the table, then set out three cups and saucers. "The kettle has just come to the boil," she assured her guests as she removed the tea set from the cabinet and vanished again.

Mr Ellison followed her. "May I carry the tea-tray for you, ma'am?" Arabella heard him ask.

"If you would, sir, I shall bring in the biscuits. They are fresh from this morning."

"Excellent."

Arabella's eyes closed. When she opened them again, a small table had been placed beside her chair with a full tea cup set invitingly to hand. Miss Eames stood beside her, offering sugar bowl and milk jug.

"I think you must be my guardian angel, ma'am," Arabella said gratefully

"Nonsense, my dear Miss Malvin. I was a governess for forty years, you know. I can recognise when a young lady is in genuine distress—and even if you had been lured into an elopement, why should I refuse to help you if, upon reflection, you regretted your action?"

Mr Ellison shifted uneasily. "Oh now, Miss Eames. Surely you would not wish to condone immorality."

"'When lovely woman stoops to folly,' you mean, sir? I do not agree with Mr Pope that all that is left to her is to die. Are we not called upon to forgive? Even the woman taken in adultery was not condemned, you remember, but told to go and sin no more. Not, my dear Miss Malvin, that I meant to imply—"

The curate reddened. "Of course not." He drained his cup. "Now, how are we to proceed?"

Arabella looked at the little mantelpiece clock. It was half-past six. "How long would it take to reach town?"

"About two hours in a post chaise," Mr Ellison replied.

Her funds should stretch to it, especially as she could have Belshaw pay off the post boy after the final stage. "I could be at home by nine." She turned to Mr Ellison. "I should prefer not to go to the inn again. Might I beg you to arrange to hire a post-chaise for me, sir?"

He looked appalled. “You surely do not propose to travel on your own? Supposing you were to be accosted again by this Lord Henry?”

“And it will be dark by the time you arrive,” Miss Eames said. “It will not do, Miss Malvin. I shall accompany you. Mr Ellison, see if you can hire two out-riders in addition to the postilion.”

“No. That would attract too much attention,” Arabella said at once. “It would be dreadful if word of this gets about.”

“Then I shall escort you myself,” the curate declared. “And instead of a post chaise, I shall beg the loan of the rector’s carriage. I shall sit on the box beside the coachman and if we put a stout groom up behind, we shall be well protected.”

Arabella was not inclined to argue with her new friends, merely insisting that they must put up for the night at Malvin House—her parents would be wishful to thank them for coming to their daughter’s aid—and that each should prepare a small valise with everything they would need.

“Now, Miss Malvin,” Arabella’s hostess said after Mr Ellison had departed to arrange for the carriage and horses, “I imagine you will like to visit the necessary before setting out again. This way.” She led Arabella through the kitchen into a small, paved yard and indicated a wooden door. “You will need this.” She handed her a small lantern. “There is a hook for it inside the door. Just be sure to replace the lid properly in the seat when you are finished.”

Chapter Twenty-Seven

Thursday evening

My dear Ferraunt,

I should be obliged if you would come at once to Malvin House.

Yours etc.

Malvin

Thomas glanced at the clock. A quarter to ten. He had just missed Lord Malvin's footman, Mrs Platts had informed him. Why had Arabella's father summoned him in such a fashion? Had she been taken ill or—a sudden terror seized him—had she changed her mind and was now resolved to break their betrothal?

He had ridden to and from Kent today—he could not front up at Malvin House covered in dust and reeking of the stables. He strode to the top of the stairs.

"Mrs Platt!"

When his landlady appeared below, he snapped, "Pray summons a hack. I'll be down directly." Retreating to his bedroom, he began to strip off his clothes. He rasped a hand over his jaw. No time to shave the evening stubble. A hasty wash in cold water and a quick change of clothes. He would do. He took the stairs, two at a time.

"Curzon Street, Malvin House," he said briefly to the driver of the waiting carriage. He would use these few minutes to compose himself. It was like going into battle. Better with a cool head.

It seemed an eternity until they reached Malvin House, with the Jehu having to weave his way through the carriages of the *beau monde* embarked on the nightly pursuit of pleasure. As soon as the carriage slowed, Thomas jumped down and hurried forward to hand up some coins to the driver. An old-fashioned berline had drawn up ahead of them, and as Thomas watched a servant climbed down from his perch behind and hurried to open the door. A visitor from the country, he thought, as a woman wrapped in a shawl alighted. He paused politely to let her pass while inwardly cursing the unhappy chance that had her arrive just before him.

She glanced up in brief acknowledgement. "Thomas!" Heedless of another lady who had to duck around her to avoid treading on her skirts, Arabella threw herself into his arms, her breath coming in great gasps as if she were trying not to cry.

"Thomas, oh, Thomas!"

"Arabella! Where did you come from? What is wrong?"

"Nothing, now that I am home and you are here."

A tall man swathed in a greatcoat jumped down from the box and came to the side of the other lady. Arabella looked around from the shelter of Thomas's arms. "Oh, may I present Miss Eames and you know Mr Ellison, I think?"

Thomas nodded without releasing his betrothed. “Come, let us go inside,” he said gently.

He felt her nod, then her clasp loosened and she looked back at the coachman. “A footman will come to show you how to reach the mews. The head coachman will tell you where to go. You will put up here for the night.”

He touched his hat. “Thank you, miss.”

Thomas kept one arm around Arabella as he urged her towards the house. The front door had opened and Belshaw stood waiting. What the devil had happened and where did John Ellison come into it?

“It was Lord Henry,” Arabella whispered as if she had read his thoughts. “He abducted me.”

“What!”

“I managed to escape, and Miss Eames and Mr Ellison came to my aid.”

“Are you hurt?”

She shook her head. “Not really.”

What did she mean by ‘not really’? Thomas thought, aware of the fine tremors that ran through her.

At last she was home. Shaking with tiredness, Arabella led the way into the hall. “Belshaw, pray send a footman to direct the coachman to the mews.”

“Very good, Miss.”

One footman departed at the butler’s nod. Arabella handed Lallie’s shawl to another and removed her pelisse and bonnet. Out of habit, she glanced in the over-mantel glass and wrinkled her nose. There was nothing to be done about her flattened hair or white face. She must go directly to Mamma. but first—

"Pray excuse me for the moment," she said to her two champions. "Belshaw here will see to your comfort." Turning to the butler, she added, "Miss Eames and Mr Ellison will stay the night."

"Very good, Miss Malvin."

"Where is my mother?"

"Her ladyship is in the small parlour, miss."

She nodded. "Come, Thomas."

Mamma was not alone. The whole family was there, even Hugo and Lallie. The four gentlemen stood grimly in front of the fireplace. Her father looked old, older even than when they had learnt of Arthur's death. The ladies had collapsed onto the sofa where Millie and Lallie each held one of Mamma's hands. They were all three bejewelled and crowned with feathers, attired in silk and lace for the evening round, but their pallor and tense expressions spoke of anything but pleasure.

"What can have happened to her? Why did I assume she had stayed to dine with Lallie? It was only when we met at the Bentons' that I realised—" Mamma broke off when she spied Arabella and Thomas. Her hand went to her breast as she rose awfully to her feet, her eyes flashing fire and her cheek scarlet.

She had flown into one of her rare rages. Arabella closed her eyes. That was all she needed now.

"There you are at last! How could you be so thoughtless, Arabella? Here is your father about to send to Bow Street! Only think of the scandal! And all because you sneaked away with Thomas like a maidservant with a follower! We had thought better of our daughter, had we not, Tony!"

"Indeed we had, my dear."

Et tu, Papa? A cold fury seized Arabella. After all she had gone through, to be scolded like a hoity-toity miss, in front of all the family, and Thomas too.

She raised her chin. "As you are too busy reproaching me for what you assume to have happened to learn what actually occurred, I shall leave you to your jobations. Your disappointment in me cannot possibly match mine in you."

"What has you on your high horse?" Matthew demanded. "You can't blame Mamma for having been worried. For all she knew, you had been abducted."

"I was," she flung at him and turned on her heel. "Come, Thomas."

"What?" Matthew grabbed her wrist. "You can't say something like that and flounce out of the room!"

As she tugged her wrist free, she felt Thomas's arm come around her waist. "I am at a loss to understand why you immediately assume that Arabella is at fault," he said coldly.

Julian raised an eyebrow. "You are very quick to defend her. What, precisely, is your part in this, Ferraunt? She is not yet your wife."

"Enough!" Hugo barked. He went on more quietly, "You are all leaping to conclusions. You must forgive your mother, Bella, if her relief spilled over into anger which she then directed at the wrong person. Believe me; we are overjoyed to see you safe and well. Will you not sit down and tell us what happened after you left Tamm House today?"

"I am sorry, Bella," Papa said. "We were wrong to judge so hastily. Please don't go."

She had been poised to depart but instead dropped wearily onto the nearest chair. They had to know the story—

better now than tomorrow. At least they were all here and she need only tell it once. Thomas took a seat beside her.

"It was Lord Henry again," she began.

When Arabella finished her account of the day's events, there was a moment of absolute silence before her family erupted into speech. They all talked at once and she knew better than to try to respond before the first explosion subsided.

Thomas seemed utterly bemused as he looked from one to the other, trying to follow the discussion. After a couple of minutes, he leaned closer to murmur beneath the uproar, "It's like an opera where everyone sings at the top of their voice but nobody listens."

She gave a little splutter of laughter. "An Outrage Septet with the females lamenting and the males swearing vengeance?"

"*La Venganza, La Venganza,*" he intoned in a deep bass and she shivered dramatically.

"That does sound very operatic. Is it Italian?"

"Spanish," he answered absently, his mind clearly elsewhere.

She suddenly felt uneasy. Surely he wouldn't call Lord Henry out? It was on the tip of her tongue to beg him not to, but then she decided against it. Perhaps she would only put the idea into his head.

"How long do you remain in town?"

"I have not yet decided. Until Monday at least."

"Will you ride with me tomorrow morning?"

"Of course—if it will it not be too much for you."

"No, no. It will help clear my head. Besides, it is important that I am seen to be in town as soon as possible.

Call for me at eight o'clock, if you please." The hubbub was finally dying down and she leaned forward. "Mamma! Did I understand correctly that you only realised I was missing when you met Lallie at the Bentons?"

Her mother turned to her immediately. "Yes. I am so sorry, Bella, and also for giving you such a scold earlier."

"We should all apologise," Matthew said.

"Only those of you who accused me," Arabella said fairly, with a smile at her uncle.

"Well, I'm sorry," Matthew said.

"And I," Julian added. "We felt so deuced helpless, you see. So much time had elapsed and we did not know where to start searching for you. And then you stroll in, unharmed—"

Arabella was about to ask would he have preferred to see her bloodied and her gown torn, when Hugo intervened again.

"I should leave it at that, Julian or you'll dig an even deeper pit for yourself."

The resulting laughter cleared the air and Arabella returned to her original query.

"What happened then? Did others notice something was wrong?"

"I don't think so," Lallie said. "We spoke quietly and then slipped away. There was quite a crush, even at such an early hour. Hugo was with me; Matthew had not yet gone out and your father and Julian planned to spend the evening at home so we did not have to send for anyone."

"Fortunately, I met Lallie before anyone enquired about your absence, Bella," Mamma said. "I don't think there should be any talk. But the important thing is that you managed to escape unharmed from that worthless wretch.

We'll discuss tomorrow what is to be done about him, but now I think you should go to bed. You look exhausted."

"First I must make you known to Miss Eames and Mr Ellison. I know you will wish to thank them."

"I'll go with you, Ferraunt," Julian Malvin announced.

Thomas looked at Arabella's eldest brother. "Do you know where Danlow lives?"

"Rickersby mentioned something about Jermyn Street. Belshaw might know."

Belshaw was indeed able to supply the address and the two men strode purposefully towards Piccadilly, returning greetings but otherwise ignoring the waves of saunterers drifting between the masculine haunts of the *ton*.

"There is light upstairs," Julian remarked when they reached Lord Henry's house.

Thomas nodded, grim-faced, and beat a tattoo with the door-knocker. "Lord Ferraunt and Mr Malvin to see your master," he declared, brushing past the man-servant who opened the door."

The man bowed. "This way, if you please."

They followed him upstairs where he set a door wide. "Lord Ferraunt and Mr Malvin, sir."

"This is an unexpected pleasure." An amiable looking young man in his mid-twenties tossed aside the latest issue of *A Sportsman in Town* and jumped up from a deep chair. "To what do I owe the honour?"

"I beg your pardon, sir." Thomas was taken aback. "We had understood that this was Lord Henry Danlow's residence."

"It was, sir, but that is no longer the case. He has sold me the lease and the furnishings. I account myself most fortunate to be able to establish myself so easily and so comfortably. I have just come to town, you know," he added confidingly. "Allow me to introduce myself—Jonathan Semper of County Kildare at your service."

"Semper? Are you Newbridge's son?" Julian asked.

"I am, sir."

Julian extended his hand. "Julian Malvin." He indicated Thomas. "Lord Ferraunt. We apologise for our intrusion."

Mr Semper waved this away. "No intrusion at all, sir. May I offer you a glass of wine?"

"Thank you," Thomas said, anxious to find out as much as he could about Lord Henry's plans from their ingenuous host.

"To be frank, I did not expect to find Danlow at home tonight, but it never does to overlook the obvious," Thomas said an hour later after they had taken leave of Mr Semper. "I am surprised to find he has sold up completely."

"He took quite a hit over that wager at Almack's. Perhaps he is following in Brummell's footsteps and is fleeing his creditors."

"Arabella said something about a yacht at Folkestone. I'll have some discreet enquiries made there."

Julian laughed. "While I make sure Newbridge's cub isn't fleeced by the first card sharp who encounters him?"

"He's a nice lad but a Johnny Raw," Thomas agreed. "Is that why you invited him to breakfast in White's tomorrow? He looked as if you had offered him the keys of heaven."

Julian nodded. "I plan to have Matthew take him under his wing. He's much nearer to him in age than I am. He'll soon have him up to snuff. As for Danlow, I'll have a word with Rickersby; make it clear that if his brother has indeed left for the continent, it would be most unwise for him to return to England."

"Indeed."

Chapter Twenty-Eight

Thomas would not have been surprised if Arabella cried off from their riding engagement, but her groom approached from the mews leading her horse just as Thomas arrived at Malvin House the next morning

The man touched a finger to his hat. "Should I take him for you, my lord?"

"Please." Thomas swung down from the saddle and handed over his reins before rapping the knocker on the Malvin door.

"Pray come in, my lord. Miss Malvin will be down directly."

Thomas had no doubt of it. She rarely kept him waiting. Sure enough, he soon heard the tapping of her boots on the stairs. She was still too pale, he thought, when she rounded the banisters at top of the last flight. When he thought of what she had gone through—abducted, dosed with that damn gas, threatened with rape and forced marriage—it was a wonder that she had not dissolved in hysterics. But no, she had had the quick-wittedness to escape when the opportunity offered, and the courage to challenge Danlow's story in the church.

"Good morning, Thomas." She tilted her cheek for his kiss. "We cannot be too long—breakfast is at nine as Mr

Ellison and Miss Eames are anxious to return home, at least Miss Eames is."

It was a dull, grey morning and there were even fewer riders about than usual in the Park. It must have rained again during the night—the streets were covered with a malodorous layer of sludge that resisted the crossing-sweepers' efforts and in the Row the ground was very soft under the horses' feet.

"Just once up and down," Arabella said. "Come back for breakfast, Thomas. We did not have a chance to talk properly yesterday. How did you come to be there just when we arrived?"

"Your father sent a note requesting me to come at once. It was waiting for me when I returned."

"Returned? From where?"

"Kent, to see a man who will be my—adjutant for want of a better word."

She frowned. "A sort of steward, you mean?"

"Not exactly. He is a fellow officer—in fact, he was a lieutenant in the 1st/52nd but has been invalided out—while a steward is more like a sergeant. Phillips will work for me, not the estate. I'm going to bring in my own man of business, too, to go through the books with him."

"Don't you trust the estate's people?"

"I don't know whether I can or not. There is a lot of resentment still towards my great-grandmother who, we were informed, had queened it in Bath at the estate's expense for over forty years."

"No, did she? How wonderful. I can just imagine her, in a grotesquely high wig, wide hoops and rouged cheeks, with all the beaux bowing and scraping to her. When did she die?"

"In 1781."

"So your cousin had more than thirty-five years to recover his position, assuming it was as badly damaged as they said. I think an adjutant a capital idea. How long do you know him?"

"Only since yesterday. Franklin suggested him—he comes recommended by Lady Franklin's brother." He smiled over at her. "You did not wish to see me so I thought I would make good use of the time and went to see would he suit."

"I received a note from Lady Franklin inviting me to dine with them—and you. It would be just the four of us, she said." She spoke very calmly, giving no hint as to what she thought of this invitation.

Thomas cleared his throat and said carefully, "I hope you do not mind, but I spoke to Franklin, asked for his advice as to our situation. He and his wife were in a very similar one last year, you see."

"I know. That is why I went to see Lallie. But I don't want to talk about that here, Thomas."

"Later then," he said firmly.

"What did Lady Tamm have to say?" Thomas asked. With half-an hour wanting until breakfast, they had repaired to the small parlour. Arabella had taken a seat on the sofa and had not protested when he sat beside her, but she seemed reluctant to open the conversation.

She looked sideways at him from beneath her lashes. "That gentlemen are not very good at reading one's mind and I should tell you directly what troubles me."

"That was sound advice. Well?"

She sat up straight and looked directly into his eyes. "While I have the greatest respect for them, I would prefer not to live with your parents, Thomas. I want to be mistress of my own home now, not only when your father dies, which I hope will not be for many years to come."

He nodded and took her hand. "Franklin helped me see the same thing. He also pointed out that both he and I are too old and too independent to return to living under our parents' roofs."

"That hadn't occurred to me, but I doubt if you would like it either. What have the Franklins done?"

"They have refurbished the dower house at Lutterworth and will remove there after the Season."

"Is there a dower house at Ferraunt Court?"

"I don't think so. When I told Franklin that, he replied, 'buy or build one'."

"That is just what Lallie said! Her father's family has what they call the 'heir's house' on the other side of the park."

He looked at her seriously. "Would that satisfy you, Arabella? I beg you will be frank with me. I can promise you your own establishment, but if we live near the Court, you will not be able to avoid my parents. The truth is, we must all four pull together. My mother is not young, and she may find her new role more demanding than she imagines, especially as she never expected to be in such a position. You, on the other hand, have been brought up to it."

She pressed her lips together. "That is why I am afraid she may resent me and—"

He raised an eyebrow. "What are you trying to say? Spit it out."

"Try to assert her position by patronising me or treating me as an ignorant girl or even her paid companion, there to run her errands. It is not that I do not want to do my share, Thomas; I just don't want to be her satellite, sent here and there at her whim, but with no authority of my own."

"You need your own command."

"That's it. You do understand."

"I do now. I'm sorry I did not realise it before. But—if we have to build, it will be at least a year before our house is ready. Would you prefer to delay the wedding until then?" He spoke as coolly as he could, although everything in him rebelled at such an offer.

"Oh, Thomas." She leaned over to give him a sweet kiss. "Once I came to myself yesterday, all I could think of was that if I could not escape, I would not be there when you called today. Belshaw would tell you I was not at home and you would think I was too cowardly to tell you to your face that I no longer wished to marry you. Then I was afraid I would never see you again." She drew a long breath. "I don't want to waste a year, Thomas, but Lallie was insistent that we have the opportunity to be private together. She said there is a big difference between being bride and groom and husband and wife and that we need privacy to allow the bond between us to grow. It sounded so beautiful, the way she described it."

He put his arm around her waist and drew her to him. "What did she say?"

She blushed deliciously. "That there is an intimacy of the mind as well as of the body, but to achieve it you must have the opportunity to freely share your thoughts, pleasures and pastimes as well as your joys and your sorrows, unhindered by others. It is hard to explain, but when she spoke, you could see how, for her and Hugo, marriage is like a—," she made a gesture with her hands as if she were shaping a large globe—"a private world, just for them."

The picture her words painted entranced him. "That is what I want too, Arabella. We shall find a way to cultivate our own Eden. I swear it. We shall start and finish each day together, make our plans and report on the success or failure of our endeavours. And we shall talk and laugh together. I shall listen to your music and read to you in exchange. Just the two of us, with no-one else interrupting."

"We need to be able to disagree, to talk freely like this and make up again."

"Kiss and be friends, you mean?" He gathered her to him. When he kissed her, her lips softened and parted, welcoming his entrance. His tongue stroked hers, advanced and retreated, advanced again, inviting her to a new dance. He retreated and, to his delight, she followed, pausing and then shyly entering and he tried to hold still under her explorations. She gasped and shuddered when he gently rasped her lips with his teeth but then she nipped his lower lip and touched just the tip of her tongue to the place, soothing it.

"To make up for the last time," she murmured.

"Arabella. Sweetheart. Have you forgiven me?"

"For what?" she asked, dazedly.

He laughed softly and pressed a line of kisses down her throat. "My dearest."

"Thomas." His name was said on a soft sigh and he felt her fingers spear through his hair, holding his head to her.

The sound of footsteps in the corridor outside made Arabella sit up and push Thomas away. "They are bringing in breakfast." She jumped up and ran to the mirror, then smoothed her hair and tweaked her fichu into place. "Let me look at you," she said as she returned to him. "Are you presentable?"

He smiled up at her as she put him to rights with a gentle touch. Her fingers brushed against his wound and she hastily took them away. "I'm sorry. Did I hurt you?"

He turned his cheek into her hand. "No."

"Is it completely healed? It does not look as angry as it did before."

"Sometimes it stings, if there is a cold wind for example, but that is all."

"Do you use a soothing lotion? I have a very good receipt for milk of roses. Lady Halworth said the admiral swore by it, especially when he was at sea and exposed to all weathers. I should be happy to make you some."

"You would make it yourself?"

She nodded. "I like to work in the still-room. Malvin women have always done so, ever since we acquired the Abbey and with it the old herbals and commonplace books."

"I seem to recall my father telling me that the Abbey library was sold at the dissolution."

"Yes, but these were not kept in the library, but by the sisters who used them daily and took them with them when they were turned out. They were offered shelter by villagers who used come to the Abbey for help and eventually found themselves back here, working for the new owners."

"Are the books still here?"

"Yes. Each Malvin daughter makes her own commonplace book of the best receipts that have been acquired over the centuries." She grinned impishly. "I have decided to omit from mine the one for viper wine which requires twelve live vipers to be macerated in canary wine for several months together with a variety of spices and is said to be good for rejuvenating elderly men. I think it more likely to kill them."

It was on the tip of his tongue to remark that that was an unlikely receipt to find in a convent, but just in time he realised that she clearly had no idea of the type of rejuvenation required.

"There is also a receipt for frog spawn water," she continued, "but I've never heard of any lady making it."

"It is surprising how effective some of these old wives' remedies can be." He smoothed the whiskers that partially concealed the scar on his face. "The peasant woman to whose cottage I was taken after the battle smeared honey on this and then put cobwebs from the cellar on top of the honey. She said it would help it heal and stop it festering. When the army surgeon came, he first pooh-poohed the notion but then had to admit the wound was much cleaner than he would have expected after three days."

"After three days?" she asked, horrified. "He only came after three days?"

"During which he had hardly slept," he said quietly. "They were still bringing in the wounded."

"Good heavens! How long did they use the cobwebs?"

"Until the wound had completely stopped bleeding and begun to heal. Then they continued with the honey, but with lint instead."

"How did it happen?"

"My horse was shot under me, then, just as I struggled to my feet, a cavalry charge came through. Afterwards, the men pulled me back into the square and bandaged me tightly."

"And after the battle you were removed to this cottage?"

"Yes. I don't remember much of it, to be honest."

"And I should not remind you. Will you try the milk of roses?"

"If you want me to." He seemed puzzled by her insistence.

She stroked his wounded cheek very gently. "You will have to become accustomed to being cosseted, Major."

"It will be a new experience, but I will try."

"The yacht was there," Mr Phillips reported the following Monday evening. "Lord Henry arrived in a great hurry late on Thursday, rousted the crew from the taverns, had his carriage lifted onto it and insisted on putting out to sea then and there, instead of waiting for the late morning tide as he had originally planned."

"Did anyone know what his destination was?"

"No, my lord. They assumed France but knew nothing more than that. The thing is, I wasn't the only one enquiring about him."

"Oh? Were the bumbailiffs hard on his heels? I understand he left a lot of debt behind him."

"That's what I thought first, but no. It was a Bow Street Runner."

Thomas whistled. "Bow Street? Did you manage to discover why?"

Mr Phillips looked solemn. "Something to do with murdered yellow-haired whores."

Thomas slapped his hand on the table. "I knew it! I knew there was something smoky about him. Good God! When I think of the danger Miss Malvin was in, it makes my blood run cold."

Chapter Twenty-Nine

Ferraunt Court, Glos.
12th June 1816

My dearest Arabella,

I trust you are well and that your wedding preparations are almost complete. My father looks forward to conducting the wedding service for us. My mother initially carped a little at the short notice, but I pointed out that all she had to do was attend the ceremony and that Lady Malvin had not complained, although the brunt of the preparations will fall to her.

Arabella put down the letter, shaking her head. Thomas had clearly decided to adopt a robust attitude in dealing with his mother. How did Lady Hawebury take it, she wondered?

Mr Phillips has spent his first couple of days riding about the estate and since then has been reviewing the books together with a senior clerk made available to me by Benson, my Cheltenham man of business whom I called upon on my way here. While there, I inspected my great-uncle's house which is a neat little property. It is let until 1820 and I see no reason to break the lease. Generally, I found the town over-full of valetudinarians, but Benson proudly pointed out the new Assembly Rooms which are to be opened next month with a Grand Dress Ball on the twenty-ninth. He (Benson) prevailed upon me to purchase two tickets for this event and also to take a suite of rooms for a week at the best inn but if you do not like to, we shall not go.

They certainly would go, Arabella resolved. It would be the perfect opportunity to make her *entrée* into Gloucestershire society and new Assembly Rooms sounded promising.

I apprised my parents of our intention to set up our own establishment—my father understood at once, but my mother had, I think, made other assumptions or, perhaps had not thought at all about how we would live. At first she was astonished and then she said, 'but I was relying on Miss Malvin being by my side', but my father said, 'Arabella's place is at her husband's side', and quoted the verses about a man leaving his father and his mother and cleaving unto his wife. He added that the same went for a woman—she must cleave unto her husband. I wholeheartedly agree with both sentiments.

Arabella gave fervent thanks that she had not been a party to this conversation.

My father went on to say that we were fortunate to enjoy such circumstances as made it possible for us to maintain separate households, to which I replied that this did not mean that we had no interest in maintaining a close relationship with them; on the contrary I expected that we would meet frequently and dine regularly with one another. I added that you were more than willing to take responsibility for some of the countess's duties if my mother so wished and suggested that you might deal with matters pertaining to the tenants and the estate, as she would have enough to do at the Court.

At this stage, my mother remarked that if the four of us were able to discuss and agree matters in a rational and mutually respectful manner, it should be possible to divide up the space in the Court so that we are not under one another's feet, as she put it, and each couple can retreat to its own private quarters. She would have no objection to relinquishing the Earl's and Countess's rooms to us—she and my father had not yet moved in there and, if she were to be honest, they had no wish to. She added that it would be easier for Venetia if she could remain in her former rooms and that between her, her governess and Mr Phillips, it was unlikely that we would be able to dine privately most days. In her opinion, it would be easier for us to retire to our apartments afterwards if we remained at the Court.

Frankly, I did not know how to respond, Arabella. It seemed churlish to reject her proposal out of hand; I felt that at the least I should offer to discuss it with you. On the other hand, I did not want to make you responsible—as she might see it—for rebuffing such an overture. Whatever we decide, we shall decide together. While I was struggling with my reply, my father suggested that he and my mother remain at Longcroft until Michaelmas. This would give Lord Malvin time to find a new incumbent and we would have a couple of months on our own at the Court, during which time we could explore it at leisure and also see what suitable properties, if any, are available in the neighbourhood.

I hope you will not be angry when I say that I agreed to this solution. My mother was greatly relieved and has ordered that the Earl's and Countess's apartments be thoroughly aired, cleaned, scrubbed, dusted, polished—what you will, but has said she will not do anything more as the decision as to how they should be redecorated must be yours, not hers.

So the countess meant to be accommodating. Arabella supposed Thomas had had no choice but to agree. And it was true that she had not really thought about the implications of adding Venetia, her governess and Mr Phillips to their household.

My dearest girl, the twenty-sixth of June cannot come too soon for me. My parents and I return to Longcroft towards the end of next week and so I shall be at your service should you have any commands for me. In the meantime, rest assured of my devotion and my love,

Your Thomas.

Malvin House
14th June 1816

My dearest Thomas,

*Thank you for yours of the 12*th *inst. I write in haste as we return to the Abbey tomorrow and you may imagine how many last minute tasks and errands there are to complete. I have given a lot of thought to Lady Hawebury's proposal. I understand why you did not want to reject it out of hand, but we are left in a nice quandary, are we not? While I am willing to make the attempt as she requests, I do not wish to devote the first weeks of our marriage to such a task, nor do I wish spend them in the company of Mr Phillips, the senior clerk from Cheltenham and a host of servants, tenants and neighbours, all of whom it will be next to impossible to avoid.*

Do you remember the night we sat in Almack's refreshment room discussing our future? Then we said that only after our wedding journey would we consider where we might live. Let us take the month of July for our honeymoon, Thomas. If we return to take up residence at Ferraunt Court at the beginning of August, we shall then have two months to explore the estate and the neighbourhood prior to your parents' return which should be more than sufficient to decide how we mean to go on.

Arabella put down her pen and reread what she had written. Surely he would not refuse her this.

Millie has kindly agreed to keep Venetia for the summer so that she can return in September with your parents and her new governess, Miss Foster, whose services I was fortunate to secure this week. She has been governess to Lady Needham's daughters these past twelve years, and remained with the Needhams for Lady Alicia's first Season, but is now no longer required by them. She is a very pleasant lady and comes highly recommended, not only by Lady N. but also by the dowager who gave Lallie the hint that she was to leave at midsummer. The Needhams have kindly agreed to let her go one week early. She joins us this evening and will travel with us tomorrow.

Millie joined me when Miss Foster called to see me and both she and Miss Lambton advised me on the questions I should ask her. It did seem strange to be putting them to a woman who is fifteen years older than I, but this is something I must become accustomed to, I suppose. The only subject Miss F lacks is Latin. Venetia is keen to continue with it and Miss Lambton says she has an aptitude for it. We—Millie,

Miss L and I, thought that perhaps your father would agree to tutor her. What do you think?

I must close if this is to go with tonight's mail. Pray give your parents my fond regards. Until next week, my dearest Thomas,

Your Arabella.

PS. Your father will no doubt remember Mr Ellison who is a former pupil of his. Do you think he would consider recommending him to my father as a possible successor? I cannot but feel obliged to him (Mr Ellison, I mean) for the way he dealt with Lord H. D.

Ferraunt Court, Glos.
15th June 1816

My dearest Arabella,

Yes! Let us honeymoon first! How clever you are, sweetheart. I cannot tell you how charmed I am by the notion of our having a whole month just to ourselves. It shall be all holiday with us. I leave it to you to decide where—I shall be happy so long as you are there.

You would have smiled to see my father's pleasure at the idea of instructing Venetia in Latin. Both he and my mother are impressed that you have found a governess who comes so well recommended and look forward to making Miss Foster's acquaintance.

I have inspected the Earl's and Countess's apartments. They are on the first floor and consist of two suites of rooms joined by a saloon and shut off from the rest of the house by a massive door. I think you will like the countess's apartments. They are in the Chinese style with wall-papers patterned with blossoming branches where little birds flit and perch. It is an indoor bower and I like to picture you nesting there.

I count the days until we meet again.

Your Thomas

Chapter Thirty

Thomas rounded the last bend of the main avenue through the park at Malvin Abbey. An exuberant game of cricket was being played on the lawn in front of the house. He shook his head, bemused, as Lord Malvin helped little Anne touch her bat to the ball bowled by her Uncle Charles. It did not roll very far but somehow the fielders took so long to retrieve it that Malvin was able to pick up his granddaughter and trot with her to the opposite popping crease to claim a notch. An older youth now faced the bowling. He stepped forward and struck the ball with a satisfying thwack, sending it soaring over the heads of the nearer players. A woman sprinted towards it, diving to catch it before it hit the ground. She sprawled full-length on the grass while triumphantly holding the ball aloft in her right hand to cheers and applause.

"Cousin Thomas! You're back!" Venetia raced towards him and he caught her up and swung her round in a hug. "Was that not a splendid catch of Aunt Arabella's? With Roderick caught out, the innings is over and we shall stop for refreshments."

"Aunt Arabella?"

Venetia nodded. "She said I could call her that, just as Hermione, Tony and Anne do, and Miles and Clarissa as well. I like it. It makes me feel one of them. I have no other aunts, you know."

"Would you prefer to call me Uncle Thomas?" He set her back on her feet and she took his hand and led him across the grass towards his betrothed, who had stood up and was dusting off her gown.

"Yes. It is what the others will call you after you are married. I don't see why you should be their uncle and only my cousin."

"And that will make them your cousins," Thomas said understandingly.

"Yes." She looked around and smiled gloriously. "There are so many of them, Uncle Thomas. Isn't it wonderful? And I am to stay here all summer. Aunt Arabella said you would not object."

"Then it is fortunate that we brought your pony, isn't it?"

"Moonlight! Where is she?"

"Settling in in the stables, I trust. You must let her rest for a day or so before you take her out."

"But I may visit her, may I not? Hermione! Come and see my pony."

"Thomas!" Arabella raised her face for his kiss. "Did all go well?"

"Very well. I left my parents at the rectory and came to find you."

She slipped her hand into the crook of his arm, but instead of going towards the crowded terrace, led him away from the players and spectators clustered around the refreshment tables to a sheltered bench in a walled garden.

"One of your private places?"

"Secluded at least."

He turned her towards him to claim a more satisfying kiss. "I missed you."

"You sound surprised."

"I'm not used to missing someone," he confessed sheepishly and put an end to the discussion with another kiss.

He looked at her lovingly. She had already been tousled from her exertions at cricket but now she was sleepy-eyed with voluptuous pleasure, her lips plump and swollen. A sweet disorder indeed.

"The banns will be called for the third time tomorrow. Only four more days and you will be mine."

She reached up and smoothed his side-whiskers. "And you will be my new-wedded lord. Shall we have a goose-feather bed, Thomas?"

"If you are not careful, it will be a cold, open field," he retorted, turning his head to press a kiss into her palm. "Have you decided where would you like to spend our honeymoon?"

"I was torn between the lakes and the sea, but in the end decided for Weymouth. Millie raves about it. You have every amenity there, she says, and there are pleasant rides and excursions, apart from walking and riding on the sands if you do not want to bathe."

"And you do not?"

"Be plunged into cold water by two stout dippers first thing in the morning?" She shivered dramatically. "I think not."

He smiled slowly. "I am sure we can think of something more enticing to do early in the morning."

Her eyes grew round and she blushed deliciously at this assertion, but she did not challenge it. His bride was not the missish sort, he thought thankfully.

"We shall have to find lodgings," he remarked.

"That's all taken care of. Millie recommended a very pleasant set of rooms on the Esplanade. The prospect from the windows is delightful, she said—she could have sat there all day looking out to sea. As it is such short notice, I asked her to write at once and enquire if they were available for Lord and Lady Ferraunt and she received the confirmation today."

He hugged her. "You would have made an excellent officer's wife. It makes me almost sorry I sold out. I'll send Martin ahead on Monday with the saddle horses."

Arabella sat patiently at her dressing-table watching Horton dress her hair. Lord and Lady Hawebury had accepted Mamma's invitation to dine. This would be the first time the two families had met since the rector's elevation or, indeed, since Thomas's and her betrothal. The Abbey was full of Malvin and Tamm relatives come to attend the wedding. The countess would be the senior lady present and Arabella wondered how she would respond to this distinction. Lady Nugent and Lallie were the only other peeresses among the guests. Strange to think that when the rector died, Arabella would take precedence over them and Mamma.

"There, miss." Horton fixed the cluster of rosebuds so that they nestled among her curls, took a step back and held up a mirror so that her mistress could see the back of her head.

"Perfect."

"A touch of pearl powder, Miss? You caught the sun a little today."

"Just a hint."

The maid dipped a hare's foot in the little box and whisked it gently over Arabella's face, then stroked a fine brush over the tiny pot of rose lip salve and skilfully applied it to her mistress's lips. Finally, she touched a little perfume to her throat and the inside of her elbows.

Arabella looked at the clock. "I must be downstairs before the Haweburys arrive. Quick, my pearls and my gloves."

Arabella dipped into a curtsey. "Lord Hawebury, Lady Hawebury."

"What's this?" the new earl exclaimed. "We'll have no 'my lords and my ladies' between us. I hope we may call our daughter by her Christian name and she should call us," he broke off, confused.

"Might I still call you, 'Rector'?" Arabella suggested after a moment. "I confess it is how I shall always think of you."

He beamed at her. "That would be most excellent, my dear—a welcome reminder of my calling. Now, as to my wife—" he began to mutter to himself. "'*Rectrix*' would not be appropriate; '*Matrona*' perhaps or '*Socrus*' which is, of course, Latin for mother-in-law."

Arabella felt more than heard Thomas suppress a cough beside her and carefully avoided looking at her assembled family. She felt sorry for her future mother-in-law whose grand entrance in rustling damascene silk was rapidly turning into a farce. She caught that lady's eye and they exchanged wry smiles before Lady Hawebury drew herself up to her full height.

"I should be pleased," she pronounced majestically, "if our new daughter would address me as 'Mother', just as our son does."

It was the only possible solution, Arabella recognised. And she always called her own mother, 'Mamma'. Think of it as simply another name or short for mother-in-law, she told herself. She took a deep breath and said, "I should be very happy to—Mother."

"Then that is settled," Mamma said. "Hawebury, pray give me your arm. You know everybody here except the Nugents, I think."

"Lady Hawebury?" Papa offered his arm to the countess and the four moved into the drawing-room, leaving their sons and daughters to breathe a sigh of relief.

"Thank you," Thomas muttered to Arabella.

"*Socrus*," she hissed. "How could he?"

"*Matrona*," Millie groaned. "How mortifying. I have to admire your mother's composure, Thomas."

The evening passed off without further incident. Lady Hawebury allowed herself to be led to the place of honour at her host's right hand and Arabella thought the rector did not even notice he had been accorded a similar privilege when requested to take his hostess in. She and Thomas were seated together and Papa insisted on drinking their health. To her horror, his eyes grew damp and he had to clear his throat fiercely before he could speak.

"To Arabella and Thomas. We wish you long life, health and happiness together."

"May you be blessed in your children and see your children's children unto the third and fourth generation," Thomas's father completed from the opposite end of the table.

This time next year she might be a mother! Arabella glanced sideways at Thomas as everyone else stood, raising their glasses. He would be a good father, she thought.

"Will you find it strange to be Lady Ferraunt, Aunt Arabella?" Hermione asked. She and Venetia were helping Arabella look through her personal belongings and decide which she would take with her to Weymouth and which would be sent directly to Ferraunt Court.

Arabella heard Venetia catch her breath. Of course, her mother had also been Lady Ferraunt. Had the girl not realised—?

"I am honoured to follow your mother, Venetia," she said gently. "I can never replace her, but I hope you will let me stand for her."

"Of course, Aunt Arabella," Venetia said quietly. "I hadn't thought about the name, but if Uncle Thomas is Lord Ferraunt, of course you must be Lady Ferraunt. I think Mamma would be happy to know I am not alone."

Arabella gave the girl a quick hug. "I am very sure of it, and she would be very proud of you. You must write and tell me how you go on here and I shall write to you and tell you about Weymouth and what is happening at the Court."

"Will you write to me too, Aunt?" Hermione said a little jealously.

"Of course, but you must promise to reply." Arabella opened a drawer and looked with dismay at the collection of fans within. "However did I acquire so many?"

"Let us see." The two girls began to open the cylindrical boxes and spread the fans on the table and day bed in overlapping arcs of ivory, cream and gold tinted with Arabella's favourite soft blues, pinks and greens.

"They look like a flight of butterflies," Venetia exclaimed.

Arabella picked up a fan of carved ivory sticks painted with flowers and linked by a ribbon of the palest gold. "This was a gift from my Aunt Henrietta; I carried it for my come-out ball—and this one when I was presented to her Majesty—I gripped it so tightly that I broke one of the ribs but they were able to replace it. My brother brought me this one from Spain—and this is from the ball where I first danced with your Uncle Thomas." She showed the girls where she had scribbled his name twice on the sticks.

A soft smile curved her lips, as she contemplated these evocative remembrances of balls and routs, soirées and musicales, and set aside those she particularly wished to keep. Gesturing to the others, she said to the girls, "You may each choose one if you like."

"Are you ready, Bella? They are waiting for you in the library."

"Yes, Mamma." Arabella cast a final look in the long cheval glass. Her new gown of pale blue striped sarsnet had turned out well. She turned, admiring the flare of the flounced hem and the lace trimming that matched the *Fichu à la Duchesse de Berri* that was tucked into the low bodice.

Mamma came and tweaked her skirts to rights. "That is most becoming." She paused for a moment and then said, "Bella, if you have any doubts or hesitations, or wish to delay the wedding, now is the time to say so. Once the settlements are signed, it would be extremely difficult to draw back from the match. Are you quite, quite sure that you want to marry Thomas on Wednesday? You know your father and I will support you, whatever you decide."

"Quite sure, Mamma."

"And you are happy with the provision that is made for you in the settlements?"

"Yes. Papa explained everything to me. He has been very generous, as has Thomas. I don't know what I shall do with so much money."

"I am sure you will think of something," her mother said dryly. "Don't forget you will have other, charitable demands on your purse. Have you your signet ring with you?"

"Oh." Arabella hurried to her jewellery box and slipped the ring onto her finger.

They descended the stairs in silence. Arabella had not realised what a momentous occasion this was, almost as important as the wedding itself.

Papa, Thomas and the rector waited for them with Julian, Hugo and Lord Franklin who would act as the trustees of her marriage settlements. Several other men hovered near the round table upon which large sheets of vellum were spread. Solicitors and their clerks, she supposed. On a side table, the taper in the wax-jack burned steadily and a fresh stick of sealing wax lay ready beside it. A tray held a number of freshly sharpened pens and an ink-pot.

As soon as Thomas saw her, he left the others and came to her. He took her hand and kissed it. "Our journey begins here," he murmured. "Any qualms?"

She shook her head. "No. You?"

He tucked her hand into his arm. "Not one. I only wish we did not have to wait until Wednesday for the next step."

"It's not even two days," she protested.

"But two whole nights," he said meaningfully, and she felt herself blush.

"Well, Hawebury? Shall we lead off?" Papa jovially waved the rector to the table.

There was a little bustle as they sat and the folio was positioned for them. A clerk dipped two pens in the ink and handed them to them.

"Here and here, my lords," a lawyer murmured.

Once the signatures were complete the clerk dripped gouts of red wax onto the parchment and the two fathers pressed their seals into them.

"The trustees," Papa said quietly. Hugo, Lord Franklin and Julian went forward. Their role was to ensure that the funds and property put in trust for her were administered properly and to her benefit and that of her children. She had been surprised at this, but her father had explained that it was necessary; they must plan for all eventualities including Hugo's early demise. Then it was Arabella's and Thomas's turn.

He smiled down at her and led her to the table where he held her chair before sitting himself.

"If you sign here, my lord, and you here, Miss Malvin," the lawyer murmured.

Thomas sent her a sidelong smile. The library was so quiet that she could hear the scratch of his pen on the vellum. When he was finished, he nudged the parchment towards her. *Arabella Clarissa Henrietta Malvin*, she wrote steadily, then drew the ring from her finger and set her seal in the little pool of wax. It was done.

Chapter Thirty-One

There she was, a shimmer of cream and gold at the bottom of the aisle. She walked steadily towards him, her hand resting lightly on her father's arm. When Thomas stepped forward to join them, her eyes met his and a radiant smile lit her face.

His father cleared his throat and began the service. "*Dearly Beloved*." He might as well have been reading the *Articles of War* for all the heed Thomas paid to him. The only important thing was their vows to each other.

"*I will*," he said firmly.

"Arabella Clarissa Henrietta *Wilt thou have this Man to thy wedded Husband, to live together…………………obey him, and serve him, love, honour, and keep him in sickness and in health; and, forsaking all other, keep thee only unto him, so long as ye both shall live*?"

"*I will*."

Her ungloved hand was soft and perfumed and he wanted to press it to his cheek. Later, he promised silently. *"I Thomas take thee Arabella,"* he began, his ardent gaze as unwavering as his voice.

At his father's prompt, he relinquished her hand and offered his for her clasp as she made her vows to him. When she finished, her lips quivered and curved beautifully. He ignored the little twinge as his lips responded. They might have stayed there until nightfall, smiling into each other's eyes if his father had not cleared his throat and held out his book to receive the ring from Lord Franklin.

"*With this Ring I thee wed*"—Thomas slipped it onto Arabella's finger, "*with my Body I thee worship*"—his voice deepened and his heart skipped a beat as he felt the slight tremor in her hand—"*and with all my worldly Goods I thee endow*."

They knelt side by side for the blessing and the final prayers. Instead of the more usual passages from St. Paul, the rector chose to read a text from the *Epistle to the Corinthians*. When he had finished, he smiled at them and said, "My dear children, if you but strive to practise charity as the apostle describes it, you will not fail in your duty to each other and to the world for, as we have heard, 'Charity never faileth'. Yet, should we fail, the apostle reminds us elsewhere that we should not 'let the sun go down upon our wrath'. Only bear this in mind, I beg you, in your dealings with one another and all shall be well."

Thomas felt a peculiar mixture of pride, triumph and gratitude as he watched his wife sign her maiden name for the last time. She was his! He managed to steal a swift kiss as she straightened, before they were engulfed in a wave of embraces. High above them, the church bells began their joyful peal.

"Is my bonnet straight?" Arabella asked him and he looked at her helplessly. She looked delicious to him but how was he supposed to know how the thing should sit?

His new father-in-law laughed. "Never try to change anything, Thomas. A wise husband looks critically, makes a minute adjustment," he touched his daughter's bonnet as he spoke, "and says 'you look beautiful, as always, my dear'."

"Papa!" Arabella protested while her mother cried, "And so wives learn that husbands are sad flatterers." She straightened Arabella's bonnet and retied the bow, but for the life of him Thomas couldn't see any difference.

"We should go." Arabella took his arm and led the little procession out of the vestry and down the aisle.

It had rained again that morning, but the sun gleamed through the thinning clouds as they emerged from the church where Hermione, Venetia and little Anne waited to scatter blossoms at their feet. Their task complete, they clustered round the newly-weds, demanding to see Arabella's ring, but soon had to make way for other well-wishers. Then it was back to the Abbey for the wedding breakfast. They would not delay long—Thomas preferred to drive directly to Weymouth without stopping overnight and wished to leave by ten o'clock at the latest.

Ruth Halworth had sniffed when told that they were not embarking on a long wedding journey abroad but would return to Ferraunt Court after a month. "Weymouth? How drearily prosaic."

Arabella had just smiled. Ruth had never understood her, and never would. She turned to look at her new husband and found him watching her intently.

"Nearly there," he said as if he had been reading her mind.

She slid nearer to him and slipped her hand into his. "Is it really only a month since we agreed to marry? When I look back at all that has happened since then, it seems an eternity."

"Was I wrong to press you for an early wedding?" he asked, peeling back the glove at her wrist so that he could touch his lips to the fluttering pulse-point. "Would you have preferred to wait?"

"No. It was time."

The lodge keeper and his wife bowed and curtsied as the carriage passed through the main gate. When they arrived at the Abbey, they found the servants drawn up outside the house, the house steward at their head.

He bowed gravely. "My lord, my lady, may I offer the felicitations of the staff on your nuptials?"

"Thank you, Openshaw." Arabella looked at the smiling faces. She had known some of them—Mrs Hampton, the housekeeper, for example—all her life.

"I must say goodbye," she whispered to Thomas. "Later there will be no time."

Her husband by her side, she slowly made the round, shaking hands and thanking each person for their service today and other days. The bows and bobbed curtsies, the murmurs of 'my lady' emphasised the change in her condition. She was amused to see that Horton, whose mistress was now the wife of an earl's eldest son, had moved up a place in the ranks and stood between her mother's maid and Millie's Agnew. And so fortune's wheel turned.

Their wedding guests, including her parents, held back until she had completed her circuit and nodded to Openshaw who, with a flick of his hand, dismissed the servants to their places and stood ready to attend his master and mistress. Maids and valets hurried away with pelisses, bonnets, coats and hats while footmen handed trays of negus against the early morning chill of the church. Then it was in to the dining room to sit at the long table where an extensive breakfast was spread, more a cold supper really, except that tea, coffee and chocolate replaced the evening white soup.

Arabella sat in a dream, mesmerised by the glint of gold on her left hand. She was now a married woman—tonight, her husband would come to her bed. She wasn't frightened, she told herself; a little apprehensive, perhaps. She remembered Lallie's assurance that she would find pleasure and happiness there. Millie had said the same. She hoped so. She liked his kisses.

"Are you not hungry?" Thomas murmured.

She looked down at her empty plate. "Just day-dreaming," she admitted.

"What may I give you?"

"Oh, one or two of those little chicken baskets." She indicated the little tartlets that were shaped like a basket with a cunning handle of pastry. "Cook knows they are my favourites."

"Then I must try one. Very tasty indeed," he remarked after a few minutes. "Is it too late to ask Cook for the receipt?"

"There is no need. It was one of the first entries in my commonplace book. I started keeping one when I was fourteen; now I have one for the kitchen and one for the still room."

"You never cease to amaze me. What other hidden talents have you, I wonder? I look forward to discovering them."

The bride cake had been cut and the toasts drunk. At last Arabella could slip away to change into a carriage dress for the journey. She was more than ready to leave the nest. She would miss her family, of course, but they would not be too far away. She hummed to herself as she opened her bedroom door. Apart from the few items she needed today, all her personal belongings had been packed and removed and already the room did not feel quite hers. In a few years Hermione might move down here.

She paused on the threshold, surprised to find the heavy curtains still drawn over both windows. Whatever was Horton thinking? Or had she simply forgotten to open them in the excitement?

"Horton?"

There was no reply.

"Horton?"

Annoyed, Arabella stalked over to the bell-cord. Her gown laced up the back so she could not even begin to undress. It was after half-past nine and it would probably take fifteen minutes to make their farewells and with ninety miles to cover, they should not tarry.

She refused to wait in this gloom. What was that strange shape between the windows? It looked as if some gowns had been thrown over a chair. She shook her head. She had never known Horton to be so lax.

Suddenly the curtain moved, allowing a beam of light to fall on the chair. Someone sat slumped there. Horton!

Arabella hurried forward, then froze at the sight of her maid gagged and bound to the chair. As her mistress neared, Horton moved her eyes frantically and tilted her head towards the door as if telling her to flee. Before Arabella could react, Lord Henry Danlow stepped out from behind the curtain and put a knife to the maid's cheek.

"One screech and she loses an eye." His flat tone made the threat more real.

He nodded approvingly when Arabella bit back a scream. "That's the way. You'll do just what you're told, my dear, or she'll pay for it." His hand moved as he spoke and Horton gave a muffled squeak. He cuffed her carelessly. "That'll be enough from you! You," he gestured with the knife towards Arabella, "will go and lock the door. Remember, if you run, you'll have her death on your conscience."

"You're mad!" Arabella cried.

He shook his head disapprovingly. "You forget yourself, my dear." He turned the point of the knife, causing a trickle of blood to run down Horton's face and stain the rag that had been forced into her mouth. She whimpered and looked piteously at her mistress.

Arabella felt sick. She might run and save herself, but how could she leave Horton with that lunatic?

"Stop dilly-dallying," his lordship snapped. "Lock the door, I said!"

She obeyed as slowly as she dared, straining her ears for any sound in the corridor outside. How could she alert the household? Dare she take advantage of the shadowed room? If he heard the key turn, perhaps he would not notice if the door were not properly closed. She must risk it. She gently pushed the door to so that the tongue rested outside the lock, then rattled the key and turned it with a loud click.

"Good girl!" He moved away from Horton, the knife in one hand and a bundle of cords in the other.

She turned to face him and looked him up and down. "What are you doing here?"

"I've come to collect my debts, shall we say? You have cost me too much, Miss Malvin."

"Lady Ferraunt," she corrected him icily.

He bowed contemptuously. "How quickly you deck yourself with your newly acquired feathers. We'll see how that upstart Ferraunt will like it if I have you first. Best of all will be if I plant my by-blow in you. I'll even leave you alive for that, provided you behave yourself. Now we shall see just how obedient you can be."

He advanced towards her, herding her back towards the bed. Step by step, she retreated into the gap between it and the chimney-breast. Reaching behind her, she found the bell-pull and tugged it as hard as she could so that the bell must jangle furiously below stairs.

"Onto the bed with you, my fine lady."

He meant to force her! Violated on her wedding day! Thomas would have to have the marriage annulled. That was if his lordship let her live. Angling her body so as to conceal the motion, she jerked the bell-pull even more violently.

"I had not thought even you could stoop so low. You dishonour your name and your house."

"What do you know of honour?" he snapped. "You, who flaunted yourself in front of all the males of the *ton*, then sold yourself to the highest bidder. I thought you were different, but all women are born fickle and whores at heart."

Behind him, she could see Horton frantically rubbing her face against the high back of the chair, trying to work the gag loose.

He was almost upon her. She released the bell-pull and closed her fingers around the heavy silver candlestick that stood on the bedside table.

"Onto the bed with you, or it will be the worse for you."

She refused to budge. She would not submit so easily. He would have to make her, and to make her he would have to be within arm's length of her. Even in the dim light she could discern his flushed face and distended nostrils. He was breathing heavily and smelled of spirits and sweat. He bared his teeth and lunged for her. Behind him, Horton screamed at the top of her voice.

"Help! Help! Thieves! Murder!"

Distracted, he glanced over his shoulder and Arabella swung the candlestick at him. He staggered back from the blow but did not fall.

"Bitch!"

He dropped what he was carrying and reached for her with both hands, his fingers curved like claws. She threw the candlestick, hitting him full in the face, and dived for the knife. Blood poured from his nose. He kicked at her but she managed to roll away. He wiped his nose angrily with the back of his hand. When he raised his foot again, she caught hold of his boot with both hands and pushed upwards. He tried frenziedly to shake her off, thrusting at her with the captured foot while hopping wildly on the other. She clung on, desperately pitting her strength against his. The edges of the boot-sole hurt her hands. Perhaps she could jerk him off his feet and then grab the knife, manage to hold him off with it. Had no-one heard the bell?

Horton screamed again and the door flew open. Suddenly the room was full of men. Lord Henry tried to turn, his arms flailing as he fought to maintain his balance. As she released her hold, Thomas seized him, spun him round and smashed his fist into his jaw. He let his victim fall, stepped over him and crushed Arabella to his chest.

"My God," was all he could say. Then, "Did he hurt you?"

"No, but Horton—" She pushed him away a little. "I must see how she is."

A footman stood beside the maid, awkwardly patting her shoulder. He had untied her bonds, but she slumped shivering on the chair where her assailant had put her.

"Oh, Miss," she said when Arabella came over. "I'm that sorry, but he was on top of me before I knew it."

"You couldn't have expected him," Arabella reassured her. "He must have taken advantage of the unusual commotion today to sneak into the house, perhaps when you were all outside. Did he hurt you badly, apart from this, I mean?" She gently touched her handkerchief to the little cut on Horton's face. "It's not deep, thank heavens."

"Not really, but he did terrify me." Horton's voice was thin and scratchy.

"You were very brave, managing to get free so you could call for help. Go and get Mrs Hampton at once, James," Arabella instructed the footman before looking at her husband. "Ferraunt, bring me that shawl if you please."

Thomas fetched it and she wrapped it around Horton's shoulders then knelt beside her, holding her hands and talking soothingly to her.

The housekeeper started when she came into the room and saw Matthew and another footman standing guard over a prone man who had not yet regained consciousness.

"What's all this? Burglars? In broad daylight? Whatever is the world coming to?"

"He must have heard about our marriage and thought to take advantage of everyone being occupied downstairs." Thomas pressed Arabella's hand as he spoke and she nodded. Best to leave it at that for the moment.

"Please look after Horton, Mrs Hampton. She was very brave. Have Bates bring my things to my mother's dressing-room. I'll change my dress there."

"Very good, my lady." The housekeeper helped Horton to her feet. "Now you come with me, Miss Horton dear, so I can dress that cut. A nice cup of tea and you'll feel much more the thing."

"My compliments to his lordship," Thomas said to the footman. "And I should be grateful if he would look in here, Convey the message discreetly—there is no need to have the whole house in uproar."

"Certainly, my lord."

Arabella began to shake.

Thomas put his arm around her. "Come, I'll escort you to your mother's apartments."

"There's no need. They are very near."

"There is every need. I don't think I shall ever let you out of my sight again." He led his wife past the recumbent body of her assailant who was now tied hand and foot. He was still breathing, unfortunately.

Lady Malvin's dressing-room was empty. "I'll stay with you until someone comes."

"Yes." She sat down abruptly as if her legs could no longer support her. "Oh, Thomas. I was so frightened. He lay in wait for me and threatened to put Horton's eye out if I did not stay. He wanted to r-r-ravish me and g-get me with c-child."

He knelt beside her, holding her close. "But you stopped him. You are the most indomitable woman I have ever met."

"I was determined to fight. I'd managed to reach the bell and knew someone would come if I could hold him off long enough. Then Horton worked the gag free and screamed."

"We were nearly at your door by then. It was a stroke of good luck that he had not locked it properly. That saved us valuable minutes."

She shook her head. "That was not luck. He hid behind the drawn curtains which made the room quite dim. He held the knife to Horton's face, and said she would lose an eye if I screamed. I was afraid to run for help when he told me to lock the door, but I turned the key noisily outside the lock."

He hugged her. "Indomitable and clever and brave. And thoughtful, kind and beautiful. To think that I feared civilian life might be dull and uninteresting!"

An hour later, a burly constable marched Lord Henry into the library.

Admiral Sir Jeremiah Halworth sat behind the desk in his capacity of magistrate. His son sat at the end, ready to act as his father's clerk. To one side, a grim Lord Malvin sat flanked by Julian, Matthew, Thomas, Lord Franklin and Lord Nugent. The other male guests sat opposite and a cluster of upper male servants stood near the door. Brought to stand in front of the desk, Lord Henry look sullenly around the room but said nothing. His bruised face had been roughly cleaned of blood but his cravat, waistcoat and coat were still liberally marked by the drying stains.

"Lord Henry Danlow, you stand accused of burglary, deprivation of liberty and assault with a deadly weapon."

His lordship made no response other than tilting his head to squint down his swollen nose.

"Ask Miss Horton to come in."

A footman left the room and returned with the maid. The cut on her cheek no longer bled but the area around it was red and swollen and glistened with salve. She seemed nervous; her hands were clasped firmly in front of her and her gaze flickered around the room but avoided Lord Henry. The Admiral peered at her over his spectacles and directed the footman to set a chair for her.

Once she was settled, he asked, "Miss Horton, do you recognise the person standing before me?"

"Yes, sir. That is the man who attacked me in Lady Ferraunt's bedchamber."

"Pray tell me exactly what happened."

The Admiral listened to Miss Horton's account of how she had been attacked, threatened with a knife, gagged and tied to a chair.

"What did he do then?"

"First, he strolled around the room, picking things up and looking at them. Then he put something in his pocket."

"Did you see what it was?"

"No, sir."

The Admiral frowned. "Please turn out your pockets, my lord."

When Lord Henry did not respond, the Admiral barked, "Search him."

At the terse command, a footman pinned his lordship's arms behind his back while the constable turned out his pockets and spread the contents on the desk.

"That's Lady Ferraunt's aquamarine cross and chain," the maid exclaimed.

The Admiral turned to Lord Malvin. "My lord, can you also identify this piece?"

"Yes. It was a gift from my son Arthur to his sister."

"Thank you. Miss Horton, I see that you suffered an injury," the Admiral continued. "Was that as a result of this attack?"

"Yes, sir. He cut me with his knife. He said he would put my eye out. I was terrified he would, sir."

"I am sure you were," Sir Jeremiah said sympathetically. "Well?" he demanded, looking at the prisoner. "What have you to say for yourself, my lord?"

Lord Henry glared contemptuously around the room but remained silent.

"Nothing? In that case I commit you to Abingdon Gaol to be tried at the summer Assizes for burglary, theft, assault with a deadly weapon and deprivation of liberty."

"That is enough to see him transported," Lord Malvin said, clearly satisfied, when he was alone with his sons and son-in-law. "What's more, we were able to bring it off without dragging Bella into it."

"I suggest you ask Sir Jeremiah to send word to Bow Street about him," Thomas said. "I understand they are looking for him in connection with some murdered prostitutes."

"Good God!" Malvin collapsed into his chair. "It gets worse and worse," he said after a moment. "I'll write to Rickersby and to Sidmouth too—make sure there is no attempt to free him quietly. Thank you, Julian." He accepted a glass of Madeira and drank deeply.

"He must be deranged," Julian said as he handed glasses to Matthew and Thomas. "He had got away safely to France but instead of remaining there, must come back to seek revenge. It's Botany Bay or Bedlam for him."

"He can hang for all I care," Malvin said. "Thank God Bella is so quick-witted. How did you get up there so quickly, Thomas?"

"One of the footmen—James—heard the bell ring violently. He was alarmed—he had never known Miss Malvin ring so fiercely, he said afterwards. He sent another servant to find me while he ran up himself. Fortunately, I was in the hall with Franklin and we raced upstairs. When we burst into the room, Arabella was on the floor. She had seized Danlow by the foot and was pushing against him with all her might. She had already clouted him with a heavy candlestick, broken his nose, by the looks of it."

Malvin smiled weakly. "Her mother used to complain she spent too much time with her brothers, was afraid she would turn into a tomboy. We should be grateful for it!"

"Yes," Thomas agreed. "Now, if you will excuse me, I must return to her."

Their wedding guests had gathered in the drawing-room where Arabella sat hand in hand with her mother. She had changed into a heavier dark blue gown trimmed with aquamarine ribbon of the same shade as Arthur's cross. As soon as she saw Thomas, she rose and came to him.

"Is it done?"

"Yes, he is on his way."

"Then let us forget him. I am determined he shall not spoil our wedding day."

He caught her to him. "My indomitable lady! Are you ready to leave or would you prefer to stay here tonight?"

"No, let us go now, even if we have to stop *en route*. Millie says The Antelope in Salisbury is very comfortable and they have an excellent cook."

He smiled. "I might have known you would have it all in hand."

Another half an hour had elapsed by the time the good-byes were said. This time the semi-circle in front of the house was made up of their family and friends. Thomas had never been hugged as much in his life or been the recipient of so many manly handshakes and claps on the shoulder.

Even his mother, who never wept at partings, had tears in her eyes. "After so many farewells when we did not know would we ever meet again, it seems like a miracle to be sure that we shall be together in a little over two months."

He kissed her cheek. "I was thinking the same, and that a letter can be written and answered within two days."

"But don't think of that now. You and your wife are right to take this time and start your married life alone. I wish you every happiness together."

"Thank you, Mother."

She looked over to where Arabella was surrounded by her family. “You must go to her. She will find it hard to break away on her own.”

“You are right.” He caught her in an impulsive hug that left her smiling as he walked over to collect his wife. Arabella seemed relieved at his arrival. Without further ado she slipped her hand into his arm and walked with him to the waiting carriage. She turned and waved as she stood on the step and then ducked beneath the door-frame. Thomas climbed in after her, the door was closed, and they were off.

Chapter Thirty-Two

Arabella woke slowly, her head on her husband's broad chest and her bare legs entangled with his. A bride had no need for night-clothes, she had discovered, although Thomas was very appreciative of the new morning gowns Lallie had insisted she include in her bride clothes. Seductive, lace trimmed confections, no more than an open negligee worn over a slip or petticoat, they were completely different to the simple round gowns that had constituted her morning attire up to now, and not to be worn outside the boudoir or dressing room. But here, where it was just the two of them, she could wear them to breakfast in their private parlour.

She lay for a while listening to the steady thump-thump of his heart. This was their last morning in Weymouth. Their rooms were everything that Millie had promised, and Thomas was the best of husbands. The very pine-apple of husbands she thought with a little giggle that had him stir and make an indistinct sound before relapsing into slumber.

She did like being married. Apart from this ravishing intimacy that grew stronger with each passing day, she loved the freedom of being able to determine her own life in a way that she never had before. They had explored the town on their first day here, written their names in the Master of

Ceremonies' book and taken out a subscription to the libraries before returning to their rooms to investigate the guidebooks they had borrowed and draw up a list of things they would like to do. Thomas was a wonderful companion and it was an additional delight to be able to attend a ball without a chaperon and walk or ride without being trailed by a maid or a groom.

She sighed and softly stroked her cheek over the silky hair that veiled satin skin. The hair on his head was curly, as was that at his groin, but everything here was unexpectedly smooth, belying the firm muscles beneath.

His cradling arm tightened and she looked up to see that his eyes had slitted open. "Good morning again, my love."

"Good morning, Thomas. I wish we did not have to leave today."

"So do I. We need not go to Cheltenham, if you prefer to stay here for a few more days."

"No, I do want to go. It's just—this is the end of our private time. In Cheltenham we will have stepped back onto the public stage."

"We'll return here next year. There is no reason why we should not have an annual honeymoon, is there?"

"None at all. What an excellent idea."

"I think so," he answered, lifting her to lie on top of him. "Perhaps you should remind me of the purpose of a honeymoon, in case I forget."

Cheltenham was overrun with visitors, drawn to the town by the unexpected presence of England's hero, The Duke of Wellington, who was to be observed not only taking the waters but also strolling with his duchess and sons.

"The landlord might have let your rooms a thousand times over for an exalted price," Mr Benson told Thomas, "but he said to me 'Who knows if his grace will come again, while we may hope to see my lord Ferraunt every year if we give satisfaction'."

"For my part, he might have had the rooms," Arabella said when Thomas related this to her. "This is worse than the Season, for the town is not able to cope with such numbers."

The inaugural ball of the new Assembly rooms was the worst crush imaginable. As a 'lady of rank', Arabella might avail herself of the reserved seats at the top of the ballroom but this, together with her recent marriage to the new heir of Hawebury, only served to turn all eyes towards her. Thomas lost no time in presenting her to his former Commander-in-Chief who wished them happy and expressed his regret at losing such a capable officer.

Although the Duchess of Wellington had the reputation of being reserved almost to the point of rudeness, Arabella liked her. She had seen her two years ago driving in Hyde Park with her nose in a book rather than exchanging greetings with other members of the *ton,* but now realised that the Duchess was extremely short-sighted and could not have recognised the occupants of the other carriages. She was content to sit and talk of her sons who only now could become acquainted with their famous father, and was interested to hear of Venetia.

"Poor child. But I am sure you will be good to her, Lady Ferraunt. Do you remain here long?"

"No, just two more days."

The Assembly Rooms were now so crowded that it was almost impossible to move. A shifting mass of bodies pressed into the ballroom, gleaming and glittering in the candle light. It reminded her of the large nets full of mackerel she had seen drawn ashore near Weymouth, the fish struggling as they were removed from their natural element. Did she imagine it, or was the air growing thin? She was suddenly suffused by a cold perspiration that caused her head to spin unpleasantly. She was trapped here at the top of the ballroom. The thought of forcing her way out against the tide of guests turned her knees to jelly. She clamped them together and took slow, deep breaths, then looked around for some means of escape. Wait—was that a servant's door set flush into the wall behind the screen? Thomas stood near the wall talking to an officer. She caught his eye and fiddled with her ear-bob. He came at once; a quick murmured excuse and they were able to make a strategic retreat to a rere-corridor where they almost collided with a servant carrying a tray of cups and saucers from the tea-room.

"Are we in danger of meeting your fellows coming against us if we go down this stair?" Thomas asked.

"No, sir. We come up the other stair from the kitchen—this one leads to the scullery."

"How well thought out," Arabella said. She caught her skirt with one hand and cautiously followed Thomas down the narrow stone steps.

"Now, my man," he said when they reached the bottom, "deliver that load and come and show us a quiet way out of here."

Arabella felt a little prickle of excitement mixed with apprehension as she dressed on their last morning in Cheltenham. She swallowed, placing her hand on her unruly stomach. It was only natural to be nervous, she assured herself. While she longed to see Ferraunt Court, she would be the young mistress from the moment they arrived. She could not rely on having Thomas always by her side; indeed it would give quite the wrong impression, as if she could not be relied upon to pick up the domestic reins without his direction and support. If she wished to place her stamp on the Court, she must do it now, before the earl and countess returned.

Thomas seemed preoccupied too, and they were content to sit quietly together, exchanging the odd word or comment. It was a new sort of intimacy, she thought, one that did not demand conversation. She sighed and laid her head on Thomas's shoulder. His arm came around her.

"Are you tired? Rest a little. About another hour, now."

"I told Phillips to have our horses brought here," Thomas said as they drew up at The Ferraunt Arms. "It's about half an hour further to the Court."

Arabella looked at the group of riders gathered in front of the inn. "I wonder what the occasion is. If it were hunting season, I would say we had stumbled upon a meet."

"There's Phillips, and that's Crofton, our land steward," Thomas said, puzzled, "and, if I am not mistaken, those others are our principal tenants."

"Oh—then they will have come to welcome us. We should alight while the horses are changed."

A cheer went up when Thomas handed his bride down from the carriage. The landlady of the inn bustled forward and curtsied deeply. "We are honoured indeed, my lord, my lady. Now, Bessie."

She nudged forward a little girl who shyly held out a posy.

"For you, mum."

"My lady," the landlady whispered.

"My lady."

Arabella bent to take the flowers. "Thank you, Bessie. They are beautiful."

"We have come to escort you and your bride home, my lord," one of the men announced.

That probably meant another welcoming party at the Court, Arabella reflected. Was she tidy? She beckoned to Horton who waited to one side, then caught the landlady's eye. "If I might have the use of a bedchamber for a moment, ma'am?"

"Certainly, my lady. This way."

"I'll just be ten minutes, my lord," Arabella murmured in response to Thomas's enquiring look. As she entered the inn, she heard him call for a round of ale for the company. She need not hurry, then.

An arch of greenery and flowers had been erected at the gate to Ferraunt Court where a large crowd had gathered. A smart band of fifes and drums stood to one side in rank and file.

"From the local yeomanry," Mr Phillips, who acted as captain of the escort, explained to Thomas through the open carriage window.

Arabella leaned over to ask, "Have they arranged for refreshments at the house, Mr Phillips?"

"Yes, Lady Ferraunt. There will be plumb cake and ale for all."

"Thank you."

The new team was unharnessed and amid a chorus of loud advice, a group of brawny men took over at the pole and swingletree. The carriage jolted and jerked as they took the strain, then struggled to get in step.

"Good heavens! They must wish to pull us up to the house," she gasped as the carriage swayed violently, throwing her against Thomas who caught and steadied her. "How far is it?"

"About two miles—the avenue curves through the park. It will be easier once they get into their stride."

The band struck up "The Girl I Left Behind Me" and they began to move, slowly at first but then more steadily. Both sides of the avenue were lined with men waiting to fall in behind them. "I expect the women and children are waiting at the house," she said.

Thomas shook his head. "Do you think so? I never expected anything like this. It is not as if they have known me all my life."

"No, but your marriage is important to them. It brings stability, you see. They will have wondered what was to happen to the earldom after Venetia's father and brothers were drowned. I am sure they are pleased that we are to live here as well as your parents."

"How should they know what we have decided?"

She shrugged. "You will find one has very few secrets. You will have to say something later, thank them for their welcome."

Arabella rested against Thomas's shoulder, looking dreamily at the greens of grass and trees and wood. In the distance, she could see the gleam of water; a lake, she thought, and beside it, some sort of folly. It would be very pleasant to stroll or ride here. It was a pity she couldn't get out and walk now—she would be glad to leave the rocking carriage. This was the second time the team of men had changed. She hoped it would be the last.

The band had a new tune. "Over the Hills and Far Away". Thomas began to sing in a low voice, just for her:

Were I laid on Greenland's Coast,
And in my Arms embrac'd my Lass;
Warm amidst eternal Frost,
Too soon the Half Year's Night would pass.
Were I sold on Indian Soil,
Soon as the burning Day was clos'd,
I could mock the sultry Toil
When on my Charmer's Breast repos'd.
And I would love you all the Day,
Every Night would kiss and play,
If with me you'd fondly stray
Over the Hills and far away.

"That was beautiful," she sighed. "You must sing it again for me, later."

"I want to kiss you now, but better not here, I suppose."

She drew off her glove, kissed her fingers and touched them fleetingly to his lips. "That must sustain you, sir."

His arm tightened. "I wanted you from that first day we met again at the gate to Malvin Abbey. I never thought I had a chance—you were too far above me."

"I am so glad that I said yes before we knew about all this." She gestured to the park and their escort. "You can never think it that I was more interested in the future earl than Major Ferraunt."

He rested his cheek against her hair. "I will never doubt you, Arabella."

She could now see the house. Was it to be her home for the rest of her life? Pray God they would have many years together.

Amid cheers from the people gathered on the lawns, the men drew the carriage onto the forecourt, halting where floral arches interspersed with pots of dark green box and white roses created a festive pathway to a great oak door. On one side of this, the servants stood ready to be presented to the heir's wife while another group waited opposite—tenants and their families, Arabella judged. Their mounted escort clattered past, heading for the stable-yard, the band took up its position beside the group of tenants and a liveried footman came forward to open the carriage door. Thomas sprang down and turned to offer Arabella his hand.

"Welcome to your new home," he said quietly.

"Three cheers for his lordship and his bride," a stentorian voice called. She stood, her hand in Thomas's, her head reeling from the deafening 'Huzzahs'. She could not recall such a fuss when Julian married Millie, but she had only been eight then.

As soon as the last echoes had died down and the carriage dragged away, the ceremonies began. Thomas presented the land steward and house steward to her. The latter welcomed her on behalf of the servants and led her around the semi-circle, introducing them. She made a point of smiling and repeating each name, down to that of the overawed little scullery-maid. Then the land steward invited her to cross over and meet the tenants while the servants began ferrying huge trays of ale and plumb cake to the crowd.

"There's ginger-ale too, my lady, if you prefer," the housekeeper said as a tankard was thrust into Thomas's hand.

"I would, thank you, Mrs Fulcher."

The tangy, effervescent drink revived her a little. The last presentation made, a Mr Bates, who had been first of the tenants to be introduced, climbed onto a small platform. He cleared his throat. "My lord, my lady. On behalf of the tenants, workers and their families, it is my honour to welcome you home on the auspicious occasion of your nuptials."

On and on he spoke. Arabella tried to listen, but her thoughts kept drifting. She slipped her hand into Thomas's arm and leaned on him as the peroration reached its climax. "And so I ask you all to join with me in drinking the health of his lordship and his bride. Long life, health and happiness, my lord, my lady, and may all your troubles be little ones!"

A roar of approval answered him. When it died down, Thomas led her to the platform, handing her up before jumping up beside her.

He was probably used to addressing his men, she thought, admiring his clear diction and air of effortless command as he expressed their thanks, honour and gratification at such a warm welcome. It had been a tragic year for Hawebury, and while those who went before them would not be forgotten, he hoped that today saw a new beginning. He looked forward to furthering his acquaintance with everyone in the coming weeks and months, and spoke for the earl and countess as well as for his wife and himself when he said that they had been called unexpectedly to this task, and would do all in their power to see that Hawebury prospered and flourished. He raised his tankard. "Drink with me to the future of Hawebury," he called, to further cheers and acclamations.

Accompanied by the land steward who decided who was to be favoured with an introduction, they strolled among the estate-workers and their families crowding the lawns. She could not speak to everyone today, Arabella knew, but she resolved to visit all the houses in turn in the coming weeks. For now, she smiled until her cheeks ached and her head was abuzz with bows, bobbed curtsies and murmurs of 'my lady'. The sun was hot and she was beginning to feel more than a little light-headed.

At last they had made the round of the lawns and could return to the house. "Let us go in," she murmured to Thomas and, arm in arm, they walked slowly beneath the scented canopy, turning at the door to wave to the crowd. Finally they could disappear into the cool shade of the great hall where the steward and housekeeper waited to receive them.

Overtaken by a wave of nausea, Arabella sank at once onto an oak settle and closed her eyes, taking slow, careful breaths. *Please don't let me be sick here.*

"Arabella?"

Thomas's voice came from a distance. Someone untied the ribbons of her bonnet and it was gently lifted from her hcad.

"Take this, my lord," a woman said.

Something pungent was held under her nose. Smelling salts. Ugh! She reached blindly and pushed away the hand holding them, then cautiously opened her eyes.

Thomas peered anxiously at her. "Are you feeling more the thing?"

"A little."

"You will be better lying down."

She was lifted and cradled in his arms. She clung to him as he left the hall and mounted some stairs. A door was opened, then another one and she was laid down on a chaise longue.

"My lady!" Horton hurried forward. She swiftly removed her mistress's half-boots and within a few minutes had her reclining under a soft shawl with a lavender compress on her forehead.

It was blissful to lie still.

"I'll let you rest." Arabella felt Thomas kiss her hand. "Send for me at once if you need me."

"Yes, my lord."

The door closed.

What an entrance to make, Arabella thought drowsily. What would they think of her?

When she woke, she felt not so much ill but—

"Horton?"

"My lady?"

"What time is it?"

"Four o'clock, my lady."

"It's no wonder I felt faint. Ring for tea. And I should like something to eat, toast perhaps. I could only face a little at breakfast and have had nothing since."

"Was it your stomach again, ma'am?"

"Yes. Why do you look so oddly?"

There was a knock on the door and Horton went to speak to the footman. When she returned to her mistress, she took a breath and said, "If I may be so bold, my lady, it's been more than six weeks since you last had your courses and, well, you have been married over a month now."

"Oh! You think I might be—?"

"With child? It is too soon to say, ma'am, but the queasiness suggests so."

"Good heavens! I had not thought it would happen so quickly."

"It only takes once," the maid said dryly. "There's no need to fret, my lady. We'll just have to wait and see."

"Yes, but." Arabella stopped. Was she ready for this? She had thought to have time to become a wife before she had to face motherhood.

Horton seemed to sense her turmoil. "It might not be that at all, my lady. With all the upset and changes of the last months you could well be late; besides, that jolting and jerking would make anyone sick to their stomach."

Arabella looked at her gratefully. "If anyone asks, we'll just say that I hadn't eaten. And, mind, not a word to his lordship."

"No, my lady."

Arabella sat up and looked about her. This was Thomas's 'blossoming bower'. It was certainly charming, if a little old-fashioned. Still, better than crocodiles' legs, she supposed. She pushed aside the shawl. "Help me out of this carriage dress, Horton. Then you can let his lordship know that I am awake."

"Did you feel as if you were trespassing when you first came here?" Arabella asked the next day as she and Thomas explored the house. Mrs Fulcher had shown his mother around, he had explained, but he only knew the principal rooms.

"I still do," he confessed. "It is seventy-five years since my great-grandfather died and since then our line has been spoken of here only in the most opprobrious terms. He hangs there on the far wall with his first wife. And there is his son, my grandfather's elder brother." He nodded towards the full-length portrait that hung in pride of place in the large dining-room.

"The one who turned him out?" Arabella considered the plump, pompous features framed by a carefully curled wig. "He must be turning in his grave to see your father installed here. Is there a portrait of your great-grandmother? If so, we should put her husband between his wives."

"I don't know. I'll enquire."

"Was any likeness taken of your grandfather?"

"There is one at the rectory, and one of my parents, too, taken when they married. My father is in full clerical garb."

"We must make sure they are hung prominently when they arrive. It will be the best way to demonstrate the change of line. Is there one of you in your regimentals?"

He hesitated before admitting somewhat shamefacedly, "Yes. My mother asked me for it and I had it done in Paris. I don't know whether it is any good, but she seems to like it."

"I can't wait to see it. Will she keep it in her own rooms, I wonder. Where are they?"

"On the other side of the great hall, in the Tudor part of the house. I imagine they were the then baron's rooms, although the furniture is later, I am told. There is a comfortable parlour and a book-room full of incunabula. That was what clinched it for my father, that and the wainscoting, which reminds him of Oxford. Come and see."

"It's like having two separate houses," Arabella said some minutes later. "They can have their own establishment here. It will seem quite natural that we do not live in each other's pockets either, although our lives will, of course, intersect regularly."

"How do you propose to manage that?"

"I think we shall let our daily rounds develop naturally. I propose to suggest that we generally dine together—as your mother pointed out, Mr Phillips and Miss Foster would dine with us even if we lived elsewhere. And Venetia too, perhaps. She is a little young, but the schoolroom must seem very lonely to her now. We shall see. If we keep country hours, you gentlemen do not linger too long over your port and we drink tea early, we may be on our own from half-past eight each evening. And we shall breakfast in our own rooms, like in Weymouth."

"Start and finish the day on our own? Promise me you will continue to wear those alluring dressing gowns to breakfast."

"If you wish," she said demurely.

He pulled her into his arms, his eyes gleaming with amusement, love and desire. “Shall you always be such a biddable wife?”

She burst out laughing. “What do you think?”

“I think you will soon have us all dancing to your piping.”

They had begun to create their special space, she thought, as he bent to kiss her. Now they just had to nourish it and let it grow.

Background Notes

This is a work of fiction, but set in a real place and time. While it would be impossible to list all the sources consulted, I wish to mention the following:

- The *'half-boots of drake's neck coloured silk, laced and fringed with dark blue and yellow kid, spotted and ornamented with* purple' (Chapter Two) are not a figment of my overheated imagination but are described in the February 1816 issue of *La Belle Assemblée.* 'Drake's neck' refers to the blue-green iridescent neck feathers of the mallard drake.
- *Thaddeus of Warsaw* by Jane Porter was first published in 1803. Thaddeus's proposal is related as follows: '*he imparted to her a concise but impressive narrative of his relationship with Sir Robert,* [his recently discovered father]. *He touched with short yet deep enthusiasm, with more than one tearful pause, on the virtues of his mother; he acknowledged the unbounded gratitude which was due to that God who had so wonderfully conducted him to find a parent and a home in England, and with renewed pathos of look and manner ratified the proffer which Sir Robert had made of his heart and hand to her who alone on*

this earth had reminded him of that angelic parent. "I have seen her beloved face, luminous in purity and tender pity, reflected in yours, ever-honoured Miss Beaufort, when your noble heart, more than once, looked in compassion on her son. And I then felt, with a wondering bewilderment, a sacred response in my soul, though I could not explain it to myself. But since then that sister spirit of my mother has often whispered it as if direct from heaven."'

- The version of *Richard III* performed by Edmund Kean and described in Chapter Fourteen was that of Colley Cibber who in 1699 rewrote Shakespeare's play, retaining only eight hundred lines of the original. Until the mid-nineteenth century Cibber's play was the standard version and David Garrick, John Philip Kemble and Edwin Booth all appeared in it.
- Susan Boyce was an actress who appeared in several roles opposite Kean, including that of Lady Anne. Her affair with Byron in the winter of 1815/16 is fact. The attempt on her life during a performance at the Theatre Royal, Drury Lane is fiction, inspired by the attack on another Drury Lane actress, Miss Kelly, on 17 February 1816 by George Barnet who was subsequently found not guilty on grounds of insanity and confined to an asylum.
- Acrostic Jewellery. First introduced by the French jeweller Mellerio in 1809, acrostic rings soon became very popular tokens of loving sentiments. Previously, Georgian acrostic jewellery shaped like padlocks with keys or hearts were decorated with gemstone

acrostics as an open declaration of love. *'In jewellery, pearls, rubies and coloured gems, the initials of which form devices or sentimental words, are now in high favour; and elegantly wrought gold ornaments of a high polish and burnish are much adopted by the British fashionists'* La Belle Assemblée 1817

- *Glenarvon*. The description attributed to Lady Holland is that used by her in a letter to Mrs Creevey of 21 May 1816
- The quotations from the Marriage Service are from the then version of *The Book of Common Prayer*
- Messrs Greenwood, Cox & Co., of Craig Court were indeed the 23rd's regimental agents. My description of Mr Greenwood as 'an affable, elderly gentleman' is based on the portrait by Sir Thomas Lawrence. and *A Characteristic Sketch of Charles Greenwood*, Boulogne, 1826
- The version of "Over the Hills and Far Away" sung by Thomas is from *The Beggar's Opera* by John Gay
- In his Autobiography Sir Harry Smith consistently uses the single form 'couple' when referring to his pack of hounds e.g. eighteen couple.

The Duchess of Gracechurch Trilogy

Set in Regency England from 1803 to 1816, *The Duchess of Gracechurch Trilogy* celebrates friendship, family and love.

Wed before she was seventeen in a made match to a duke's heir, heiress Flora Hassard quickly learns that her new husband has very little interest in getting to know his new wife. Supported by her mother-in-law, she creates a happy home for herself and her children while 'donning the Duchess' in society where she uses her position and influence in the ton to befriend young wives "*whose husbands are, well, distant, shall we say? They are safe in that circle, or as safe as they want to be. The older women keep an eye out for the younger ones, warn them of the worst rakes, that sort of thing; keep them out of harm's way.*" *(*Perception & Illusion*)* Flora is content, but her contentment has come at a high price—she has had to turn her back on love.

Books One and Two of the Trilogy tell the stories of two of the brides Flora befriends while in Book Three Flora herself takes the lead. ***Note: While Books One and Two can be read***

in either order, The Duke's Regret contains spoilers for the first two books and should be read last.

Book One: **The Murmur of Masks**

Eighteen year-old Olivia, daughter of a naval officer is desperately in need of security and safety, following the sudden death of her mother. Unaware that his affections are elsewhere engaged, she accepts Jack Rembleton's offer of a marriage of convenience, hoping that love will grow between them. When Olivia meets Luke Fitzmaurice at a ball given by the Duchess of Gracechurch, Luke is instantly smitten but Olivia must accept that she has renounced the joys of girlhood without ever having experienced them.

An unexpected encounter with Luke at a masquerade ten years later leads to a second chance at love. Dare Olivia grasp it? Before she can decide, Napoleon escapes from Elba and Luke joins Wellington's army in Brussels. Will war once again dash Olivia's hopes of happiness?

Reviewers said. "*I read it very quickly as the story was very compelling and the characters really came to life and engaged me." "Depicts both the harsh reality of the battlefield and the pleasures and challenges of society life in England.*"

Book Two: **Perception & Illusion**

Cast out by her father for refusing the suitor of his choice, Lallie Grey accepts Hugo Tamrisk's proposal, confident that he loves her as she loves him. But Hugo's past throws long shadows as does his recent liaison with Sabina Albright. All too soon the newly-weds are caught up in a comedy of errors that threatens their future happiness.

Lallie begins to wonder if he has regrets and he cannot understand her new reserve. She resolves to find her own sphere, make her own life and is delighted to be welcomed into the circle of the Duchess of Gracechurch. When a perfect storm of confusion and misunderstanding leads to a devastating quarrel with her husband, Lallie feels she has no choice but to leave him. Can Hugo win her back? Will there be a second, real happy end for them?

Award winning author Nicola Cornick said of Perception & Illusion: "*it was a real pleasure to read a book so well-rooted in the manners and mores of the period. I also loved your protagonists and the depth you gave to their emotional journeys and to the rest of the characters and story. Bravo! It was a lovely read.*"

***Book 3:* The Duke's Regret**
A chance meeting with a bereaved father makes Jeffrey, Duke of Gracechurch realise how hollow his own marriage and family life are. Persuaded to marry at a young age, he and his Duchess, Flora, live largely separate lives. Now he is determined to make amends to his wife and children and forge new relationships with them.

But Flora is appalled by his suggestion. Her thoughts already turn to the future, when the children will have gone their own ways. Divorce would be out of the question, she knows, as she would be ruined socially, but a separation might be possible and perhaps even a discreet liaison once pregnancy is no longer a risk.

Can Jeffrey convince his wife of his sincerity and break down the barriers between them? Flora must decide if she will hazard her heart and her hard won tranquility when the prize is an unforeseen happiness.

"*Well-researched and strongly recommended.*" The Historical Novels Review

All three books are available as eBooks and paperbacks; there is also a box set of the whole Trilogy. Amazon UK https://amzn.to/2xhAe1t:

Amazon US https://amzn.to/2KKfdVY

A Suggestion of Scandal

If only he could find a lady who was tall enough to meet his eyes, intelligent enough not to bore him and had that certain something that meant he could imagine spending the rest of his life with her.

As Sir Julian Loring returns to his father's home, he never dreams that 'that lady' could be Rosa Fancourt, his half-sister Chloe's governess. They first met ten years ago but Rosa is no longer a gawky girl fresh from a Bath Academy. Today, she intrigues him. Just as they begin to draw closer, she disappears—in very dubious circumstances. Julian cannot bring himself to believe the worst, but if Rosa is innocent, the real truth is even more shocking and not without repercussions for his own family, especially for Chloe.

Driven by her concern for Chloe, Rosa accepts an invitation to spend some weeks at Castle Swanmere, home of Julian's maternal grandfather. The widowed Meg Overton has also been invited and she is determined not to let such an eligible match as Julian slip through her fingers again.

When a ghost from Rosa's past rises to haunt her, and Meg discredits Rosa publicly, Julian must decide where his loyalties lie.

"*A smooth read; providing laughs and gasps in turns. Readers will enjoy the cool-headed Miss Fancourt, while hoping that Sir Julian puts the pieces of the puzzle together quickly! A host of other loveable and detestable characters keep the entertainment moving through the trials, tribulations, and victories of love.*" Historical Novels Review

https://amzn.to/2NE7J4A Amazon UK,
https://amzn.to/2LPrzb7 Amazon US

Lightning Source UK Ltd.
Milton Keynes UK
UKHW010123051022
409926UK00004B/86/J